STEP OVER RIO

MARTHA EVERHART BRANIFF

To Jacquelyn,
Wishing you the best!
Marty Braniff

❖

The Way Things Are Publications
Los Angeles

1ST EDITION

Manufactured in the United States.

Published by The Way Things Are Publications, Los Angeles.

Jacket design by Pacific Coast Creative, © 2011.

ISBN-10: 0-9839641-1-4
ISBN-13: 978-0-9839641-1-7

http://www.marthabraniff.com
http://www.waythingsare.com

STEP OVER RIO is a work of fiction. Incidents, characters and dialogue are products of the author's imagination and are not to be construed as real. Any resemblance to actual events or persons, living or dead, is entirely coincidental.

Printed on acid free paper. Interior pages are Sustainable Forestry Initiative (SFI) certified. Meets all ANSI standards for archival quality paper.

For David

Acknowledgments

Many thanks to my publishers, Jennifer and Mark Havenner, and my editors: Jennifer Havenner; Julia DeGraf; and Angela and Mark Hooper.

With heartfelt gratitude to Judy Berger for her expert counsel.

I deeply appreciate the time and brainpower of my friends who read Step Over Rio and offered advice and support: Suzan Glickman, Chris Rogers, Nancy Mudd, John Oehler, Jeanne Klein, Judy Simon, Charlotte Jones, Patty McGrath Morris, Rick Nelson (in memorium), Marcia Gerhardt, Jack Thomas, Jamie McGrath Morris.

And to my friends and colleagues whose ideas, professional expertise, and encouragement have been critical for me: Jackie Pelham, Jane Wagner, Kathy O'Neil, Harvey Stone, Sue Barnum, Harvey Simon, Sue Mize, Judy Wilson, Susan Berk, Jane Moser, Judge Michol O'Connor, Maud Lipscomb, Trish King, Grace Givens, Peggy Harrison, Charlie Romney Brown, and with kudos to the Special Agents at the US State Department, Diplomatic Security Service; the US Marshals; Adrian Garcia, Sheriff, Harris County, Texas; and Manny Perez, Former Navy Seal.

My children who always root for me: Beth Harp, Jim Braniff, IV, Blakely Rickett, and their spouses: Mike Harp, Shannon Braniff, and Jason Rickett.

Of course, my grandchildren: Harrison Harp, James Braniff, V, Haley Harp, Brooke Braniff, and Caden Rickett.

ONE

In Guatemala City the night is chilly and damp. A bright moon appears from behind clouds of handspun silk and illuminates cardboard shanties built by desperate Indios *who come in search of work. Their hovels are strung as far as the eye can see into every park and over every grassy knoll.*

Lomas de Santa Faz, *the* barrio *where Fernando Sifuentes lives, has houses made of pilfered cinderblocks and scrap metal. Inside the dwellings, babies sleep on dirt floors, mothers squeeze last trickles of milk from cartons found in other people's garbage, and* La Sombra, *the men of death, prowl the streets for young ones they deem unfit to live.*

On a curb in the plaza, Fernando sits and comforts Rodrigo, who can barely walk, his leg a festering wound. Suddenly the boys hush their chatter. Three armed men round the corner near la zapatería *and call Fernando's name. He scrabbles to his feet and dashes down the closest alley. Sweaty hair sticks to his forehead. When he races past a gang of scrawny street kids, they stuff their noses into paper bags and breathe the cheap delight only cement glue can bring. Neighbors peek from their windows. They see Fernando out of his mind with fear, but they do not offer help.*

Heading for a dead-end road, Fernando knows he must force these men to kill him so he will not suffer torture. "Hey, you stupid pigs," he yells. "I am not a Latin Angel anymore." He throws the bloody bandage that his brother, Alex, had removed from Rodrigo's leg before Alex ran to get a first-aid kit from Casa Maria, the orphanage where they live.

The men draw near and aim their guns. They are dressed in camouflage jackets, shiny boots, and dark caps pulled low on their foreheads. "God will not forgive you," Fernando whispers, stepping closer to the killers. Strident rattles burst his eardrums. His nimble body crumples to the ground, his "Just Do It" T-shirt rips open as brown curls and heavy lashes are splattered with flesh. Blood seeps into the alley's cracked concrete.

The autumn moon sheds saffron light on the killers' backs as they bend over Fernando's body. The short man, known as The Surgeon, removes a military knife from a clip on his belt, snaps the button on its handle, and flashes four inches of serrated steel. Kneeling, he fits his broad hands into surgical gloves, turns Fernando's face toward him and makes the Sign of the Cross.

Somewhere close, a dog yelps, a baby wails, and children sift through litter blown to the curbside by an oblivious wind.

*

Alex Sifuentes hugged the metal first-aid kit close to his chest and hurried past a group of teenage boys roasting skinned rodents on a makeshift cook-fire. Its flames shone on their sallow faces as they took turns inhaling cement glue. Soon they would be meaner than rabid dogs. Alex counted on his past friendship with this gang, the Latin Angels, to keep him safe from attack, although experience told him that the desperate little thieves could swarm at any minute, relieving him of the first-aid kit, his clothes, and his shoes.

"Hey you," a voice called.

Slowing his pace, Alex glanced at a blank-faced boy with pimpled skin who lowered a sack from his nose. The kid's eyes held a fiendish glow. Alex wanted to run, but he knew any unexpected move could set the boy off.

"*La Sombra*," the boy said, slurring his words, "is chasing Fernando."

Alex dropped the kit and raced to the plaza, now empty and jarringly silent. Fernando, his clever little brother, would surely escape *La Sombra*. Alex sprinted past the crumbled fountain, past *la paneria*, all bread removed from the windows for the night, and past rows of mended shoes in *la zapatería*.

Surrounding the plaza, slanted dwellings butted against each other, lining narrow passageways that spread out like the spokes of a wheel. Shouting Fernando's name, Alex tore up and down the alleys. Lanterns and open stoves shot sparks of orange light, and fetid smells of human waste merged with scents of cooking oil, but Fernando was nowhere along the teeming streets of *Lomas de Santa Faz*. Panic filled Alex's soul as it had the night he'd watched his young mother cough and wheeze until she'd lost her desire to take one more breath on this earth. Red rims encircled her eyes. Her forehead and limbs burned with fever as she held both sons' hands, one boy on each side of her cot. With a last gasp, she'd told them of her wish.

"Go to *Rio Grande*," she'd said. "I want for you . . . America . . . just a step over *Rio*." Her clammy fingers had wilted in the tight grip of Alex's hand, and no matter how fiercely he'd held on, her spirit had slipped from his reach.

Sudden voices from across the plaza, three men in black knitted caps, snapped Alex from the memory of his mother's deathbed. Crouching behind a pile of broken cinderblocks, he peered around the side, accidentally knocking a cluster of stones onto the pavement. A square-shouldered, mustached man spun on the heel of his boot. Their eyes met.

Alex ducked a spray of bullets that shattered store windows and chinked into the rough-edged mound where he hid. Chips of pulverized rock stung his eyelids, and his rubbery legs buckled. He couldn't decide what to do. Leaving now would delay his search for Fernando, but he needed help. *Father Chiabras, Father Chiabras*, he repeated under his breath. The priest's name shored him up, prevented him from falling into despair, kept him focused.

Alex determined he could disappear into the *barrio's* crevices and crooked lanes—an endless maze for those who didn't live there. When bullets riddled the cinderblocks again, he dashed for the path that led to a neighborhood food center, a clapboard building with wide covered porches for the hungry people who spilled over from the tiny waiting room. And near the building, an underground sewer, the secret link to *Casa Maria*.

At the rear of the center, Alex hunkered between two trashcans crammed with rotting vegetables. In the distance, boots crunched dry ground as the men shouted something about hunting the second rabbit they'd kill tonight. Refusing to listen, Alex held on to hope.

Less than a hundred feet from where he squatted, the mustached man waited near a cracked fire hydrant. His sharp eyes scanned the area around the clinic. Flattening his body, Alex belly-crawled behind a row of shrubs and down a concrete slope, the surface rough and painful against his palms. When he reached the mouth of the sewer, he bit his lower lip at the thought of being trapped below. Many of his friends had found refuge from *La Sombra* in these pipes, but this offered Alex no consolation. Blowing air from his lungs and taking a last glance at the moon, he wedged his lanky body into the close space. His knees and hands sank into sticky sludge as he crawled toward a pinhole of gray light.

To keep his mind off the vile odor and the wet rats brushing against his bare arms, Alex imagined what had happened after he left Fernando. Every evening, he and his brother helped Father Chiabras bring food to the street gangs, their friends from days past. Three years ago, when he and Fernando had been members of the Latin Angels, Alex had possessed a keen sense of danger, but working with Father Chiabras had tamed his cunning. Still, he was more skilled than his little brother. If only Alex had stayed with the wounded boy, Rodrigo, and sent Fernando for the medicine box.

A sick tingle filled his gut. If Fernando was alive, every second counted. Alex crawled faster. His palms stung and his head split with grief, but he kept sucking shallow breaths as he drew closer to the end. At last, he lifted his head from the hole and inhaled fresh air. *Casa Maria* was right across the road.

Thrilled to see the simple adobe house and no sign of the men, Alex pulled himself from the sewer. He sprinted to the small veranda, thrust open a heavy wooden door, and burst into a room crammed with bunk beds, desks, and chairs. Kids of every age gathered around him, their quizzical expressions and bronzed faces full of questions.

"You stink!" Pablo held his nose.

Alex pushed the boy out of his way. "Where's Father?"

"In the garden," said Elena, a nine-year-old orphan Alex had adopted as his little sister. Her amber eyes narrowed into slats and her forehead knitted into a frown. "What's the matter with you, pushing Pablo?" She slammed a wooden bowl filled with purple berries onto the dining table and thrust a checkered dishtowel at Alex. "Clean your face."

Snatching the towel, Alex fled to the courtyard.

"Father, *La Sombra* is in the *barrio*. Fernando is missing!" Alex's voice evaporated into the thick warren of his throat. All he could do was pray for the safety of the brother he'd raised since their mother's death, the two of them so close they knew each other's thoughts and dreamed each other's dreams.

"*Madre de Dios.*" The priest snatched up the hem of his brown robe and followed Alex through the house into the empty street. He was a humped little man with wisps of curly gray hair around his forehead, and Alex loved the lightning in Father's eyes. It was always those clear blue eyes, shining like wet marbles, distinct from all others. Always, Father's see-through gaze forcing Alex to think about what he was going to do or refuse to do.

"*La Sombra* was here just minutes ago," Alex said as he and Father crossed the road.

Ignoring the priest's command not to follow, the rowdy bunch of *Casa Maria* kids scuttled along behind them. But Father didn't argue or send them home because at times like this, the kids did what they pleased regardless of his orders. These children knew the street, their instincts sharp and untamed. Now, they shadowed Alex and Father, who ran against a north wind kicking up dust from the road until a red Jeep rounded the corner and sped toward them, its glaring headlights, angry eyes, its silver grill, hungry teeth.

"*La Sombra*," Father said.

Alex pointed to the food center. The kids dashed up beside him and Father as they all swarmed onto the pillared porch. Close behind them, the Jeep bounced over the grassless yard, heading straight for a post where Elena stood. If it kept its course, it would smash into her. Father Chiabras flapped his arms at the Jeep. When it kept coming, he flung his hand in a wide arc, shoving Elena backward. Alex grabbed the terrified child, her eyes brimming with tears, her clammy hand clenching his as the Jeep suddenly veered from its course and stopped.

The other kids raised their fists and shouted at the Jeep.

"Bastards!"

"Chicken fuckers!"

"Silence!" Father's strident voice cautioned. "Stay behind me." He strode forward, shielding his eyes from a brightness that obscured the murderous men.

The kids huddled, defenseless against the growling Jeep. To Alex's relief, the doors didn't open. Instead, the monstrous thing ground into reverse, roared backward through the yard and careened into a wide street leading from the *barrio*. Father Chiabras remained in his defensive stance, shielding the kids until the vehicle had vanished.

"Did you see those men, Alex?" Father called, his chalky face dotted with perspiration.

"The one with the mustache." Wincing at his memory of the wicked man, Alex walked toward Father. "And if we can't save

Fernando, I do not care if he kills me."

"No death wishes." Father gripped Alex's upper arm.

Alex slumped.

Blue eyes flashing, Father began to pace. "*La Sombra* went for one of my kids, a warning for me to stop telling the UN about how they murder our children." Tears spotted his cheeks. "And yet, how can I stop?"

"You can't stop," Alex said with resolve. "But I will get those men."

Father Chiabras placed a finger on Alex's lips, but Alex avoided the priest's eyes. Shuffling his worn athletic shoe against the pavement, he swore a secret oath on the blood of *Jesucristo*: someday, he would inflict the worst possible hurt on the mustached man and his friends, he'd twist a knife into the bastards and grind it into their livers. If he failed, he'd lie down and die from his life so hard to live—sixteen years in this mean, forsaken city.

As the group snuck down a tight walkway between the hovels, Alex glared at the squatters who gawked from their staked-out squares of land. The empty plaza greeted him like a sad friend, as Rodrigo, the boy with the infected leg, staggered toward them from *Calle Roja*, his eyes glassy, his clumsy hands dangling beside his scrawny body.

"He has seen the devil," Elena whispered.

"Where's Fernando?" Alex asked, his voice a distant choking sound.

Rodrigo shook his head. "Don't go down *Calle Roja*, Alex," he said as he approached. "Do not go."

Weighted with dread, Alex closed his eyes, certain that he must go.

TWO

A dreary dawn arrived as the sun spread its spider arms of orange and yellow light through the polluted haze of Guatemala City. Alex trudged into the cemetery with a spade slung over his shoulder, much like a soldier carrying a gun. A wealthy patron who admired Father's ministry had donated the tiny block where over twenty murdered children were buried. While Father Chiabras and four older boys searched for an empty space, Alex bent down and ran his fingers over the rough white crosses: Tomás, 12 *años*. Fatima, 17 *años*. Marcos, 14 *años*. Now there would be another cross: Fernando, 13 *años*.

Alex had dug graves here before, but today, he was numb. He withdrew a worn, plastic-covered photograph taken long ago in a picture booth, two grinning boys in front of their beautiful mother. The boys' bright expressions were eager and laughing, as if they had a future. Alex stared at the picture of his family before he tucked it in his pocket to face the torturous task. His chest burning with bile that continuously forced its way into his throat, Alex promised himself he would never care about anyone again, except Father Chiabras … maybe.

"Here under the tree," Father said, pointing to a barren patch between some twisted roots. The priest stuffed his chocolate-colored robe beneath the braided cord around his waist, then grabbed a shovel. Muffled voices and humid air pressed on Alex's body as he watched the priest's spindly leg force the spade into crusty earth and heard the first crunch of the ground breaking. Powerful and agile for a man in his fifties, Father Chiabras's bony arms, thinning hair, and pale skin masked a steady strength.

For over an hour they dug, until at last, Alex helped the boys lower Fernando, his mutilated face wrapped in their mother's red, yellow, and green *huipil*, her favorite poncho.

Soon, the younger children arrived carrying flowers and singing. Elena found her way to Alex and reached for his hand. Refusing her touch, he took up his spade and flung more soil on top of Fernando's body, shovel after shovel of cruel dirt, until the roar of a motor startled him. He wiped salty sweat from his eyes and glanced toward the road. When Alex spotted the red Jeep, his trembling hand clutched the spade. He moved his tongue around his mouth, touching his teeth, imagining how it must have felt if Fernando was still alive when those bastards cut out his tongue.

The Jeep kept circling the graveyard—around and around—until Alex thought he'd scream. The others saw it too, and although he knew they held their fright inside for his sake, the stench of terror hung in the air.

"Keep shoveling and do not look at them," Father Chiabras said.

Alex kept his head down but his ears alert.

Father approached, patting Alex's shoulder. "They know you saw them. I am making arrangements for you to leave the city."

"But I don't want to leave you." Alex tried to hold his tears but he couldn't. Good times, he thought, are like falling stars, gone in a split-second before you can enjoy them. Bad times last forever. He kept thinking this one thing over and over. It served to quell his fear and the growing certainty that even though he'd proclaimed differently the night before, he didn't want to die.

"I have talked with Santiago, the *coyote*. He will take you to America."

"Father, it will cost so much money. Over a thousand US dollars, I've heard."

"More than that." Father smiled and patted Alex's arm. "Our patron gave me the money."

"But people say bad things about Santiago," Alex said in a hushed tone. His heart felt as if it were being squeezed by an iron fist.

"Perhaps some stories are true, but Santiago has given me his word. He will take special care of you." Embracing Alex, the priest continued, "When you arrive, you will work in Houston. There, you can learn a trade, and someday return to me and the children."

"I'm scared."

"It has to be, dear Alex." Father nodded at the circling Jeep. "It has to be."

*

Alex stood alone in the dorm room of *Casa Maria*. Recalling each kid's name and face, he memorized little things about his friends: high-pitched giggles, bad dreams, longing for disappeared parents, favorite stories, and joyful screeches when someone learned to write their name. He may never again see the cloth dolls and wooden trucks hidden under pillows, notebooks to practice letters, straw crosses above each bed, the cross above Fernando's bed. Alex slumped onto that bed made only yesterday by his brother's hands. When he traced his fingers over the folded blanket, a draft passed through the room, reminding him that dead souls frequently returned to their favorite places.

Burying his head in Fernando's pillow, he smelled his brother's scent and heard his voice calling. It wasn't an anguished cry, as Alex imagined it would be, but a soft whisper, the way Fernando used to talk after Father Chiabras had put out the lights and commanded them to go to sleep.

"*Beware of the rat,*" Fernando said.

Alex shot up from the pillow and listened to be certain he'd heard Fernando. A gauzy image of his brother materialized above the pine dresser.

"What do you mean 'the rat'?" Alex gaped.

"*I have been sent to tell you,*" his brother continued. "*Take special care after the rat arrives.*"

Hopping off the bed, Alex reached to hug his brother, but the apparition dissolved into the highest dresser drawer, left open by one of the children. Alex rushed to the drawer, searching madly through the folded shirts and shorts, feeling unusual warmth in the clothes. Fernando had been there, he was sure of it. Taking a deep breath to treasure the soapy aroma of the freshly laundered clothing, Alex resolved not to tell a soul. They'd think he was *loco*.

He flew into action, fueled with a new enthusiasm brought on by the certainty that he'd see Fernando again. Alex stuffed a backpack with his other pair of jeans, a T-shirt, some books Father had taught him to read, water bottles, and a supply of tortillas wrapped in a rag. Lastly, Alex removed Fernando's pillowcase, folded it into a neat square, and gently placed it in his pack.

From the corner of his eye, he spied Elena lingering in the doorway. "When will you come home?" She asked in a hoarse voice too old for her age.

Alex went to her immediately. He squatted to meet her inquiring eyes, round as soup bowls. "I will miss you, *chiquita*," he said.

"But when?" She thrust her hands on her hips.

Alex shook his head but couldn't mouth the words. He hoped he lived through this day. He hoped he'd make it to the States. He hoped to return and help them all, but saying these things could bring bad luck. Instead he signed himself and went to kneel in front of Maria de Guadalupe's altar. Elena tiptoed up behind him, and he felt her presence, innocent but very strong, as Fernando had been. Alex stared at the altar strewn with dried flowers, locks of hair, and children's drawings, all gifts to the Virgin. He lit a candle and watched the silver plume curl from its flame, but a bleak, uneasy feeling filled his soul. No matter how hard he tried, Alex couldn't pray.

Accompanied by a group of younger children who traipsed into the dormitory, Father padded barefoot across the tile floor. He still wore his blue nightshirt, his eyes encircled with dark lines. "It is time," he said.

"*Sí.*" Alex hitched his backpack over one shoulder, kissed Elena's soft cheek, and felt her lashes brush his face. Then he hugged the others, inhaling their sweet and sour puppy-dog odors, collecting more memories for his trip.

When they reached the door, Father removed a gold cross from his neck and placed it around Alex's. "Wear this under your shirt, or they will take it from you."

Alex examined the cross's plain hammered surface with no figure of *Jesucristo*. Alarmed, he met Father's gaze.

"Our Lord's body is missing," he said. "Where is He?"

"He's in your heart, dear Alex." Father wrapped him in his sinewy arms.

All the kids gathered to say good-bye, but their jabbering ceased at the clack of the doorknocker. After Father checked the peephole and unbolted the lock, a short, wiry man known as Santiago bustled in. Alex had seen him in the streets, unmistakable with his gelled hair, diamond-studded ear, sun-cracked skin, and dark stubble framing his mouth stuck in a permanent sneer.

Alex stepped forward to identify himself to the *coyote*, but Father Chiabras pulled him back for a final blessing. As he lifted his hand,

Santiago grumbled something about being late already and doing Father a big favor.

Alex's heart fluttered like a trapped bird in the rib cage of his body. He studied the man's hard face, so unlike Father Chiabras. For three years he and Fernando had lived at *Casa Maria*, soaking up everything Father could teach his unruly minions. Alex had believed it would be his home forever. Now the hour to leave had come, and he didn't think he could go.

Guiding Alex toward Santiago, Father pressed a card into Alex's palm. "Find this woman. She went to Houston to help our people there. Her house is called *Casa de Luz*."

"I remember her." Alex's spirit lightened as he thought of the energetic little nun's lilting laughter and constant encouragement. She'd worked with Father when Alex first came.

"Do not be surprised," Father said. "She is no longer a nun. Now, she calls herself Obispa."

Alex started to ask more about Obispa, but his mind was full. He inhaled the warm air inside *Casa Maria*, then strode toward the door.

America, he thought, remembering his mother's wish. *A step over Rio.*

THREE

As she parked her car near a crumbling curb in the *barrio*, Elizabeth Grant spoke the woman's name out loud. "Obispa." It was the popular name of a well-known shaman, revered by everyone with whom Elizabeth had spoken as she developed a series on Guatemalan illegals who'd fallen victim to US slavery rings. She'd chosen this subject because of the deplorable poverty in Guatemala, recent data about trafficked children, and other human rights tragedies she wanted to document—all in hopes of winning a Pulitzer.

She glanced at the gunmetal sky. Clouds shrouded the afternoon sun, and a gloomy mist had settled over the city, a herald for the icy rain predicted to arrive at nightfall. Elizabeth tightened the belt of her gray raincoat, girding herself for winter air and longing for Houston's summer days when sunlight stretched into lazy evenings.

Before she left the Beemer, a '95 wreck she should have traded for cash, she finger-combed her hair and bunched it into a clasp at the nape of her neck. Withdrawing a business card from her purse, she stepped onto the sidewalk near a brightly painted sign, *Casa de Luz*.

The brick bungalow tucked behind two sprawling oaks was a cut above the other shabby homes on the street and offered a promising counterpoint to the electric-blue cantina, *Noche Azul*, at the end of the block. Elizabeth hurried up the walkway over four beveled stones placed in a perfect square, a hole chiseled into the center. She climbed red cement steps, walked across a wraparound porch, and peered through a window at hundreds of glittering votives. *Casa de Luz*, she thought, "House of Light." The pleasant scent of burning wax spread from the interior as if its balm could heal the shabby street. Brightly painted quetzal birds, two-headed snakes, and a spotted jaguar, Mayan symbols she remembered from her Central American studies, guarded the door on both sides.

Before she pressed the bell, a diminutive woman with brown-sugar skin and a heart-shaped face opened the door. She held a lighted candle, its flame casting shimmers onto her creamy cotton smock as shadows danced across her face.

Taken in by violet flecks glinting in the woman's eyes, Elizabeth caught herself staring, quickly recovered, and offered her hand. "*Navidad Maria Cid?*"

"Please, call me Obispa." The woman spoke in accented English. "Come in." Cupping the flame on the taper, she turned to face a line of unlit candles among the throng of flames and began to light them one by one.

Elizabeth stepped into a vestibule that led to the living room, where more votives brimmed from iron stands and flickered off the somber-hued fabrics of a cushy sofa. Haunting flute music from *la mísa católica*, the Catholic Mass, floated in the smoky air.

"What's with this candle thing?" Elizabeth asked the shaman, who was still busy lighting.

Obispa pivoted, her violet eyes an enigma. "I have read your articles about my people in the *Chronicle*. I thought you might be Hispanic, but your light skin and yellow hair. It is not possible, *sí*?"

"I'm mostly English, I guess," Elizabeth said. The shaman made her nervous. No, it was more like fearful, and Elizabeth seldom felt uncomfortable in an interview. There was something intensely personal about how this woman held her gaze and seemed to look right through Elizabeth. Biting her lip, she asked, "Where do you want me?"

"Want you?" Obispa raised an eyebrow, then to Elizabeth's surprise, she returned to lighting candles.

"I mean, where can we have our interview?" She stifled an antsy sensation.

The shaman didn't speak again until after she'd bowed her head in front of twenty-four freshly lit tapers. "Welcome to my *Casa de Luz*. Please, come sit beside me." She glided to the sofa and patted her hand on a cushion.

Elizabeth remained standing. "Why did you light all those candles?"

"I perform this ritual with every new visitor," she said. "My little flames give me insight into your desires and conflicts, and at times, I have visions of your future."

Elizabeth felt herself moving from nervousness into downright irritation. Time was precious to her, and she'd wasted a boatload of it driving halfway across town to interview an eccentric woman who maybe saw things, things Elizabeth really didn't want to know about. The shaman didn't appear to be interested in the interview topics Elizabeth had outline on the telephone, yet, she felt compelled to try. As the chant drifted through the room, she took a seat next to the shaman and withdrew a digital recorder from her purse.

"No." Obispa held up her hand. "You may not use that machine. We will have a conversation."

Elizabeth stuffed the recorder into her bag and glanced away. Piercing eyes watched her from mask-covered walls, vibrant red and blue devils, spitting fire and eating children amid orange-whiskered jaguars and phantasmal snakes turning into people, humans evolving into lizards, frogs into birds. She blinked and felt her mind slipping off-kilter in the shaman's sanctuary.

When Obispa began to speak, Elizabeth slowly withdrew a pen and pad in hopes that the woman wouldn't object to notes.

"Since I left the convent, I have worked with Father Chiabras, a priest in Guatemala City, to establish a network for our people who come to the US."

"You were a nun?" Although Elizabeth had intended to focus on trafficking, her astonishment steered the conversation.

Obispa nodded. "But now, I have taken up the healing practices of my grandmother, a shaman of our tribe who was also a bonesetter and a midwife."

"I guess it's my urban living, but I've never actually met anyone from a 'tribe.'"

"I am a Quiché *Indio* from northern Guatemala. We are descendents of the ancient Mayans, and my people who live in the US need a *curandera* who practices traditional ceremonies."

"So, are shamans and *curanderas* the same?"

"No," she said. "But I am both. A *curandera* has gifts to cure the sick, while a shaman performs ceremonies to heal the human spirit."

"I think I see the difference," Elizabeth said, scribbling fast. "Tell me about your name, Obispa. It means bishop, right?"

"*Sí.* My people have honored me with this name."

"And you deliver babies, like your grandmother?"

"Absolutely. Birth and death are the greatest miracles."

Obispa folded her petite hands in her lap. Her entire persona emanated a sense of peace and satisfaction, the exact opposite of Elizabeth's tumultuous existence, running from investigation to investigation, frantic for stories to create a buzz for her readers, and sandwiching in her duties as a mother.

The shaman gestured at the masks. "My grandmother taught me herbal medicine and shamanic rituals to cure tormented souls. You see, the devils on my wall are artistic expressions of interior demons."

Elizabeth refused to consider her own helter-skelter existence or to look at the creepy masks again. "How long were you in the convent?"

"For eleven years I served my order, the Sisters of Mary, but when they sent me to the Houston *barrio*, I experienced a desire to minister to my people in a more complete way."

Through an arched door leading into the dining room, Elizabeth spotted an icon of the Virgin of Guadalupe. Before she formulated a question about this apparent contradiction, Obispa seemed to perceive it.

"I am a Christian who understands ancient rituals. For example, when a couple gets married, I perform a ceremony on four stone slabs, symbols of the corners of the Earth and the corners of their new house. Spirits who control the four directions receive my offerings, and they bless the bride and groom. Afterward, I light twenty-four candles, sprinkle rose petals and drink *aguardiente*. It is important to have this ceremony for my people."

"I understand," Elizabeth said, recalling the four stones in front of *Casa de Luz*. Unaccustomed to writing so fast, she jotted some details, intending to clarify them at the end of the conversation. "And what is this '*aguardiente*' you mentioned?"

"It means 'burning water.'" The shaman's lips parted in a devious grin. "But really, it is the drink you call rum." Reaching for the teapot on a side table, she poured a cupful of a steaming brown liquid and handed it to Elizabeth.

Its fragrance wasn't rum or any other alcoholic beverage she could discern. Chocolate perhaps. Elizabeth gutted up and sipped. Yes, a bittersweet cocoa.

Aromatic vapors permeated her facial bones, descended into her limbs, and ushered in a rare sense of relaxation. To speak out loud seemed a transgression now amid the flute's melodic drone in this house that smelled like an ancient cathedral.

After allowing herself to enjoy a moment's peace, Elizabeth slowly refocused. "Tell me more about your work," she said.

"When Guatemalan people come here, I help them find a place to live, a job, childcare, the essentials for a good life."

"My editor wants me to interview someone who's been a victim of human trafficking."

"Your articles have revealed many of our problems, *señora*, and I am very grateful. But I cannot give you names. I will tell their stories for them."

"That won't work," Elizabeth said. "I need a personal interview."

The shaman rose and ran her fingers over the edge of a votive stand. "My people are afraid to talk to reporters."

"I can't get a front-page spread unless someone speaks to me directly, and I know you want their stories to get maximum attention."

"It will not be easy." She threw her hands in the air, then quietly brought them to her chin as if in prayer.

"See what you can do. I'm sure we can work something out."

"There is one man who was forced to work on a North Texas ranch to pay for his passage. When he escaped, he came to me. I am trying to find him work now."

Elizabeth could barely contain her thrill at the prospect of interviewing an indentured worker. "I'll make every effort not to reveal his identity, and maybe I can find him a job."

A smile graced the shaman's lips. "Perhaps it could be arranged." Obispa resettled herself beside Elizabeth. "I will speak to him."

Elizabeth felt the time was right to ask the urgent question she'd been holding back. She cradled the cup in her hands before swallowing the last drop of cocoa. "As you know, I just started the series, and I've been focusing on illegals who are forced to work in cantinas. After I wrote the first article, I started receiving anonymous tips on my cell."

Obispa tilted her head.

"Last week, a person with a muffled voice told me about a raid led by sheriff's deputies and agents from the State Department. It was true, all right. I went straight to the cantina, but the cops wouldn't let me in."

The shaman's eyes probed her. "Did the caller threaten you?"

"Not at all."

"If the person had tried to scare you or hurt you, I would suspect

Tulio Mola."

"Mola. Yes." Elizabeth's throat tightened. The man was a drug lord and suspected murderer who had a stranglehold on the *barrios*. "You know him?"

"He is depraved." Obispa gazed at her wall of masks. "He has visited my *casa*, and he has put his hands on me."

Elizabeth's pulse hammered at this unexpected turn in the interview. What had Mola done to this woman? Her mind swimming for a response, she could find nothing to say. She wasn't good at consoling people; in fact, she was lousy at it, so she edged closer and placed her hand on top of the shaman's tiny hand, now balled into a fist.

FOUR

Luke Santa Maria scrutinized the totems adorning a brick bungalow called *Casa de Luz*. The house seemed to glow from within, a hot coal simmering in dusk's half-light.

Seated in the passenger seat of an '11 Chevy sedan, he drummed his fingers on the dashboard of the obnoxious surveillance vehicle provided by the State Department's Diplomatic Security Service. Even more obnoxious was his partner Dominic Fontana's rhythmic snores and slack jaw. Luke jiggled the cord attached to Dominic's earphones and clicked off the audio player wedged between his thighs. No response, so Luke tugged a strand of Dominic's black ponytail. Nothing.

He envied his partner's ability to nod off, sometimes minutes before a raid, but all too frequently, Dominic would awaken in a state of hyper-agitation, fueled by unpredictable rage. Still, in spite of these eruptions, he operated more effectively than most DSS agents, and for as long as Luke could remember, he'd covered for his heat-seeking missile of a partner.

"Yo! We're running tight." Luke punched Dominic's arm.

Dominic's facial muscles twitched. "What?" He yawned, squinting into the early evening fog. "Where's Grant?"

"She's been talking to your new CI for over an hour. I don't like it," Luke said.

"Obispa's been an informant before. She won't tell that reporter squat." Dominic eased off his earphones.

"We can't afford any glitches." Luke rubbed his five-o'clock shadow. "I plan to stop Grant's meddling."

"From what I've heard about her bitchy ways, you'll have a battle on your hands." Dominic winked. "But hey, she's a looker. Could be fun."

Ignoring the innuendo, Luke tapped his watch and gave his partner the look. "Have you forgotten the time?"

"I want you to meet Obispa, just in case I'm out of pocket," Dominic said.

"A memorable visit, I'm sure."

Dominic shrugged. "After this is over, I have intentions."

"Does this mean you're going to clean up your act?" Luke chortled. "Death to the ponytail?"

"Not squeaky clean like you, GI Joe."

Luke scanned the house again, this time wondering about the woman who was interesting enough to snag Dominic's attention. "Aside from carnal intentions, what's your take on this 'shaman'?"

Dominic angled a knowing look at him. "First off, I'd say she has principles."

"Principles?" Luke had heard that one before.

"Yeah. The lady's like me. She believes gangs, drugs, and prostitution are bringing her people down—lower than she's gonna stand for."

"What's her story?"

"Nothing subversive or anti-American." Dominic opened a tin of breath mints. "It's simple. We pay well, and she needs the money."

Luke considered the financial thrashing he'd just experienced in his divorce. Splitting everything fifty-fifty had cleaned him out. "We all need money."

"Yeah, but she's a former nun who helps people with food, housing, clothes. You know the kind." He popped a handful of mints into his mouth.

"And her Guatemalan connection?"

"A Catholic priest who's been working with homeless kids for years."

"Makes you wonder. I mean, with all the scandals about priests and kids."

"Naw."

"The guy could be a pervert."

"No arrest records and the street says he's a good guy. Has contacts at the UN."

"You don't sound like my partner." Luke threw a wad of paper at him. "Find out more about this priest," he said, certain now that Dominic was thinking with his dick rather than his brain.

FIVE

Her hand still on Obispa's, Elizabeth Grant shuddered, remembering what she'd learned about Tulio Mola while writing a series on Houston children born to gang members. Mola's name had surfaced as the ruthless leader of the Latin Angels. He'd been arrested several times but had always eluded charges. At the time, Elizabeth had wondered why he hadn't been prosecuted, but she'd never investigated. She'd begin her query now in the shaman's House of Light.

"Tell me about Mola," she said.

"He is very tall. In the past, he wore a black vest with no shirt, and you could see his skeleton tattoos. Now he has shaved his head, buys expensive clothes, and always wears a leather jacket. He runs prostitution, drugs, and extortion rings in the *barrios*. And worse, the man has no conscience." When Obispa spoke, the nearby flames wilted as if extinguished by an invisible hand.

"What happened when he visited you?"

"I had just opened my *casa*. He and one of his thugs came into this room without knocking or ringing my bell. My candles could not breathe in the presence of those wicked men." Obispa folded her hands and stared at her lap.

"Mola wanted money for the Latin Angels to protect me, and I said I would never give him anything. The snake unzipped his pants and shoved himself against my body. I slapped his face. He pushed harder. I was trembling, but still, I confronted him with what I knew. 'You are a seventh son,' I said. Mola stepped away as if I had the plague. And what I said was true, *Señora* Grant. Tulio Mola's father was a Guatemalan curer who had clairvoyant powers."

The shaman's piercing gaze fell on Elizabeth.

"You may not believe me, *Señora* Grant, but when Mola was a baby in his mother's womb, he made such fiendish howls his father declared the child would be born without a soul. If it had not been for his mother's mercy, the family would have killed him at birth, but she secretly took him to an orphanage."

"How do you know these things?"

"In my country, the street has a wagging tongue."

"What did Mola do to you?" Elizabeth found the word rape catch in her throat.

"The seventh son is evil, but not more powerful than I."

Elizabeth wanted to press the shaman for details, but she couldn't make herself.

Speaking in low tones, Obispa smoothed her skirt. "The day of that visit, I told Mola never to return to my House of Light. He zipped his pants but did not take his vulture-eyes off me. He slapped a piece of paper on the table and demanded fifty dollars a week for protection. I refused again. His thug ripped my precious *tigre* from the wall and jammed it under his boot."

She gestured toward an orange and black whiskered tiger mask centered in the middle of the devils. "I did not beg him to preserve my mask. Instead, I gripped the amulet around my neck and told Tulio Mola if he ever came here again, I would send the Black Moth to eat his heart and call upon the airs of the damned to torment him."

Madly scribbling, Elizabeth glanced at Obispa's stunning but intense face.

"Mola fears the Black Moth curse, and he knows I will do these things to him, so he left with his thug, who did not crush my *tigre*."

"You're very brave." Elizabeth pressed her lips together, then fell into silence, considering the Black Moth and the airs of the damned. She'd save those questions for later. At the moment, she had to get this train back on track.

"Since you've been leading the movement to expose trafficking in the *barrios*, I hoped you'd have an idea about who my mysterious caller is. The person has a Spanish accent."

"Maybe one of the children who works at those hideous cantinas?"

"I doubt a kid would know about these raids," Elizabeth said. "Today, I received another call. *Zona Azul*. Seven o'clock tonight."

She shrugged, remembering the club, *Noche Azul*, right down the street. "Two cantinas in this area have *azul* in their name."

The shaman's face fell into a frown, and her mouth tightened. "Those 'blue' cantinas are owned by Mola and his gang, the Latin Angels. They enslave girls and boys. I have seen them dancing with the customers."

"I'm afraid they're doing more than dancing."

"It is an abomination." Obispa bit her lower lip. "Go to the raid, *Señora* Grant, and write everything you see happening to my people."

Elizabeth nodded. She felt a trickle of empathy for this woman, an emotion that seldom surfaced from Elizabeth's hard-nosed veneer.

"It's so peaceful here," she said, basking in the soft sheen of shadows.

"*Casa de Luz* is restful for some, for others, it is not." Obispa walked into the dining room and bowed in front of the Virgin of Guadalupe. She selected a burning taper, reseated herself, and held the candle so near Elizabeth's cheek, it felt as if it might singe her lashes.

"This flame tells me you are a driven woman," she said.

Unsettled, Elizabeth studied the shaman. She could have easily guessed about Elizabeth, and besides, anyone who dealt with people all the time could read a person's motivations.

"You want to be recognized more than anything."

Caught off-guard again, Elizabeth snapped an abrupt reply, blurting information she hadn't intended to give. "My daughter, Kate, says that all the time."

Obispa continued, her voice a hush of certainty. "There is a deep valley between you and your daughter."

"Stop it. She's a teenager."

"There is more—"

"Look. Kate has an attitude." Elizabeth's stomach quivered. She wanted to say the hell with fortune telling, but she couldn't afford to lose the fragile trust she'd built with Obispa. "Speaking of my daughter, I need to get home for supper." Elizabeth forced a smile, trying to hide the untruthful tone in her voice. It would be quite a while before she'd be eating with Kate. She was going to the raid at *Zona Azul*.

"Your daughter misses you." The shaman stared at Elizabeth. "Do you spend much time with her?"

"Most nights," she said. "After work, I pick up takeout meals. We eat together." Elizabeth checked her watch. Six p.m. She snatched her coat and headed for the door.

Obispa followed. "In your house, there are problems."

"There are problems in every house." Elizabeth tromped down the red cement steps, and when she reached the four square stones, she turned toward the shaman, hands on hips, her voice shrill and shaky. "And by the way, you sound just like Kate."

SIX

Luke Santa Maria watched the leggy *Chronicle* reporter, Elizabeth Grant, climb into her Beemer and rev the engine. How much trouble could she be? No one knew better than Luke how a poorly timed news story could damage an investigation, but on the other hand, he'd negotiated cooperative agreements with the media on several occasions.

After the reporter had rounded the corner, Dominic moved the Chevy forward, parking the crap-mobile in front of *Casa de Luz*. Grabbing his jean jacket, Luke swung out, closed the door, and waited on a patch of dry winter grass. When Dominic remained in the car, Luke peered through window to find his partner inspecting his reflection in the rearview mirror.

"Jeezus, Dom! Get a move on."

Dominic straightened his collar, methodically subtracted an envelope from the glove box, and slipped from the car. They hadn't reached the door before it opened to reveal a petite woman with exotic lavender eyes and chiseled Mayan features. Now Luke understood his partner's interest, a lovely presence, to say the least.

"Agent Fontana, so nice to see you." Obispa's voice was breezy and warm, as she touched Dominic's arm, allowing her hand to linger for a moment.

"Obispa," Dominic said. "This is my partner, Luke Santa Maria."

Luke held out his hand and was surprised at her hardy shake. She stood aside so they could enter the room, heavy with the scent of melting wax. Although Dominic had described *Casa de Luz*, Luke hadn't imagined the multitude of primitive artifacts or the spooky flute music that mingled among the thousand beacons of light. When the State Department had sent him to Central and South America, he'd developed a fondness for folk art, but this stuff was out of his league.

"Where are you from?" Obispa asked Luke.

"Born and raised in Amarillo," he said, pulling his gaze from the art display back to the shaman. Suddenly Luke found himself offering more information than she'd asked for. "Our family was a rarity in North Texas. My grandparents on both sides came from Italy."

Tilting her head with an amused smile, she said, "Ah, an Italian."

Dominic and Luke followed her into the glimmering room, past statues of saints and pagan masks. She paused at the front window and opened the lace curtain. Dominic groped in his jacket and passed her the envelope. She opened it and meticulously counted the bills twice before folding the money into her pocket. All CIs checked their payments, but Luke found himself ticked off at her apparent distrust. He questioned whether Elizabeth Grant had also paid the shaman for information about the cantinas, and God knows what else.

From the front window, Obispa gestured toward *Noche Azul*, the "Blue Night" cantina at the end of the street. The parking lot was a pantheon of vehicles: pickups, wreckers, and lowriders at the rear, versus expensive cars conspicuously parked near the front door. "The ruin of our *barrio*," she said.

"Not for long," Dominic replied, his lip curled. "We're gonna make those bastards wish they were dead."

Obispa's eyes darted at him. A good hand-length taller than the shaman, Dominic peered down at her, his scowl softened, all evidence of hostility evaporating into the smoke-laden air.

"Just joking," he said.

My partner's going down, Luke thought.

"Tell us what you've seen," Dominic said to Obispa.

"White vans arrive at night and unload groups of boys and girls who are taken inside by the drivers," she said.

"Define *young*," Luke said.

"Teenagers. Some look younger, ten to twelve. It is hard to tell in the dark, Agent Santa Maria."

"How often do they come?"

"Every two or three weeks. Another van should arrive in a few days." She stepped to a teapot resting on a spool-legged table. "Would you like some cocoa?"

Luke tapped his watch and glanced at Dominic. The raid at *Zona Azul* was at seven p.m.

"We have a few minutes," Dominic said with an impish smirk.

Luke acquiesced, reasoning that *Zona Azul*, the sister cantina to *Noche Azul*, wasn't far from the shaman's, and Dominic knew the streets.

Spying an overstuffed chair, Luke sank into its cushions, his arms spanning the armrests, his hands dangling over the ends. Dominic and Obispa settled on the couch next to each other. As she poured the cocoa, Luke eyed her ceramic teapot, a plump frog with a serpent's head for the spout. Everything in the house was evolving into something else, but he decided to quit analyzing what he didn't understand. Maybe he'd learn something. When the shaman handed Luke a cup of cocoa, he enjoyed the tasty warmth in his mouth, sipping and listening, first to her quiet fury about the exploitation of illegal kids, followed by an account of her shamanic practices.

"And now before you leave, I will read your candle," she said to Dominic.

With poise, she rose from the couch and bowed at an altar where she withdrew a taper. The altar, a small end table pressed against a wall between myriad votives, held a crudely carved statue of a man with birds resting on his arms and a docile wolf beside him. The statue stood among vases of dried flowers and a smattering of carved, brightly colored wooden animals.

"Good old St. Francis loved the critters," Luke said, staring at the statue and recalling a visit to Assisi with his grandparents.

Obispa didn't comment. Returning to the couch, she positioned herself close to Dominic and brought the candle to his cheek. The flame sparkled in his pupils. When he smiled, it gleamed off his teeth.

Luke leaned forward. "Are you reading his face or his palm?"

"I am reading his fire," she said. The shaman's eyes seemed to trace every line on Dominic's face as she brought the candle closer and closer until he flinched, arching his back as if he couldn't stand the heat. She slowly shifted the candle to his other cheek. Luke wanted to say *enough*, but he understood the need to show cultural respect to this CI.

After switching the candle from cheek to cheek several times, Obispa's serene expression vanished. For a moment, Luke took her sudden gravity as an end to the ceremony, but then there was more silence, and he suspected she was trying to hide what she'd seen in

Dominic's candle. The shaman touched her finger to her lips and ran it through the flame again and again until Dominic gently clasped her wrist.

"'Fess up, Obispa," he said. "What do you see?"

"I do not reveal my visions."

"Then what's the point?" Luke asked. "He deserves to know."

After quiet deliberation, she said to Dominic, "I will give you a protection."

"Protection from what?" Dominic jerked his head away from the candle. "Let's put that thing out." Inhaling a mouthful of air, he puckered at the flame, but she touched his lips with her fingertips.

"Never blow out a fortune." She rose and placed the candle in its holder. "It is the worst luck."

"What does that mean?" A gloom crept into Dominic's eyes.

That did it. Now the witchy woman had spooked his partner, who wasn't easy to scare by any means. "We're outta here." Luke stood up.

Obispa removed a small oval buckskin bag from her neck and looped it around Dominic's. "My talisman will keep you from harm."

Dominic fingered the pouch.

"There are other ways—" she began.

"Unless you have more information about *Noche Azul*, we're leaving," Luke said.

Dominic raised himself from the couch and trailed Luke to the car like a cowed dog. When they reached the sedan, Luke heard Obispa calling his name. She stood on the porch and held up his jacket. With a sense of dread, he jogged back to retrieve it from the shaman, her diminutive body frozen as if she were a statue and her crystalline eyes drifting past him to something only she could see.

Luke wasn't sure if he was genuinely afraid for his buddy or if he was being suckered into fear by a feral, demented creature. "What's the problem with Dominic?" He asked in a low voice after he took his jacket.

Obispa drew her hands in front of her mouth, bowed her head, and didn't answer.

"Shit," Luke said under his breath. "This was a bad idea."

SEVEN

As they drove through the *barrio*, the evening fog created an eerie mist on the car windows. Luke stared through the windshield at clusters of cans and piles of litter lining the curbs beneath a haze of streetlights. He winced when Dominic weaved the car from side to side on the battered street, a rough scar running the length of the neighborhood. But tonight Luke decided to keep his *bad driving* comments to himself because he felt certain his partner was spooked by Obispa's mumbo-jumbo. To tell the truth, Luke was uncomfortable, too. He'd never forgotten the creepy stories about Dominic's parents consulting shamans and *curanderos* when he and Dom were growing up.

Dominic swerved to miss a pothole, then steered the sedan into a hardened rut, bounding to a halt near a chain-link fence a half block from *Zona Azul*. All the homes were surrounded by fences, their windows secured with burglar bars. In shadowy spaces between the houses, Luke could see huddled silhouettes of street people sharing cigarettes, or maybe they were teens who'd snuck outside to smoke weed. A pungent aroma in the chilly night air told him the latter was the case.

Luke and Dominic left the car and strode past unmarked sheriff's vehicles toward *Zona Azul*, a trendy Mexican restaurant and bar. It had a rap for attracting West Side yuppies and downtown loft-dwellers, as well as people from the *barrios*—quite the chic thing nowadays for the thirty-something crowd to mix with the unwashed masses.

"Knock 'em dead," Dominic said as they headed toward the DSS surveillance van.

Luke grinned, relieved to see a twinkle in Dominic's eyes.

A sheriff's deputy in a starched tan uniform approached. "Some of my men are at the rear. We'll stop anyone who leaves." He spoke above the din of *Tejano* music. "The cantina's back door leads into a room where the kids are kept, and a hallway from that room opens into the restaurant."

Nodding the ready, Luke drew his SIG Sauer. "We'll go through the front with you guys," he said to the deputies. As they approached the building, the shaman's candlelit face appeared in Luke's mind. He glanced at Dominic. "Watch your ass, buddy."

Zona Azul was bloated with boisterous music, a hectic beat in a helter-skelter milieu. Waiters skated back and forth from a fancy indigo bar to bright-blue booths with mosaic tabletops. The ceiling swayed with *piñatas* floating above a host of curious patrons, all of whom were now fixed on the officers who'd just entered the restaurant.

Dominic took the arm of a doe-eyed, spongy-breasted hostess and asked in Spanish for her to point out the manager's office. She gestured to a closed door near the far end of the bar, and one of the deputies headed that way. Luke led the others toward the backroom, where he hoped to find evidence that juvenile prostitutes were working to pay off their debts to *coyotes* and the cantina owners.

They invaded a room with velvet wall coverings, plush sofas, and dim wall sconces that reminded Luke of a Victorian saloon. His gut tightened. Young girls, some looking no more than ten or eleven, garbed in filmy blouses, their midriffs exposed to their pubic bones, danced with men old enough to be their grandfathers. He counted seventeen patrons and twelve girls. There were two doors, the one they'd just entered and another in the corner leading to the rear parking area where the deputies waited. Cigarette smoke stung his nostrils, and he noticed several lines of cocaine disappearing into anxious noses. He and Dominic flashed their badges.

"Diplomatic Security Service." Luke spoke in both English and Spanish, asking everyone to remain calm and to cooperate.

Bodies flew out the rear door into the arms of waiting deputies, who marched them back inside straightaway. When the group realized their escape hatch was blocked, an uneasy calm descended. Deputies handcuffed the male suspects and searched them for weapons. Huddling in the middle of the parlor, the girls wailed and clutched each other's waists while the jukebox howled a Mexican rock song.

Dominic's forehead beading with sweat, he aimed his SIG at the jukebox and fired into its belly. As the machine blinked and sputtered, the girls shrieked even louder. "Goddammit, *chicas*, you're safe with us." He pivoted and jammed his gun under the cheekbone of a blond guy who'd been pawing one of the girls. "We rescued you from these mother-fucking kiddy rapists."

The deputies gawped at Dominic as if deciding whether to participate in the harassment or to stop him. Luke immediately stepped toward his partner, but he was startled by rapid bursts of light slashing through the smoky air. He spun around to see Elizabeth Grant whoosh in from the restaurant behind a rotund, red-faced man armed with a professional camera.

Dominic's color drained when he spied the reporter. He swiftly stuffed his gun into his belt and cuffed the quivering blond. A front-page picture of Dominic roughing up an arrestee would undoubtedly put an end to his outbursts. And most likely his career.

The flashes kept coming. Agitated prisoners flung their cuffed arms in front of their faces and yelled rich insults at the photographer. Taking advantage of the commotion, a bony girl attempted to squeeze between Grant and her cameraman. The reporter took the girl's arm and had the audacity to question the child in Spanish.

"You can't take pictures," Luke called to them. "And no interviews."

The girl edged over to the cluster of other girls. Shrugging, the camera jockey stepped out of the room, but Grant didn't budge. Dressed in a black sweater and pants, she stood, arms akimbo, tapping her long, slim foot on the floor—all in all, a determined bitch of a woman.

Two prisoners, a meaty man with a handlebar mustache and a grizzled soldier type who kept spitting on the floor, burst into laughter.

"Hey, copper, you're being pussy-whipped," the mustache said.

"Are you really cops? I've never heard of the fucking Diplomatic Security Service." The other guy grinned and spat again.

"Sounds un-American to me," someone called.

Ignoring them, Luke strode toward Grant. She'd regret this public defiance. "I need you to leave," he said.

"No way," she replied.

Edging past her, Dominic snarled behind her back, then said

to Luke, "I'm going to check the manager's whereabouts." Luke felt somewhat relieved. Dominic had recovered from his fury and perhaps from Obispa's candle-visions.

"Why did he shoot the jukebox?" Grant asked.

Luke fought to maintain a polite air because he didn't want her writing about Dominic's angry bout with the jukebox or his harassment of the blond suspect. "Ms. Grant, you cannot stay here, and under no circumstances can you interview these girls."

"You know my name," she said, her chin tilted upward, her neck muscles taut.

"Correct. And now, you're outta here."

"The hell I am." Her green-flecked eyes seized upon him with a curious mockery. "What's your name, Officer?"

Ripping a card from his pocket, Luke shoved it at her, then checked the situation. One deputy was herding prisoners out the door into sheriffs' vans destined for the county jail. Another wrote the wide-eyed girls' names on a notepad as they gripped each other's hands, holding tight in a cluster.

"What's going to happen to those children?" Grant asked.

"You never stop." Luke took hold of her elbow. To his surprise she acquiesced, stepping with him through the doorway that led to the restaurant.

"I said, what will happen to the children?"

"They'll be taken to a victims' shelter, but eventually most of them will be sent back to their own countries, and that's a horror story in itself." Luke spoke with no visible emotion, taking care to conceal his feelings. He felt a world of sadness for illegal kids who attempted to enter the US, and he was glad for the ones who were able to make lives for themselves here.

"They gave up everything." Grant's quiet voice left the impression she felt genuine sympathy.

Her tone could have been a ploy to lull him into saying something he'd regret, so Luke pressed his lips together, stifling a careless comment. "Come with me," he said instead. "We'll talk about this another time."

"You'll give me an exclusive?"

Against his better judgment, Luke nodded, and to his surprise, she pivoted and walked with him into the restaurant. They slipped sideways between tables piled with half-eaten *fajitas*, bowls of chips, and melting margaritas. He quelled a frivolous urge to chug a tequila and forget his mission of capturing the *coyotes* who smuggled kids into the country, and even more, the people who used them once they arrived.

When they reached the front door, Grant immediately strode toward Dominic, who was questioning a man Luke took to be the manager.

"Excuse me," she said. "Why'd you shoot the jukebox?"

Dominic blinked. "Not now, Ms. Grant."

"Everyone knows my name."

"Outside," Luke said, gesturing toward the door.

They marched to a covered porch where the photographer was waiting.

"Give me the camera, sir," Luke said to him.

"Last I heard, this is a free country," Grant said.

"Last I heard, you're not allowed to take pictures of juveniles."

Glancing at Grant for orders, the photographer shifted his weight from foot to foot.

"God damn," Luke said. "You can take a picture of the cantina, that's all."

In a haughty voice, Grant requested the camera, and the photographer handed it to Luke.

After he'd removed the memory stick and returned the camera, he called to a pruning peacock of a deputy who combed his hair and slouched against a squad car. "Yo, Johnny, escort these people outta here."

"You got it," Johnny said with a Hollywood smile. "I'm sorry I let them in, but they seemed so official."

Luke grimaced at the rookie, then said to Grant, "Call me for details."

"I will." She abruptly turned. Her willowy figure descended the steps, her head high, her shoulders arranged in perfect posture.

Luke presumed this was the first skirmish in a battle between them, so he relished the momentary pleasure of her retreat as well as the sight of her long legs gracefully carrying her into the night.

EIGHT

Alex huddled shoulder to shoulder with eight other teenagers, legs bent, bodies crunched between wooden crates. Their eyes smarted, and their lungs burned in the stifling air and ever-present haze of dust. They traveled in the rear of a truck whose sign read "Blue Agave Tile, *Ciudad Juárez*." On the first occasion they were allowed outside to stretch their legs and breathe fresh air, Alex had taken pride in reading the words painted on the truck and telling the others what they said.

Inside the truck, he passed the hours concentrating on light shards that crept through the linear vents. Depending on weather and time of day, the quality of light changed, sometimes casting fuzzy patterns, sometimes crisp designs on the crates. Alex employed another pastime when he tired of these light games. He counted the turquoise tiles brimming from frayed boxes, but he always returned to the glimmers of sunlight crosshatching his companions' faces, like the sparks of hope each one held inside.

Wiggling his toes to relieve persistent legs cramps, Alex brushed his foot against Mariella, a slender teenage girl with startled, olive-shaped eyes. She'd been in the truck when he'd first twisted himself into this crippling corner. Mariella had told him she was Panamanian, but that was all she'd reveal. Shortly after they met, more teenagers had come onboard, four boys and twin sisters from remote parts of Mexico, and now the group pressed against each other, smelling each others' bodies, maneuvering arms and legs to assuage their misery. As the journey progressed, each kid began to cough. Their chests ached, and their throats burned from breathing the vile powder that puffed from the boxes and fell into their hair with each bump in the road.

Forming animal shapes with his hands, Alex acted out silly stories he'd once used to entertain Elena. Everyone laughed, and he felt relief from the maddening rumble, the stench of vomit from a boy who'd been overwhelmed with motion sickness, and the acrid scent of urine. When one of the kids could no longer hold water, they all yelled and banged in unison on the truck's floor. Alex was certain the *coyote*, Santiago, heard their pleas, but he seldom stopped. The result was always the same, urine-soaked clothes. And if they complained, Santiago cut their water ration from two small bottles a day to one.

Each morning the weather was cool, but even so, the truck's cloying air fueled by warmth from their bodies became insufferable by noon. Alex advised the kids not to move in the midday heat, and he mesmerized himself by listening to the thwacks and crackles of tiles as they drove onward. Santiago told them travel would be slow through Mexico because he had business in cities along the way, but if no gangs or other *coyote*s stopped them, the trip should take about eight days.

Resting his head against a crate, Alex blanked out his terror of being captured by a gang as he listened to his travel companions recite their histories, complaints, and curses. Repetition of their stories began after the second day, a constant river of sadness.

"As soon as I could walk, my mother, she was only sixteen, man, she left me near the dump where I was born (fourth time) . . . In San Jose, my brother and I sniffed paint, glue, anything to get high. We were so cold and hungry (second time) . . . My sister's boyfriend gave me dope, but he beat us bad. I ran away to find my father. He picks grapefruits in Florida. He'll get me a job (fourth time) . . ."

Alex had heard it all at *Casa Maria*, but his curiosity increased when the kids cajoled Mariella into telling her story. The sun was fading from the slatted vents, but Alex could see her caramel skin, wide forehead, and deep-set eyes. Earlier, she'd knotted her unruly black hair at the nape of her neck and secured it with a broken pencil. As she spoke, she kept touching the purple linear scars on her forearms. He'd seen them before on Guatemalan street kids who practiced bloodletting to relieve their misery, but he never understood why they did it.

"I cut myself," she said shyly. "Deep cuts."

"How does that help?" Alex's harsh tone sliced the air. He hadn't meant to be so blunt.

"The doctor who sewed me up told me to get away from my father," Mariella said, her lips spitting each word. "So I stole money from him and ran. But my father was a wild bull, looking everywhere for me."

An angry fly buzzed in Alex's ear. He concentrated on the insect's drone, making a futile attempt not to hear another word of Mariella's tale. He didn't want to know anything more about her father, or her scars. And yet, he couldn't drown out her words.

"When my father found me . . ." Mariella's voice faded, and her eyes seized on the truck's ceiling, as if she were hypnotized by a ghost floating there. Even shyer than before, she dropped her heavy lids and stroked the scars with her delicate fingers.

A creeping silence followed, causing the group to grumble, nudge, and pinch each other as they often did when things became unbearable, but then, as if to quiet them, Mariella continued.

"I got here because some street kids introduced me to Santiago." She pulled her knees to her chin. "That's all I have to say."

Admiring her refusal to reveal more, Alex thought Mariella had probably retreated to a safe place deep inside herself. He was practicing that same ritual, resolute in his decision not to mention Fernando's death, and he controlled the impulse to do so now by occupying his thoughts with the passage of time. If Alex figured right, they'd cross the US border tomorrow by truck, not by wading through the Rio Grand as Alex had once supposed. They'd been traveling twenty-four hours a day since Santiago had picked up another driver whose face and skin reminded Alex of a diseased rodent. Alex secretly named him "the rat man."

Finally, he dozed into shapeless daydreams of *norte*, a country of opportunity, the land of freedom. He slept for a long time until he sensed the truck slowing, then jolting to a shaky halt.

"We could be at the checkpoint between Juárez and El Paso," Ramón, the sick boy, whispered. He'd made this same trip three times, had been caught three times, and had been ushered back to Chiapas three times. Alex wanted to ask Ramón about the border, but he didn't dare utter a word. No one moved. Outside the truck, people shouted above automobile engines revving and dying, revving and dying. Alex gulped deep breaths of stale moldy air, particularly unpleasant and sticky now that they'd stopped.

The kids' eyes gleamed, wet with excitement, but each time the truck inched forward, noxious fumes crept through the vents, forcing them to gasp and stifle coughs. The heat of the day created a furnace. The twin girls' heads drooped as if they'd fainted. Splinters from the wood floor pricked Alex's butt, and his legs burned and twitched. Both feet went numb. Mariella's eyes glassed over, her hand fell on her lap, and her head flopped onto Alex's shoulder. He wasn't sure how long he could stand the unbearable weight of her.

Time crept, minute by miserable minute, until an abrupt lurch followed by a forward thrust signaled movement at last. The truck was picking up speed.

"I think we're almost in Texas," Ramón said. His thinning hair, skeletal face and yellow teeth reminded Alex of a picture he'd seen of a dying horse.

The kids strained to straighten their hunched bodies as best they could. Alex couldn't wait to stretch his legs and find water to wash out the foul space. Surely Santiago would allow this, but Alex's hope waned when they didn't stop for a break. His excitement about the successful border crossing slipped into boredom again, and although the road was smoother than the ones they'd traveled so far, the never-ending journey went on and on with Ramón retching and the twin sisters weeping because they had no water.

Water. Alex swallowed hard. An immense thirst clawed at his throat, and he thought again of the *Rio Grande*. This wretched truck wasn't what he'd imagined when his mother had wished that he and Fernando could come to 'America, just a step over rio'." He began to feel woozy and confused about whether he was awake or asleep.

When Alex heard Santiago's voice, distant and hollow, he had no recollection of how much time had passed or when the truck had stopped.

"Get out, you pigs," the *coyote* commanded as he cracked the paneled door "And on your way, if you make these boxes fall, I'll leave you for the buzzards."

The cool air lightened Alex's misery. He rubbed his eyes and rotated his shoulders. Everyone was studying the narrow space, a passage of protruding sharp-edged tiles where they had to wedge their bodies. Although they had left the truck numerous times, the boxes had now shifted. One mistake could mean a cut arm and sure infection, or worse, a toppled stack. Alex motioned for the others to go first, so he could hold the boxes as they crept forward. "Watch the box on the left," he said as Ramón stumbled. "Help him, Mariella."

She fell in behind Ramón and braced his waist with her hands. "You can do this," she whispered. "Just take your time."

"Hurry up, you fuckers," Santiago said as they stepped into the dull light of early evening.

The rat man sneered, smelling of tequila, as he watched Alex join the boys near a twiggy scrub brush, where they hid themselves from the girls and sighed at their long-awaited collective leak. Feeling tremendous relief, Alex gazed at the vast prairie in front of him, an expansive ocean of American sand. Barren mountains on the far horizon and an eerie silence reminded him of how he envisioned life on the moon. Alex smiled at this thought. Maybe Santiago had taken them to *la luna*. But no. Between the mountain peaks, there was *la luna*, lying on her back with her two ends pointing heavenward. Father Chiabras called this position a horned moon, and he said it meant good luck.

But Alex didn't feel any good luck when Santiago refused to allow them to clean the truck. Instead, the *coyote* insisted they focus on a moss-green cabin to the right of the road, so far away Alex could barely see it.

"Where are we now?" Alex asked.

"South Texas. And that's an immigration checkpoint." Santiago aimed his grimy finger at the distant shack. "It's your job to sneak around it. If you don't get caught, I'll pick you up on the other side."

Alex's heart quickened. Even though Ramón had warned him this might happen, Alex couldn't quell a smoldering fury. "After all we've suffered, we have to get by immigration on our own? What did we pay you for?"

"You pigs will do what I tell you." Santiago motioned for the rat man, and both men held out their hands. "Give us everything in your pockets. You'll get it back when I pick you up."

"We gave you everything," Alex said.

With a sudden smack to the cheek, Santiago sent Alex stumbling backward. The *coyote's* mouth clamped into a smirk. "And hand over that cross around your neck you've been hiding."

Alex sensed his face flush, the beat of his pulse so strong it throbbed in his teeth. Refusing to speak, he glared at the *coyote* with the absolute certainty he'd die rather than give up Father's gift.

"You'll have to kill me."

Santiago stepped sideways, his cruel eyes never leaving Alex. As other kids surrendered a few photographs and coins, the rat man handed them each a half-filled water bottle. Then without a word, both men trotted off and left them alone in a vapor of truck exhaust.

Alex took stock of the group, who began squabbling among

themselves in sharp tones.

"We go together in a pack," one of the twins said.

"The best way is to go in pairs," Ramón explained. "Two pairs on each side of the road."

The grapefruit picker's son kicked at the dry earth. "No. Together is the way."

"I agree with Ramón," Alex said.

The group cast doubtful glances at both Alex and Ramón.

"We should do it Ramón's way," Mariella said. "He's been here before."

Alex nodded his appreciation of her support, then searched their weary faces. When no one offered resistance, he removed the cross from his neck, kissed it and offered for others to do so. After all lips had kissed the cross, they bowed their heads as Alex restrung the chain around his neck. The last flicker of sunlight vanished from the horizon, and except for the grinning moon and a sprinkle of stars, they were abandoned in a vast wild place where men and animals would hunt them down in a relentless pursuit.

NINE

Exasperated by her evening at *Zona Azul*, Elizabeth trudged up the flagstone walkway to her condo. At least she'd had the opportunity to set up an interview with Luke Santa Maria. And Diplomatic Security Service? Something new every day. She unlocked the door, flung her coat over a hall tree, and glanced at the walls adorned with portraits of Kate, taken every year from the delightful days of her daughter's childhood to the present time, when things had turned sour between them.

"I'm home," she called, heading for the kitchen.

Kate squatted in front of the refrigerator's open crisper, her mass of light ginger curls cascading down the back of her soccer uniform shirt, her hand groping in the empty produce drawer on a quest for food.

"Oh-my-god." Kate's lingo was laced with animosity. "I just got home and there's nothing to eat in this house, not even a snack." She shifted from her futile search and telegraphed her best scowl Elizabeth's way.

"I picked up Chinese," Elizabeth said.

"Chinese again? Are we having it for breakfast too?"

"I thought you liked Chinese," Elizabeth replied in an apologetic tone, determined not to get down and dirty.

"What I'd like is food in this house when I get home from soccer." Kate grabbed for the next drawer in pursuit of one edible piece of anything.

Deflecting the ire in Kate's emerald eyes, Elizabeth said, "If you want snacks, why not go buy them yourself?"

"Shopping's your job. You know, like a real mother." Kate stuck out her lower lip as if she were a scolded child. She withdrew a head of lettuce from the last drawer, peeled off the green slimy leaves and chomped into it.

"I had to work late."

"What else is new?"

"How was your game?"

"You are so lame. You don't even care."

The knot in Elizabeth's throat grew. "Listen, you little prima donna. I work hard to make sure you have everything."

"Is that what I have, Mom? Everything?"

After Kate had launched the zinger, she chewed furiously, her mouth spewing specks of lettuce. Elizabeth didn't answer, and it wasn't because she didn't want to. She simply couldn't conjure up a retort.

Slapping soccer cleats against the stone floor, Kate marched out, leaving Elizabeth to glower at the humming refrigerator, door ajar, a machine oblivious to the roller coaster upheavals in this house. She stifled an urge to grab her daughter and rave about their disparate paths. Instead, she tramped to the microwave, crowded to-go cartons onto its rotating tray, and mindlessly stared at the white boxes circling round and round. Unexpectedly, Obispa's words seeped into consciousness. *There is a deep valley between you and your daughter.*

When *bing, bing, bing* signaled the food was warmed and ready for eating, Elizabeth dumped the entrees onto paper plates, set the table with plastic chopsticks and called Kate as if nothing had happened.

Slinking into the breakfast room and slouching at the table, Kate twirled the glass noodles around her chopsticks. Elizabeth settled across from her and resolved to bridge the gap Obispa had so aptly described.

"I wish we could get along." She stared at a glob of sweet-and-sour sauce spreading along the edge of her plate. "Just today, I told a woman you were the most important person in my life."

"You're seeing a shrink," said Kate, sucking noodles off the chopsticks.

"No." Elizabeth paused. "She's a shaman."

"You mean like a witch?"

"Not exactly."

"A witch doctor then. You told a witch doctor about me?"

"She isn't a witch doctor." Elizabeth pinched her lips together and tried to regroup.

Kate stood, stabbing her chopsticks into the egg fu yung, her eyes blinking tears. "A perfect ending to a perfect day. My mother tells some hag sorcerer about me, and my father announces he's getting married."

"Your father called you?" Elizabeth was shocked. The jerk barely showed his face.

"Yes."

"Well, I wouldn't get upset about his romances. He has one a month."

"What a bitch."

"Don't you dare talk to me that way!" Elizabeth's jaw tightened. The conversation had turned to shit.

"I'm talking about the bitch Dad's going to marry. She looks like a facelift gone bad." Kate plopped into the chair, laced her long fingers together beneath her chin, and gave Elizabeth a chilly look. "But you'll never marry anyone. Wanna know why?"

Elizabeth didn't want to know.

"I think you like women, and not in a normal way, if you get my drift."

"You are so wrong." Elizabeth's voice trailed off. Her heart hurt from Kate's spiteful comment. "I like men, Kate. It's just—"

"Name one."

Elizabeth couldn't win. She hadn't had a date in months. Slowly, she folded her napkin, walked to the sink, dumped her uneaten food, and flipped on the disposal. As its motor ground, an utterly zany idea struck her, a marvelous solution, and it could work.

"I just met a really nice man who asked me to call him," Elizabeth said, pivoting to face her daughter, conniving to kill two birds with one stone. She reached for her purse on the counter and snatched Luke Santa Maria's card. She'd schedule an interview with the rough-hewn Don Juan. A handsome guy, but a government agent and no match for her sophisticated crowd—still, he'd do in this pinch.

Elizabeth was delighted with herself as she dialed Santa Maria's cell phone. Undoubtedly, he'd still be dealing with the *Zona Azul* situation and wouldn't answer. She'd talk like she was setting up a date. Kate would never guess.

Then Elizabeth realized she'd have to call the man something other than Agent Santa Maria. What would she say? With every ring, her anxiety mushroomed.

Kate's green eyes watched Elizabeth like a hawk. "How can I be sure you're calling a man?"

"Oh, for God's sake." On impulse, she offered the phone. "Listen to his voice message."

Sidling up to her, Kate plucked the cell from Elizabeth's hand and cradled it against her ear. Suddenly, she screwed her mouth. "It's not a voice message, Mom. It's the guy—"

Elizabeth seized the phone.

"Santa Maria here," the man said.

Mute, Elizabeth gulped.

Kate rolled her eyes. "This is tragic."

"Can I help you, Ms. Grant?"

"Uh, yes." She couldn't believe she'd stooped so low. "You mentioned we could meet."

"That was fast."

For the first time in years, a blank screen appeared in Elizabeth's brain, and she simply couldn't respond.

"What do you have in mind?" He asked.

"I don't know."

"Say something better than that," Kate whispered, jabbing her mother in the ribs.

"I would enjoy seeing you again," Elizabeth said in a wooden voice.

"Really?" The agent sounded incredulous, and rightly so.

"Yes, yes. It was such a strange circumstance," Elizabeth said. Shit and double shit. She was a certified idiot nailing herself to the cross.

"God, you're lame." Kate shook her head.

"How about tomorrow at my office, ten a.m.?" he asked.

"It's a date." Elizabeth clicked off before Luke Santa Maria could reply.

"Mom," Kate said, blowing a strand of hair from her eye. "You need help—bad."

TEN

Determined they would make it past the immigration checkpoint, Alex swallowed his fear and spoke with bravado. "Pair off," he said, hoping the group's prior protests would die down.

Mariella slid her hand into Alex's. "I'll go with you," she said, the certainty in her voice daring the others to complain.

No one moved.

"We can't stay here." Ramón pointed to the sky. "They have planes that fly low and take pictures. If you hear anything, hide in the brush. Cover yourself with weeds."

"When you run," the grapefruit picker's son added, "my father said to keep down and not say a word."

Everyone nodded. The whistle of a west wind and yelps of unseen animals held them together in the huddle.

"Pray those are coyotes," Ramón said. "And not the search dogs."

"They are coyotes," Alex said. "As a boy, I lived in the country. Don't worry." He delivered the lie with skill. Until now, he'd never left the *barrios* of Guatemala City.

After touching fingertips for the last time, the kids parted in pairs. Alex and Mariella took the lead on the side where the checkpoint loomed like a death sentence. Ramón and a scrawny boy from Acapulco followed them at a distance.

Alex's instinct told him they should walk at least a half mile away from the road, then pass parallel to the checkpoint, but in the dark, how could they tell for sure? Mariella excitedly pointed to a solitary beacon, a small light perched on top of the checkpoint. *Gracias a Dios.* They'd go until they could barely see its glow, then pass the shack and hug the road.

Hand in hand, he and Mariella ran over packed earth as hard and cold as city streets. Alex's limbs tingled with new life, with the energy of free air, a magical force he couldn't explain. Even though it had been eleven hours since Santiago had given them their daily ration of two tortillas and an orange, Alex's stomach didn't cry out for food. Mariella also seemed to float beside him, a spirit girl with no body weight, until Alex skidded to a halt, and she tumbled into him.

A huge, deformed animal crouched close to the earth, moving up and down not more than a hundred feet away. Mariella's fingers dug into his arm. They ducked behind a prickly cactus. As if the black monster weren't enough, howling dogs approached from behind. Where was his hope now? Alex didn't say these words out loud, of course, because he didn't want to frighten Mariella more that she already was.

"Can you see Ramón?" Alex scanned the land behind them.

"I see nothing."

Dogs yelped and howled, their barks pulsing louder and louder across the plain, but the monster stayed in its spot, humping up and down, a carnivorous creature devouring its dinner or screwing a doomed victim. Alex and Mariella decided their best chance was to run around the creature while it was busy. There was no time to consider alternatives.

Alex took the lead, running as fast as he had the night Fernando was murdered. Mariella sprinted beside him. Tiny groans and squeaks met their ears as they neared the monster. The raw sounds made Alex slow down.

"Don't stop," Mariella whispered, tugging on his arm. "It will eat us alive."

Unable to believe his own stupidity, Alex chuckled. He stepped up to the inky menace, reached out and touched it. Mariella grumbled under her breath, but she didn't leave his side. She was probably more afraid of being alone than of witnessing the beast devour Alex.

"Mariella," Alex said, running his hand over a low metal rail. "This is a machine. I think it's pumping oil."

"Are you sure?"

"I'm sure it isn't alive, but I'm not positive what it's doing."

"Hey, Jack," a man's voice shattered the night. "Dogs going this way."

Winking flashlights skipped across the level landscape. Alex grabbed Mariella's arm jerking her toward the low railing.

"Hop over," he said as he hurdled the rail.

"But—"

"Now!"

She hiked her long legs over the upper bar and jumped inside with him. Thinking harder than he ever had before, Alex slapped both hands on the sides of a narrow, flat-topped piece of steel slanting up toward the moving parts. He could see the undulating motion of two huge forms resembling hammers. The head of the lower hammer traveled parallel to the slanted steel he was touching. The other head was farther away, thrusting a pipe in and out of a shaft. Oh, that he and Mariella could shrink themselves and slither into that hole in the sand.

She tugged on his shirt and pointed in the direction of a nearby ridge where large dogs sniffed the ground. Simultaneously, they heard the startup and ensuing snarl of an airplane motor.

Alex shuddered. To run seemed ridiculous. They'd be out in the open where dogs could pick up their scents. His mind wracked in urgent thought, Alex slapped his hand against the steel, his fingers tracing a sticky substance. He rubbed his palm across the beam. "Grease." Without hesitation he smeared it on his face.

"It's grease, yes." Mariella applied the black substance to her face too. "And there's oil or something slippery under my shoes."

Arms and legs were next until they had covered their skin and clothes in gooey blackness and foul-smelling oil. Motioning for Mariella to follow, Alex mounted the narrow slanted plank as if it were a horse. He used his arms to pull himself forward toward the swinging hammer, which was large enough to crush him if he fell under it. Glancing back, he watched Mariella struggle. She straddled the steel, but she wouldn't make it to the top before those miserable bastards got to them.

Alex slid back to her. "Get off. You go first."

"I'm strong, it's just . . ." Sinking to the ground, she sent him a sheepish look.

Wiping his hands on his jeans, Alex motioned for her to climb ahead of him, so she hitched back on, her ebony-ringed eyes never questioning his commands. From the ground, Alex pushed her up the plank. His temples bulged with strain. He ground his jaw. Mariella scooted as best she could until she neared the hammer where she could go no higher.

"When it comes toward you again, get up on the hammer," Alex said, knowing full well she'd resist.

"But I might fall," she said in a hush.

"If you want to stay in this country, you will do it."

Mariella grasped the sides of the hammer as it came toward her and edged herself onto its rocking beam. She grasped the narrow ridges on either side until she was able to flatten her body. In excited disbelief, Alex hurled himself onto the plank, but he overshot his mark, slamming his chin into the solid surface. His teeth dug into his tongue. The taste of blood flooded his mouth, and the pungent smell of lubricants launched waves of nausea, but he kept his course toward the hammer.

"Move up, Mariella," he said.

"This way," a man called.

"They're here," Alex whispered as he crawled onto the rocking steel cradle. It was at least a foot wide—more than he expected. His greasy hands sweated, his grasp on the rim precarious.

Around the perimeter of the pumping machine, two gray dogs sniffed and pawed. A man's silhouetted figure held a flashlight as he circled the platform. The dogs trotted behind him. Suddenly the man aimed the beam on the lower girder, moving the shaft of light up toward the hammer. "Goddammit! I lost their trail," he yelled.

Jesucristo, Alex prayed. *Any minute he's going to realize where we are.* He pressed his cheek against the rough plank and watched the man flick his light over a lonely patch of brush.

"Yo," a distant voice called. "I've got two live ones over here."

*

Alex couldn't determine how long he lay on the plank before the men, their slobbering hounds and an airplane with red eyes faded from sight. Despair covered him like a heavy blanket. He felt bottomless, rootless, and empty. All he could think about was poor sick Ramón and the other boy whose name Alex couldn't recall. They had most likely been caught, and the pain of that was unbearable. Fighting an instinct to dwell on what would happen to the boys, Alex instead considered Ramón's resolute goal to live in the US regardless of the long journey, filthy trucks, rotten food, and men like Santiago.

The crunching metal shaft propelling downward into dry ground reminded Alex of the sharp jabs of the *coyote*'s cruelty, yet Ramón never succumbed to Santiago's evil prodding, and out of respect for his friend, Alex would never do so again. As his cheek rested on the rough steel *en el silencio del noche*, he wondered what dark grace had protected him and Mariella from the border patrol.

At last the voices, yelps, and motors dissolved. Alex glanced up and saw Mariella sliding off the girder. She hung from the hammer, prepared to jump. His melancholy evaporated.

"Wait!" He said, hopping to the ground and grasping her knees.

They both collapsed on the cement platform, too weak and bewildered to move, but the thought of Santiago leaving them in this dangerous place forced Alex to stand. Mariella's bright eyes seemed enormous as her blackened face looked up at him.

"We have to find Santiago," he said, trying not to sound alarmed, calculating the odds of meeting up with the bastard and his rat-faced accomplice.

"I want to wash off," Mariella said in a whine. "The smell is awful."

Alex's temples throbbed with sudden anger. "This grease saved your life, Mariella. Think of poor Ramón."

*

"Line up." The rat man smoked a hand-rolled cigarette and flicked his long fingernail at the loose tobacco on his shirt.

The exhausted kids, their number dwindled to six, tramped to the door of Blue Agave hell. The sky painted itself in shades of plum and pink, sunrise on its way, and the earth glowed in honey hues, soothing colors that didn't ease Alex's pain about Ramón. The air was fresh though, and he breathed as much as his lungs would hold. Alex memorized shapes of oval cacti ripe with tiny green fingers, scraggly bushes, and clumps of low brown brush, mind-fodder for the long hours ahead.

"We lost twenty-five percent of our profit." Santiago's left eye twitched as he hiked his unbelted jeans and sauntered toward Alex. "I bet it was your fault." He slugged Alex in the gut.

Gasping, Alex doubled over. Santiago's spite stung worse than his punch.

"Get in the truck in the order I tell you." With his rough, oversized hands, Santiago arranged the kids. Alex was first, Mariella last.

Alex glanced at her before he climbed in. She waited with her head down. Good. At least she wasn't giving Santiago the satisfaction of seeing her misery at still being coated with grease. After they'd eluded the border patrol, Alex tried to locate a creek or a well, but his search proved futile in this waterless land.

The space inside the truck felt roomy without Ramón and the other boy, and then Alex realized Mariella wasn't yet in, nor had Santiago closed the back door or started the motor. He heard a muffled whimpering outside.

The grapefruit picker's son crouched near the crawl space. Venturing a look, he swung toward the group. His face was pasty, dark eyes blinking. "They're raping her."

Alex felt as if he'd been slammed in the stomach a thousand more times. He fought his way across the kids and shoved the boxes aside, spilling cartons of tile. First he saw the rat man with his zipper open, stroking his erect member with one hand. Santiago pinned Mariella on the ground, ripping at her pants, prying her legs, pumping his body over her fragile frame like bullets shot into the ground.

"Stop, you bastards!" Alex hurled himself at the rat man, who reached into his jacket and thrust a huge pistol into Alex's chest. Mariella's anguish pierced the morning as she clawed at Santiago's face and attempted to buck him. Alex closed his eyes, certain the *coyote* would shoot her. But instead of gunshots, engines of a reconnaissance plane rumbled nearby, followed by the faint barks of dogs.

Jumping to his feet, Santiago hopped around, trying to zip his jeans. The rat stuffed his swollen penis into his pants, angled the gun toward Alex's temple and waved him back to the truck. Mariella pulled on her jeans and struggled to stand.

"Leave the bitch," Santiago said.

"But the money," the rat man complained.

"Do what I fucking tell you."

Santiago's cheeks bled from Mariella's scratches, and Alex choked with the brutal realization. The *coyote* would take revenge for her resistance. The rat's gun forced Alex into the truck as Santiago raced to the driver's side. Still, Alex managed to yank Father's precious cross from his neck and pitch it to Mariella. The last thing he saw was her scrabbling in the dirt near the spot where his cross had landed. The door slammed in Alex's face, and within seconds, a motor groaned and came to life.

"Please don't leave me!" Mariella wailed.

Alex imagined her desperate tears. "Mariella!" he screamed. Over and over, he jerked the inside handle. Her fists pounded on the other side. But the truck took off, abandoning her for the border patrol or a cruel death in the desert.

Separated from the other kids by fallen boxes of tile, Alex crouched near the door and wept, his grief an open sore. On the streets of Guatemala City, he'd honed a keen ability to survive, but his strength and savvy had never been foolproof. He couldn't save his brother, and now Mariella was gone. If Santiago had been alone, Alex might have been able to stop him, but with two men, it was impossible.

Suddenly, Alex remembered Fernando's warning: *"Take special care when the rat arrives."*

ELEVEN

Balancing an apple, the *Houston Chronicle*, and a frothing latte, Luke shouldered open the office door. He walked through DSS reception, walls papered with terrorists, both candids and mugs—Osama himself front and center, a red X across his face. Dominic lounged in their cramped conference room, his stitched gray boots propped on the table as he read reports and devoured an onion bagel.

"Yo," Luke said, taking a peek over Dominic's shoulder at the file he was reading.

"All the kids in last night's raid have work permits, visas, or birth certificates."

Luke scanned the profiles on a couple of the teens. "They have bank accounts with large balances, just like the ones we arrested last week."

"Thousands of dollars," Dominic said, popping the last morsel into his mouth. "Money they'll never see."

"Zadie Gutierrez is the cosigner," Luke remarked, pointing at a bank document.

"Zadie operates *Noche Azul* down the street from Obispa's, and she says the place is swarming with older men, young girls, even boys." Dominic gazed at his diet cola, then guzzled the caffeine with gusto.

"*Noche Azul* may be the processing center so to speak before Zadie sends the kids to different cantinas."

"Sounds right to me."

Sipping froth from his latte, Luke inhaled the fragrant aroma, stalling his delivery of an important piece of info that would make Dominic furious, so he delayed his news until he finished the coffee. Dominic immersed himself in a pile of visas as Luke said, "I asked Cole to stop by and look at these documents."

Dominic's upper lip curled. "The fucking guru is lowering himself to meet with us?"

"Don't start."

"We're as sharp as he is. Why do you keep calling him?"

"He's an expert, and you know it."

"Just because Cole's father took you in, it doesn't mean he's anything like his old man," Dominic said. "Hell, my mom would've taken you if we'd had the money."

Luke didn't relish Dominic digging up childhood events that continued to poison the present. It was painful enough for Luke to visit his father, and his trips to the pen seemed to be getting further and further apart. "Goddammit, Dom—"

"One more thing." Dominic's black eyes trained on Luke. "I can't figure why Cole keeps helping us. Everyone else he works with dishes out profit and fame for him."

"Why, Dominic, you know I love you," a velvet baritone boomed from the doorway.

Luke twisted to see his lawyer buddy, Randall Cole, stroll into the room. He was a tall man with cropped russet curls, a deep tan, and well-formed shoulders. Cole was impeccably groomed from his camel hair coat and striped French cuffs to his Ralph Lauren loafers. He shook hands with Luke, but all the while his steel-gray glare was aimed at Dominic.

Dominic looked away, searching the area and fingering a bakery box on the chair beside him. He withdrew another bagel, tore the leathery crust with his teeth, and returned Cole's frosty stare.

Irritated with their nonsense, Luke went right to business. "Here's what we've got," he said to Cole.

The big man looked with disdain at the hard-backed government chairs and chose to remain standing. Ignoring Cole's arrogance, Luke handed him an overstuffed folder. He wanted the lawyer's input and worried about Dominic's temper if Cole prodded him.

"Going to our reunion?" Dominic asked Cole, his sour mood seemingly lifted.

"Nah. Business is booming. You guys should join me and make some real money," Cole replied.

"Not interested." Dominic withdrew a red and silver tin from his shirt pocket and opened it, offering mints.

Cole took a few. "You still sucking this shit?"

Dominic nodded and they all laughed. Luke felt the tension ease. He was anxious to move on.

Crunching the mints, Cole examined the bank documents as Luke pointed to the other stacks on the table. "Work papers, visas, even some birth certificates."

Dominic lowered his boots to the floor. "Best forgeries I've ever seen."

Luke glanced at his watch—ten sharp. "I'll be back," he said, moving toward the door. Elizabeth Grant would be roaring in there any minute, and he didn't want her talking to Cole, a publicity hound if ever there was one. If the lawyer started bending her ear, they'd never get Cole's opinion about the forgeries.

Before he left, Luke checked the temperature between the men. "Behave if you can," he said, but his words were meant for Dominic. He was sure his partner understood.

"Get a load of this," Dominic said, gesturing for Cole to sit beside him.

Cole groaned. "I guess it's just you and me, babe."

Hearing Grant's voice, Luke slipped from the conference room. He moved quickly to the reception area, stood in the doorway, and watched her. Wearing a hunter-green pantsuit, she grilled the receptionist with a modern version of twenty questions about the DSS. When Luke cleared his throat, the reporter ceased her interrogation and turned toward him.

"I've heard of FBI, CIA, and ICE, but what the hell is DSS?"

"Come to my office and I'll answer your questions, or die trying."

An devilish expression found its way to her lips. "I want your story first. After that, you can die all you want."

He'd wager a month's salary that Grant's statement about his dying wasn't a joke, and he'd also bet her piranha personality wasn't a facade for a kinder, softer woman. She strode beside him into his office, a cubbyhole with an ochre metal desk littered with files and framed photos of his nephews. Instead of sitting, as Luke expected, Elizabeth Grant drifted toward the wall and began reading the inscription on one of his service citations.

"Former Navy Seal. Silver Cross. I'm impressed."

"I thought it'd take more than a couple of military awards to impress you, Ms. Grant."

Reeling around, she grimaced, almost hurt, a reaction Luke hadn't bargain for. "I respect service to our country," she said tartly, but this time, she chose not to fire away at him with her sharp tongue. Instead, her lips dropped into a pout, and she turned back to his awards.

Propped against the edge of his desk, he eyed the nape of Grant's neck beneath strands of blonde hair piled on her head, and he detected the slightest scent of honeysuckle. The longer she kept reading, the more nervous her silence made him, but he reached his limit when she began to study his football trophies and eyed his barbells resting in the corner. He didn't have the time or the patience to deal with a temperamental female. He'd spent the last three years trying to live with his now ex-wife, and that didn't work out too well. So when doubtful about how to treat a woman, Luke began cutting to the chase, taking the offense, and getting things over with. Today would be no different. "Who's giving you tips about our operations?" he asked.

"You won't believe it," she said, her voice hard and distant. The piranha reemerged as she faced him eye to eye.

"Try me."

"An anonymous person with a Spanish accent called on my cell. Twice now."

Considering this feeble explanation, Luke shrugged. Her eyes sparked dynamite, indicating she recognized his skepticism, but then her persona flipped to the hurt little girl she'd been a moment before. Probably a technique she'd developed to lure unsuspecting males. This woman was a skilled Siren of the first order.

"I'm not lying," she said. "The caller muffles their voice, so I can't tell if it's male or female."

"I need more than anonymous. Is there a number?"

"No. It says private caller. That's all I can give you." She turned again to his sports trophies. "And now, I'm changing the subject. Did you go to St. Joe's High in Amarillo?"

Elizabeth Grant gave Luke the jitters. "Graduated in ninety," he said.

"I didn't want your age," she said. "I don't get that personal."

"Yeah." He snickered. Luke knew she was moving the conversation away from the informant but decided to go along. He'd get the information from her later—one way or the other.

She continued as if she hadn't detected his mockery. "I went to St. Joe's too. A year ahead of you."

He frowned. How could he have missed her? "You're talking St. Joe's up in the Panhandle?"

"I was taller than most boys, so I became a bookworm. Needless to say, I didn't make the football games or know any jocks like you." She gestured toward his trophies.

Where the hell was this going? Next thing, she'd want the whole story about Luke's father, if she didn't know already. Most people in Amarillo knew. Most people would never forget. He drummed his fingers on the desk and stacked messy piles. Finally, she sat down across from where he stood, crossed her legs, and shook her foot. Whenever she stirred, the scent of honeysuckle unsettled him.

"Until I began my series on human trafficking, I'd never heard of the DSS. What exactly do you do?"

Luke seated himself in a chair next to her and explained. "We protect the US embassies, and our other focuses are identity fraud, indentured servitude, and terrorism. DSS takes the lead on the trafficking cases we originate. ICE and locals are usually involved too."

"Would you talk to my recorder?"

Luke shook his head, thinking she'd argue, but Elizabeth Grant didn't miss a beat.

"Tell me how indentured servitude relates to child trafficking."

"Trafficked kids are indentured, meaning they're forced to work with no hope of leaving their jobs, ranging from restaurants, ranches, citrus plantations, private homes, you name it. But sadly, most teenagers are used as prostitutes." He moved to his computer and clicked on Homeland Security. "Check this site. You can sign up for daily updates on national and international trafficking."

"Thank you." Grant withdrew a pair of silver readers and a notebook from a sleek black purse. She studied the computer screen and copied the information.

Luke continued, "Drug cartels are trafficking teens now because it's so profitable. They might use *coyotes* to smuggle them across the border or they smuggle them across themselves, then they employ US gangs that force the kids into the sex trade." Luke sighed. "Everyone benefits except the victims. We now believe that profits from human trafficking are second only to illegal drugs."

"Now that's a headline," she said, peering at him as her glasses inched down her nose. "So, gangs like Mola's Latin Angels are involved."

"They could be," he said.

"When's your next raid?"

Luke smiled. He couldn't help it. He found the damn woman alluring. Tedious, but alluring. "I'm sure your anonymous informer will anonymously inform you."

"Not funny."

"When the time's right, I'll let you know, and you can come with our team. We can't jeopardize our position at the moment."

"And what position would that be?"

Luke rolled his eyes. This was going to be a long morning.

TWELVE

Noche Azul's blue neon sign flickered below a dome of dusk-pink clouds, and beneath the sign, a black surveillance van with a green "Jose's Liquor" logo painted on its side. Inside the van, Luke Santa Maria glanced at his watch. Nine p.m. Impatient and restless, he forced himself to settle at a laminated console, open his laptop, and review a profile on *Noche Azul*'s cantina operator Zadie Gutierrez.

The van's driver DSS agent Jeff Collins slowly maneuvered the vehicle through the parking lot, an uneven surface ruptured by gnarled roots from live oak trees. Collins backed the van into a space with excellent side and rear views of the cantina. He was a young guy with goggle glasses and a dull brown crew cut, a rookie who was a little too timid for Luke's taste. However, he had to admit Collins was a skillful navigator in crowded places.

"Refresh me on the finer points of this techno-spy machine," Jeff said, switching off the ignition.

This was Jeff's first field action, and Luke presumed he was anxious. "The roof-rack antenna and video camera lets us see and hear what's happening on the lot," Luke explained as Jeff joined him to watch the monitor attached above the desk. Luke focused the lens on a parade of Mercedes, Chevy convertibles, and souped-up Hondas cruising for a space. The brick cantina, originally a 1930s home with an inviting veranda, leaded-glass bay windows, and a carved wood front door spoke of past grandeur. Now, the numerous shaded and barred windows tainted its charm.

Luke pointed to another antenna camouflaged as a standard cellular model located on the front passenger side. "High-speed transmitter for the body wires and cell phones we're using to talk with the undercover deputies."

"Got it," Jeff said.

"According to our CI, over the past few weeks, several white vans with a Blue Agave logo have unloaded Hispanic teenagers and taken them into the back room. This morning, the folks at Corpus Christi immigration called to say another van was headed for Houston. I immediately arranged for *Noche Azul*'s electricity to be cut and for one of our guys dressed as a power company employee to repair the lines. This agent planted A/V equipment in the cantina's back room and the electricity was restored within an hour." Luke gestured toward the rear of the building and Jeff nodded.

They watched couples stroll arm in arm into to the cantina, and raucous *Tejano* music blared each time the door opened. Buttoned-down city councilmen types ducked from expensive cars and escorted jeweled women in leather minis. Longhaired dudes with tattooed arms and diamond-studded ears pranced alongside Hispanic *contessas* whose plunging necklines took you to heaven.

"The back room seems to be the best place to record both on-mike and camera, " Jeff said. "Away from that damned music."

Luke nodded then glanced up as the side door opened. Dominic clambered in. He wore jeans, threadbare at the knees, a navy sweatshirt, Obispa's talisman, and his black Astros cap. Below the cap a red bandana covered the top of his forehead, and his braided hair dangled through the cap's back opening. He'd replaced his diamond ear stud with a large silver loop.

"A postmodern pirate," Luke said.

"More hip than starched shirts and kakis," Dominic quipped.

"Just what I need—a wardrobe consultant." Luke leaned back in his chair. "What did you learn on your walk through the *barrio*, Mr. Versace?"

Dominic grinned. "Sheriff's boys swept the area and picked up four Latin Angels."

"Get anything from them?" Luke asked.

"*Nada*, but I'm pretty sure they were lookouts for the cantina."

Luke considered how little DSS could actually prove, but he believed Zadie Gutierrez fronted for the Latin Angels' prostitution enterprise in the "blue" cantinas. The Angels ran all crime in this *barrio*: ecstasy, crack, meth, H, weapons, and prostitution—both sexes, all ages. Their leader, Tulio Mola, was a brilliant sociopath. To connect the dots, DSS needed substantial information from this cantina's proprietor, the infamous Zadie, and of course the *coyotes*.

"If that van ever gets here, we're going to keep those *coyotes* awake till they squawk," Luke said.

Dominic grinned, but his mind was clearly on something else. "I'm curious whether the Blue Agave vans are stolen, or if there's a front company."

"Cole's network is investigating the Blue Agave," Luke said. "The company's out of Juárez."

"Fucking figures. Juárez is the ninth level of hell," Dominic snorted.

"We can see most of the backroom," Luke said to change the subject away from Juárez and to avoid a potential Dominic rant. He gestured toward the grainy video monitor. "The mike and camera are in the ivy hanging basket."

"There's definitely not as much noise. I think the mike will pick up," Jeff said.

Relieved about the sound, Luke glanced at a magazine article he'd started a few nights before, but a persistent scuffing noise thwarted his concentration. With a Swiss army knife, Dominic scraped grit off the soles of his boots while he hummed along with music from the cantina. When finished, he swiveled in his seat, drummed his fingers on the armrest, and glanced out the window.

"Goddammit, I'm trying to read," Luke said.

"Sorry to interrupt your literary experience, sir, but guess who's here?"

"I knew it," Luke said as he glanced out the window, snatched a two-way, and buzzed the undercover deputy who was roosting in a blue convertible parked nearby. Good-looking Johnny McCullough, dressed in an outlandish orange leisure suit groped for his handset.

"Johnny, you hear me? That black Beemer belongs to a *Chronicle* reporter. This could be trouble."

"I met her at *Zona Azul*," came Johnny's voice.

"You had the pleasure," Luke said, keeping a keen eye on Elizabeth Grant's aging 530i wedged into a space thirty feet across the drive from them. "Don't let her out of your sight."

Grant and her photographer simultaneously opened their doors. Luke caught sight of her long legs below a tight knit skirt. Her hair was twisted and held with a clasp, and she wore pointed-toe boots, a pale yellow jacket, and rimless glasses. Grant started toward the cantina, followed by the obedient photo jockey.

"Poor guy trots behind her like a dog," said Luke.

"Maybe she's in heat." Dominic chuckled.

"Could be good for me." After he spoke, Luke chided himself. He was usually cautious about his "women" comments to Dominic because of the relentless razzing that would ensue. Too late now.

"Start panting, big dog." Dominic growled and yipped. "A little heat couldn't hurt you."

"Heads up," Jeff said. "White van approaching."

"If the driver sees Grant's cameraman, we're fucked." Dominic bolted for the door.

"Wait. I don't want her to know we're here," Luke said. He hollered into the two-way, "Johnny, deep-six that reporter. Now!"

The deputy hopped from the convertible and caught Grant's arm. Although he flashed his badge, she was having none of it. A heated discussion ensued as the Blue Agave van veered into the lot, its darkened windows obscuring all occupants. At a cautious speed, it approached Grant and Johnny, then slowed to a halt.

"The driver must be watching the show," Jeff said.

Waving his hands and yelling obscenities, Johnny maniacally pounded on the Beemer. As if she were stunned, Grant slowly opened her door and eased back into the car, but the photographer kept clicking until Johnny grabbed the camera. After more words were exchanged, the photo guy finally slipped into the front seat.

"Johnny shoulda been an actor," Dominic said with a hint of irony.

The Blue Agave van idled between the DSS van and Grant's car. To get a sharper view, Luke and Dominic moved to the screen connected to the roof-rack video camera. He could see Grant's stony expression as she attempted to back out, honking angrily at the Blue Agave.

Luke's temples pulsed. Even when the van crept past the ruckus, heading toward the rear of the club, Grant kept honking. "If she screws this up, I'll kill her, goddammit."

The reporter finally whipped into the street and drove toward the front of *Noche Azul*, Johnny following in his convertible. After they'd disappeared, the dust-streaked van idled for several minutes beneath the mammoth oaks, whose leaves reflected a radioactive glow from the cantina's neon sign. Luke's pulse quickened as the driver's door opened. Scuffed boots hit the ground. A man wearing reflector glasses, a white T-shirt, and jeans scuttled to the rear and opened the door. Three teenage boys and two girls groped their way out, helping each other step to the ground. Another man rounded the van but remained in the shadows behind the line of captives.

"Every time I see this, I get more fucking pissed," Dominic said.

"Yep," Luke said with a groan. Time and again, he'd found it tough watching these half-starved, desperate kids.

The group trekked across a grassless yard scattered with autumn leaves. Nearing the cantina, the tallest boy slowed his pace and glanced around. His face was smudged with grease, his jeans ripped, and his athletic shoes mended with duct tape. The *coyote* hammered the boy's shoulder, shoving him into the girls, who appeared to be identical twins. With balled fists, the boy squared off at the driver, but the man turned his back on him. The second *coyote* reappeared and helped herd the kids through the cantina's rear door.

"That boy has guts," Dominic said. "I'm impressed."

Jeff motioned to the monitor. "Coming in like a charm."

The backroom was covered with a dizzying wallpaper of tropical birds, its edges frayed above a battered wainscot. Luke and Dominic slipped on earphones as a hefty woman entered. She wore a rose in her dark shoulder-length hair, a flowing low-cut dress, and a gold chain bearing a jeweled cross nestling between her enormous wrinkled breasts.

"I give you Zadie Gutierrez, former prostitute, now proprietor," Dominic said. "Other occupations include dominatrix, kiddie-porn queen, and mother of four felons. In short, *una bruja*."

"Is that code?" Jeff asked.

"Spanish for 'witch,'" Luke said with mild amusement. "The lady with a black heart."

"Get a load of that cross." Dominic chortled. "Vampires beware."

Zadie strutted toward a café table in the center of the room. The *coyotes* helped themselves to beers from a bar in the corner, and the second man, whose image had been obscured, came into view. Scraggly hair brushed his shoulders. Puffy eyes, lined face, and a permanent sneer evidenced a life hard lived.

"A new crop, just in time for the weekend. Good work, Santiago," Zadie said in the gravelly voice of a heavy smoker.

"Santiago," Dominic repeated. "The other guy is obviously second string."

"We haven't seen either of them before," Luke said.

Santiago handed Zadie a manila envelope, then ordered the browbeaten teenagers to form a line while the other *coyote* opened a second beer. Strolling in front of the kids, Zadie prodded their teeth, fingered their hair, and touched the girls' breasts and the boys' genitals. When she thrust her fleshy fingers into the tall boy's crotch, he grabbed her wrist.

Waving a knife, Santiago lunged. The kid twisted to avoid the weapon, but the *coyote* held the knife at his neck, pricking his skin. Blood trickled from the boy's punctured flesh.

"You are my slave, black face and all," Zadie said, speaking in a mixture of English and Spanish commonly known as Tex-Mex.

The boy touched his wound and stared at the floor.

"Look at me, you son of a bitch." Her Spanish was full force now.

He lifted his head.

"Take off your clothes," Zadie said, thrusting her finger at the group.

The twins gasped.

"Now," the *coyote* snarled, stalking them with his knife.

Untwining their arms from each other's waists, the girls slowly lifted their shirts, while the boys' fingers fumbled with snaps and pulled down their jeans.

"Enough," Luke said.

Guns at the ready, the agents hurried from the van and met up with the sheriff's deputies who'd been waiting for their signal.

"Take the front," Luke said to the deputies as he caught a glint of streaking tangerine, Johnny McCullough in his lounge-lizard suit racing toward them.

"I got sidetracked watching that reporter. She's still out there," Johnny whispered.

"Go," Luke said, nodding toward the other deputies, who were heading toward the front.

With a dramatic gesture, Johnny drew his gun and hurried to catch up with his team.

"He's going to fuck this," Dominic said.

Luke shook his head. He, Dominic, and Jeff headed for the rear of the cantina and crept to the crooked wooden door. A smoky film escaped into the night as they burst into the room.

THIRTEEN

Killing time in front of *Noche Azul*, Elizabeth slouched in her car, seething with thorny impatience. *Cha cha boom, cha cha boom, cha cha—aye, aye, aye, aye, aye.* She tapped her foot to tunes blasting from the cantina, while Joe, her photographer, retrieved another camera from his bag and wandered down the block in hopes of catching some action.

Abruptly, Elizabeth straightened her spine and took note. A streak of orange, the undercover deputy who'd been watching her, dashed from the noxious convertible and disappeared around the side of the cantina. He returned shortly with a group of uniformed deputies. They entered the cantina *en masse*. Bravado encouraged Elizabeth to follow them, but reason cautioned that she'd probably be escorted out. This time she'd be patient. Still, she called Joe and asked him to stay close.

Elizabeth drummed her fingers on her laptop and decided she'd had it with waiting inside the car. She might miss something. Computer in tow, she stepped into a pool of streetlights and placed the laptop on the hood. She created a file and wrote an introduction to her article in case tonight's story ever materialized. Her informant hadn't been wrong about the other raids, but this bust at *Noche Azul* gave the phrase "slow as molasses" new meaning.

*

Naked and exposed, as if he were a chicken hanging in the market, Alex bowed his head in shame. He felt dizzy and confused. Long hours in the van with little water and only an orange to eat had made him weaker than he'd ever been. He glanced at his friends. The boys muttered under their breath, then closed their eyes. Sobbing, the twins hugged each other, a useless protection from the evil eyes of Santiago and the rat man. A wasted effort, thought Alex, his anger suddenly surpassing his embarrassment. After what they'd done to Mariella, he knew they'd eventually do the same to him and the others. He would rather die in that cantina than live by these bastards' rules, and for a minute, Alex was no longer afraid of anything. But his chest tightened as the fat lady and Santiago approached him.

"*Now's your chance.*"

Alex blinked at a gauzy apparition of Fernando perched on Santiago's shoulder.

"*You must do something,*" Fernando said.

Summoning his courage, Alex sidestepped Santiago, snatched the flowered tablecloths, and tossed them to the kids, then he grabbed one for himself before Santiago could reach him. They had just covered themselves when Alex heard a noise. Fuzzy purple dots floated in front of his eyes, and he found himself looking over his shoulder as the back door swung open. Zadie, the rat man, and Santiago also turned to see what was happening. Voices sounded in echoes. Alex steadied himself on the arm of the grapefruit picker's son.

"Diplomatic Security," a man with a ponytail yelled in Spanish. "You're under arrest." Two other men followed him. One was very tall, the other very short. To keep them straight, Alex named them *los tres Señores*: Tall, Short and Ponytail.

Santiago's cigarette dropped from his mouth, and he whisked his hand into his jacket, but *Señor* Tall struck him in the jaw.

"Face the wall," Tall said, swiveling Santiago, pressing his cheek against three wallpaper parrots, and removing the switchblade from the *coyote's* back pocket. *Señor* Short forced the rat man to stand next to Santiago.

Ponytail approached Zadie, who stepped backward into a café table. Her plump fingers picked up a stack of papers Santiago had given her, but when *Señor* Ponytail jammed his gun into her temple, she dropped them to the floor and plopped into a chair.

"Take over," Tall said to Short, who held a gun on Santiago and the rat man.

The State Department men spoke in a language Alex took to be something between English and Spanish, and he picked up most of their words, but when *Señor* Tall joined Ponytail and Zadie, she growled at them inaudibly. *Señor* Ponytail then withdrew more papers from his jacket and showed them to her. "Here's your fucking warrant, *señora*."

Zadie snatched the papers in her left hand while her right hand, every finger ringed with rhinestones, traveled down her fat belly, but *Señor* Tall grabbed her wrist. He winced as if he smelled the same pungent perfume Alex had noticed when Zadie had attacked him. Patting her skirt's swirls and folds, Tall removed a handgun from her pocket.

"A true *bruja*," he said to his partner as he tucked the gun into his belt.

Señor Ponytail nodded and grinned.

Zadie certainly did match Alex's image of a *bruja*. And this witch wasn't going down easily. Her eyes, huge blinking orbs, watched *Señor* Ponytail stoop over to pick up Santiago's documents from the floor, and Alex assumed these papers were very important because she tried to kick Ponytail with her sandaled foot.

"Dog fucker," she yelled in Spanish. "Hey, everyone! This cop fucks dogs."

Alex was sure she was strung out on meth or crack, but the men ignored her ranting. *Señor* Ponytail zipped the papers he'd collected from the floor into a brown case, pulled up a chair, and scooted close to Zadie. He said, "Who you working for, *amiga*?"

"Prick." Zadie spit on his boot.

Señor Tall glanced at Alex and the other teenagers, flowered tablecloths wrapped tightly around their bodies. When he walked toward them, Alex stepped out in front of the group, committed to be their guardian. The twins began to sob again as Tall gathered their frayed clothes, a ragged mixture of urine-soaked shirts and jeans reeking with the stench of rotted meat. Alex was wary when *Señor* Tall handed over their clothes, but the man met each kid eye to eye, then he showed them his badge. "I'm Agent Santa Maria with the US State Department. No one's going to hurt you."

"Bullshit," Zadie said. "He's going to rape you."

A creeping despair worked its way up Alex's spine. At first he'd been glad to see the State Department men, but now he realized he would be sent back to Guatemala.

"Go behind the bar and get dressed," *Señor* Santa Maria said.

They scurried away from him as if fleeing a dangerous animal. After dressing, they squatted on the floor, whispering about their bad luck, but all murmurs stopped when the agent squatted down in front of them. Alex watched him study their faces, and he thought the man looked kind. His name was Santa Maria after all, meaning holy Mary or saint Mary, and this must be a good sign.

"Tell me about your trip to Houston, and I'll see what I can do to get you work cards," *Señor* Santa Maria said.

"How can you do that?" Alex asked. The doubt in his voice hung in the air. This must have been a trick the man used to lure kids into doing what he wanted.

"Don't talk to that pig!" Zadie shrieked.

Although he couldn't see her, Alex had memorized the *bruja* from head to foot. He cringed.

The agent stood. "Shut up, Zadie," he said, and then he paused, laughing.

Curious, Alex motioned for the others to stand. They all scrabbled to their feet in time to see *Señor* Ponytail remove the bandana from his head and stuff it into her mouth. Her pig-eyes popped as she tried to breathe. Alex and his friends snickered, afraid to laugh out loud.

Señor Santa Maria chuckled. "Take it out, Dom," he said to Ponytail.

The kids smiled at the sight of *Señor* Ponytail slowly pulling the red scarf from Zadie's mouth and throwing it on the floor. One of the twins took a small step forward, and Alex noticed a purple scar above her right eye that flawed her cocoa-colored skin, and when she opened her mouth to speak, he could see her discolored teeth. Funny, he'd never noticed these things before.

She pointed to the faucet in the bar. "*Agua, señor, por favor?*"

Agent Santa Maria hurriedly filled glasses with water and passed out the drinks. They gulped so fast, water dribbled onto the fronts of their shirts. Then they gathered around the sink, cupped their hands and splashed water on their faces and arms. The cool liquid refreshed Alex, and the dancing black dots momentarily disappeared.

"*Gracias, señor,*" Alex said, then lowered his voice. "We have not eaten in a long time."

"Soon as we finish here, I'll get you all the food you can eat," the agent said, then he touched the grease on Alex's cheek. "What happened to you?"

Alex drew back. The others grouped around him and stared defiantly.

"I didn't mean to startle you," Santa Maria said, glancing at a smudge of grease now on his finger. "But I need to know what these *coyotes* did to you."

No one spoke.

"How can we believe you about the work cards, *señor* ?" Alex changed the subject. Telling him what had happened to Mariella would be too painful. He couldn't do it.

The agent took out his badge again and gave it to Alex. As he examined the gold metal object, his grease-stained hands trembled and the dots reappeared.

"As I said, my name is Luke Santa Maria. I'm with the US State Department."

Alex returned his badge and cast a quick look at his *compadres*. Sudden sparks in their hollow eyes and the slightly forward bend of their bodies signaled newfound hope.

"First, I need your names," the agent said, tucking the wallet in his pocket.

"My name is Alex Sifuentes."

"Hi, Alex. I'm glad to meet you." Smiling, he offered his hand.

Alex twinged at this simple act of kindness after so many days of misery, and he suddenly couldn't stand to hold the secret any longer. Taking a deep breath, he glared at Santiago and the rat man. "These men raped and murdered our friend, Mariella." As Alex spoke, he could feel his eyes moisten.

"*Sí*," said one of the twins in a whisper. "They left her to die like an animal in the desert."

"I'm so sorry," the agent said. "Do you know where they left her?"

Alex opened his mouth to answer when a man in an orange suit accompanied by a uniformed policeman strutted into the room. They herded a group of men and teenage girls, clothes hanging half-off their slender bodies. The girls looked beaten down and ashamed, bras undone, skirts hiked to navels, blouses rumpled. Their frightening conditions confirmed to Alex what his fate would have been if the agents hadn't found them, and he began to cry for Fernando and Mariella and Ramón, and for all the lost children.

FOURTEEN

They left her to die like an animal. Luke was sickened by the girl's words about their friend Mariella. He determined to find out more, maybe the Border Patrol could find her, but at the moment, he had a pressing situation. Why the hell hadn't Johnny put these arrestees in the sheriff's vans?

"Just look at this sleaze we found in a room off the restaurant," Johnny said to Luke and Dominic.

The men ranged in age from early twenties to late fifties, all of them in one stage or another of zipping their pants or wriggling into their shirts.

"Get these people out of here," Luke said, knowing full well Zadie wouldn't say a word or make a slip in front of this scum.

Johnny's chest puffed like an angry rooster. "So this is the thanks I get for busting these guys?"

"We'll talk later. Now move them into the vans, and call Protective Services about the girls." As Luke walked toward Johnny to emphasize his point, one of the suspects, a burly hirsute man, drew a small handgun from his jacket, shot randomly at the ceiling, and broke toward the door leading into the cantina. Johnny tackled him. The half-naked girls scuttled toward the other door. Jeff dashed to block their exit.

Drawing his SIG, Luke strode across the room. He wrenched the weapon from the shooter and ground his cheek into the wall. "You're in the sewer, *hombre.* Assaulting a police officer, not to mention sexual assault of a minor." As he cuffed the guy, Luke noticed the other suspects casting covert glances at each other. Trouble was still brewing.

"Heads up, Dom," he yelled.

Dominic aimed his sidearm at the men.

"*Señor* Luke, Santiago is getting away!" Alex Sifuentes pointed at the *coyote* sneaking toward the back door.

Stunned, Luke wondered why the hell Jeff hadn't cuffed the bastard. He aimed the SIG at Santiago, but the *coyote* grabbed one of the girls, using her as a shield until he reached the doorway, then he pushed her to the floor and vanished before Luke could get a clean shot.

Luke ran past the screaming girl. Outside, he scanned the lot, a bleak landscape cast in eerie blue light. No sign of Santiago, but a revving motor and the smell of diesel fuel caught his attention. Luke spotted the Blue Agave van and chased behind it as it gained speed, heading for the street in front of *Noche Azul*.

*

She'd just finished writing a description of the cantina when Elizabeth's ears caught a single cracking sound, surely a gunshot. People poured outside and clumped together in the front, a morass of drunks stumbling around, waking up the *barrio*. In nearby houses, silhouetted figures pulled back curtains and peeked between blinds, but no one ventured outside.

Elizabeth debated whether to make a stealth entry into the club or to nab a fleeing patron and beg an interview. She watched Joe aim his lens at the crowd and click off one frame after another. Some people shielded their faces, others shook their fists. They probably wouldn't talk to her now, but Elizabeth was ecstatic. This story would be a sensation, maybe even make the front page in spite of the obstacles laid down by that Day-Glo-costumed jerk, Deputy Johnny something or other, and in spite of the fact she hadn't nailed down all the facts, just yet.

"Well, look who else came to the party," she said to herself. Things were getting better by the minute.

Luke Santa Maria brandished a pistol and elbowed his way through the diehard club-goers, who spotted his weapon and scuttled out of the way. At the same instant, a white truck with Blue Agave painted on its side reeled from the parking lot and sped past her, its license plate coated with dust, a foul odor puffing from the exhaust pipe, the breath of its passing too close for comfort. Elizabeth placed her laptop in the car and perched on the trunk, a prime observation point.

Santa Maria sprinted into the street. Holding his gun with both hands, he spread his legs and fired a couple rounds at the vehicle. Elizabeth's ears rang from explosive pops as she stood to watch. The van's back windows shattered, but the vehicle kept going, ten houses away now, heading toward an intersection.

Elizabeth jumped in her car and shouted at Santa Maria. "Need a ride?"

He whipped around, glared at her, and seemed to be checking the area for another option. "Against regulations," he said, breathless, his dark hair mingling with sweat on his forehead.

Elizabeth nodded toward the van escaping down the street. "Time's a'wasting."

"What the hell." Luke sprinted to the passenger side of her car and slipped in. Cradling his gun, his eyes knifed into the unspoken tension. Regardless of circumstances, Elizabeth prized the sizzle of his energy—but now wasn't the time to ponder the DSS agent's finer points.

"Get a move on." Luke slapped the dash.

"Who're we chasing?"

"A *coyote*."

The truck had two blocks on them and was wheeling onto Navigation Boulevard. Gunning the motor, Elizabeth sped through the *barrio*. She kept her eyes on the road, but her peripheral vision caught Luke withdrawing a telephone or a two-way radio, she couldn't tell.

"I need backup," he said. "Navigation. Approaching that Catholic church, yeah, Lady of Guadalupe. White van headed toward Canal."

Ignoring a red light, Elizabeth rounded the corner at Navigation and headed for Canal Street. She sped by corrugated metal warehouses, sprawling machine shops, and strings of dilapidated row houses built in the Great Depression, now occupied by indigents and transients.

Luke fumbled with knobs on the Beemer's rooftop window until it slid open. He jutted his upper body through the narrow space and fired at the truck. The piercing reports throbbed in Elizabeth's ears and whittled at her nerves, but the shots were to no avail. The Blue Agave's taillights glittered as if they were the crimson eyes of a

Cheshire Cat, and the truck held its lead.

Suddenly, Elizabeth heard a train whistle. The car quavered from its proximity to a powerful engine. Maybe she was driving alongside it. Should she stop? The last two coherent things she remembered were spotting several sets of railroad tracks on the poorly lit street and Luke yelling, "No signal guards!"

Night air roared with a wicked din. On the left, an approaching train screeched, its wheels spitting sparks. All oxygen was sucked from Elizabeth's lungs. Electrified by a Morse code of panic, her right leg rammed the accelerator to the floor. "Drive!" she screamed to herself as she skirted the iron horse by a hair.

The instant they made it past the train, Luke twisted toward her. "Heads up!" he yelled, but it was too late.

A rumpled man, pushing a grocery cart crossed their path, ambling along, unaware of three tons of steel about to sweep him into oblivion. Elizabeth stiffened her arms and punched the brakes in a desperate attempt to reverse her forward thrust.

Phantom shadows moved in slow motion. Luke's hands seized the steering wheel. Swerving to change their course, he missed the man, but the car's front bumper caught the chrome shopping cart and hurled it into the air. She glanced in the rearview at the man gazing at his flying cart, his life's possessions sailing above the street.

Luke barely controlled the Beemer as its right wheels bounded onto a curb in front of a dry-cleaning store. When the bottom scraped cement, the car joggled to a halt, and the mayhem ceased, although a scathing high-pitched bleat pulsed in Elizabeth's ears. All she could see was her rigid foot planted on the brake and Luke's hands gripping the wheel. She blinked her lids and pressed her cheek against the sleeve of his leather jacket. Perspiration moistened her neck, and a yeasty odor laced with gasoline permeated the air. She sensed the car was tilted at an angle, half on the curb, half in the street, and her head throbbed to the tune of a siren's blare. Chopper engines reverberated overhead. Sheriff's deputies whizzed past.

Tilting her head sideways, Elizabeth studied Luke's profile, a five o'clock shadow around his jaw, his eyes alert and fixed on a bower of scraggly trees, and beyond the trees, the van's rear lights evaporating into a diaphanous mist.

He withdrew his hands from the wheel. "You okay?" He touched her shoulder.

Trembling, she nodded, vowing not to admit how rattled she was, as her hair clasp fell off and her hair tumbled onto her shoulders.

The last thing she wanted was Luke Santa Maria's sympathy, and he was looking pretty sympathetic.

"You take it easy," he said, leaving the car and opening her door before she could get her mind on track. "You should stand up and move around a bit." He offered his hand and she took it. When Elizabeth stood up, the street felt as if it were a boat rolling on uneven waves, an ocean spray in her face. Fumbling, she gripped Luke's wrist for support. He reached around her waist, guiding her to a bench in front of the laundry. He parked himself beside her, and she felt an urge to lean into him again, but Elizabeth stymied that impulse. She knew better.

"I'm okay, really," she said, stiffening her shoulders.

"Just making sure." Luke smiled before he released her waist, then he strolled around inspecting the car. "No serious damage," he said. "I can't believe the shopping card didn't take out your bumper."

Cryptic and way too nice, she thought as he got in the car and backed the Beemer off the curb. He probably wanted to influence her pending article on the *coyote*'s escape at the bungled raid.

After steering the Beemer to level ground, Luke helped Elizabeth stand, braced her elbow, and ushered her into the passenger seat. As he slid behind the wheel, his face was a mask, impossible to read, but when he clicked the ignition, he shot her a grin.

"Thanks for the lift," he said.

FIFTEEN

Alex's hope dwindled after Luke Santa Maria ran from the cantina to chase the *coyote*. What if Santiago killed the agent and came back? What if the agent forgot about them? He flinched at gunshots from outside and instinctively looked around for the rat man, who slouched against the wall near *Señor* Short. At least the rat's hands were cuffed.

The room was turning loud and crazy. Alex was afraid. The girl Santiago had used as a shield was wailing with no one to comfort her. Zadie spit at *Señor* Ponytail again, and this time he punched her in her gut. She doubled over, coughing and shrieking. Mr. Orange barked a laugh at Zadie's distress as two of his prisoners broke for the back door.

"This is a goddamn fucking circus!" Ponytail yelled, firing his gun above the prisoners. "Back in line."

The men halted, the room went silent except for the twins' nervous twitter, and Alex knew what had to be done now that Santiago was gone. He hadn't come all this way to be sent back to Guatemala City. Whispering to his *compadres*, he said, "I'm going to find Luke Santa Maria and make sure he gets those work cards for us."

"No, Alex. Don't leave." Shaking their heads, the girls lowered their lids, thick lashes brushing their cheeks, but both boys gave a hardy nod.

"It's worth a try," said the grapefruit picker's son.

Alex sent a rueful smile at his friends, then, snatching his backpack, he made the Sign of the Cross. While the confusion with the arrestees continued, he crept, hugging the wall until he slipped silently into the cantina. To his surprise, he found the room deserted and half-eaten meals left on the tables. He stuffed his pockets with chips, gulped a glass of iced tea, and ventured outside. Clusters of people milled on the front lawn talking to several uniformed policemen. Alex worked his way to the back of the building unnoticed. But Luke Santa Maria wasn't there.

The air smelled like scorched coffee, and sirens blared in the distance. A slight breeze feathered his hair before a chill seized him. His legs buckled. Alex squatted between waxy-leafed plants alongside a brick wall. His eyes were seeing fuzzy shadows everywhere, and his stomach cramped with a vengeance. The thought of eating the chips in his pockets made him want to vomit, but he was alert enough to notice the cantina sat on brick legs, a couple of feet off the ground.

Crawling beneath the building, he thought of nothing but sleep. The musty air and damp earth stole all warmth from his limbs, so he curled into a ball, backpack for a pillow, then scooped leaves and dirt around his body for comfort. Shots and car motors held his attention for a while. He imagined the brawl thundering on as his mind drifted in and out of consciousness. Entering a long-forgotten memory, he found himself playing in the cobbled streets near *Casa Maria*, splashing with Fernando and Elena in a broken hydrant's refreshing waters.

*

A dull glow edged into the space between the loamy earth and the cantina's under floor. Rubbing sleep from his eyes, Alex thought it must be morning. He could see raindrops tapping the surface of shallow puddles in the gravel parking lot. The thunder he now heard came from the mouth of God, not from the guns of men. His throat burned, and the pinching sensation in his stomach made him miserable, but worst of all, his thirst was so intense he was willing to chance being caught. Alex crawled outside, cupped his hands and slurped the falling water, but this didn't satisfy him, so he ventured into the lot and drank great gulps from a muddy puddle.

Relief came when he realized the night had passed, and now he was free to search for Obispa. Maybe she could help him find Luke Santa Maria. The rain was letting up, but drops from the leafy canopy plopped onto his shoulders and arms. A fresh golden light shimmered though puffed clouds, and the air smelled pure. Alex started to go under the house again, but the cheerful sounds of children's voices piqued his curiosity.

Stealing along the sidewall, he ventured to the front of the cantina, where he stopped cold. A yellow ribbon encircled the entire yard. What could this mean? A group of school children carrying backpacks and umbrellas clustered on the sidewalk. Fingering the ribbon, they squealed and pointed at the cantina's turquoise columns. Some of the windows were smashed, shards of glass scattered across the porch, and the door was secured with a brown padlock.

One of the little boys spotted Alex lurking near the corner of the house. Before he could duck into the bushes, the boy ran to him. His light chocolate skin and sepia eyes told Alex he must be Hispanic, but he spoke in brisk English. "Did you see what happened last night? My mother wouldn't let me watch, but I heard the guns and sirens. It was cool."

Alex swallowed hard. He understood very little English, but he caught the part about whether he'd seen what had happened. "Yes," he said. "Cool."

Waving his hands and bouncing on his tiptoes, the boy yelled at his friends. Alex could tell he was urging them to come over because the youngsters, two boys and two girls, galloped toward him. The first thing he noticed was their sparkling clean shoes and socks. The boys had identical short hair, shaved close around the ears, longer on top. They wore blue, green, and white checkered shirts with ironed collars and blue slacks. The girls' blouses matched the boy's shirts, but they had blue pleated skirts and blue hair bows in their long dark hair.

The children's questions bounced from their mouths so fast, Alex put up his hands as a signal for them to slow down. He hesitated to speak in Spanish for fear of being discovered.

A plump girl with intense green eyes and ebony curls tilted her head. "This morning, Obispa told my mother the police have shut down the cantina forever."

Alex wondered if he was dreaming the most incredible dream of his life. "Obispa?" he asked.

"Everyone knows Obispa. She takes care of the whole neighborhood, and she's my mother's best friend," the girl continued in a singsong voice, jutting her chin at Alex. "My name's Concepción. What's yours?"

"Alex," he replied to the girl's obvious introduction. This time he was certain she'd reported something about Obispa. He had to chance it now—his future and his friends' futures depended on finding the former nun. He would speak in Spanish. One of them would understand.

"I haven't had the pleasure of meeting Obispa. Can you show me where she lives?"

The children gawped.

Snickering, Concepción answered him in Spanish. "You don't know her?"

The others shuffled their feet and moved closer together. They were wary, or at least Alex thought the veiled looks on their faces indicated suspicion. These kids could tell their parents about him, and he couldn't let that happen. His heart skittered and thumped. The spots reappeared, dancing and swirling in furious circles.

Fingering his backpack for the crumpled paper Father had pressed into his hand at their parting, he showed it to the children. "A priest, Father Chiabras, gave me this information and asked me to visit Obispa. He is her friend from Guatemala." He emphasized the word "friend" in hopes of impressing them.

The group huddled around Father Chiabras's note of introduction written to Obispa.

"Our family is from Guatemala too," the smallest boy said.

Feeling a tinge of relief, Alex bit his lip. "So am I," he said. "And I bring an important message to Obispa from her friend. Please, show me where to find her."

The boy who first approached him lifted his shaded eyes from the note and grinned, revealing two missing front teeth. "See that house with the sign across the street?"

Alex squinted at the words on the sign, a jumble of rainbow-colored letters. Something was dreadfully wrong. One minute he was sweating and the next he was freezing. Still, he concentrated on the sign. "*Casa de Luz?*" he asked.

"That's where she lives," said the boy.

"Everyone knows where Obispa lives." With hands on her hips, swishing and sassy, Concepción's air of confidence highlighted her conviction that the entire world knew Obispa.

"You are so kind." Alex tried to smile, then groped for the brick wall to steady himself. The children's voices faded as a buzzing in his ears became louder and louder, driving him crazy, sucking him into a swirl of warped confusion before the world went black.

SIXTEEN

Luke and Dominic strode into Randall Cole's office located on the sixtieth floor of an uptown building with a panoramic view of Houston's skyline. The paneled room smelled of rich wood and expensive cigars. Reading a brief, Cole sat at his mahogany desk and glanced up when they entered. "Welcome to my world," he said. As he leaned forward to shake hands, his silver cufflinks clicked against the desk's flawless grain.

Settling himself into a butter-soft leather chair, Luke admired the painting of a blue woman with haunted eyes hanging behind Cole's desk. "One of my favorites," he remarked. "Tamayo's *Mujer Azul*."

"A foxy *chica* ." Dominic grinned. "Just your speed, Cole."

"Yeah. The one *muchacha* who never gives me any sass." Twisting his neck, Randall Cole studied the painting, then his gray eyes fell on Luke. "If you'd gone to law school with me, you'd have ten Tamayo's by now and we'd be partners."

This was the second time in a week Cole had made an overture about working together. "Sorry, Randall. No fast lane for me."

"You call busting slavery rings the slow lane?" Cole said.

"A different lane." Luke stared at him.

"If you change your mind—"

"Cut the foreplay, boys. We've been here before." Dominic slapped a handful of mints into his mouth and crunched. Cole flashed an irritated look. Dominic crunched louder, and Luke found it difficult not to laugh. Cole, with his two-thousand-dollar Armani suit, custom shirt, and manicured fingernails posed a sharp contrast to Dominic's braided hair, cracked leather bomber jacket, frayed jeans, and cowboy boots.

Luke suspected Cole persisted in trying to hire him because Randall's father, Mason Cole, had wanted it that way. After Luke's mother's death, Mason Cole had raised Luke as if he were his own. When Luke graduated with honors, the elder Cole had generously offered to pay for Luke's law school, but Luke figured he'd taken enough favors and needed to do something on his own.

Anxious to move on, Luke cleared his throat. "What you got, Cole?"

"Come with me," he replied with a noticeable air of conceit. He led them down a hallway past the senior partners' richly appointed offices into a workroom crammed with fax machines, scanners, printers, telex, and paper shredders.

Drumming his tanned fingers on a fax-copier, Cole elevated his voice above the mundane din of office equipment. "We checked the birth certificates you got at *Noche Azul*. I put my sexiest baby lawyer on it, right, Rebecca?" he called to a shapely, well-dressed brunette who was in a cubicle across the hall. The woman lowered her eyes.

Luke wondered how Cole got away with being a rank sexist in this day and age. Still, it must be nice to have a host of beautiful women to do his bidding.

"The certificates were obtained from county health departments across the state," Cole continued. "We think the thieves emailed or faxed copies of stolen driver's licenses to these departments, ordered birth certificates, and paid via the Internet. As far as most health departments are concerned, a person's license confirms their identity.

"Watch this." Cole slipped his license from his wallet, made a copy, scanned, and emailed it. "Just before y'all got here, I logged on to Canyon City's website and sent them my Amex number. They're expecting my license. Within a week, I'll have a notarized copy of my birth certificate. You can even pay to have them overnighted."

Cole motioned them back to his office where he clicked on the Internet and brought up Houston's health department. "Even Houston still uses this procedure."

Luke studied the instructions on the screen. "Homeland will stop this shit soon, I'll bet," he said.

"In whose lifetime?" Cole smirked. "The locals will resist. They need the revenue."

"Even if they change the procedure, someone can always be bribed," Dominic said.

Cole folded his large frame into the armchair behind his desk. "Precisely. Everyone has their price."

"There's a flaw in your hypothesis," Luke said.

"I doubt it. I've never met a man I couldn't buy." Cole's tone sounded wistful, as if he wished it weren't true.

"I'm talking about your driver's license theory," Luke said. "Not the people you bribe."

It was always like this with Cole, difficult conversations. The guy was top of his class at Harvard Law, had a mega-immigration practice and an international reputation. Still, he couldn't stop himself from reiterating that Luke had chosen a lesser profession or from goading Dominic into acting like a child. Even though Cole was always the richest and smartest, he seemed to resent Luke and Dominic, his buddies from the poor side of town.

Ignoring Luke's doubts about his license theory, Cole glided his hand over an eighteenth-century humidor as if caressing it. "Want a *Cohiba*? The best Cuba has to offer."

Luke grimaced and shook his head, but Dominic took a hand-wrapped cigar. Biting off the tip and curling his tongue around it, he spit the severed end into an oiled wooden trashcan. Cole watched Dominic's antics. In obvious disdain, he raised his neatly trimmed sandy brows, opened his drawer, and withdrew a circular cigar clipper with an inside blade. He sliced off the end of his cigar, flicked a flame from a silver monogrammed lighter, and puffed until the obnoxious thing lit up. Luke's eyes stung and he stifled a cough.

"Do you want a light or do you prefer rubbing stones?" Cole asked Dominic.

Before Dominic could match the zinger, the lawyer shifted his imperious gaze to Luke. "Back to your objection about how birth certificates are obtained. I assume most licenses are stolen from people in the larger cities."

"They are," Dominic said, reaching for the lighter.

Cole puffed on the cigar and rolled the smoke over his palate. "The thieves gamble that a majority of stolen license owners were born in big cities. They order copies of notarized birth certificates from the larger health departments, and they usually hit the jackpot."

In the past, Luke had dismissed this scattershot approach to gaining birth certificates illegally. He reasoned that the small slavery rings they'd been busting wouldn't have the savvy to train someone to keep up with the paperwork. Now he was inclined to consider the possibility. "If this operation is as large as I think it is, they have people assigned to the task."

"Without a doubt," Cole said.

"Zadie Gutierrez had visas and work cards too," Dominic added.

"A consulate employee probably forges them." Cole tapped an ash into a crackled amber bowl.

"We have several agents checking the border consulates," Luke said. He could barely tolerate the smoky room. Eyes watering, he covered his mouth to restrain a sneeze.

"What makes you think the forgers are located on the border?" Cole asked.

"Odds." Dominic glanced at Luke's misery, took a last draw from the Cohiba, and snuffed it into the bowl. Examining the extinguished cigar, he tucked it into his jacket pocket.

Cole winced. "Don't ignite yourself."

Dominic patted the pocket where he'd stored the cigar. "I'm saving my fire for the *coyotes* who're fucking those kids."

"How admirable—" Cole began.

"One more thing," Luke said. "We're hoping to get significant information from a boy we picked up last night. I may need your clout with Judge Montoya. If the boy starts talking, I want him out of detention and into witness protection."

Cole held smoke in his mouth until he spoke. "Really, now. What could he tell you?"

"Where he met the *coyote* Santiago, for one thing. And if the victims paid up front or agreed to pay when they got here or if their families are being extorted."

"What's the kid's name again?" Dominic asked.

"Alex Sifuentes." Luke recalled the tortured face of the brave young boy. "He told me that Santiago killed a girl who was traveling with them."

"I'm going to burn that bastard when we get him." Standing, Dominic began to pace. "I'll get Sifuentes from detention, and we'll have a heart to heart."

Cole's brow knitted into a deep furrow. "But the *coyote* escaped, correct?"

Dominic threw up his hands. "He sure as hell did. In one of the stupidest—"

"Don't even go there," Luke said. "We got his *compadre*, but he's just a driver and doesn't know much, or so he says." He heaved himself from the chair. Removing a Houston area map from his pocket, he spread it on Cole's conference table. "Take a look."

As the men bent over the map, Luke pointed out a smattering of red dots.

"Except for *Noche Azul* and a couple of others, the cantinas we're investigating are outside city limits."

"Fewer cops and less harassment," Dominic remarked.

"I'm sure you've noticed, several of the bars have 'blue' in their name," Luke continued.

"A signature," Cole replied.

"And the van comes from a Juárez tile company called 'Blue Agave.'"

"If they're making tile in that fuckin' city," Dominic said, "they have connections."

"That's one point on which we agree," Cole said.

A sudden refrain from *The Battle Hymn of the Republic* blared through the room.

Cole's eyes darted around his office. "What the—?"

"I'm innocent." Dominic held his hands over his head.

Luke snatched his cell phone from a pouch on his belt and listened to the rapid-fire report. As he rolled up the map and grabbed his jacket, he asked the caller to slow down.

"Something's up," Dominic said to Cole. He trailed Luke to the door.

Luke closed his phone. "They found the van in Greens Bayou close to Hobby Airport."

"Any sign of the *coyote*?" Cole asked as he trotted after them.

"As I said, we have one of them, but he's just a flunky. Santiago has vanished."

SEVENTEEN

The street where Obispa lived reminded Elizabeth of the quaint block in Amarillo where she'd grown up, except, of course, for the abundance of trees and the looming presence of *Noche Azul*. As she drove through the afternoon sunshine, brick and stucco bungalows burst from straw-colored winter grass, their wide porches, cracked sidewalks, and chimneys brilliant in the crisp December air. An occasional tile roof shone red. Clusters of oleanders bordered the houses, and the spreading arms of water oaks graced every yard.

When she passed *Noche Azul*, a group of boys played soccer near the cordoned-off area, even though the grass was wet from last night's downpour. One of them bounced a black and white soccer ball with his knee. It hit the curb and careened toward her car. The boy rushed for the ball. Elizabeth rammed the brakes against the floorboard and swerved the Beemer to miss him. Seemingly oblivious to the near accident, the kid retrieved the ball and booted it beneath the yellow police tape. A gaggle of other boys swarmed after him as he dashed toward the hedge near the cantina's front steps.

Still reeling from last night's near miss with the homeless man, Elizabeth felt her heart thump so loudly she couldn't speak. Any other day she would have jumped from the car and read the boys a stern warning about death at an early age, but today she calmed herself and stayed focused on her interview with Obispa about last night's raid. Parking in front of *Casa de Luz*, Elizabeth scooped up her notebook from the passenger seat and stepped out of the car. As she locked the door, she heard frantic screams coming from the cantina.

"Obispa!" The boys who'd been playing soccer were running toward her at a breakneck pace. "¡Obispa, venga!"

The lead boy was lanky, built like a string marionette, arms and legs flailing in all directions. His crazed black eyes and wild gestures told Elizabeth the soccer game was over. They zoomed past her onto Obispa's porch, where they pounded the door with their skinny fists. Elizabeth picked up the meaning of their shouts: a little girl's shoe, her leg sticking out from beneath the bushes, her body not moving, maybe asleep, maybe dead. Yes, really dead.

The shaman drew the window curtains and stood in front of her thousand flames. When she saw Elizabeth with five bellowing boys, she hurriedly opened the door. The balm of burning candles didn't calm the children, who launched into a set of gory descriptions. Elizabeth felt a surge of revulsion and panic. For the first time in her career, she was having difficulty with a murder.

"This could be bad," Obispa said to Elizabeth. "You should wait here."

"Not on your life."

Obispa hiked her white woven skirt and tucked it into a green sash. The women flew down the street behind the children. As they ran, Elizabeth's hand groped in her bag for her new smart phone; although she fiercely hoped she wouldn't be using it to call the police.

The boys raced ahead and ducked underneath the yellow tape, then abruptly stopped. Huddling, they waited for Obispa and Elizabeth, their frightened expressions saying it all. Beneath the bushes near the soccer ball, a patent leather Mary Jane shoe and a fleshy caramel leg bent backward at an odd angle. The boy who'd kicked the ball in front of Elizabeth's car held back branches of an oleander bush as Obispa and Elizabeth approached.

"It's Concepción!" he screamed. "She's dead. Someone cut her face!"

Despite the cool air that might delay the stench of death, Elizabeth sniffed an odor like rotten garbage as she approached the muddy earth where the body lay. She couldn't imagine how the girl had died, but one look at her blood-streaked legs and torn clothes sealed the fact that it was a hideously violent death. The lower part of her face was covered with coagulated blood, and her arms were gray. Elizabeth thought her dark almond-shaped eyes were open, but a wave of nausea made her look away.

"We can't disturb anything," she said. "I'll call the police."

Obispa's violet eyes glistened with tears, but her tight lips revealed a smoldering anger. "She was only twelve years old."

"Did she work at the cantina?"

"Absolutely not. Concepción went to the parish school. She was her mother's pride and joy."

Elizabeth's trembling fingers punched 911. She walked away to report the death, then returned to stand by Obispa.

"Could this be related to last night's raid?" Elizabeth asked.

Obispa didn't acknowledge her question. Instead she knelt near the body and began chanting in an unfamiliar dialect.

"Obispa, you need to move away from the body," Elizabeth whispered. "Evidence."

The shaman jerked around. "My people come here to escape atrocities, and now this. I will finish my prayer before I move. No one will interfere." She bowed her head and continued the haunting lament.

Elizabeth knelt too. She put her hand on Obispa's shoulder, feeling slightly comforted when the shaman didn't shrug her off. Forming a half-circle, the boys fell on their knees. No one spoke until a blare of sirens broke the solemn moment.

"I'll do anything to help you and your people," Elizabeth said to Obispa. "You have my word."

"I will remember your promise."

The activities around Elizabeth churned in slow motion and seemed to be happening in another dimension. The Houston police, apparently taken with their prayerful group, approached and politely asked them to move when they finished, just as an ambulance screeched up and two medics hurried into the yard. They were followed by a cruiser from the Sheriff's Department. By that time, neighbors were standing on their porches and trickling over to see what had happened, but they didn't cross the yellow tape still in place from last night's raid.

Obispa's hand was cold as she gripped Elizabeth's wrist. A short, plump woman wearing a red and yellow headscarf crossed the street and headed their way.

"Concepción's mother," the shaman said. "She must not see her child like this. She will go mad." Obispa trudged toward the woman.

The world turned blacker than anything Elizabeth had ever experienced. Kate's face crept into her mind—Kate, her precious daughter whom she'd been neglecting because she was an ambitious, hard-nosed bitch. She sat on the curb and put her head in her hands as Concepción's mother began to wail. Every bone in Elizabeth's body wanted to flee this horror, but she had to get the story, and she knew the officers would need to question her. Glancing at her phone, she keyed the number of the one person who might be able to shed some light on the girl's death.

His voice was breathless and impatient, as if he were being interrupted from an important mission.

"Santa Maria here. Is that you, Ms. Grant?"

Elizabeth felt her throat constrict, and she didn't try to constrain her sorrow. "It's me, Elizabeth," she said softly. "There's been a murder."

"Where are you?" The shift in his voice from irritation to concern was instant.

"Sitting on the curb in front of *Noche Azul*. Someone butchered a twelve-year-old girl."

There was a long silence on the other end, and when Luke spoke, his voice sounded weary. "I'll be there in ten minutes. Are the police—"

"Yes, plus medics and two sheriff's deputies. The police and the deputies are arguing about who's in charge. I can't hear everything they're saying. Something about the murder occurred in the city, but the lead investigation is located in the county. Does that make sense?"

"Let me speak to the officer in charge. I don't want that body touched until Houston forensics gets there."

"The medics are examining her. I can't tell who's—"

"Give me whoever looks like they're in charge." His manner was cold. "And don't leave until I see you."

Although Luke's commanding tone irritated her, Elizabeth scurried to the closest deputy, whom she now recognized as the guy who had been at the raid. He'd been dressed as a pimp in an orange leisure suit. Beneath creased eyebrows, his dark eyes kept darting to the girl's body and then to his clipboard as if he wasn't sure what to do.

She thrust her cell in his face. "It's Agent Santa Maria."

"Bad news travels fast," said the deputy.

Elizabeth wanted to slap him, even though the man probably wasn't making light of the tragedy. As he took the phone and listened, she glanced at the name on his badge, John McCullough, and she remembered. Luke had called him Johnny.

"Hey, boys," McCullough yelled at the medics and other officers. "State Department says to back off until forensics gets here."

Consoling the mother, Obispa kept her from rushing forward to see her daughter. The shaman's gentle voice tried to soothe the woman, whose shoulders shook with each sob, while an officer kept the boys corralled. There was nothing else to do but wait for Luke to arrive, and for the deputies to take her statement, so Elizabeth returned to the curb.

Sitting on the rough concrete, chin in her hands, she couldn't imagine the anguish Concepción's mother was feeling nor could she get the little girl's crumpled body out of her mind. To distract herself, Elizabeth considered the second hand on her watch, following its journey around and around. But after several revolutions, the details of Concepción's murder inched back into consciousness. A cold shiver shot through Elizabeth—a little girl alive in one sixty-second revolution, dead in the next.

It was after 2 p.m., and she needed to inform the paper of her whereabouts. Groping in her purse for her cell, she realized Johnny, the deputy, must have pocketed it. She pulled herself up from the curb and stretched her arms.

At that moment, Luke and his sidekick, Dominic Fontana, roared up in an Chevy sedan. Elizabeth instantly recognized the car as the one parked near Obispa's house the day of their first interview, but circumstances didn't warrant questioning Luke at the moment. She removed a pad from her pocket and made a note. Why was DSS watching the shaman?

Luke gave her a cursory glance on his way to the crime scene. *Hello, to you too*, she thought, edging closer to the deputies.

"Forensics is on the way," Johnny yelled the minute he saw Luke.

Luke nodded approval and started to speak, but everyone's attention was drawn to a hulky, six-foot medic who turned from Concepción's body. He breathed heavily and ambled toward the group with a grim expression. This mountain man looked like the kind of guy who'd never get rattled. But he was rattled all right, Elizabeth could tell. She bent her body under the tape and stepped closer.

"Some sick fuck cut out her tongue," the medic said in a hushed voice.

"Goddamn, son of a bitch." Dominic's black eyes threw off sparks, reminding Elizabeth of *Zona Azul*, where he'd roughed up one of the suspects and shot the jukebox. She was starting to understand his rage.

"Dominic, I need you over here," Luke said as he made his way to the girl's body.

Dominic followed him. "You know those motherfucking gangs copy the death squads," he said loudly. "Kill an innocent kid, send a message to the neighborhood—it shuts folks up real fucking fast."

"Yeah, I know."

Although his behavior seemed extreme, Dominic Fontana appeared to be genuinely tormented. Elizabeth jotted the disturbing information about possible gang involvement in the girl's mutilation, but she wasn't anxious to print this shit. Glancing at Obispa and the grieving mother, she decided to let her editor make the call, but either way, she wouldn't allow a byline.

"Latin Angels?" Johnny asked, moving closer to Luke and Dominic.

"Suspects, sure, but there's nothing yet." Luke squatted in front of the girl's shoe. "Jesus!"

Fist clenched, Dominic walked up and down the damp honey-colored grass in front of the girl's body until Luke stood up. Mumbling to each other in inaudible tones, both men stared at the ground and shook their heads.

From the corner of her eye, Elizabeth spotted a dapper mustached man dressed in a blue suit and red bowtie. He carried a large container reminiscent of her father's tackle box. Must be the medical examiner. Luke gave the man his card, and Dominic began interrogating Johnny about what had been disturbed before they arrived. Stepping back from his partner, Luke sent Elizabeth a troubled look, lifted the tape, and gestured for her to follow him to the curb.

"How do you stand this?" she said, returning to her spot near the oak tree.

"The same way you do, I guess." Luke lowered himself and sat beside her. "I'm surprised you're not on the horn."

She hesitated, not willing to express how awful she felt, especially to Luke. "I would be, but that idiot, Johnny McCullough, has my cell, and since you ordered me to let him speak to you, I hold you responsible."

"Guilty as charged." Luke twisted to face Dominic and Johnny. "Yo, John-Boy, throw me the lady's phone."

With a bewildered expression, Johnny groped in his pockets. Finally he hurled the phone at Luke, who rolled backward onto the sidewalk, stretched his long arm, and caught it.

"I can't believe you. That phone is expensive."

"You asked how I stand this. Rolling on the ground is a diversion."

Acquiescing, Elizabeth smoothed her long black skirt over her knees. "Do you think I should print the stuff about possible gang involvement?"

"You're asking me?"

She slatted her eyes and thinned her lips, her best hostile look, although Elizabeth didn't feel any ill will toward Luke, and she suspected he knew it.

He bent over and ran his fingers through the dirt near the curb. "More than before, I need to know how you got wind of *Noche Azul.*"

"An anonymous caller. I swear."

"We could trade information—off the record, and when we break this case, you'll get the exclusive." Luke shifted his concentration from the patterns he was drawing in the dirt. His forehead was creased as his eyes scanned her face.

"You still think I know my informant," Elizabeth said.

"It's a huge operation: identity fraud, slave labor, and child prostitution. The story will probably get you a prize."

Glancing toward the dead twelve-year-old and thinking of Kate, Elizabeth hesitated. "Maybe I don't want a prize."

EIGHTEEN

Alex shot straight up in bed, a nightmare crawling beneath his flesh. Santiago and the rat man pursued him through a stinking sewer. Seconds passed before he realized he was in a strange bedroom, no *coyotes*, no sewer. His head was cool now, and the dancing spots had disappeared. Daylight crept into the room from the edges of drawn curtains, and a pungent white vapor, its odor reminiscent of the medical clinic in Guatemala City, floated from a copper bowl resting on a small wooden table near the bedside. The red flame below the kettle evolved into faces of the children he'd met in front of the cantina. Rubbing his eyes, Alex guessed they had brought him to this place, but how long had he been there?

He slipped beneath a soft woven blanket and willed himself to sleep again, but his curiosity wouldn't allow it, so Alex propped a pillow against the headboard and sat up. Suspended above a roughhewn desk, a carved *Jesucristo*, blood dripping from his wounds, caught Alex's attention, and he reached for Father Chiabras's cross. Then he remembered he'd given it to Mariella, and with scant hope, he prayed it had kept her safe.

Other walls in the room bore masks of snakes winding around human heads and of humans evolving into lizards. Glowering, Alex thought of *La Sombra*, vile serpents disguised as men, spitting their venom at innocent children.

When he spotted the embroidered birds on a *huipil*, the Guatemalan version of a *pancho*, hanging above the bed, a wave of homesickness washed over him. Alex commanded himself to concentrate on something besides Guatemala. He thought of the Blue Agave truck, the hideous trip, and Santiago, and the ghostly reflection of Mariella glided into his mind. Alex knew instantly that this vision was different from Fernando's apparition. It seemed as if Mariella were inside his head, probably a result of his desire to believe she was still alive. He waited for her to speak, but instead, he heard women's voices coming from another room.

Tossing the blanket aside, Alex tiptoed toward a closed door. On his way, he felt comforted by the sight of his backpack lying on the desk. He padded down a hallway to a sitting room that glittered with more candles than he'd ever seen, even in the great cathedral. The women's voices came again. Alex figured they must be close. Although they spoke in English, he picked up several words and realized he understood more of the language than he thought.

And from their conversation came talk of *La Sombra*.

"The boy is not safe with me," one of them said.

He recognized the words "boy" and "safe," but that was all.

"Since he's illegal, it's going to be a problem."

Alex clenched his jaw in fierce resentment. He knew "illegal" all too well. He'd been illegal all his life—born to a sixteen-year-old girl who'd left her impoverished rural roots in an attempt to survive in the city. His *santa madre* died trying to care for her sons. Alex never knew his father, nor did Fernando. The sexual acts that created each boy had earned their mother enough *quetzals* for a week's worth of food, and this was his mother's honest explanation for two absentee fathers.

Stepping from the candlelit corner into the open, Alex spotted two women at the far side of an adjacent room. They stood near a glossy black dining table and an altar honoring the Virgin of Guadalupe. He recognized Obispa from her days at *Casa Maria*. The other woman, the one who said he was illegal, had golden hair and her shoulders were draped in a woolen shawl. His anger at her comment flared as he approached them.

"Alex, you are awake." Switching to Spanish, Obispa was the first to speak. "Welcome, my friend. How you've grown." She opened her arms to embrace him.

Alex stepped back. He didn't want to hug anyone. Turning, he stumbled into a wooden kneeler in front of a homemade altar, and he quickly knelt before the Virgin's icon.

"An angry boy," the golden-haired woman said under her breath to Obispa. "And with good reason."

Again, Alex understood the words "boy" and "angry." From his place on the kneeler, he whipped around and glared at Obispa. "Tell *la señora* if she must talk about me, to speak in Spanish."

The lady blinked her green cat-eyes. "You're right," she said in his native tongue. "I was thoughtless."

"Alex Sifuentes, this is my friend, Elizabeth Grant," Obispa gestured from him to the lady.

"*Con mucho gusto*," he replied, but he didn't stand or offer a more polite greeting in the manner Father Chiabras had taught him to do in the presence of elders. He signed himself and resumed his prayer of thanks to the Virgin for bringing him this far.

"When you have finished praying," Obispa said, "come in the kitchen. I will make you something to eat."

Alex nodded. He could hear soft clicks of the women's shoes against the wooden floor as they left the room.

A pleasant breeze drifted from the open window, and gentle corn-colored light filtered through palm fronds planted in a center courtyard. The air smelled of recent rain, reminding him of the damp cold locked in his bones since he'd hidden beneath the cantina. Alex shivered. He'd never felt so alone.

*

Standing behind the boy, Elizabeth watched Alex Sifuentes wolf down a plateful of steaming huevos rancheros and fresh tortillas. She couldn't think of anything to say, her mind was still reeling from Concepción's murder, so she heaved the heavy iron skillet from the stove and began to scrub the pan in which Obispa had prepared the eggs.

The shaman positioned herself across the breakfast table from him while he ate in silence.

"Alex," Obispa began as he scraped the last morsels from the plate. "Father Chiabras told me about Fernando, and I want to say how sorry I am."

"*La Sombra* murdered him." Alex bowed his head. "I couldn't save him."

Elizabeth thought the day had peaked with sorrow, but the boy's halting voice and his revelation about his brother's death engulfed her. Slowly, she dried her hands on a dishtowel and seated herself at the end of the table between Obispa and Alex, who continued the story about his saga in Guatemala City.

"And now they want to kill me in order to stop Father Chiabras from telling the UN about the other murdered children." He slammed the table with his fist. "And what Father says is true. We have graveyards full of kids. I know. I helped bury them."

"Since you're out of Guatemala, why do these *La Sombra* people care about you?" Elizabeth asked, hoping her Spanish was good enough for him to understand.

"*La Sombra* cares." Alex gave her a cold stare, then dropped his eyes to focus on his trembling fingers. "*La Sombra* is everywhere."

Obispa leaned close to him. "I do not want to alarm you, Alex, but the gang in our *barrio* works with *La Sombra*. They will soon know you are here, if they do not already know. Many of their members are aware that Father Chiabras and I are friends. For these reasons I have determined it is not safe for you to stay with me, even for a day."

"But where will I go? I've come all this way."

The boy's desperate expression pressed on Elizabeth's heart, but his stubborn glare gave her pause. "We could find him a place in one of the immigrant shelters."

"Eventually we can, yes, but all the shelters have waiting lists. And Alex is different. He is Father Chiabras's prize student, honest and hardworking. He needs a home." Obispa cast her eyes at Alex. "You must understand why I am worried for you. This morning an innocent girl was mutilated near *Noche Azul*. After the raid last night, the Latin Angels are sending a message to our *barrio*—do not talk to the police."

"How was she mutilated?" Alex asked, pushing his plate away.

"They cut out her tongue," Obispa replied in a whisper.

"That is what they did to Fernando." His voice broke.

Elizabeth gasped. Obispa drew a long breath. No one spoke.

Finally, the shaman placed her hand on top of Alex's. "You have been through so much, and now you are hearing about another atrocity. But this murdered girl is the reason you cannot stay with me." Speaking in a firm tone, she gestured toward Elizabeth. "We are in luck. Earlier today, *Señora* Grant promised to help our people in any way she can."

It took a second for Elizabeth to realize that Obispa was suggesting the impossible. She couldn't take Alex in, care for two teenagers, and deal with two rivers of raging hormones. And besides, she was already botching the job with Kate. Speechless, Elizabeth blinked at the shaman, then slowly shook her head.

"It is all right, *señora*," the boy said, studying her reaction. "I have lived on the streets. I am a fighter."

"This has nothing to do with you, Alex," Elizabeth replied. "It's my situation—"

"Perhaps your situation needs an innovation, a new approach, a different way." Obispa's skirt rustled as she stood. She stepped to the kitchen counter, plucked a tapered candle from its brass holder, and rubbed it back and forth in her palms.

"For God's sake, would you stop with the candles," Elizabeth said holding her head in her hands, staring at the table, a barrage of logical objections piquing her brain. What would Kate do if Elizabeth brought Alex Sifuentes home without advance warning? Plus the danger he posed if a death squad or a gang came after him. She bit her lip and searched for a reply.

Alex scooted his chair. Elizabeth heard him scrubbing his plate, the sound of water running from the faucet, the clink of silverware. Her instinct to take him home with her expanded and contracted, a taffy-pull of give and take, a yes and a no, mingling with her admiration of his courage and resolve.

NINETEEN

Luke conspired with Javi Padilla, the mayor's anti-gang director, as they waited for Zadie Gutierrez to be brought from lockup to the interrogation room. Luke had invited Javi to be present at the questioning because of his extensive knowledge of gang members, specifically, Tulio Mola, local boss of the Latin Angels.

Luke and Javi had first met when Javi was a lieutenant in the Houston Police Department before his career took an unexpected turn. After discovering Javi's talent for working with gang members he'd known since childhood, the mayor had created the position of anti-gang director and offered him the job.

As usual, Javi's hair was trimmed short, and he was impeccably dressed in a crisp white shirt, kelly-green tie, and navy blazer. His polished chocolate-tone loafers twinkled beneath creased tan slacks, giving him the air of a Spanish gentleman, a far cry from his humble beginnings in a Houston housing project. Luke frequently speculated privately on how Javi's face had been scarred, but he never asked.

Zadie flounced into the room, her chubby fingers drifting along the rough sheetrock walls before she wedged herself into a metal chair opposite the two men. The hulking female guard who escorted her waited outside the door. Zadie reminded Luke of a circus elephant that could go berserk without warning, but for the moment, the elephant was rapt in peaceful bliss, batting her eyelids at Javi Padilla. She leaned forward and adjusted the V-neck of her orange jumpsuit, revealing a wrinkled, craggy cleavage.

"You've moved up in the world," Luke began. "Once a piggy

little prostitute fucking Tulio Mola. Now a full-fledged madam."

"What would you know, cocksucker?"

"I know a lot," Javi said. "You and Mola have been together since he slimed into Houston from Guatemala. He controls the northeast side, and you do his bidding."

A muscle quivered above Zadie's corpulent upper lip, and her coy demeanor toward Javi melted. "Don't act so cool, *hombre*. You've been hanging around gangs in the projects since you were a *muchacho*. But *los cholos* wouldn't have you, so you joined the other side."

Javi's response was smooth as butter. " Someone cut up a twelve-year-old girl. We think Mola's behind it. I thought you were better than that, Zadie."

Staring at Javi, Zadie withdrew a piece of toilet paper from her brassier, exposing more crinkled brown flesh. She dabbed her eyes. "I know nothing about the girl, but you're wrong about my Mola. He only plays nice."

Luke smirked. "Look, Zadie. We can help. Mola's going to smoke you. You're no use to him now."

"He's paranoid as hell," said Javi with a hint of compassion. "I'm sure he's worried you'll squeal to save your ass."

The elephant fidgeted in her chair, and with that massive body, there wasn't much wiggle room. "I want my lawyer," she whined.

"I hate to repeat myself, Zadie, but Mola's homeboys will whack you one way or the other," Luke said.

With a guttural snort, Zadie bent forward and spewed a glistening ball of spit that plopped onto Luke's shirt. He clenched his jaw. Adrenalin skyrocketed, commanding him to choke her fat neck, but Luke's reason warned him to cool it. Hoping indifference would deprive the bitch of any pleasure, he impassively removed a tissue from his pocket and wiped the spittle.

Javi drilled his fingers on the table. "You can turn state's evidence, go into witness protection, or you can keep your mouth shut and die."

Luke placed a hand on Javi's shoulder. "Whoa, buddy. I'm sure this lady knows the rules." He cut a sharp glance at Zadie. "We've got you cold on human trafficking. You don't want to go down as accomplice to murder."

"*¡Chinga a tu madre!*" Zadie yelled at him. "I was in this fucking jail when the girl was murdered."

"So you were," Luke said. "But it was prearranged. Her body

was found on your property."

"Supposedly your property," Javi interrupted. "I've heard Tulio Mola owns the cantina."

"I own *Noche Azul*, you *puta*." Despite her fierce demeanor, Zadie's voice dropped a notch. Her imperious attitude seemed to be slipping.

Luke glanced at Javi, who gave him a quick wink, then, with a steely gaze, Luke placed his card on the table. "Give us what we need, and you'll be safe from Mola."

"Witness protection is foolproof." Javi stood and sauntered toward the door. "Our offer's good for twenty-four hours."

"It's your life, not ours," Luke added. He scooted his chair back, making a scraping noise like nails ripping across a blackboard. "You know how to contact us," he added with a gesture toward his card lying near Zadie's chipped glitter-pink nails.

She straightened her shoulders, snatched the card, shredded it, and threw the pieces at him. Luke and Javi turned their backs and strolled from the interrogation room past barred iron doors. At the front desk, they warned the duty officer to put Zadie on full-time watch and to see that she had no visitors.

"We don't want Mola's boys to get her," Javi said.

The officer agreed as Luke spotted Dominic bounding through the front door, jiggling his mint tin in one hand and swinging a briefcase in the other.

"*Hombres.*" Dominic pocketed the mints and shook hands with Javi, but he summarily frowned at Luke. "The Sifuentes kid—"

"We took this boy into custody at *Noche Azul*," Luke explained to Javi. "He told me the *coyote*, Santiago, killed a girl after they crossed our border."

The anti-gang director's cheek quavered beneath his eye. "Mola and his people are poison."

"Yeah, the creep's a bottom feeder," Dominic said. "But we have another problem right now, man. Sifuentes isn't in detention, and there's no record of his admission."

"We've been counting on information from that boy," Luke said.

"I talked to the kids who were with him," Dominic added. "One of the twins 'fessed up. Sifuentes sneaked out of the cantina after you went for Santiago. He's looking for you, Luke."

"*Mis amigos*, I must leave for a meeting. Send me the info on Sifuentes, and I'll put out the word. Maybe my network can find the boy." After shaking hands, Javi made his way through a gaggle of visitors and disappeared through the jail's frosted-glass doors.

Luke glared after him. "Jeezus. This investigation is jinxed. First the *coyote*, now the kid."

"Calm down, *amigo*. Throwing fits is my shtick."

Luke trudged from the low brick building, an eyesore among towers of glass skyscrapers. The afternoon had sunk into cloudless cold with brisk winds whipping through crowds on the sidewalks. Zipping his leather jacket and stuffing his hands in his pockets, Luke strode ahead of Dominic. He wanted to be alone.

But Dominic stayed close, whistling loudly, strolling up beside him at the corner of Texas and Congress. "I do have some better news."

Luke slatted his eyes and stepped off the curb before the red light changed. As they crossed the street and headed for the lot where officers parked free, Dominic continued to whistle, bugging the hell out of Luke, who relished wallowing in his foul mood.

"Okay. What's the news?" he said, more to stop Dominic's whistle than anything.

"We need a CI in the Angels to find out who murdered that girl, right?"

"Yeah."

"I just called Obispa to see if she knew anyone, and she said that if the candles give her a sign, she might have a person for the job."

"Well that's simply marvelous," Luke said. "Some psycho lumps of wax are going to screen a CI for the State Department."

"That's about it." Dominic grinned. "And it's free."

TWENTY

Alex was amazed when *Señora* Grant decided he could stay with her. He felt certain she didn't want him, but he went along with it because he felt Obispa was right about *La Sombra* and their US gang connections. He grabbed his backpack full of clean clothes Obispa had washed for him and followed *la señora* to her car. Settling into the soft cushion of the front seat, he sensed he was being thrown into another world. He could tell the car was old, yet he'd never ridden in such a nice one, nor had he ever worn a seat belt. He watched her pull a strap across her chest, so he pulled on a similar ribbon-like belt beside him. It didn't release. He yanked harder. If *Señora* Grant knew how anxious he was, she didn't show it when she reached across his chest and magically clicked the belt into a silver buckle beside his hip.

"*Gracias*," he said in a half-whisper, catching the sweet scent of flowers.

"*Por nada.*"

She turned on the radio as they sped onto a lighted highway, and it made Alex nervous when she quit looking at the road to search for a station.

"There's lots of Latino music, here," she said in Spanish. "I thought you might enjoy some."

"*Gracias*," he replied, but he shut the happy music out of his head. Alex glanced at his tattered backpack and frayed jeans, quite a contrast to the rich leather seats and glossy dashboard. Thank

God he'd been able to shower before he left Obispa's, but somehow he knew he couldn't scrub away the filth and memories of life in that truck, the blue tiles' sharp corners, and Santiago hovering over Mariella. And even though Obispa trusted this fancy lady, how could Alex be sure she wasn't taking him to a horror worse than the truck? He longed for Father Chiabras, for little Elena's reassuring embrace, for Fernando's impish smile.

Señora Grant drove into the driveway of a white stucco two-story house, or kind of a house that attached to what appeared to be another house. Alex wondered how many people lived there, but he didn't ask. When she pushed a button in the car, the paneled garage door opened, and Alex felt as if they were entering a cave. He shuddered. This house reminded him of a wealthy section of Guatemala City, a place called *Zona Nueve*, where he'd visited with Father to meet one of *Casa Maria*'s patrons.

Before she opened her door, *Señora* Grant smiled at him. "I have a daughter your age. Her name is Kate."

Nodding, Alex fumbled to remove his seat belt. He retrieved his backpack, slung it over his shoulder, and followed her into a spotless kitchen. He assumed *la señora* would have him clean her house in order to earn his keep. He could do that, no problem, but what niggled at the edge of his mind, causing him to lose his breath, was meeting her daughter. Alex had never met an American teenager, but the minute they entered the kitchen, he heard her earsplitting music.

"Kate, I'm home," *Señora* Grant yelled, but there was no answer. "She can't hear me," she said to Alex, leading him through a high-ceilinged room adorned with giant paintings splashed with bright colors.

Filled with awe, he cautiously trod over cushy rugs laid on top of stone floors and dared to run his fingers across a soft white couch. Alex trailed *Señora* Grant up a circular stairway and down a carpeted hall to a closed door. Biting his lip, Alex nervously pushed his straggly hair off his forehead and tucked runaway strands behind his ears.

"Kate." *La señora* opened the door.

Alex's first sight of Kate Grant was unforgettable. Her light-colored hair fell over slender shoulders, and her eyes were blue-green like turquoise jewelry the *Indios* sold at market. She wore a pink shimmering blouse and jeans. Reading a magazine, she sat on a white rug.

Señora Grant spoke above the music. "We have a guest."

The girl's beautiful eyes drifted over Alex, and although it wasn't a friendly look, he couldn't stop staring at her. She was slim—shaped like a movie star. Her mother entered the room, walked to a cabinet loaded with slick black machines, and turned off the music.

"This is Alex Sifuentes," she said in English, returning to stand by Alex.

Kate didn't offer her hand, and he detected her scorn. If only he owned better clothes and had left the tattered backpack downstairs, she wouldn't know how poor he was. As the stiff silence continued, pride seeped into Alex's bones. He wouldn't give this girl the satisfaction of knowing how her attitude hurt him.

"Is he staying for dinner?" Kate asked, shifting her intensity to her mother. "Because if he is, there's nothing to eat in this house."

"Alex will be living with us for a week or so. He escaped from Guatemala."

"That's just great, Mom." Kate turned around, cranked up the music, flopped on her bed, and thrust her nose into the magazine she'd been holding.

Although he didn't understand all her words, Alex felt like a worm. He vowed to get out of this hateful house at the first opportunity. He'd heard about spoiled American teenagers and guessed he'd just met one. Most certainly, he wouldn't get to know her, no matter how beautiful she was with her head bowed low, her nose buried in a magazine to show anger or lack of interest, he couldn't tell. Then Kate glanced at him, and Alex launched a most spiteful look. For a moment, their eyes locked.

"Come with me," *Señora* Grant said softly. "I'll show you to your room." Her face was sad, and in spite of his previous anger at *la señora*, Alex found himself feeling sorry for her.

Satisfied that Kate had gotten his telegraphed message of disdain, Alex tramped downstairs and settled into a bedroom as large as the entire dorm at *Casa Maria*. He propped squashy pillows behind his head and flipped on the TV using the device *Señora* Grant had showed him. Hoping to find a Spanish station, he jumped from one channel to another, fascinated by a feast of moving delights: cartoons, football games, real-life helicopter rescues, and rock singers. When a knock on the door burst his visual consumption of the best things America had to offer, he glanced at a clock and realized a whole hour had passed. Alex flew from the bed to answer the door.

"I bought some hamburgers for dinner." *Señora* Grant looked happier than when he'd seen her with her daughter. "Are you hungry?"

"*Sí, señora*," he said.

"Before we eat, can we talk for a minute?"

He nodded, and she gestured for him to sit on the bed. She folded her long body into a fat armchair across from him. "Sometimes Kate can be difficult. I apologize for her behavior, and I want you to know it has nothing to do with you," she explained in Spanish.

Questioning how he should reply, Alex swallowed hard. "I think I understand. Sometimes my brother would throw fits. There was nothing I could do to stop him."

"The other thing I want to say is, I'm so sorry about your brother."

Alex inhaled a deep breath to keep from revealing his distress, then he noticed Kate standing in the doorway. He didn't know whether to acknowledge her, but *Señora* Grant couldn't see her daughter, so why bother? Anyway, she'd been so mean, he decided ignoring her was best.

"Our mother died when I was ten," Alex continued. "I raised Fernando, and in order to survive, we joined the Latin Angels until Father Chiabras took us in."

"There's a Houston gang called the Latin Angels." *La señora's* face showed concern, maybe even fear.

"I know," he said.

"Are you sure the Guatemalan Angels aren't the ones who killed Fernando?"

"I am sure because I saw the men who did it."

Señora Grant seemed more worried. "Now I understand why Obispa is afraid for you."

Alex didn't respond. He couldn't stop himself from glancing at the enchanting Kate. Her eyes were wide, and she looked ashamed or distressed, he couldn't tell, but either way, he hoped she was miserable.

"Can I come in?" Kate asked.

Señora Grant stiffened, but she didn't answer. Alex didn't know what to do. He still felt the sting of Kate's rudeness, but he nodded at her in spite of his hurt. She came to the bed and sat beside him. Alex ran his fingers through his hair with the hope it didn't look too messy.

"Look, *hombre*. I'm sorry about being such an asshole when you came in with Mom."

Alex couldn't believe his ears. The girl spoke Spanish.

"You're forgiven," he said.

"Thank you." She leaned even closer. "I heard Mom say your brother is dead."

"They killed him—"

"Who killed him?" Kate's elevated voice startled Alex.

"*La Sombra.*"

"The Shadow?"

"Yes, the Shadow."

Silence filled the room, but Alex didn't feel uncomfortable. It was as if the women were mourning with him, and he was deeply touched by their compassion. No one spoke until a phone rang from another room. *Señora* Grant excused herself to answer it, leaving Alex alone with Kate, who didn't move from the bed.

*

Expecting an anonymous tip, Elizabeth reluctantly checked her cell and was relieved to see Obispa's number. She flat didn't have the stamina to cover another raid and was looking forward to hamburgers with Alex and Kate, even if her daughter would likely protest about the nutritional quality of the takeout meal.

"How's Concepción's mother?" Elizabeth asked.

"I have sedated her with an herbal potion. She will never get over this." The shaman hesitated. Elizabeth could hear her breathing into the receiver.

"Concepción's death is hard for you too."

"Yes," Obispa said. "And Alex? How is Alex?"

"I think he's fine. He and Kate are talking. It was a shaky start, but she's warmed up."

"I am glad." Her voice trailed off.

Elizabeth felt helpless in her effort to console Obispa about the girl's death, but when the shaman spoke again, Elizabeth noted Obispa's voice had suddenly turned aloof. "An agent from the Diplomatic Security Service has contacted me. He needs an informant to join the Latin Angels."

"Let me guess." Elizabeth recalled Luke's car parked near the shaman's house on the evening she had her first interview with Obispa. "Luke Santa Maria."

"No."

"Dominic Fontana, then."

"It does not matter who spoke to me. These matters are confidential. What I am trying to say is Alex could do this job."

"You've got to be kidding. A few hours ago you were afraid for his life. Now you want him to join that gang?"

"There are three Houston gangs that have Guatemalan connections. We cannot be sure *La Sombra* is in touch with the Angels," she said. "Our people need him, Elizabeth."

Elizabeth knew there were things she'd never understand about cultural attitudes, but she wasn't rolling over on this one. "Not after what he's been through."

"If Alex cooperates, the government will provide his papers."

"I'll get his papers," Elizabeth said. "Without exposing him to the kind of perverts who killed his brother." Her temple throbbed against the receiver. Her head ached with confusion.

"My candles say he will be safe."

"That's ridiculous. No one's safe in a gang."

"Your heart is melting for the boy," Obispa said in a hushed tone. "This is noble."

Elizabeth said good-bye. She didn't ask the shaman to explain her last comment, an obvious contraction and too much for one day. After taking a moment to regroup, she hollered for the kids to join her in the kitchen. The three of them spent the evening visiting over greasy hamburgers, milkshakes, and crispy fries—without a single "bad diet" comment from Kate.

TWENTY-ONE

Elizabeth overslept, and for once, she didn't care. She lolled at the breakfast room table, scanning her latest copy of the *New Yorker* and visiting while Kate blended a yogurt shake for herself and Alex. He sat across from Elizabeth, his circled eyes and lean frame screaming for healthy food and a boatload of vitamins. Kate would boost Alex's heath, and Elizabeth would find a solution to his illegal status. As much as she hesitated to admit it, Obispa's wisdom was proving to be right—everything, that is, except her insane idea about Alex joining a gang.

After seeing Kate off and cautioning Alex to rest, Elizabeth stopped at the grocery, loaded up on produce, and stocked the fridge. She asked herself why she hadn't done these things for Kate and vowed to change her slipshod ways.

The morning was hectic at the *Chronicle*. Elizabeth edited her follow-up article about Concepción's brutal murder, then she took a late lunch. From the window of a French café across from the newspaper, she watched the afternoon sun dive behind a nasty cloudbank marching in from the north. The palpable gloom matched her sadness. She pulled out her computer and reread her account of Concepción's death, but she couldn't stand to submit it yet. Elizabeth ate in robot fashion, paid the bill, and didn't return to work. She cautioned her assistant not to tell anyone where she was going and gave no explanation to her editor, who disapproved of family time off.

Kate had taken up running in order to improve her soccer

performance, and so, in spite of threatening weather, Elizabeth hurried into the bleachers at the Lamar High School track. Hoping she hadn't missed Kate's event, she sighed relief when she spotted her and her team members on the field, stretching and jogging short distances, telltale signs they hadn't run yet. Elizabeth removed her stadium seat from its zipper bag and settled in.

Smiling to herself, she remembered Kate's enthusiasm at last night's dinner when she'd given Alex her freshman Spanish book and showed him how to use the Spanish-to-English dictionary. Elizabeth didn't have the heart to ask him if he could read, but when Alex glanced through the book and read several Spanish words, she was delighted. Everything about this boy, from his manners to his eagerness to learn, spelled "smart."

A whistle blew from the field, and Elizabeth did a double-take. The race didn't involve Kate, but she spotted Luke Santa Maria climbing the bleacher stairs two at a time. When he sat down beside her, she halfway resented his presence, an intrusion into this special new thing she was doing for her daughter. On the other hand, she was pleased. The man was damn good to look at, something she'd been doing a lot of lately.

"You're following me." Her accusatory tone held a teasing edge.

Luke grinned, then gave her a serious look as if he'd caught himself from saying something he might regret. "I left a message on your cell earlier. I finally called your office and convinced your assistant to tell me where you were. Apparently, it's a secret."

"I'm on break. Cell's off."

"Not afraid you'll miss a tip?"

Ignoring his jibe, she pointed to the runners. "That's my Kate. Number nine in red and white."

Luke scanned the track. "An athlete and a beauty. Great combination. I see a strong resemblance to you."

Elizabeth felt flush, embarrassed by his compliment. She was falling for this guy, and that was a mistake. They had nothing in common but their mutual quest to expose human slavery.

"Do you have kids?" she asked.

"Nope."

Elizabeth was tempted to ask if he was married, but she thought better of it. Somewhat assuaged, she noticed he wore no ring. "So, tell me something about yourself that I'd never guess."

He gave her a quizzical look.

"Like a hobby."

"In my spare time, I do wood carvings, small totems usually. I particularly enjoy Northwest Coast Indian art." Luke smiled. "Your turn."

"I don't have an artistic hobby other than looking at art, but I attend lots of gallery openings and buy paintings when I can afford it."

"Anything else?"

"Well, I run six miles every other day. Back to you."

"Okay. In college I learned to fly small planes," Luke said. "I still have my license, though I don't get much practice these days."

"Now that's an accomplishment," she said. "I'd like to learn. It's on my list." Maybe Elizabeth was wrong about not having anything in common with Luke Santa Maria.

"I know an instructor when you're ready."

"Thanks." Emboldened by the friendly revelations, Elizabeth continued the questions game. "Tell me about your family."

"A soap opera not worth watching," Luke said.

"I like soapy memoirs. Go ahead," she said.

Luke shook his head.

"Come on. It couldn't be worse than my nutso family."

Luke's face conveyed an unreachable sadness, and yet Elizabeth persisted.

"Surely you trust me," she said, watching his reaction.

"You? The consummate investigator?"

"Actually, I'd rather be your friend," she said. Elizabeth meant it. The game was over. "But just now, I wasn't acting like a friend. Forget my interrogation."

"It's not a pretty story, but here's the short version."

"No. I was out of line."

Luke stared straight ahead as if he were mesmerized, and when he spoke, Elizabeth absorbed his every word.

"As a young kid, I remember my dad being a successful geologist, but he drank too much Scotch, a lethal combo with his bipolar disease. When I was fourteen, he lost his job. Crazy drunk, he raged home and pulled a gun on my mom, who was fixing dinner. She pleaded with him, begged him to get help. I heard a shot and ran to the kitchen in time to jump him before he killed himself." Luke paused, sucked in a breath. "There was nothing I could do for Mom."

"I'm sorry, Luke." Shocked and humiliated, Elizabeth sat mute, staring at her hands, strange numb appendages folded in her lap. Why had she been so pushy? Finally, she said, "Do you want to say more?"

"Nah."

"I understand." Elizabeth fixated on the races, but her only thought was of Luke's story. Minutes passed without conversation. At some point she had to say something, had to move on, had to find a conversation topic that might lighten the mood. "So, what's up? Why are you—"

"I need your help."

"Sure," she said, willing to do almost anything.

"Would you contact Zadie Gutierrez, the woman who ran *Noche Azul*?" he asked. "Say you'd like to write her side of the story. Maybe you can convince her to cooperate with me, that witness protection would be a good thing."

Elizabeth shook her head. "She'd need more than witness protection if I saw her right now. I'd be homicidal. The bitch was involved in Concepción's murder."

"That's the point, Elizabeth. Zadie knows who killed the girl." Luke rolled his eyes. "I can't get anywhere with her, or I wouldn't involve you in this. But you could pretend you're interested in her, flatter her, and during your interview, tout the witness protection program."

"I've never felt so sure about not interviewing a suspect," Elizabeth said, regretting her offer to help him. "Trust me, you want another reporter for this job."

Bam! The gunshot made Elizabeth jump. She dug her fingers into Luke's arm.

"It's just the hundred-meter," he said with a wry smile.

Elizabeth's cheeks heated up again as she inched away from his arm and watched the race. When Kate sprinted ahead of the other girls, she jumped up. "Go, Kate!"

"She's going to win," Luke said.

But nipping at Kate's heels, a tall girl with copper hair and polished brown skin broke into the lead, and her daughter missed first place by a stride.

"Damn," Elizabeth murmured. "She almost had it." She hid her disappointment when Kate waved. "Great run!" she yelled.

Kate flashed a huge smile, then Elizabeth noticed her daughter was seriously focused on the stands. Kate had spotted Luke.

After the meet, Luke accompanied Elizabeth to congratulate Kate. He didn't bring up Zadie again, and Elizabeth was relieved but a little surprised at herself. A few days ago, she'd have jumped at the chance to get to Zadie, but Concepción's murder shouldn't be upstaged by a story about Mola's madam. If anything, she'd do a story about the girl.

A sudden north wind ruffled Luke's hair, and he zipped his black leather jacket. Elizabeth buttoned her coat while Kate slipped on her warm-ups. Praising Kate's performance, Luke took a closer look at her medal. When he glanced at his watch, Kate batted her lids and grinned at her mother, an obvious sign of approval. If Luke noticed the nonsense, he acted oblivious. Elizabeth observed the sheen in his blue eyes, the sharp line of his jaw, and near his ear, a tiny cut from shaving too close. No matter how she tried to stop herself, she enjoyed observing intimate details about this man.

Kate beamed at the silver medal. "I can't wait to show Alex."

"Your boyfriend?" Luke asked.

Elizabeth raised her finger to her lips, but Kate didn't see the signal.

"He's just a friend from Guatemala," Kate said as she strung the red, white, and blue ribbon around her neck. "Mom met him at the witch doctor's."

Luke's eyes flashed.

"What's his name again?"

"Alex—"

"*Sifuentes?*"

"Yes," Kate answered, biting her lip and turning to Elizabeth.

Elizabeth felt Luke's penetrating gaze as she scrambled to think of something to say.

"The kid who escaped *Noche Azul?*" He cocked his head. "I need to see him."

"He's our guest," said Kate, aiming a defiant look at Luke.

Luke stepped toward Elizabeth. "He may have info on that *coyote.*"

"He just lost his little brother and survived a miserable trip," Elizabeth said, and then she paused with a knowing look. "I've got it. You're the one who talked to Obispa. You want Alex to join the Angels as a CI."

Luke shoved his hands into his pockets. "What are you talking about?"

Elizabeth thought in the end, Luke would probably win. Still, she would try to prevent him from getting to Alex until the kid regained his equilibrium. By then, she might have arranged a student visa or a work card. "I intend to hire Randall Cole to help Alex."

A sly grin spread across Luke's face. "Randall's a good friend, practically like my brother. His father took me in—"

"Please don't interfere. Alex is great kid." Elizabeth grabbed Kate's arm and headed off.

"You can't obstruct a State Department investigation," Luke called.

"Watch me."

On the drive home, it occurred to Elizabeth that Luke had been about to tell her Randall Cole's father had taken Luke in after his mother's death. A complication for sure, but Cole was the best immigration lawyer in Houston. She'd hire him anyway—if he'd take the case. It also occurred to Elizabeth that she was fighting again with someone she cared for. This time, Luke Santa Maria. It wasn't fair the way life dished out random dilemmas, difficult relationships, steel bullets in the chicken soup.

Her cell rang. The ID read: *Private Caller*. Another tip. Another raid. More bullets.

TWENTY-TWO

Except for the occasional night he crashed at his townhouse in the city, Randall Cole spent most evenings on his ranch, a thousand-acre spread in rural Waller County, forty-five minutes from his Houston office. He poured a whiskey, then strolled into the great room, where he settled into a chocolate-brown leather chair to review profiles of potential jury members. His clients in this landmark trial, a Florida citrus plantation, were being sued for sexual harassment by the EEOC on behalf of a Latina farm worker. She'd worked for the company for twenty years. Cole hadn't been able to trip her up during depositions, and he suspected the woman was telling the truth about the ranch supervisor's repeated sexual assaults. But he'd still win this case for the owners. He had no doubt.

After highlighting names of jurors who'd most likely enjoy a cash infusion, Cole laid the file in his lap and watched phantom light patterns scatter on the beamed ceiling. Outside, a crimson glow, vestiges of the dying day, blanketed the grasslands as Texas longhorns meandered from the pasture to their feeding troughs. Cole surveyed his herd crowding into the two-story red barn until his attention was drawn to a lithe silhouette flitting across the veranda.

Grabbing a jacket on his way to the portico, he shouted at the delicious teenager, Muñeca.

Obedient as expected, she came to his side. Cole took her arm, dragging her to the sporting clay range several yards from the house.

When he flipped a switch, the evening sky instantly retreated, and the shooting range flooded with light in the foreground. He inserted electronic earplugs and adjusted his protective glasses, then screwed a full choke into the barrel of his favorite twelve-gauge, over-and-under, a handcrafted Italian Perazzi. The choke constricted the spread of the shot and was intended to break targets at fifty yards. Cole insisted on the most difficult settings for the clays that were electronically thrown from towers stationed around the range.

Muñeca quickly knelt on the ground and gripped a black cord with a button device at one end. Her breasts were visible through a sheer pink dress with a Peter Pan collar and a wide sash looped into a bow. Glistening hair adorned with lush satin ribbons gave her the appearance of a child, and no matter how cold it was, she wore no more than he demanded.

Shouldering the Perazzi, Cole leaned forward on his left foot, pressed the stock to his right cheek, squeezed the palm-swell against his hand, and yelled, "Pull!"

As a saucer-shaped ceramic clay flew from the hundred-foot tower, Cole swung his twelve-gauge to create a lead. Moving the barrel underneath the clay, then upward in front of the target, he pulled the trigger. The shot stream collided with the orange and black saucer, its pulverized fragments falling to earth. He was damned pleased.

"Pull!" he shouted again at Muñeca.

When no clay appeared, he pointed his gun at her.

"So beautiful," Cole said in Spanish. "But so stupid."

Her wide eyes signaled fright, and he felt himself grow hard. He loved instilling terror into little girls.

"Goddamn it, Muñeca, pull faster."

When she didn't react, he bent and seized her hair. Muñeca whimpered. Cole caught the pain in her face and yanked her hair again. Forget foreplay, he was ready now. But a shadow fell across the lawn near the place where Cole held Muñeca.

Tulio Mola sauntered toward them. The gangster sported a short-sleeved silk shirt emphasizing his muscled arms. In one hand he held a cracked leather bomber jacket slung casually over his shoulder, in his other hand, a briefcase. A horsehair belt cinched his slim waist above dark twill pants. Head freshly shaved, Mola wore an earpiece for his cell phone. His eyes, keen as a raven's, fell on the trembling Muñeca.

"Beating up on *chicas* again?" said Mola, his English heavily accented.

Less than amused, Cole released the girl. No fucking her now.

Business ruled. "Did you teach that *barrio* a lesson?"

Mola's wicked smile revealed a mouthful of brilliant white teeth. "No one in that *barrio* will ever rat on *Noche Azul* or any other cantina again."

"Why is it I doubt your fucking proclamations?"

Mola rolled his eyes, uncapped a Corona, and settled at the polished oak bar on the veranda overlooking the shooting range.

"Learn some manners. Don't sit until you're invited." Cole glanced at Muñeca, whose rapt attention focused on Mola as if the goddamn dick could save her.

"You little bitch," Cole said.

At this, Muñeca fell on her knees, her whole body shaking, exactly as Cole had taught her to behave when she displeased him. This girl was the best fuck he'd ever had, and Cole was tempted to tell Mola to beat it, but he had issues to discuss with the Latin Angels' jefe. Frustrated, he ejected shells from the Perazzi and laid it on the bar.

"Did you find out who's been talking to Elizabeth Grant?" he asked.

The gang leader opened his crocodile briefcase, revealing a stack of drivers' licenses. "The Angels had a good week."

Mola's saucy maneuvers around critical questions annoyed the shit out of Cole. "There's an organized movement in those *barrios* to oust our cantinas," he said. "I want it stopped."

"A twelve-year-old girl—dead and defiled—sends a message, *mí amigo.*" Mola flipped through the stack of driver's licenses.

"Defiled—that's more than excellent." Cole swigged from a Jack Daniel's bottle and swirled the whiskey in his mouth.

"We'll reopen *Noche Azul* when the State Department calms down," Mola said.

"Keep processing the licenses, but stop the trucks for a few weeks. Let them think *Noche Azul* was a small operation." Cole glanced around to see if Muñeca was listening, but she'd snuck away, maybe in her bed waiting for him, her soft brown legs spread beneath pink lace. Cole's brief fantasy was interrupted by the clang of Mola's cell. The gang leader adjusted his earpiece, listened for a moment, then removed the headset.

"Sandoval," he said. "DSS just hit the Blue Adobe, arrested kitchen help, busboys, even the manager. And worse, they found the kids who work other shifts, the ones living out back, the one's we handcuffed to their beds." Sheer hate exuded from Mola's pores.

"And that goddamned *Chronicle* reporter took pictures."

The Blue Adobe was Cole's showcase restaurant located in the posh Woodlands area. No prostitutes. No drugs. Just excellent food. Thinking he'd misjudged the breadth of Luke Santa Maria's mission, his concern bordered on alarm. "Their focus is wider than I realized."

"I thought you had those *putas* under control."

"It seems we have both lost control, *amigo*: me of the State Department, and you of the *barrios*."

Mola lowered the lid of his valise, paused, then clicked the locks. "I have made arrangements for our friend Zadie, and you need to handle the DSS."

"Government agents can't be erased like a two-bit whore."

Mola sniffed at the evening air. Cole felt the man's black eyes drill holes into his secret thoughts, visions of payback, retribution, and reprisal for Mola's arrogance. *Calm down*, he told himself. He needed this motherfucker more than ever. In an uneasy silence, Cole watched Mola chug his beer and turn to leave. Cole stalked behind him as the gangster strolled through the ranch house as if he owned the place.

"My new baby," Mola said, opening the front door and ambling to his black Porsche Carrera GT convertible. He placed his briefcase in the trunk, patted the leather headrest, and dropped into the driver's seat. Cole grasped the door before he could close it.

"A boy named Alex Sifuentes escaped from the *Noche Azul* raid. Find him."

"Do you want us to kill him, or do you want him brought here so you can fuck his brains out?"

Cole stifled an impulse to slam Mola's face into his hundred-and-twenty-thousand-dollar dashboard.

"Kill him."

With an insolent smirk, Mola started the ignition and roared off. Gravel flew in his wake as his car disappeared.

Covering his mouth to keep from inhaling the dust, Cole remembered one of his father's favorite sayings: "There's no sweet music when you dance with the devil."

TWENTY-THREE

Alex gawked at thousands of lights high above him magically attached to a glass ceiling. In doing so, he bumped into several people as he stumbled alongside Kate through the Galleria, a huge building filled with all kinds of shops: toys, gifts, jeans, dresses, books, computers, everything imaginable. Finally, she stopped so he could lean over a rail and watch people glide, twirl, and jump on a silver surface that filled the entire center of the building. Alex had never seen anything like this, but he didn't want to ask stupid questions. In the middle of the strange surface stood the largest Christmas tree he'd ever seen.

Kate must have sensed his bewilderment. Touching his shoulder, she said, "They're skating on ice. It's a sport in the United States, like baseball." Her Spanish was great!

Nodding, Alex looked closely at their bladed shoes and realized they really were moving on top of ice. "Can I do it?" he asked, certain he could fly over the ice as fast as he could run through the *barrios*.

"Yes, but not tonight. We're on a mission."

Alex frowned. Earlier in the evening, *Señora* Grant had gone to see Obispa. She warned them not to leave the house, but after she left, Kate decided to take Alex to this enchanted place anyway. Although he worried about disobeying, he couldn't resist Kate's invitation.

Kate motioned for Alex to follow her into a record store, where she placed earphones on his head. Alex listened to some Latino tunes, and then she bought three CDs for him.

"*Gracias*, Kate." He knew he must be blushing.

"De nada. And now, we're going to Scissors," she announced.

He shot her a puzzled look. What could this "scissors" mean?

Together, they picked through the crowd until they entered a sweet-smelling shop with tall chairs, lighted mirrors, and young people hanging out listening to rap music. Some of them sat in the tall chairs, while others worked on customers' hair. Kate pulled Alex over to a skinny girl with spiked red hair. She wore five silver rings in one ear, and her painted blue eyelids matched her fingernails.

"Stella, this is my friend Alex." Kate's clear eyes sparkled. "He needs a cut—bad."

Explaining in Spanish, Kate gestured for Alex to hop in the chair, but he looked at the floor and shuffled his shoe. With suspicion he studied the elevated chair, similar to a chair in the dentist's office where Father had arranged for *Casa Maria* kids to have their teeth checked. Not a happy day for Alex, who had six cavities.

"*Hombre*, what's the matter?" Kate squeezed his hand. "Stella's a wiz. She'll be finished in no time, and think how handsome you'll look."

He looked in the mirror at his thick mop, its uneven lengths reminding him of the last time his hair had been cut—by Elena and her friend. They'd used a dull pair of school scissors and ended up nipping his ear.

"You're right, Kate." Alex climbed into the chair.

While fussing and patting him, the girls spoke to each other in English. Alex strained to understand, recognizing some words and memorizing others he didn't understand, words that sounded important.

"Should we wash first?" Stella asked Kate.

"Nah. Just wet it and chop. He took a shower earlier, and he's too scared."

"I am not scared," Alex protested.

Kate gave him a shrewd look and poked his chest. "Catching on, aren't you?"

He didn't get everything she said, but he understood "catch."

"I am catch," he repeated.

"Yes, you are one good catch," Stella said as she swathed his chest in a black drape and fastened it at the back of his neck.

"I am good catch." Alex peered at the girls for approval, and Kate nodded with a giggle. Delighted he'd made her laugh, he straightened his shoulders. "I open eyes when finish," he said with a grin.

After a tense minute of remembering the dentist, Alex relaxed into the sensation of Stella running her fingers through his hair, followed by a soft swish of scissors. The cut took less time than he'd imagined, and when Kate told him to look in the mirror, Alex wished he could have enjoyed the amazing experience a little longer.

"*Voilà!*" Stella squealed. "He's perfect."

Alex raised his lids. His eyes popped. The scraggly Guatemalan boy he'd been a few minutes before had vanished along with his hair. It was cropped short on the sides with a small fringe hanging over his forehead, like famous baseball players he'd seen in magazines. And all the ends were even. He couldn't believe it. A wave of self-consciousness swept over him. He glanced around to see if other people were staring, but no one even noticed his transformation.

A teenage boy sitting next to Alex had several pieces of silver paper wrapped on the tips of his hair. When Kate saw Alex gawking, she gently elbowed his arm.

"Don't stare," she whispered. "He's getting his tips highlighted."

"Tips." Pretending to understand, Alex focused his attention on Stella, who jutted her chin forward and winked at him.

"*Muy bonito.*" Alex fingered his hair, then he lowered his voice as he pointed to black locks scattered on the floor. "*Muy feo.*"

"You are so cute!" As Stella wet her lower lip, Alex leaned forward to get a better look at the metallic dot in the middle of her tongue.

Kate stepped in between them. "Time's up. We need to buy some clothes."

Alex ran his hand over the thinning leg of his shabby jeans. "These are okay."

"But you need more, and your shoes are taped together."

Nodding agreement, Alex couldn't believe his good luck. Twenty-four hours ago, he wanted to die from loneliness, and now he'd stepped into heaven. He jumped from the chair and grabbed Kate's hand. "Let's go."

Digging into her purse, she nodded toward Stella. "Hold on, *amigo*. I have to pay."

Feeling sheepish at his mistake, Alex sensed the blood run from his face. He slogged alongside Kate to a counter up front. While she gave Stella her credit card, he watched the mall people. A group of Latino girls with mid-thigh skirts and low-cut waistlines revealing their bellybuttons passed in front of him. One of the girls reminded him of Mariella. She had the same black curls, deep-set eyes, and friendly smile. Suddenly, all Alex could see was the expression on Mariella's face when Santiago and the rat man had left her in the desert. Could this girl be Mariella? Could she have escaped? Forgetting Kate and everything else in his newfound life, he shoved his way into the crowd lest she disappear.

"Mariella, Mariella!"

Eyes wide as saucers, the girls spied him bounding toward them and backed up against a rail overlooking the ice rink. The beautiful girl whom Alex mistook for Mariella no longer wore a smile. Glaring at him, she hunkered in the middle of the others. Alex chewed the inside of his mouth, his head spun, and his dinner stuck in his throat.

"I am sorry. I was hoping," he blurted. "But Mariella is dead."

"You think we look dead?"

The girls' shrill retorts floated down to the ice and up to the rooftop. The heftiest girl in the bunch lunged at him.

Pivoting to run, Alex smacked into Kate.

Had she seen his ridiculous behavior? He didn't want to know.

"Who's Mariella?" she asked.

TWENTY-FOUR

❝ My name is Mariella Guzman." Her throat burned, and a bitter wind chapped her lips.

"How long have you been here?" The man's accented voice sounded far away.

"I can't remember." Earlier, when Mariella had tried to reach the porch of a gray weathered house, she'd collapsed, too weak to keep walking. She must have fallen asleep in the sandy soil near the steps. Now she could make out a brown-skinned woman and man standing above her, and she thought they were Latino. Maybe they spoke Spanish.

"*Hablan español?*"

"*Sí.*" The woman nodded.

Mariella's mixed-up mind flooded with relief. "I've been walking for days, drinking water from ditches." She tried to sit up and fell on her back. Bending, they helped her to stand.

"Every time I take a breath, a knife stabs my lungs."

"You're sick. Come to our house. It isn't far," said the man, his strong arms and kind eyes a welcome refuge. "You can rest there. We've helped others like you."

They moved slowly along a road filled with shells, passing small houses set far apart from each other. Mariella's ears rang with an unfamiliar noise. She wondered if she was near a highway, or if the lack of food was making her hear things.

"What's that sound?" she asked.

"We live near the ocean," the woman explained, directing Mariella down a side path. "The Gulf of Mexico."

For several days, Javier and Soledad Morales fed Mariella hot soup, fresh juices, and homemade tortillas. During her recovery, she learned they lived in a beach community on the outskirts of Corpus Christi, Texas, near the Gulf of Mexico. When she regained her strength, they took her to the ocean and told her the sea air would heal her even though it was winter and the wind off the waves held a clammy chill. They said they'd helped many teenagers like her, and they even remembered someone called Santiago, who came into the *barrios* of Corpus Christi looking for boys and girls who'd escaped from him.

Mariella shuddered, stuffing memories of Santiago into a hidden place where wounds festered but never healed. "He's an evil man."

"We know," Javier replied.

"My mother lives in Houston," Mariella confided to Soledad one morning while they were eating a delicious breakfast of oatmeal and cinnamon toast. "She's very sick. I must find her."

"Sometimes I go to Houston to visit my *nietos*. I could take you there," Soledad said.

"I have no money to pay you," Mariella replied sadly.

"*No problema.* I'll have company for the trip, and you'll have a ride. This is good luck."

"Yes, it is!" Mariella's heart leaped. "How can I ever thank you?"

Soledad sighed and gave Mariella a look she took to be pity or shame or some other emotion she couldn't read, but in her happiness, she dismissed it.

"When will we go?"

"I'll make arrangements," Soledad said. Swallowing the last bite of her cereal, she picked up the bowl and went to the sink.

Mariella thanked her again, cleared her place, and attacked a stack of laundry she'd promised to fold. While smoothing the shirts with her hands and stacking the towels, she dreamed of her mother's radiant face, so happy, the last time she'd seen her, leaving on a bus with a new lover. Mariella had been six years old when her mother fled Panama and the brutal hand of Mariella's father. She now recalled with some resentment her mother's unfulfilled promise to bring her to America as soon as she could. But that was the past.

Now Mariella would find her, and they'd live together, everything forgiven in this marvelous country.

To make time pass quickly, Mariella spent hours on the beach collecting shells. She never expected to find anything as beautiful as the ones she discovered in the shallow waves. Now she had gifts for her mother.

When the morning of their departure arrived, Soledad gave Mariella a short black skirt, a fuzzy blue sweater and a blue jean jacket.

"Now you'll look like a regular teenager," Soledad said.

"*Muchas gracias.*" Mariella's eyes filled with tears as she put on the skirt and sweater and folded her old clothes into a paper sack. "You're so kind."

Soledad snatched her orange and yellow poncho from a hook on the wall. "Get in the truck." Opening the front door, she hurried into the damp morning breeze.

Surprised by her gruff manner, Mariella promptly trailed her.

"Where's Javier? I want to say good-bye."

"He got a day job on the road crew."

In some ways, Mariella regretted leaving this special place where the roar of the sea had made her forget her problems. She wistfully sent a silent farewell to sandy yards, weather-beaten houses, and salt-laden air. The turquoise and white truck with rusted side panels and peeling paint reminded her of a splotched metal heap covered with scabs. Mariella hopped into the passenger seat and placed the sack on her lap for warmth. Looking at the battered dashboard and metal floor, she figured there would be no heat.

Soledad cranked the stubborn engine until it let out a popping sound, grumbled for a moment, and calmed into a purr.

The drive to Houston took six hours because the ancient truck smoked up several times, and they had to stop at gas stations to fill it with water. Mariella breathed through her mouth to keep from smelling the gas fumes leaking into the cab, but she didn't complain. Soledad had saved her life and was generously taking her to find her mother.

Opening the bag, she searched her jeans pocket and removed the folded paper Alex had given her, the one she'd guarded with her life, the address of a woman called Obispa.

"Do you know where Winburn Street is?" she asked.

"Houston has millions of people and millions of streets. When we get to my daughter's, we'll call a taxi."

"But I have no money for a taxi."

"Do I have to tell you everything?"

"I don't know," Mariella answered. "Maybe."

"When the taxi takes you to the house, tell the driver to wait. Go inside and beg that Obispa woman for money."

"If no one's home, what then?" Mariella felt a swimming sensation in the base of her stomach. "Or what if Alex's friend refuses to pay?"

Soledad didn't answer. She gripped the steering wheel so tight her knuckles blanched and her eyes squinted as she stared at the windshield. Seconds passed before she replied. "If no one is home, or if the bitchy friend refuses to pay, you can run like hell, or you can offer to fuck the taxi driver."

Mariella's chest muscles tightened. She lowered her head. Why had Soledad lost patience with her?

In silence, they chugged along. To occupy her mind, Mariella read the signs: "Victoria," "Edna," "El Campo," "Wharton," "Rosenberg." When they came to a place called Sugar Land, she wanted to ask why it was called this funny name, and farther down the road, it was hard to contain her enthusiasm when she spotted colorful billboards advertising Houston businesses. But she didn't breathe another word, worried she'd made Soledad angry enough.

As they entered the city, there were so many cars Mariella feared they'd be crushed. They moved slowly in a line of traffic crossing a high bridge rising above all other bridges. Buildings glittered in the afternoon sun and surrounded the bridge on all sides. Finally the traffic thinned out, and they approached a park filled with the tallest trees Mariella had ever seen.

"How beautiful," she muttered to herself.

Soledad drove the truck toward the exit lane and continued alongside the park until they left the highway beneath a green metal sign: "Durham and Shepard."

"We need gas," Soledad said.

Mariella noted the gas gauge pointed to half-full as they veered right onto Durham, a street filled with red and yellow plastic flags strung above rows of shiny new cars.

"Soon Javier and I will have money to buy a nice car." Soledad guided the truck into a gas station and stopped at a pump. "And you're going to make it happen."

Mariella started to ask how, but then she knew. Near a metallic pump, Santiago crushed his cigarette on the ground and focused his wretched smile on the truck.

Mariella's throat thickened, her eyes brimmed with tears. "Soledad, please don't leave me with him, please." Jiggling the handle, she shoved hard, then beat the door with her fists. When it didn't open, she threw all her weight against it, again and again and again.

"Don't bother," Soledad said. "The door can only be opened from outside."

TWENTY-FIVE

Icy rain accompanied by a sudden plunge into the low thirties didn't dampen Elizabeth's zeal for the late-night field trip she and Obispa had arranged. In front of the House of Light, windows twinkling as always, she grabbed her umbrella and prepared to run. As she stepped from the Beemer, a woman screamed from inside the house. Elizabeth dove back into the front seat. Another agonizing scream before she closed the door. Heart skittering, she reached for the Glock hidden in the glove compartment, a recent purchase she'd made after an investigative reporter had been assaulted. Gun in lap, she dialed 911. The dispatcher promised a patrol car would arrive within five minutes and cautioned Elizabeth to wait. She signed off, slipped the pistol into her raincoat, and dashed for the porch. She drew the gun and tiptoed to the front door, left carelessly ajar. Its hinges creaked as she entered the candlelit parlor.

Another wail burst from the kitchen. Someone was torturing Obispa. Elizabeth tiptoed into the dining room. She could see a Hispanic man in his early twenties standing near the kitchen door clutching a speckled red-combed rooster by the feet. The scene reeked of voodoo.

Although doubt clouded her resolve to pull the trigger, Elizabeth aimed the gun and moved toward the man. "Stop whatever you're doing," she shouted.

"¡Dios!" He frantically waved the chicken. "No shoot, no shoot!"

"A baby is being born, Elizabeth," Obispa called breathlessly. "Push! I can see the head."

Elizabeth sagged as her adrenalin charge melted. She slipped the gun into her pocket and trudged into the kitchen.

Stumbling into the refrigerator, the man's eyes sparked fear.

"*Lo siento, señor*," Elizabeth said to him, raising both hands sans pistol.

He edged closer to the woman lying on the table, her knees bent, her face cherry red. The poor chicken looked as if it had given up on life, only twitching when the woman hollered.

"Harder," Obispa said. She was perched on a swivel stool between her patient's legs.

Propped on her elbows, the mother-to-be sucked a heroic breath, let out a titanic roar, and bore down with all her strength. The baby, glommed with blood and a white pasty substance, burst from between her legs.

Obispa caught the infant in her gloved hands. "It's a boy," she said to the parents. The shaman's forehead trickled with sweat droplets as she hastily drew fluid from the howling baby's nose with a syringe, swabbed his ears, and washed his pink squirming body. She then laid him on his mother's stomach and massaged her abdomen. The new mother moaned as the placenta emerged. Placing the spongy red afterbirth alongside the baby, the shaman snipped and tied the cord.

As Obispa positioned the baby at the mother's breast, strident banging on the front door startled everyone. The father looked up with concern.

"Oh, brother," Elizabeth said. "It's the cops." She ran to the door. "I made a mistake," she hurriedly explained to two uniformed deputies caped in rain slicks, guns at the ready, storming past her into the parlor. "I heard screams. Then I found out Obispa was delivering a baby. I got so excited, I forgot—"

"Where's the baby?" one of them asked.

She led them to the kitchen. The young father, his daze lifted by the unexpected presence of the law, gripped the flaccid chicken and stepped toward the back door. The officers kept their guns drawn and looked around.

"Is anyone else in the house?" a deputy asked.

"No." Obispa's voice was terse as she pulled a sheet over the mother. "Please leave."

"Not before we're sure no one's in danger, ma'am."

Elizabeth had been in such a twit for forgetting to cancel the cops, she hadn't looked closely at the officers, but now she recognized that voice, Johnny McCullough. Catching a glimpse of his badge, she remembered the idiot who'd hamstrung her at *Noche Azul* and had later forgotten to return her phone.

"I give you my word," the shaman said. "The screaming came from this woman."

Holstering his gun, Johnny apparently believed them, and Elizabeth felt a measure of relief. Then it struck her.

"What are you guys doing here? This house is inside city limits."

Johnny moved his tongue over his upper teeth, taking his own sweet time in answering her. Finally he spoke. "It's like this, Ms. Grant. After the mess at *Noche Azul*, the Sheriff's Department is sharing jurisdiction on places of interest like this area, and since me and my buddy here was close, we took the call."

"I see," said Elizabeth, resisting the urge to correct his grammar.

"Just doin' our job, ma'am."

While the other deputy stepped into the dining room and called an incident report, Johnny moseyed over to the father.

"Got your papers?"

"He doesn't speak English," Elizabeth said.

"That more'n likely means he don't have papers."

"Doesn't," Elizabeth corrected him under her breath.

"Leave him alone." Obispa's voice was shrill. "He's a new father."

"Yep, I see that. He and the missus got themselves up here to *Tejas* just so they could have a bona fide little citizen." He gestured at the father. "Your ID, *por favor, señor.*"

"This man hasn't committed a crime," Elizabeth said.

"Times are a changin', ma'am. I'm empowered to send these suckers home." Johnny thrust his hand at the father. "Your ID, *por favor.*"

"Deputy McCullough," Elizabeth said evenly. "I'm writing a series about the challenges new immigrants face in our *Land of the Free.*" She strolled over and stood next to the father. "One of those difficulties is police harassment. Would you like to be the star of my next article?"

"Is that a threat, Ms. Grant?"

"No, sir. It's a fact." Elizabeth reached into her jacket for a pocket recorder and waved it.

"Then consider this fact." Johnny McCullough's hand fell on the handle of his gun. "The fire marshal and Harris County Health Department will be interested in what's going on here."

"I have an idea," Elizabeth said. "Let's call Agent Santa Maria."

"Not a good idea."

"Better yet, Agent Fontana. He throws a fit every time—"

"You've made your point." Johnny drilled Elizabeth with a final glare and sauntered out with his sidekick. Taking a blatant survey of the living room, he turned to Obispa and Elizabeth. "There outta be a law against this shit." He flung his arms toward the masks.

"Don't say a word," Elizabeth said. The shaman squeezed her hand.

After the cops left, Obispa comforted the parents and checked the baby, who was now sleeping. Elizabeth helped clean up, then the shaman opened a drawer in the sideboard and removed a shoulder-length black veil. "Last vestige of my life as a nun."

"You're wearing it because?"

"It may help our investigation. Latino men cannot resist confessing to a holy woman."

The fabric framed Obispa's face in such a way she resembled a newborn herself, her smooth mocha skin, eyes blinking and bright. But her determined mouth pursed as she withdrew a small notepad from her pocket.

"My people say they have seen young teenagers working in these cantinas." The shaman handed Elizabeth a list scribbled in green ink. "*Hurican Azul, Caliente Azul,* and *Vocan Azul.*"

As Elizabeth reviewed the list, Obispa gave the father instructions to call her if anything unusual occurred with his wife or child, and especially if *la policía* returned. He left his wife's side and shuffled toward Elizabeth. His dark-chocolate eyes were moist, his lips quivered.

"*Gracias, señora.*"

"*De nada.*" Elizabeth's heart warmed as she shook his hand. It was the first time she'd actually looked at him, just a kid really.

After more good-byes, she and Obispa dashed to her car and torpedoed their soaking umbrellas into the backseat. Elizabeth plowed the Beemer through the driving rainstorm across deserted streets onto Interstate 59 North. Her knuckles whitened as she gripped the steering wheel.

"Johnny McCullough is a creep."

"Thank you for coming to the rescue."

"Deputy Dog is scared of me now, huh?"

"He did not want an article depicting him as a bad cop," Obispa said.

Elizabeth's grin faded. "Still, I'm worried he'll call the fire marshal."

"Or force me to stop delivering babies." The shaman gazed out the window.

"You could ask Luke to talk to Johnny," Elizabeth said, wondering if she should be the one to contact him. Bottom line, she felt miserable every time she thought of their confrontation about Alex, particularly after Luke's revelation concerning his parents. If she and Obispa located more cantinas tonight, Elizabeth would let Luke know immediately. Perhaps that would smooth things over.

The rain dwindled to a drizzle the farther north they traveled. Elizabeth exited the interstate onto Mount Houston Road, a street sullied with billboards advertising massage parlors, tent revivals, and real live, nude women.

"I have always been curious about why they say 'live' nude women," Obispa said. "Certainly no one wants dead nude women."

"Don't bet on it." Elizabeth chuckled as she sighted a dimly lit warehouse next to a bleary sign: *Hurican Azul*. With high hopes, she and Obispa entered the smoky cantina, but after finding no teenage workers there or at the other two bars, their fervor waned.

"Maybe they move the kids from cantina to cantina." Obispa's tone was sour.

"Could be." It was after one a.m. Elizabeth's head throbbed, her eyelids drooped. She cracked the window for a blast of cold wet air as they headed toward the interstate.

"Wait! Look, down there," Obispa said.

Groaning, Elizabeth hooked a U and crept down a narrow unnamed street as tight as any alley she'd ever driven. In spite of the hour, the parking lot of *Carnivál* was crammed with lowriders and pickups.

Frosty night air stung their faces as Elizabeth and Obispa trekked toward the cantina's chipped red door. When they entered, the sweetly pungent scent of marijuana met their nostrils. Blue and white Christmas lights, *piñatas*, and doilies glittered from the ceiling, and on the walls shimmering gold guitars, lace fans, and silhouettes of flamenco dancers. A carved wooden bar spanning the entire front wall sported glass shelves lined with more lights, blinking onto bottles of tequila, wine, and assorted whiskeys. On both ends of the bar, margarita machines swirled icy sips of paradise.

Next to one of the machines, Elizabeth noticed two men gawking at them. Both had shaved heads, wore leather jackets, and weren't your average clean-cut guys.

"Tweedledum and Tweedledee are staring at us," Elizabeth said.

"Tulio Mola." Obispa's voice was a gasp. "How did I not see him?" Her fingers clutched an oatmeal-colored amulet that had been tucked inside her blouse. Pressing it to her lips, she whispered, "Mola is giving me the *mal de ojo*."

"The evil eye? You're kidding."

"When we return to my *Casa de Luz*, you must help release me from his spell."

"If you say so." In dismay, Elizabeth realized the shaman was in earnest.

She struggled to reconcile her logical beliefs with the lure of the shamanic world, a place of mystery, ritual, and omens. As Elizabeth formulated a question about Tulio Mola's *mal de ojo*, a live band burst into spirited music. Six men wearing black jackets embroidered with white flowers pounded their rhythms with mallets on a huge instrument that resembled a xylophone.

Obispa clapped her hands. "They are playing the *marimba*, the instrument of my country."

The dance floor, surrounded by tables and booths, quickly filled with couples. Obispa continued to clap her hands to the music's contagious energy, and before long, Elizabeth found her exhaustion slipping away. They settled into a red plastic booth tacked with bronze nail heads. Elizabeth glanced at Tulio Mola, the skid of his eyes searching the room, lighting on the booth where they sat.

"*Señoras*, would you like a drink?"

Elizabeth shifted her gaze to a lovely teenage girl, uncommonly thin, with liquid brown eyes and a sad mouth. She wore a blue fuzzy sweater above a slick black miniskirt.

"Pray for me, Sister," she said to Obispa as she withdrew a pad from her apron.

"I will pray for you," Obispa said. "Tell me your name."

Obviously frightened, the girl angled her eyes toward the bar.

"We'll have two Sprites," Elizabeth said.

The girl left without giving them her name. On her way to the bar, some greaseball grabbed at her butt. She kept walking. The greaseball followed, but Mola's evil twin stepped into the man's path, and the sleazy guy melted into the crowd.

"Looks like Baldy-Number-Two has clout around here," Elizabeth said.

Obispa leaned forward and whispered, "Since he is with Mola, no one will cross him. I think his name is Hector Sandoval."

When the waitress returned with their drinks and a check,

Elizabeth placed a twenty-dollar bill in her hand. "Let us help you."

Shuddering, she took her tray and rushed to the next booth. Out of nowhere, the greaseball popped up in front of her. She dropped her tray, glasses shattered.

Elizabeth shot from the booth and met the jerk eye to eye. "Leave her alone."

The girl squeezed close to Elizabeth's shoulder. The greaseball backed off. Elizabeth was surprised, but then she sniffed a sweet aftershave, and she pivoted to face Mola's *compadre*, an acne-scarred man, head shiny as a pool ball, braided neck muscles visible through his black silk shirt. The *marimba* band pounded another lusty tune, couples swayed on the dance floor, and happy lights waggled above. The gangster glared at them. Elizabeth put her arm around the terrified waitress, and from the corner of her eye, she saw Obispa tramping toward them.

"Please, Sister, I will handle this," the man said.

"*Gracias, señor*, but we do not need your help."

His mouth momentarily twisted before his lips broke into a gold-capped smile. "My name is Sandoval."

Obispa nodded. "This girl . . ." She glanced at the waitress.

"Mariella Guzman," the girl said.

Obispa continued. "Mariella is leaving with us."

"No, she isn't." He pointed toward the entrance. "You must go now, Sister."

"*Señor* Sandoval, we won't leave without Mariella." Elizabeth spoke with respect, her knowledge of machismo warning her not to be aggressive.

Sandoval fiddled with a black rosary hanging around his neck. Kissing the crucifix, he rolled his eyes heavenward and said, "*Las problemas de la vida.*"

Obispa was having none it. She took Mariella's arm. "She is coming with us."

"Dear Sister, you want this sweetest flower to keep her beauty?" Sandoval caressed Mariella's neck. "She is so lovely."

Flinching, Mariella said to Obispa, "I cannot stay here. Help me."

"*Chinga tu madre.*" Sandoval's fingers dug into Mariella's waist as he forcefully shuffled her to the rear of the cantina.

Din buzzed in Elizabeth's ears as she and Obispa followed. She imagined Kate imprisoned by this obscene man, Kate—disfigured, raped, killed if she didn't behave, but when Elizabeth gripped the cool handle of the Glock tucked in her raincoat, its killing power didn't shore her up. Her instructor's cautionary voice rolled in her head: "Never pull a gun unless you're prepared to use it."

When they reached the back door, Sandoval forced Mariella outside, brandished a silver knife and held it at her neck. Crammed together on a small cement patio, no one spoke. Elizabeth surmised Sandoval was weighing his options, most of which were in his favor. Chiding herself for not pulling the gun inside where someone might have helped, she recalled the greaseball's paralysis when Sandoval had stepped in. No one inside would have helped them because Mola was there, and no one would help them now. And another frightening truth—Elizabeth wasn't sure she had the guts to shoot anyone. She felt a growing despair.

"We're locked in a standoff," Elizabeth said to Sandoval. "*Houston Chronicle* versus the Latin Angels. My newspaper will be happy to report this incident."

"If you write one word, Mariella will suffer." Sandoval squinted at them. "And now my dear ladies, give me your cell phones."

"Not on your life," Elizabeth said.

"You are correct. It will not be on my life." He pressed the silver blade against Mariella's face, pricking her cheek with the tip.

"*¡Aye, señor!*" Mariella wriggled to free herself.

Obispa threw her cell at Sandoval's feet. He kicked the phone into the yard, then raised his brows Elizabeth's way. Squeezing the Glock's handle, she withdrew the gun.

"Drop the knife and let her go."

"You can shoot me, *señora*, but not before I ram this knife through her eye."

Sandoval pricked Mariella's cheek again. She moaned. Elizabeth winced, then glimpsed at Obispa, whose blistering stare was riveted on something behind Elizabeth.

"Remember the Black Moth," the shaman said, her eyes a cauldron of contempt.

Elizabeth felt cold steel at the nape of her neck and knew Obispa wasn't speaking to Sandoval.

"*Señora* Grant, I have been waiting to meet you. *Por favor*, toss your gun."

Elizabeth's gut churned as she reluctantly obeyed. After the weapon hit the grass, she angled her head to see Tulio Mola, his vacant stare and malicious grin terrifying.

"And now your cell." While steadying his weapon at her neck, Mola reached around Elizabeth's waist. His hand casually drifted upward along her rib cage, touching her breast with his fingertips. She cringed, the force of his gun still pressing on her as she threw her phone.

Obispa said, "You will regret this, Tulio Mola."

"No, I will not." He sighed, his glance a blatant appraisal of Mariella. "A rare beauty."

Sandoval lowered the knife, then scooped up the phones and gun.

Mola ushered Mariella into the cantina, but before he slammed the door, he said, "Never come back to *Carnivál*."

TWENTY-SIX

Mariella wished Mola and Sandoval would rip her to pieces, a quick death, her troubles over in an instant. Once inside the cantina, Mola's grip on her arm tightened, and Sandoval stayed disturbingly close to her side.

"This one will bring favor, but I will test-drive her before she goes to the ranch," Mola said to his partner as he guided Mariella to a barstool. His fierce eyes violated her body before he ever touched her, and the light in Mariella's soul began to fade. This time, she wouldn't pray for deliverance as she had on the truck ride to *Tejas*, or in the desert when the *coyotes* left her, or on her trip with Santiago after Soledad's betrayal. Mariella now understood her mother's blank expression on all the occasions she'd been beaten by her father, and she knew what her mother had told her was true: "*Hell is on earth, mi hija. Every person burns for their own sins. And no matter what, God does not help.*"

After offering a glass of tequila and crushed ice, Mola twirled a silver pillbox around on the bar before sliding it into his pocket. She was sure he'd put some medicine in her drink, so Mariella eagerly bowed her head over the chalice of liquid relief, sipping the cocktail that would weaken her will and deaden her memory.

Mola ran his finger along her jaw, made kissing sounds with his lips, and caressed her thigh, but she didn't push his hand away or resist his wet mouth on her neck. Cupping her breast, he stood, spread her legs so they grazed both sides of his hips, and drew her to his chest. After placing her hand on his hardened cock, Mola glanced sideways and nodded to the bartender, a plump, brooding girl. "Give my *chica* another drink."

The man smelled like the tobacco shop in Panama City where Mariella and her friends used to panhandle, and his hard marble face made her think that *el Diablo* lived inside his head. Mola passed a fresh margarita in front of her. Gulping it, she promised herself when the opportunity came, she'd end this misery any way she could.

The cantina blurred into a blue haze. Mariella's hands tingled. Both men gripped her underarms and urged her to walk with them.

"Is your name really Mariella?" Mola asked.

Her tongue was so thick she could hardly speak. "I can't remember," she whispered, stumbling into a bedroom. Or was it the backseat of a car?

*

At an all-night gas station down the block from *Carnivál*, Elizabeth dialed 911 from a payphone. Repulsed by the receiver's musty odor, she breathed through her mouth as she talked.

"Elizabeth Grant here. I just witnessed a kidnapping at *Carnivál*."

Outside the booth, the shaman signed herself and rocked on her heels while Elizabeth elaborated.

"Yes. A man named Tulio Mola kidnapped a teenage girl, Mariella Guzman." Elizabeth gave the operator the address, hung up, and slapped a high-five on Obispa's palm. "They're in the area and they're coming."

The women sprinted to the Beemer and sped back to the cantina in time to see a sheriff's patrol car park on the street. As she drove up behind them and snapped off the ignition, Obispa groaned.

"*¡Madre de Díos!* Look who is here."

With contempt, Elizabeth watched Johnny McCullough and his partner swaggering toward her. He bent over as she rolled down the window.

"I thought I recognized your car." He grinned. "We can't go on meeting this way."

In hopes of assuaging the fallout from their nasty encounter earlier in the evening, she said, "I'm so glad it's you, Deputy McCullough. We need your help." She slid from the Beemer and took off toward *Carnivál*. "Let's go."

"Not so fast. What happened?" He nodded at his partner, who handed him a clipboard.

Elizabeth reiterated the story about Mola and Sandoval.

"Are you sure it was Mola? This kind of crap isn't his style."

"Of course I'm sure. And he has Mariella. We know because she works for us."

"What kind of work does she do?"

"Translates documents," Elizabeth said.

"Housework," Obispa offered simultaneously.

"Mariella does housecleaning and translating," Elizabeth added in haste. "Plus, some nights she works here as a waitress."

Johnny took his own sweet time scribbling his notes.

"Can you do this later? She may still be in the cantina."

The deputy shifted his weight and threw back his head. "Last name again?"

"Guzman," Obispa said in an overly loud voice.

"Are you related?"

Obispa dabbed her eyes. "Please, help us find her."

Johnny nodded to his sidekick. "Oh, what the fuck." He gave Elizabeth a hard look. "I'm not such a bad guy, you'll see."

Elizabeth compelled herself to smile sweetly, then led the way as the four hurried into the cantina. The *marimba* band was packing up, and patrons were settling their tabs. Elizabeth scanned the room for Mariella, Mola, and Sandoval. The trio had vanished.

The deputies began questioning a bartender and several customers about the girl, while Elizabeth and Obispa checked the cantina, then dashed to the rear and searched the parking lot.

"We are batting zero, as you Americans say." Obispa shook her head.

"Yes, we are." Elizabeth's scant hope sank into a dark place, and she couldn't get Mariella's headline out of her mind: "*Innocent Girl Dies in the Hands of Lewd and Treacherous Men.*"

"I can tell you right now, those *hombres* at the bar are not going to share information if they want to live," Obispa said as they returned to the cantina. "The only way to get Mola is through the Tunnel with a curse as foul as he is." She removed the veil and smoothed her hair. "I will prepare an evil scourge."

TWENTY-SEVEN

The animal shelter reeked with odors of eau de canine, something like Luke's house might smell after this, but he decided to go for it anyway, no matter how much trouble it was. A pooch would be the next best thing to a family. Luke realized his divorce and the looming prospect of a childless life had everything to do with the decision he was about to make. Of course, a dog wouldn't ask for help with homework, but canine-as-kid-substitute could work, providing a warm body to meet him every night with a wag and a bark, no chatter, no flack. It'd be fun. Luke smiled to himself.

While he waited for the animal care worker to show him the kennels, yelps and howls met his ears. Luke sipped a latte, his third of the morning, and replayed his vexing situation with Elizabeth Grant. His irritation ballooned. Why the hell had he told her about his parents? His mind skittered through all possible reasons, and loneliness shot to the top of the charts. Great. He'd confided in a woman who had no heart, but Luke knew this wasn't exactly true. Elizabeth was going all out for Alex Sifuentes. He shook off his muddled thoughts when the shelter worker, a young man named Sam, strolled in.

He led Luke down aisles lined with chain-link pens occupied by shepherds, retrievers, and chows. The dogs stretched their bodies upward against the cages, their paws flopping through holes in the links. Luke stroked the head of a pregnant yellow lab but shook his head at Sam.

"No mommy dogs."

"If you want a small dog," Sam said, "we don't have any right now. They go fast."

"What's the biggest one you've got?"

The boy's lips barely parted, and his eyes danced with amusement. "That would be Andre."

"Is he French?"

"No, he's Andre the Giant."

"Let's give the boy a look."

"He's down at the end in our largest pen."

Andre, a brindle-haired Great Dane–German shepherd mix with a sleek body, snoozed in the corner. When he heard Luke and Sam, he sprang to his feet.

"Good reflexes," Luke said.

"A great watchdog, but he's gentle as a lamb." Sam unlatched the pen. "Go in and give him a pat."

Luke studied the dog's canines and wondered how truly gentle he was. He'd no sooner slipped into the pen than Andre's paws sprawled on his shoulders and his sandpaper tongue lapped Luke's cheek.

"How much does he weigh?"

"I'd guess around a hundred and thirty."

Andre's breath smelled like he'd swallowed a tank of catfish.

"I'll let you get acquainted," Sam said. "Come to the office when you decide."

Luke nodded, then removed Andre's paws from his shoulders. "Sit." He used a commanding voice.

Andre plopped on his haunches as Luke heard the door to the shelter swing open. He peered from the stall and waved at Dominic, who was marching toward him in double time. All spruced up, he wore an ironed white shirt, blue sport coat, and jeans with no holes. His hair was slicked into a tidy ponytail and his second-day facial stubble had vanished.

"What the hell?" Dominic crunched a mint, licking white flecks from his lips. "It took me thirty minutes to get here—a goddamned puppy farm in bum-fuck-Egypt."

"I think outside the box."

Dominic squinted at Andre, his wagging tail, hanging tongue, and drooling saliva. He whistled under his breath and surveyed his partner.

"You need a good lay."

"That's me—looking for love in all the wrong places." Luke knuckle-rubbed Andre's head, left the stall, and locked it behind him in spite of the dog's whimper.

Dominic snooped around, strolling among the pens and pausing to look at a doe-eyed basset. The hound resembled a seventy-pound overstuffed hot dog baying in low C. Its ears dragged the ground, and its weight prevented it from hoisting itself against the chain link. Nonetheless, the clever critter coaxed Dominic to bend down and scratch its ears.

Presently, Sam returned to the kennel, and Luke gestured toward Dominic, who by now was talking to the dog while the basset belted out a mournful story.

"Meet Horace," said Sam, sauntering up behind the romantic pair.

Dominic jerked at the sound of Sam's voice and stood up. "I've never seen this kind of dog in person."

"Not many bassets in Houston. They're mostly East Coast, but we don't hold it agin' 'em. They're real friendly." Sam handed an application packet to Luke. "If you want Andre, here're the papers."

Luke nodded and flipped through a mound of forms. "This is like adopting a child."

"Takes about thirty minutes, but think what you get on the other end."

The other end was what Luke worried about. "You're sure Andre's house-trained?"

"Positive."

Dominic whistled, giving Luke the nod, a clear sign something was brewing.

"My partner and I need to talk," Luke said, showing Sam his badge.

Orbs wide as a bug-eyed Chihuahua, Sam pointed to a conference room. "Be my guest, Officers."

"Say, Sam," Dominic said. "I think I'll take Horace."

Luke burst into laughter.

"Don't crack yourself up," Dominic said.

Sam flew to his office and hurriedly returned with an adoption packet as if he were afraid Dominic would change his mind. Dominic thanked him and ambled into the conference room. Closing the door behind them, he flipped Luke a copy of an e-mail he'd received from Randall Cole.

"Cole located a Blue Agave tile company in Juárez. I'm going to check it out."

"My friend at Homeland says seven out of ten businesses are

closed down there, so if they're doing business in that hellhole, they must be paying protection. Either that or they're a front for the Juárez cartel."

"I called the tile store, and a live person answered. I didn't ask him if he worked for a cartel." Dominic grinned. "Anyway, I'm flying out at noon and I'll be there by four, just in time to stick it to the boss-man before he leaves for the day."

"Did you let our guys at the consulate know?"

"Don't do my thinking for me, bud." Dominic's lips narrowed into an edgy smile.

"Sorry, man. It's my Type-A rearing its nasty head." Luke stood and held out his hand.

Dominic reached across the table and slapped Luke's palm. As the tension eased, Luke slipped into his chair and scanned the shelter's application.

"Jeezus. Social Security number, driver's license, next of kin."

"Checking our history for dog abuse." Undaunted by the paperwork, Dominic began to scribble information, then grinned at Luke. "So, will you keep my new pooch until I get back?"

"Con artist."

"You're the one who dragged me out here."

"I did, and I'll keep that hound of yours." Luke sucked a quick breath and watched his partner bow over the application in serious concentration. "About Juárez."

"Yeah?"

"If ICE reports serious fighting today, don't cross."

Dominic's eyes flashed.

"That's an order, Dom. I'm not kidding." Before his partner could respond, Luke's cell blared the *Battle Hymn*. Still holding Dominic's glare, he answered, "Hey, Johnny, what's up?"

Dominic slapped his forehead. "Let me guess. He shot himself in the balls."

Breathless, Johnny spewed a report to Luke. "Another girl's been murdered. Off Mount Houston. We're at the scene, a bar called *Carnivál*. I was here last night, in fact—"

"Slow down." Luke felt a blister in his gut. He hesitated to let Dominic in on the girl's death but decided he should know now, or there'd be a worse explosion later. He switched to speakerphone. "You need to hear this, Dom."

Johnny's voice trembled. "An hour ago, some garbage guys emptied a dumpster, and they saw a body falling through the air into their truck. She looks around fourteen." He paused. "Only fuckin' fourteen, man."

"Goddamn son of a bitch." Dominic slammed the table.

"I didn't know you were there, Dominic," Johnny said.

"Why *Carnivál*? We didn't raid the fuckin' place."

"Be there in twenty minutes," Luke said.

"Johnny!" Dominic's neck bladed with anger. "She was Latino, wasn't she?"

"Good chance. Dark hair, light-brown skin. Real pretty. She's cut up bad, and from the looks of it, she was raped. Man, I can't take another one of these."

"You can't take it?" Dominic was yelling now and pacing. "You can't take it? Think how it must've been for her."

"Johnny, no one disturbs a thing until forensics gets there," Luke said.

"Yeah, yeah. I know the drill, but I'm afraid the garbage guys pulled her from the trash."

"Don't let another person touch her."

"Yes, sir."

Luke clicked off. He stacked the adoption papers and stood. The room was alive with Dominic's furor, his face white, his eyes far away, focused on the long-ago event that framed his police work. "Fuck Juárez. I'm coming with you."

"No," Luke said. "I need you to get to the bottom of this."

"Yeah, let me do the scud work."

"It was your lead," said Luke, containing his exasperation. "And it's just as important as this murder investigation."

"I don't agree."

Luke shook his head. "We aren't going to find the killer before you get back. We'll be lucky—"

"Have it your way." Dominic waved his hands in the air, then hustled to the door. "You always do."

The door slammed. Luke slumped at the table. He listened as dogs whined, barked, and howled into the empty morning that had begun with a glimmer of humor and promise, now hollow and mean. And for the second time in a week, he shared Dominic's rage.

TWENTY-EIGHT

Elizabeth had been impressed with Randall Cole's reputation as one of the state's primo immigration lawyers, but in person, he was a flaming asshole. As they discussed Alex's situation, Cole jotted notes, leaned back in a creamy calfskin chair and swiveled. Seated in another dream chair upholstered with the same leather, Elizabeth waited for his comments. Impatient for the guru to make a proclamation, her attention shifted to Cole's tiger-oak desk, an edifice as bodacious as the state of Texas itself.

"I find it amazing the boy escaped from *Noche Azul*," Cole's baritone voice boomed. "DSS doesn't usually lose detainees during a raid."

"I was there, and it was chaos, lots of opportunities," Elizabeth said. "The reason I need your help is that Agent Santa Maria, whom I believe you know, wants to interrogate Alex now." Elizabeth decided to leave out the idea of Alex becoming a CI. If by some strange circumstances, it ever came to pass, she didn't want to put the word in the street.

"Ah, Luke Santa Maria. I never call him 'agent,' you know."

"No, I didn't know."

Cole smirked and leaned forward. "Luke's aware the boy's living with you?"

"Yes, and I've asked him to wait to question Alex, but I'm not sure he will. And equally important, I want to start the ball rolling on a student visa."

"Why don't you want the boy questioned?"

"Because Alex needs help. He recently lost his brother and his best friend."

"Or so he says. Kids like him, I call them 'street rats.' They've all lost somebody. Suffering's their lot in life."

Elizabeth gawped at his eminence, Randall Cole, a powerful white man who'd probably never experienced an ounce of pain in his privileged life. "Alex is not a street rat, Mr. Cold, I mean Cole."

Scoffing, Cole fiddled with the top of his Montblanc pen, idly screwing it on and off. "Since Luke knows the boy's with you, this could get complicated."

"That's why I chose you, because of your experience, and particularly because of all the problems illegals are facing now." Elizabeth folded her arms and tried to dismiss his smug air.

"Bring him in at ten tomorrow. We'll talk."

"Can you take the case in spite of your friendship with Luke?" Although she asked the question, her intention to engage Cole had waned.

Opening the lid of an inlaid wood humidor, he removed a cigar, ran it under his nose, and admired its leaf. Elizabeth winced.

"Don't worry, I'm not going to light it."

"Thank God."

As his tongue drifted over the cigar's smooth mocha surface, Elizabeth thought he might kiss the damn thing. Uncomfortable with his antics, she recalled an urban myth she'd once heard—the final leaf of a fine Cuban cigar was applied by a virgin who rolled it against her inner thigh.

Cole laid the cigar on his desk and changed courses, apparently oblivious to her disgust. "I've read your recent articles, Ms. Grant. On several occasions, it seems, you've had prior knowledge of these raids."

"I have my sources, but what does this have to do with Alex?"

"Nothing actually, but in my practice, sources are critical. Would you be willing to share yours?"

Elizabeth felt her cheeks burn. "My source is anonymous, but if I did know who it is, I wouldn't tell you."

"I'll reward your source, and I'll waive my fee to represent the boy."

"His name is not 'the boy.' It's Alex."

Cole snickered. "You're not saying this kid is your source—"

"I'm saying to call him by his name. Even street rats deserve respect."

"I wasn't expecting you to be such a bleeding-heart, Ms. Grant."

Elizabeth couldn't abide the unctuous creep one more second. She admitted to herself that she'd made a huge mistake and would have to find another lawyer . . . fast.

"You and I aren't a fit, Mr. Cole." She stood, left his office and scurried down a hallway.

"Wait a minute," he called. "I have to let you out."

Cringing at the sound of Cole's footsteps behind her, Elizabeth paused at a locked door to the reception area. He pawed a release button, and she quickly entered the waiting room. Ripe with frustration, she'd hoped Cole would arrange asylum or at least a visa for Alex, and now, every instinct warned her to get away from him. She blinked tears, blaming her rare emotionality on the fact she and Obispa had lost Mariella at *Carnivál* and had stayed up all night looking for her. But crying now certainly wasn't an option, because the primo jerk-off had followed her into the waiting room.

"I apologize if I offended you, Ms. Grant. I do want to help Alex."

Elizabeth didn't answer. Her knees weakened. She was immobilized by the profile of a swarthy man talking to the receptionist in a low voice. The odor of cigarette smoke mixed with the same sweet aftershave she'd smelled last night hit her nose. Noticing their presence, the man stopped whispering and turned. For a moment, Hector Sandoval held Elizabeth under a spell of utter shock. Had he tailed her?

"So, we meet again," Sandoval said, running his piggish eyes up and down her body.

"Where's Mariella?"

"Ah, *señora*, the last time I saw her she was at the cantina."

"I went back last night. She wasn't there."

"I have no control over where the girl goes."

Cole moved closer to Elizabeth. "What's this about?" he asked.

"It's a domestic dispute." Sandoval burst into a wicked laugh. "A family squabble."

"You sicko bastard." Elizabeth wanted to slap him down and stomp him like a snake.

"Apparently, I have the wrong office." Sandoval gave Cole an odd look, then headed for the door.

Something strange here, but no time to analyze. Elizabeth glanced at the lawyer, whose laser-sharp glower was transfixed on the back of Sandoval's muscle shirt. "Call the sheriff," she said. "This man is wanted for kidnapping." She started for the door, her goal to find Mariella clouding all prudence.

"I'll call the sheriff, but you can't leave. God knows, he could be dangerous." Cole stretched for her arm.

"Go smoke your cigar."

Elizabeth sidestepped him, dashed into an empty hallway, punched the elevator button, and put an ear to its door. After a few seconds, she still didn't hear mechanical movement in the shaft, so she removed her boots and raced down the stairs. After sixteen floors, her knees ached, her back protested wildly, and her efforts were in vain. Sandoval had vanished. She hurried from the lobby into the street. Looking both ways, she noticed two strangers leaning against her car, parked a half block down.

The sidewalk, crowded with downtown lunch traffic, offered her a modicum of protection. With her boots draped over her arm, Elizabeth marched toward the tattooed, earringed men. One was just under six feet, his body a steroid-induced mass, and like Sandoval, his grinning mouth was chocked with gold. The other guy brought to mind a fur-laden caterpillar, hair in wooly disarray, body squat and flabby, not a candidate for a muscle shirt.

When she spied her four slashed tires, she halted.

"Lay off the Angels, lady." The tall man twirled a toothpick with his tongue, then let it loll in the side of his mouth.

The gangsters shoved past Elizabeth and sauntered down the street. Determined to make them pay for the damage and thinking they might be with Sandoval, she followed them to a seventies-era gold Cadillac. She dropped her boots on the sidewalk and opened a notepad, but they didn't seem to care if she recorded their license. Shaking from anger more than fear, she scribbled three letters and three numbers. When she finished, Elizabeth fixed on the Day-Glo yellow scrotum loaded with gigantic testicles dangling from the rear bumper.

Mr. Muscle massaged his crouch. "If you think those are big *cojones*, lady, you should see mine."

With a mixture of revulsion and fear, she punched Luke's cell number. The hell with their argument about Alex. She needed his help, and he'd have to respond.

"Don't bother with the cops. We're legally parked," said the caterpillar.

"I'm calling the State Department."

"Now we're scared."

Elizabeth seethed as she listened to Luke's phone ring. She'd see these guys in hell.

"Santa Maria." His voice was hushed, and she could hear men talking in the background.

"Is this a bad time?"

"Couldn't be worse. What do you need?"

"My tires have just been slashed by two goons. I can't prove they did it, of course, but they're leaning on their most-likely-stolen Cadillac watching me."

"Jeezus, Elizabeth! Where are you?"

"Downtown, near Main and Congress."

"Get away from them." Luke hesitated. "Go to Javi Padilla at City Hall."

She cupped her hand over the phone and whispered. "The mayor's gang guy?"

"Yeah. Tell his watchdog secretary I sent you. Give him a full description of those bastards."

"What if they follow me?" she said as she headed for City Hall.

"Just keep walking. I'd come for you, but there's been another murder, a teenage girl near a cantina called *Carnivál*."

"My God." Elizabeth's first thought was Mariella Guzman. Her words tumbled out, telling Luke about the girl and the *Carnivál* ordeal with Mola. "Obispa and I shouldn't have left her. Mola probably killed her."

"Listen, Elizabeth Grant, you and that shaman stay away from him. He could've killed you too." He made no effort to disguise his anger. "Why the hell didn't you call me?"

"I should have." She swallowed hard, a red pain blazing in her head. "And even if the kid isn't Mariella, another girl has been murdered. Probably because of me."

"Don't blame yourself for Tulio Mola's shit." Luke exhaled a long breath into the receiver. "I know this is bad timing, but I've got to talk to the Sifuentes kid."

Elizabeth resolved not to tell Luke about her meeting with Randall Cole. He'd find out soon enough. "Not until we see a lawyer."

"Look," Luke continued, "if Alex goes undercover in the Angels, he won't need a lawyer. State will take care of everything. We need him, Elizabeth."

She glanced at the gangsters snug in their Caddy. Someone had to stop them, but she couldn't imagine what these ruthless psychos would do if Alex joined them and they discovered he was a mole. Still, he was a streetwise kid, a former Angel, and perfect for the job. Elizabeth twisted a lock of hair around her finger. "It has to be Alex's decision," she said.

"I'll see him this evening."

"Don't get your hopes up."

"Alex is my hope," Luke said.

TWENTY-NINE

Dominic Fontana kept the car windows closed, a barrier against the fetid fumes and deafening din. He ground his teeth, a habit triggered by insufferable situations. At the moment, he was loathing the marriage of US greed, its appetite for drugs, and Mexican desperation. He maneuvered a PT Cruiser, his tacky rental *du jour*, into an El Paso checkpoint established for government officials, a line much shorter than the other queues, where cars stacked up for blocks.

His badge prompted a grave nod from a Border Patrol officer. "Watch your back," he said. "Twenty-two murders this morning, and those are the ones we know about."

Dominic nodded. Luke's order skimmed through his mind as he drove the Cruiser onto Mexican soil. He'd been to Juárez one other time, the brutal summer of 2004, to accompany the body of his murdered niece, Juana, back to her hometown in Oaxaca. She was the light of Dominic's life, a lovely girl and excellent student. She'd abandoned her studies to follow a fucked-up boyfriend who'd promised her paradise in Juárez.

At the time of Juana's death, she lived in a shanty near the *maquiladoras*, factory after factory of international sweatshops, many deserted now in the wake of the silent slaughter. In this sewer of humanity, his niece was numbered among the hundreds of girls who'd been raped, mutilated, and murdered, an unhealed wound in Dominic's heart and unending fuel for his wrath. Her murder had never been solved in spite of his efforts, and he doubted it ever would.

Checking directions to Blue Agave, he steered his car toward *Avenida Lincoln,* a strip of craft stores and tile factories. He noted the graffiti-strewn facades and signs advertising leather coatings, solvents, Styrofoam, and water purifiers. Water purifiers? Now that was fucked up. The bastards made water purifiers using laborers who had no running water in their hovels.

He worked himself into a lather, like he'd done at the animal shelter, but when he spotted the Blue Agave, his social justice rant with himself dissolved. The factory occupied an entire block and was bordered by a six-foot cinderblock wall topped with barbed wire. A gaudy blue and purple mosaic sign towered above the place. Dominic veered into a gravel drive and peered through a thick iron gate. The yard beyond overflowed with cast sculptures and colorful hand-painted tile stacked near white vans similar to the one that had transported the kids to *Noche Azul.*

He slid from the car, removed a digital camera from his briefcase, and zoomed in on the trucks' license plates. Before clicking a single shot, he spotted the nose of an AK-47 and the guard who aimed it at him.

"*Señor,*" the man said. "No photographs. This is original artwork."

"Original?" Dominic clucked to himself as he pocketed the camera and flashed his badge. "*El jefe. Pronto.*"

The stump of a man probably of Mayan descent, scrutinized Dominic's badge and lowered his assault rifle. His stiffened torso exuded suspicion, but he opened the gate and wheeled in the direction of an adobe building centered in the complex. "*Vamanos a la oficina.*"

Dominic followed him through a turquoise painted door, and the guard disappeared down a hallway. Heavy air ripe with linseed oil and chalk tweaked Dominic's nose. He studied a showroom chocked with shelves of mosaic wall decos, statues of the Virgin, and a gaggle of saintly figurines whose names he didn't know.

A towering man ambled into the room from the hall. Crudely handsome, he had a razor-thin mustache, dark cropped hair, and gnarled knuckles on his monstrously large hands. He wore a lime-green shirt and stylish stonewashed jeans. "Diego Velasquez, *señor.* How can I help you?"

"US State Department," Dominic replied, badge in hand.

Velasquez's brow folded into a crease, and Dominic intended to stoke this bastard's concern into a bonfire. When operating alone, he used techniques unauthorized by his rule-bound superiors, including Luke, with whom he hadn't shared his plan. He'd done his homework on Velasquez and intended to get everything he needed in one visit. Dominic wasn't coming back to Juárez.

"You transport illegal kids along with your tile, Velasquez, and I aim to hang you for it."

"I beg your pardon?"

"Pardon my ass."

"My trucks are filled with tile and sculptures. There's no room for people."

"That's because you stuff 'em in like animals."

Diego Velasquez snorted as he sidestepped toward a conference table in the middle of the showroom. A glitzy Spanish-style chandelier gleamed above him. He lit a *cigarillo*, drew the stogie to his lips, and inhaled.

Ambling over to get in his face, Dominic leaned over the table's polished edge. "Let's talk about your family in Villa Real, the nicest part of this goddamn pit." Dominic paused, waiting for the comment about Velasquez's family to sink in. "There's something you need to know about me. When I come to Mexico, I act like a Mexican cop." He waved his hands as if he were a certified nutso. "There're no rules down here, man! I love it, so either cooperate, *Señor* V, or you won't be seeing your wife and daughters *por mucho tiempo*."

Velasquez opened his mouth but emitted no sound.

"And your workers will be interrogated." Dominic gestured toward a barred window. Outside men and teenage boys pushed dollies overloaded with terra-cotta pots into corrugated metal buildings. "My guys are going to tear your plant apart looking for evidence. I told them not to worry if they smashed everything."

"There is nothing to hide, *señor*." His shaggy eyebrows knitted together, eyes askance, Velasquez took drags and blew smoke as he spewed one bullshit explanation after another.

Dominic quickly tired of the bastard's drivel. He dropped his business card on the table. "Talk to me now, and we'll work a deal."

The man snarled.

"If that's the way you want it, man." On his way to the door, Dominic assumed a cool veneer. "We're watching your house. Pretty little girls you've got, real pretty."

The manager groaned. Dominic loitered at the door and glimpsed a third-rate train stir up swirls of dust as it wobbled to a halt near a loading area. Hordes of peons swarmed from the factory like ants after honey. Some hoisted crates from the train while others checked the contents and funneled them inside.

"I have told you everything I know, *señor*." Velasquez stubbed his cigar into a mosaic ashtray.

"Your poor girls. Their papa in jail. No one to protect them in this nasty town."

"You fucking pig."

Dominic withdrew the SIG, pointed at a shelf behind Velasquez, and blasted St. Francis into oblivion. Cement exploding around him, Velasquez shielded his eyes as Dominic blew a lower shelf of figurines, then fired at a row of Virgins of Guadalupe. Pulverized rock and a montage of glass peppered the air.

"You will regret this," Velasquez said.

Striding back to the stunned manager, Dominic ground the gun barrel into his temple, and the man's breath quickened, revealing a heavy smoker's wheeze.

Finally, Velasquez spoke in an unsteady voice. "You should talk to the owner of the Blue Agave, Rufino Banderas. He lives in El Paso." He scrawled an address on Dominic's card, still visible beneath the rubble.

"Does Banderas arrange the transport of illegals?"

"He sends our products to Texas. That's all I know."

"Interesting word—products." Dominic moved again toward the door, his gun dangling from his index finger. "Warn Banderas, and I'll be back to take you out."

On impulse, he sighted the heavy iron chain holding the chandelier and pulled the trigger. Metal and glass crashed onto the table in front of Velasquez, thrown off guard, tripping backward over a chair, scrambling toward the hall.

THIRTY

Frazzled and exhausted, Elizabeth Grant tramped into Javi Padilla's office to report the Angels who'd slit her tires. The guard-dog secretary about whom Luke had warned her was missing in action, probably at lunch. Padilla lounged at his desk, devouring a pile of tamales and drinking atole, a thick, warm Mexican beverage. He wore a sleek Italian suit, monogrammed shirt and gold cufflinks.

She'd heard from her City Hall contacts that Javi was the most sought-after bachelor on the mayor's staff, but now she knew it wasn't because of his looks. Although he had thick black hair, bedroom eyes, and a friendly smile, the bony ridge of Javi's nose made a zigzagged path above his nostrils, and a purple scar slashed his left cheek. The disfiguring injuries didn't fit with the gossip about his dashing success with the ladies.

Elizabeth tapped on the doorjamb.

Swallowing a bite of tamale, he motioned for her to come in.

"Elizabeth Grant, *Houston Chronicle*." She offered her hand.

"I know who you are," he said. "Lunch?"

"I couldn't." Elizabeth's stomach howled for food, but the spicy aroma made her queasy after her roller coaster night with Obispa and the maddening morning with Randall Cole.

"Sure you could. The atole is delicious today, chocolate and cinnamon." Javi swiveled in his chair to open a drawer in an oak credenza behind him. "I'm always prepared for guests."

He slapped a paper plate in front of her, poured half the atole into a Styrofoam cup, and forked over two tamales. "Best in town. I buy them from Lucinda, the vendor in front of City Hall. You've seen her."

"Yes." Elizabeth always wondered if street food passed health inspections. Now she was about to find out. Slumping into a chair opposite his desk, she peeled off the soft husk and picked at the grease-soaked pork stuffed in cornmeal. Between nibbles, which at another time she might have enjoyed, Elizabeth gave Javi her account of Mariella's disappearance and the horrific night she and Obispa had spent at *Carnivál*. She concluded with the slashed tires.

"I can only imagine what Mola did to that girl," she said quietly.

"Since there's no evidence of a crime yet, I doubt the sheriff will haul Mola and Sandoval in for questioning, and *Carnivál* is out of my jurisdiction."

"No one will search for her?"

Javi pressed his lips. "I'll put out a bulletin on her immediately."

"Thank you. Her name is Mariella Guzman."

"Every day we round up homeboys hanging in the downtown area. Fifteen minutes, there'll be a lineup of our latest actors. Maybe they'll know something about the girl. More likely, they'll have info on the goons who did your tires, but you can bet they won't tell us."

"Well, if anyone does identify those men, I'll be only too happy to press charges."

"That's good. Most people won't." Javi slipped a disc into his computer. "Take a look at our superstars." He clicked on a series of black and white photos. Gang members, hands and arms tattooed with flames, snakes, and naked women, grinned as if they were posing for a family portrait. "Tulio Mola and Hector Sandoval," he said, pointing at two familiar faces. "They run prostitution, drugs, extortion, human trafficking, you name it."

"Yes, I've seen them in action," Elizabeth said.

"And get this. My aide discovered a site for a studio that records gang-specific music."

A gravel-mouthed, demonic chant emanated from Padilla's computer, and Elizabeth shuddered at the hypnotic sounds of a repulsive dirge swirling in the room.

Noting the web address, she said, "Turn it off."

"Scary stuff, huh?"

"Indeed it is." She paused. "Can you tell me why Mola hasn't been arrested?"

"Off the record? No story, no tweets, no blogs."

She hesitated. "For how long?"

"For as long as it takes to get evidence that'll put him away for life."

"I give you my word." Elizabeth hoped she could keep it.

"Our locals are cooperating with the State Department. Mola's suspected of masterminding the execution of three federal agents."

Thinking of Luke, Elizabeth's concern grew from an uneasy feeling about his safety into an edgy fear. She thought of asking Javi about the DSS cantina-busting operation, but she didn't want to give any hint of her arrangement with Luke to share information.

Javi continued. " While we're waiting for the lineup, I'll give you some gang trivia, and stop me if you already know this stuff. In our area there are at least two hundred and twenty-five gangs with around ten thousand members."

"Unfortunately, I did know that."

"In Latino countries, gangs are called *Maras*, short for *Marabuntas*, killer ants who attack in groups. They have tattooed codes. The Angels' code is 121 at the base of their right, middle three fingers, and their password, *sureno*, means 'south of the border.'" Javi swigged the atole. "They control northeast Harris County, and most of their cantinas are located outside city jurisdiction except for a couple. *Noche Azul* comes to mind."

Elizabeth's shoulders tensed. *Noche Azul* would forever be a nightmare. " Her eyes skidded over the paltry notes she'd written. "A little girl, Concepción—"

"I know about Concepción." Javi raised his eyes to the ceiling. His voice clotted into low-toned words. "When I was twelve, I learned about gangs the hard way. My parents moved to the Gulfton ghetto because I was a good student, and they wanted me to attend Bellaire High. The Southwest *Hermanos* controlled the area. Still do. When I refused to join them, they left me for dead." He rubbed the buttons on the front of his white cotton shirt. "Besides the job they did on my face, my chest is covered with knife scars."

Elizabeth's hand flew to her mouth. She mumbled a lame "I'm sorry," but Javi's revelation made sense. He wore his facial disfigurement as a badge of survival and courage.

Apparently unperturbed by her reaction, Javi gestured toward the walls covered with honorary plaques, photographs, and citations. "When I was asked to create the HPD Anti-Gang Program for the mayor, I jumped at it. My goal is to keep my experience from happening to other kids." He twisted his lips, then bent over his computer and clicked the mouse again. "Get a load. Rival gangs send messages on the net or text each other. This was posted yesterday."

The poorly worded, misspelled message read: "Fuk all you litle bitch ass lollypops puro southwest hermanos de la Gulfton. im gona put a bullet in yo head bitch ass. 8bal."

"Someone's going down," Javi remarked. "And Eight Ball's gonna make it happen."

Elizabeth scribbled the web address. "Can you stop it?"

"I doubt it." He glanced at his watch and stood. "Let's take a gander at the homeboys."

"One quick question." Elizabeth chose her words judiciously. "Since the DSS hasn't been able to nail Mola, illegal kids who he brings into Houston are still being exploited, right?"

Javi's nostrils flared. "We're moving forward, but most human trafficking cases don't bring stiff sentences. I'm sure you've heard about those Dallas men who were prostituting Honduran girls aged nine to thirteen. They only got five years."

She scowled.

"The grim news is this: if the DSS doesn't get Mola for murder, he'll be out in a few years, or get off completely if he has the right lawyer."

"What a crock."

"Yep. We want him for life." Javi moved toward the door and motioned for Elizabeth to follow. "Mola was a street kid who fought against the Guatemalan death squads. Now he copies them."

"Death squads as in *La Sombra*?"

Javi raised his brow. "Not many people know *La Sombra*."

"Let's see if your dragnet caught my fish," Elizabeth said, not wanting to discuss Alex or how she knew about the death squad.

Then, suddenly gripped by the thought of gang-style revenge like Javi had suffered, she measured the consequences of filing charges against the Angels, and in her mind's eye, Kate's face appeared.

THIRTY-ONE

Elizabeth's adrenalin-induced energy had drained into relief when the Angels who'd slashed her tires weren't in Javi's lineup. Exhausted and longing for sleep, she retrieved her car from the tire repair shop and drove to *Casa de Luz*, faithful to her promise to help Obispa remove Mola's curse—*el mal de ojo*.

The shaman was in rare form, wide awake and lively. Placing a straw pallet on the living room floor, Obispa stepped to a side table brimming with her accoutrements: a caramel-colored hen's egg, a carved wooden crucifix, a prayer card, and an empty jelly jar.

Elizabeth sighed. "How about some hot cocoa?"

"No eating or drinking before the ceremony. Remember?"

"I forgot." Elizabeth decided not to tell her about the tamales and atole sitting heavy in her stomach, and especially not about the murdered girl at *Carnivál*. Obispa would feel the same burden of responsibility that Elizabeth did. No use in distracting her until after the so-called ceremony.

"What is the matter?" the shaman asked.

"Things haven't been going well. The lawyer for Alex didn't work out, and a couple thugs slashed my tires."

"Ah! Mola has cursed you too. You must be cleansed."

"It wasn't a curse," Elizabeth mumbled, but then she eyed the pallet and thought she might catch some shut-eye during the ceremony. "How about me first?"

"No, I must go first," said Obispa, her approach thoughtful, almost contemplative, as she quietly lay on her back on the reed-woven mat.

"Okay, let's get on with it."

Obispa raised herself on one elbow. "First," she said. "You must assume a peaceful attitude."

Fat chance. Elizabeth nodded as the shaman issued instructions.

"Place the crucifix on my chest. Take the prayer card and candle from the small table."

"Why am I not surprised about the candle?"

The shaman drummed her fingers with tight-lipped disapproval.

"I promise to be good."

"The Apostles' Creed is written on the card," Obispa explained. "Say the prayer while walking around me three times, making a Sign of the Cross with the candle over my head, my stomach, and my feet each time."

"That I can do, but what about the egg? It's making me nervous."

"Be patient, *hermanita*. After you have done as I told you, crack the egg into the jar, then hold the jar over my forehead while you recite the Creed again."

"Raw eggs make me gag."

"Elizabeth."

"Sorry."

"After you have done these things with no sign of resistance within your soul, you will take the jar with the egg and place it beneath my bed, which is located in the last room down the hall."

"Does this mean I'll have a raw egg under my bed too?"

"It does. And you must bring me your egg before sunrise tomorrow. The last of the ceremony is the burning of our eggs."

A big part of Elizabeth wanted to say forget this hocus-pocus, but an inner voice cautioned her she might need extra protection right now. With no more wisecracks, she handed Obispa the crucifix and delivered a flawless performance. Afterward, the shaman completed the same ablutions over Elizabeth, then she screwed the top on the both jars containing the broken eggs.

"And now for some cocoa." Obispa disappeared into the kitchen and returned with a steaming cup of her prodigious brew.

As Elizabeth sipped the curative liquid, she felt exhaustion slip away. Her mind renewed, she began to review the scant details she knew about the second murder at *Carnivál*. The same voice that had warned her about needing protection from the *mal de ojo* now demanded she tell Obispa about the dead girl, who might be Mariella. Elizabeth finished her cocoa before she began. While she spoke, the shaman fell to her knees on the pallet, her body a stone Madonna. Elizabeth was describing the young girl's body falling from the dumpster into a garbage truck when her cell rang.

"It's Luke," she said to Obispa. "He should have her identity by now." She flipped on the speakerphone, and they listened to the agent's weary voice.

"Her name is Nuria Izquierdo. An eighth-grader, thirteen years old," Luke said, sounding miserable. "Like the other victim, no known gang connection."

"Nuria means *luminosa*," Obispa said and busied herself, preparing a miniature altar next to the one she'd made for Concepción. "A light has been snuffed."

Elizabeth watched the shaman while Luke continued. "Her parents aren't home, neighbors say they work, but we haven't located them."

"Was she mutilated?" Elizabeth asked quietly.

"Same as the first girl."

"How's Dominic taking it?" Elizabeth asked, remembering his extreme distress at *Noche Azul* after he'd seen Concepción's body.

"Maybe that's the only good thing about this situation. Dominic's in El Paso to check out a lead."

"Dominic?" Obispa abruptly turned, her face etched in dread.

Not wanting to unnerve Luke, who sounded beyond rattled, Elizabeth covered the receiver with her hand. "What's the matter?" she asked.

"I see Dominic," Obispa whispered, "and the Black Moth."

THIRTY-TWO

At dinner, Alex devoured a grilled steak, more meat than he'd ever eaten at one time. He piled on a second helping of potatoes and wolfed down two pieces of chocolate cake. After he and Kate cleared the table, *Señora* Grant instructed them to study. She seemed distracted, deep in thought, not her usual friendly self. When they were alone in Kate's room, Alex decided to ask Kate about her mother's mood.

"*Su madre*," he began.

Kate thrust her hands on her hips, blowing a strand of hair from her lovely forehead, spitting her reply in perfect Spanish. "She's always thinking about herself. Elizabeth Grant, the super reporter, Elizabeth Grant, the primo investigator." Kate plopped into her chair and rummaged through a pile of notes on her desk. "From now on, don't ask about my mother."

Alex didn't like being scolded, but he reminded himself not to mention that subject again. Sitting on the floor, he opened Kate's Spanish book. He'd wanted to trace the words with his finger, but Kate wouldn't allow it and made him study without pointing. She hunched over her desk, working on something called "Geometry." Earlier Alex had noticed all the shapes and numbers in her Geometry book, and after he'd mastered English, he would ask her to teach him about this "Geometry." That is, if he was still around.

"*Mi abuelo es viejo*. My grandfather is old." He read the words out loud, taking great care to say them perfectly. When Kate didn't pay him any attention, Alex picked up a CD cover to examine the red background and the anguished expressions of the longhaired musicians. "*Slip . . . knot.* This says *Slipknot.*"

"Yes!" Kate bounced out of her chair and plopped beside him on the floor. "You're doing great. Would you like to hear their music? They're the best hard rock group ever."

Nodding, Alex felt Kate's electricity when she took the CD from him. He pretended to play an invisible guitar as he stole glances at her perfect body, her rounded breasts beneath a tight sweater, her long legs brushing against his. Inhaling her scent, a sweet breeze in springtime, he forced his hands to keep strumming, strumming, strumming silent chords. She slipped the CD into a shiny black player and rotated the knob all the way to the right. Earsplitting music crashed around them. Kate leaned close, her breath on his cheek.

"What do you think?"

Alex's throat tightened. His heart thumped to the beat of the throb between his legs. If he stayed in that room one more second, he'd grab Kate, caress her hair, and kiss her. "I have to go." Scrambling to stand, he grinned sheepishly at her puzzled face then hurried to the door, where he collided with *Señora* Grant, her green eyes flicking some kind of bad message. Alex wondered how long she'd been standing there. If she knew how he felt about Kate, she'd throw him in the street, and he wouldn't blame her.

"Alex, please come to the living room," she said.

"*Sí,*" he said, his voice a scratch, his tongue tangled in his throat. Alex was certain now. *Señora* Grant suspected his love for Kate.

As Alex followed her down the hall, Kate hollered at her mother above the blaring beat. "We were just taking a break. We've been studying!"

Alex turned to see Kate hanging out her door, but *Señora* Grant didn't respond. She just kept walking toward the living room.

"Mom."

La señora pivoted. "This isn't about the music or studying. I need to talk to Alex alone."

"It's not fair." Kate stomped toward them. "He's my friend."

When Alex heard Kate's words, his spirits sank even lower. She thought of him as a friend, he liked her as a girlfriend, and her mother was getting ready to kick him out. Maybe life had been better with Father Chiabras—not so many difficulties, not so many temptations.

The three of them entered the sparkling white living room with furniture and floors so clean it must have been what heaven was like, although the surroundings didn't feel like heaven at the moment. *La señora* gestured toward a fluffy cream-colored couch. Alex peeked at his hands to be sure they weren't dirty before he lowered himself onto the cushion. *Señora* Grant sat opposite him in a yellow chair the color of *pan dulce.*

"I'm not leaving." Kate marched around a low glass table and planted herself right next to Alex.

As the doorbell rang, *la señora* rubbed her temples with her long graceful fingers.

"Agent Santa Maria's here. Do you remember him, Alex? He led the raid at *Noche Azul.*"

In the haze of all that had happened in the past few days, Alex still recalled the kind agent who'd offered a work permit if he cooperated.

"*Sí.* I will tell him about Santiago," he said, hoping this was the right answer.

"He needs information about the *coyote,* but I think he also wants your help with the Latin Angels—"

"What do you mean, *señora?*"

"He needs an informant to join that gang."

"How could you, Mother?" Kate's anger was a bullet.

"I didn't want to involve you in this, Kate, but since you insist, be quiet and listen." *Señora* Grant sighed. "And before you make a judgment, you need to consider what's happened."

La señora stood as if she had a pain in her back and headed for the door. When the tall agent came into the room, Alex remembered him even better, but Luke Santa Maria had changed in some way. He was different—his gloomy expression, his hesitance, his tentative glance at *Señora* Grant were unlike the man Alex had met at the raid.

"I'm Luke Santa Maria," he said in Spanish.

"*Señor* Santa Maria. I remember."

"Call me 'Luke.'"

Surprised the agent would ask Alex to use his first name, he felt more at ease. After shaking Alex's hand with a strong grip, Luke's attention fell on Kate. He smiled and nodded toward her. "Hi, Kate."

"Hi." She clamped her lips, and Alex could feel the chill. He was sure Luke caught it.

Luke cleared his throat. When he put his arm on the armrest, Alex spied a holstered gun beneath his tweed jacket.

La señora sat in the yellow chair, so Alex and Kate faced them, separated by the glass table and a bowl of fresh white daises.

"I hear you were a member of the Latin Angels in Guatemala

City."

Anxious to cooperate, Alex scooted to the edge of the sofa and showed them a tattoo on his right fingers. "This is the Angels' mark."

Everyone bent forward to view the small black numbers: one-two-one.

"What do they mean?" Kate asked.

It pained Alex not to tell her, so he explained. "When Fernando and I left the gang, we swore an oath never to say what the numbers mean." He stared first at Kate, then at Luke to let them both know he wouldn't break his promise.

"I didn't come here to ask about the code," Luke said, shifting in the chair, his large hands on his knees in what Alex thought was a rather stiff position. "I came to ask your help, Alex. The State Department needs a confidential informant, a CI, we call them, to join the Houston Angels. This means you'd receive training by men in my office. You would learn how to join a US gang, to get information for the government, and many other things we can discuss later."

"*Dios.*" Alex imagined the consequences of this sort of commitment.

"Every minute counts, or I wouldn't be asking you. Two girls have been murdered, and we're sure the Angels did it."

Alex hesitated. "I'm sorry for the girls, *señor*, but I must explain. In Guatemala, the Latin Angels, we stole food, cigarettes, and sometimes glue. Things we needed to survive. Little crimes, nothing like our American brothers." He was determined not to reveal the violent gang life he had led and withheld information about his proven skills as a street fighter.

"You're asking Alex to make a huge sacrifice," *Señora* Grant said. Standing, she moved behind him and put her hand on his shoulder as if she were urging him not to join the gang. When she spoke to the agent, her voice was overly loud. "*La Sombra* killed his brother, Fernando, and they may have connections with the Angels here."

"All the more reason to stop another killing." Luke's sky-blue eyes seemed to be searching for Alex's reaction.

Bowing his head, he tried to concentrate, but the voices of his mother and Father Chiabras whirled in his head. One minute Alex thought they were telling him to join the gang; the next, they were saying no, never get involved with those murderers. When he lifted his eyes, Fernando's ghost floated into the room and settled on the armrest of the chair where Luke sat. Alex squinted to make sure he wasn't dreaming and gulped a mouthful of air. Fernando sent him a pining smile, as if he truly missed being together with Alex on earth.

"*This will be a dark night,*" Fernando said.

Alex knew there was truth in his brother's warning, just as there had been truth when Fernando cautioned him to beware of the rat, the man who helped Santiago rape Mariella and leave her to die in the desert. "What will happen?" he said out loud, seeing nothing but Fernando, listening only for his brother's answer.

Before Fernando could respond, Luke spoke. "After your training, a CI who deals with the Angels will arrange for you to meet some gang members. We think you'd have to go through their initiation."

Alarmed at what Luke said about initiation, Alex's attention shifted to the agent. He asked him, "What if initiation means I have to hurt someone?"

"If that's the case, we'll get you out," Luke answered.

"What should I do?" Alex said to Fernando.

Luke replied. "I can't tell you, Alex. But unless we arrest the leaders of the Angels, there will be more murders."

"*You are your brother's keeper,*" said Fernando, his body melting into the chair.

"Wait!" Alex sprung to his feet. "Don't leave until you tell me what to do."

"I'm not leaving." Luke cocked his head and gave Alex a hard look.

"No one's going anywhere, Alex." Kate put her hand on his wrist.

He momentarily drew calm from her touch, but as he watched Fernando dissolve, Alex called out again, "Please don't go away. I need you!"

"This is too much for him, Luke." *Señora* Grant rounded the sofa and settled beside Alex.

Kate thrust her arms across her chest, and Alex could see that Luke again noticed her disapproval.

"I don't like this either, Kate," Luke said. "But if Alex becomes a CI, the State Department will grant him asylum."

"Yeah," Kate said. "If he lives to enjoy it."

"We'll train him to protect himself and to escape if he's in danger."

Twisting his lips, Luke looked at *Señora* Grant. Alex detected a certain energy between them, and he watched her reaction. She kept her eyes centered on Luke, but she said nothing. The room rolled in unnerving silence until Kate tugged Alex's arm and rose from the couch.

"Let's go to that movie we talked about," she said.

Standing to follow Kate, Alex felt a mixture of fright and shame. He couldn't imagine joining the American gang. His strength was hand-to-hand street fighting, but he had no skills with guns and knives. Alex knew he wasn't a coward, but in the past few days, he'd begun to care about his life, about having a future in this country. Remembering Father Chiabras's kindness toward all people, Alex's heart told him he should have no part of the Latin Angels.

But there was the problem of Fernando's messages. What could the dark night mean? For sure, Alex would stay awake and guard Kate tonight while she slept. He could sit on the floor outside her room. As for being his brother's keeper, did Fernando want Alex to avenge his own death or prevent the deaths of others?

"Call me if you change your mind," Luke was saying. He reached into his pocket, withdrew a business card from a small leather case and handed it to Alex.

"We'll talk soon," *Señora* Grant said to Luke as she accompanied him on his way out.

Alex and Kate passed the front door, left slightly open, and he heard *la señora*'s voice. He paused. Kate jerked his hand, but he refused to budge.

"I want to know what your mother thinks about me joining the Angels," he said in a low tone. "Maybe she really wants me to."

"You won't understand what they're saying."

"You could whisper to me in Spanish."

With a conspiratorial nod, Kate gestured for him to follow her into a downstairs office, where a door led to a front walkway near the porch. They stole outside and hunkered in the bushes just in time to see Kate's mother and the agent arguing by the front door. Every time they spoke, Kate interpreted their words, her cool breath in Alex's ear.

THIRTY-THREE

Saffron light glimmered from gas lamps on either side of the door as Elizabeth stepped onto the porch with Luke. He lowered his eyes as if examining the stitches on his polished black boots. Finally, he peered at her. A single crease deepened the middle of his forehead.

"I'm worried about that 'don't leave me' business with Alex. Is he disoriented?" Luke asked.

"Not that I've noticed, but after what he's been through—"

"I'm aware of what he's been through, Elizabeth. Do you think I don't understand? I've had my losses."

"Yes, you have." She pondered the unhappy similarities between the agent and the boy. Luke had been about Alex's age when he'd lost his parents. She asked softly, "Want my opinion?"

"I'm sure I'll get it." His voice sounded tired, bitter even.

"You're right to want Alex as a CI, but Kate and I are right too."

"Where does that leave me?"

"Can you find someone else?"

"Not anytime soon, and certainly not someone like Alex."

When he didn't continue, the lull in conversation heightened Elizabeth's urge to escape, a feeling she frequently had when life became too complicated. What she needed was a no-brainer ending to this horrendous day. Slipping off her heels, she curled her toes against the cool bricks.

"I'm going for a run. Wanna come?"

He shook his head. "Not tonight."

"You're no fun."

"In case you've forgotten," Luke said. "I have two unsolved murders and no time to play."

"True," Elizabeth said, considering the erratic behavior she displayed toward Luke—one minute his adversary, the next his friend. Extreme maneuvers. War games. She was forty years old and still creating battleground relationships and escape hatches, but, war or not, she knew she didn't want Luke Santa Maria to retreat from this skirmish. Selecting a topic she bet would hold his interest, she said, "I met with Randall Cole today. When I left his office, Hector Sandoval was in the waiting room."

Luke cocked his head.

"They acted like they didn't know each other, but I'm not so sure."

"No chance," Luke replied. "Cole wouldn't let his pristine snout breathe the same air as that thug." He took a long breath and glanced at the starless horizon. "I guess someone in his firm could represent Sandoval, but Cole would relegate that to a baby lawyer, as he calls them."

"That's my point. He knows you're after the Angels, and he didn't tell you about Sandoval."

"Look, Elizabeth, Randall's not involved with a gang leader. We lived together during high school. He just bailed me out of a divorce snafu. He advises me on immigration issues. Case closed."

"All I can say is that asshole was in Cole's office, and he hasn't told you." Elizabeth's voice held a righteous flare.

"He will. It just happened this morning."

She kept on. "There's something sleazy about Cole. He called Alex 'a street rat.' And then he pressed me to tell him my source on the raids."

"The comment about Alex is off base, I give you that. But I asked for your source too. Am I a sleazebag?"

"No—"

"And your source is anonymous, so you couldn't tell Cole." Luke leveled his gaze, his eyes moving back and forth in a rapid, inquiring manner. "Right?"

"Right." Elizabeth planted her palms on her hips. "He tried to bribe me."

"Since when are you above bribery? You'll deal with the devil if you think there's a story in it. I know your tactics."

"You know my tactics?" An irrational ire shot through Elizabeth.

"Does the State Department have a dossier on me?"

"Don't flatter yourself." Glancing at his watch, Luke huffed off toward a white Chevy truck, his personal vehicle, she guessed.

Elizabeth waited for him to say something. When he clicked his door opener instead, she marched down the walk and stood behind him. She felt puffy and miserable, but she wouldn't withdraw from the frontline. "The night I met you, I thought you were arrogant, but you're not only arrogant, you're rude and you rash judge people." Her words hung in the air like a noose.

Eyes the color of washed-out seersucker, Luke pursed his lips. He methodically hoisted himself into the front seat. Elizabeth expected him to slam the door, but he closed it quietly. She pivoted, refusing to watch him leave. As the truck's motor droned into a fade, she wandered up to the house, unable to quash a harsh critique of her latest performance, and this time she didn't get off to the hostilities.

Elizabeth had shunned relationships for years after a dreadful divorce from a distant man who rarely bothered to see his precious daughter. With Luke's arrival, a puzzling verve eroded her steadfast resolve to avoid romance. She halfheartedly attributed this new development to Obispa's spells, but Elizabeth knew better.

"Kate? Alex?" she called as she tromped past the office. The stereo was off, the house silent except for the creak of the garage door opening. The kids must be on their way to the movie Kate had mentioned. What the hell. Elizabeth was going for a run.

She threw on white sweats and her favorite cushy runners, snatched a house key, and hit the street. Jogging slowly at first, Elizabeth felt soothed by the familiar cadence of sole against earth. She picked up speed when she reached Potomac, a boulevard lined with chic townhomes and trees whose leaves never changed color in Houston's two seasons: sweatbox and faux winter.

The cold night crept around her, but Elizabeth preferred the humid chill to summertime, when running outside felt like taking a dip in warm spit. Block after block, she glided through a low mist, occasionally glancing at the dusk-pink sky. The clouds, looking as if they'd been infused with Pepto-Bismol, captured the glow of headlights and held their beams close to the earth. This kind of evening, when Houston's pollution grew palpable, Elizabeth was frequently thrust into a claustrophobic, doomsday mood, and she groused at a car passing her on the left, a little too close for comfort.

By the sixth mile, however, her endorphins engendered a complete recovery from the doldrums. Humming snippets of a song, she headed for home in a much better mood until a car swerved into her path. A slice of cruel light shattered her reverie and clouded her vision.

Attempting to hop the curb, Elizabeth twisted her ankle and fell forward. Rough pavement stabbed at her hands as blue-white lights held their course. Frantic, she crawled over the curb into a narrow swath of grass and lay down, spooling over crisp winter blades onto the sidewalk, scrambling behind a hedge and peering through its branches at a black sedan.

The car's front tires skirted the curb to her right, perilously close to a thin band of lawn in front of the hedge where she hid. She shielded her eyes from the headlights and hunkered into a squat. Her sprained ankle made it impossible to dash for the white stucco town house behind her.

Elizabeth fully expected someone to leave the sedan. When no one did, she surmised the driver planned to run her down, but he would have to ram the hedge or back up and go around it to get to her. Not waiting for the attack, she belly-crawled to the town house gate.

Wheels screeched. The stench of burnt rubber hung in the air as the driver reversed and headed for the town house driveway. In spite of a spiking jab in her ankle, she stood up at the iron gate and pushed. No luck. Screaming, she repeatedly banged the doorbell with her fist.

"What the hell?" A white-haired man in striped pajamas appeared on the balcony above.

"That car's trying to run me down!"

He brandished a handgun at the car crashing into his driveway. The driver must have spotted him because he slammed on the brakes. The uncommon fracas caused neighbors to peek from upstairs windows while anxious voices floated over courtyards walls. In the midst of bedlam, a green car with a pizza sign on its roof sputtered up to the curb. A deliveryman sprang from the car, sprinted to Elizabeth, and grabbed her wrist. She instinctively scratched at his face.

Chuffing, he leaned away from her fingernails. "Houston Police," he said.

As the pursuing car torpedoed down the street, Elizabeth's dubious savior keyed a speed dial on his cell with his free hand, ordering a "be-on-the-lookout" for the black sedan, and kept a firm hold on her wrist with his other. She eyed the guy. Latino, about thirty. Terrifying thoughts poked at her brain, warning that he could be another attacker. Elizabeth tried to wriggle from his grasp.

"HPD, ma'am." He fumbled in a back pocket. "Let me show you—"

"Get away!" she rasped.

"Hold it, Romeo." The man on the balcony pointed his gun at the maybe cop.

"I'm an undercover officer, sir. Sergeant Diego Buendía," he called to the man. "All I have in my hand is a wallet."

"Throw it on the ground and back away from her."

The pizza man released Elizabeth and threw his wallet.

A silver badge stared up at her, and she studied it carefully. "He's legit," she called to her hero on the balcony.

The man lowered his firearm. The folds of Sergeant Buendía's frown slipped into relief as Elizabeth slumped onto the grass, dew seeping through her sweats. Lightheaded and dazed, she found herself memorizing the sergeant's features, a young version of Dominic Fontana if ever there was one.

"Sorry, I'm staring, but you look like a guy I know."

"*No problema.*" Buendía flashed a glitter-white smile.

She noted his Lady of Guadalupe T-shirt and smelled an aroma of pepperoni wafting on the breeze. "Do you really have pizza, or am I delusional?"

"Tell me what happened." His kind eyes, a welcome sight.

"What are you doing here?" she asked.

"You have friends in high places."

THIRTY-FOUR

Dominic breathed deeply. Away from the desperation of a haunted Juárez, things looked better, and he enjoyed the El Paso evening horizon through the dusty windshield of his fat-ass PT. A funky melon sky melted around the earth like a man embracing woman. Dominic chuckled. The heavens must be celebrating the stunt he'd just pulled on Velasquez.

Cruising Franklin Drive, he checked the address Velasquez had given, a five-story terra-cotta brick affair, its windows coated with metallic film, no doubt a protection from the searing desert sun, ever-present even in winter.

Once in the lobby, Dominic explained his mission to the building's security guard, a man drowning in a khaki uniform several sizes too large. His long fingernails, unkempt hair, and ochre teeth brought to mind a renegade groundhog clambering from his hole to please the State Department, eager to answer any question about Rufino Banderas.

"How long has Banderas officed here?" Dominic asked.

"Since before I started six months ago," said the unarmed and therefore impotent security officer. He scratched the stubble on his chin. "Funny thing, though. I've never seen him."

"That's strange."

"But the cleaning lady, Orilla Tomás, talks to him in Spanish. She's up on five now." He tapped on a cell phone clipped to his belt and scribbled his number on a scrap of paper. "If she doesn't cooperate, call me."

"Good work, partner."

The groundhog beamed. "Let me know what else I can do."

"You bet, little buddy."

In the elevator on the way to floor five, Dominic punched his cell and gave Banderas's name, street address, and suite number to his liaison at El Paso PD, sweet-smelling Lourdes Ortiz. They'd worked together on other cases, and at one time he'd had designs on her. Now he was content to envy her happy marriage and growing brood of kids. Always good-natured, Lourdes agreed to bring a search warrant and her most talented forensic guy to join Dominic.

The fifth floor was lit by fluorescent tubes and reeked of a strong cleaning solvent. Dominic strode down a moss-green carpet until he reached Banderas's office and, not surprisingly, found it locked. Checking an open closet nearby, his eyes fell on a woman's double-wide butt, her body bent toward a bucket. As Dominic approached, she straightened and pivoted toward him, her gray uniform a blunt contrast to her fried-bleached hair slicked into a ponytail. Her jet-black eyes sat close together above a pug nose and overly red lips. Her left fingers curled, withered by muscle strictures, and Dominic wondered how she performed her cleaning tasks.

He flashed his badge. "Orilla Tomás?"

She shrank into the shelves crammed with window cleaners, rags, and white plastic bottles.

"US State Department," he said in Spanish, betting a dollar to a dime she was illegal. Dominic smiled to ease her fear. "Don't be afraid. I just want to ask you some questions."

Orilla covered her mouth and slinked farther into the corner.

"My questions aren't about you, *señora*." Dominic used his kindest voice. "The security guard told me you've met Rufino Banderas."

"*Sí.*" Her voice was barely audible.

"Is there anyone in his office now?"

She shook her head, her dark eyes slatted, her crippled hand jammed deep in the apron pocket.

"I need you to open the door."

"*Sí.*"

Toppling a mop, Orilla sidled past Dominic. When they reached Banderas's office, her good hand removed a key from the hook on her belt. Dominic rechecked the brass plate: "Rufino Banderas, Attorney at Law," then drew his gun. Fuck the warrant, he was going in.

Mouth agape, Orilla shuffled backward as Dominic swung

the door open. Stark disappointment met his astonished gaze—an unfurnished office, devoid of human habitation. He moved around the space, pointing his weapon in every direction, checking the closet, finding it empty. Frustrated, he holstered the SIG and glanced out the window at the orange light streaking a lavender sky. It occurred to Dominic that the office faced due west, with no metallic protection on the windows.

"Does he ever work here?" Dominic asked Orilla, who'd crept into the doorway.

"*No mucho, señor.* Sometimes he comes for a short time." She bit her upper lip. "I keep his machines. He asked me to hide them for him."

Dominic's pulse quickened. "Show me."

Orilla returned to the broom closet, moved two amber bottles of floor wax to the side, and pointed at a glossy cream-colored fax and a scanner tucked behind them. Dominic's eyes searched for a clean cloth and found something better, a carton of disposable gloves. He whipped on a pair, stacked the machines and headed for the vacant office. When Orilla didn't follow, he looked over his shoulder at her lingering near the closet, fidgeting with the handle of a bucket.

"Come with me," he called. "You aren't in trouble."

She waddled toward Dominic. Her watchful eyes remained glued on him while he set the fax and scanner on the floor of Banderas's office, plugged them in, and called Lourdes again.

"I need an artist too," he said. Dominic updated the policewoman on his findings and endured her flack for entering the office without a warrant, then he hung up and spoke gently to Orilla. "A police artist is coming. I want you to describe Banderas to him."

Orilla's shoulders stiffened. She twisted a strand of hair and tucked it behind her ear.

"Do you have work papers?" Dominic said.

"*Señor,* please—"

"After you describe Banderas, I'll get the papers for you."

"How, *señor?*"

"Remember, sugar, I'm with the State Department." He showed her his badge again.

Orilla ran her calloused fingers over its raised letters. "Sometimes there are deliveries," she said. "I save them for *Señor* Banderas."

"Do you have any now?"

She shook her head. "But one time when he didn't know I was watching, he opened a brown envelope filled with small cards, driver's licenses, maybe."

"That's very good, Orilla. Banderas has hurt many Latinos, and you can help us stop him." Dominic squatted by the fax, pushed the button to print all the numbers in the address book, and faxed the list to Houston. After he was certain the fax had gone through, he dialed Luke's cell. When he didn't get an answer, he left a message.

"We need a profile on Blue Agave owner, Rufino Banderas, and the manager, Diego Velasquez. Could be the same *hombre*, not sure yet. FBI, Homeland, or ICE may have something." He elaborated on his discoveries and started to hang up. "Hey, man, sorry about this morning. I'm chewing mints and staying cool."

It took three hours for the El Paso team to finish their work, with Lourdes questioning some fifth floor occupants, forensics scouring for evidence and prints, and Dominic hand-holding Orilla while she talked to the artist. She described Banderas as a man with few remarkable features: no moustache, no scars, no damaged skin, no limp. He was very tall with big hands, she was sure of that. Orilla's description of the hands gnawed at Dominic. Too hungry to immediately act on his suspicion, he figured his adrenalin would click after food. True to his promise, he secured Orilla's personal information and explained that someone from State would contact her about work papers. Beaming, she hugged him and said goodnight.

On his way out, he briefed the zealous security guard and gave him a copy of Banderas's description, so the poor guy would feel he was in the loop. It was after eleven when Dominic drove the Cruiser five blocks to the Camino Real Hotel, his pad for the night. He dumped his duffle bag in the room, then found the bar, where he swigged a Jack Daniel's and inhaled a plate of deluxe nachos. Even though it was past midnight, he decided to take a walk, savoring the cool air, rethinking his session with Velasquez. The manager had given up Banderas too fast, and the office was probably a tactic to throw him off, but Velasquez hadn't counted on Orilla, or on Dominic's discovery of the fax numbers.

Within minutes, he found himself in front of the El Paso Museum of Art. He studied the grillwork resembling rectangular solar panels arched above six square-edged pillars and admired a series of glass cases displaying photographs of murals painted in the museum freight elevator. These paintings depicted grotesque people with shortened limbs, gnarled feet, and enormous hands.

Something about those hands inflamed Dominic as he considered how many people had suffered at the hands of Diego Velasquez, and

Velasquez was most certainly Banderas. In spite of Luke's warnings, or the certain danger Juárez promised, Dominic was jazzed by the thought of busting Velasquez at home, at night, for a bedtime story.

As he trekked back toward the hotel, Dominic's ears picked up a growling noise behind him and identified it as the annoying gurgle of a souped-up car. He twisted slightly, spotting a lime-green lowrider, its hood alive with fluted red flames. A teenage *cholo* rolled down the back window and motioned to him.

"Hey, dude, know where Valencia is?"

Picking up the pace, Dominic shook his head and continued toward the Camino Real. The car followed.

"Valencia Street?" the kid called. "I got to find it."

Dominic started to speak, but his voice caught midway in his throat at a whoosh from the corner of his eye, a stealth approach from behind. He'd fucked up big time. Someone poked a gun in his ribs and eased him toward the lowrider.

When they reached the car, the young hood in the backseat opened the door. He had spiked henna hair, a pitted complexion, and glassy lupine eyes. Probably higher than shit. Dominic inched his hand toward his weapon, but the hidden gunman snatched the pistol along with his cell and cuffs, then shoved Dominic into the backseat with the pock-faced bastard who thrust an AK-47 under his chin.

"You don't want to do this," Dominic said. "I'm State Department."

"We know, man!" howled the *cholo*. "Welcome to Marco's house of fun."

"Are you Marco?"

"I am," he said with a wicked smirk.

"What do you want?" Stalling, Dominic searched for a way to take these guys out.

"To fuck your mother, man."

"We might fuck you too, cocksucker." The garbled voice came from the front seat, and both men guffawed.

How could he have been so stupid? He'd taken a walk at one in the morning and done nothing to protect himself. "What's this about?" Dominic asked, hardly able to move his jaw with the gun barrel pinching the soft tissue under his chin.

"Shut up, you motherfucking, dog-ass pig."

"Make up your mind. Am I a dog or a pig?"

Dominic was instantly sorry for the wisecrack. Marco plowed the butt of the AK-47 into his stomach. Gagging, he doubled in agony as

Marco threw a serape over him and pressed his spine with the gun until Dominic jackknifed onto the floorboard, his neck bowed, head rammed against the door. Pain radiated from his gut as bourbon spurted from his stomach into his throat.

Folded in a fetal position, Dominic sucked shallow breaths through his mouth in an effort not to smell the serape's fetid odors. *"Arrogance never serves you."* Luke's brotherly advice floated into his head. *"And besides, you're too smart for that behavior."* Forcing himself to swallow the sour liquid in his throat, Dominic knew he had to get a grip, and after that, he had to slide his hand to the Ruger strapped in his ankle holster.

THIRTY-FIVE

Elizabeth slouched at the breakfast room table. She stared at gray and white forms in an abstract painting and wished for a taste of painterly emptiness she could call peace. The chaos was hard to digest. Two hours ago, a pizza delivery boy/undercover cop had rescued her from death-by-auto, leaving no doubt about the driver's intentions.

Grasping three small bags of ice, Kate nudged a chair over to Elizabeth so she could prop her legs. Her daughter had metamorphosed into a sweetheart child with tears in her eyes and concern carved all over her face. She placed baggies filled with cool relief on Elizabeth's palms and ankle.

Alex hung close to Elizabeth too. Cheeks pallid, eyes sharp and darting, he looked as if he'd seen a ghost. "I glad the policeman save you," he said.

"Very good English." Kate smiled at him, but it didn't seem to brighten Alex's spirits.

He shifted in the chair. "I wish I warn you," he said. "It was a dark night."

Elizabeth leaned forward. "What do you mean?"

Shrugging, he bit his lip.

Uneasy about his behavior, Elizabeth asked again in Spanish. "What did you mean when you said 'dark night'?"

Alex's eyes filled with tears, and he muttered in Spanish as if he were afraid to speak. "Something my brother told me."

Elizabeth took his hand, heavy in her raw palm, but Elizabeth's pain was inconsequential compared to the hurt this boy had endured, the loss of his mother, his brother, his country.

They sat that way for a while, Alex with his head bowed, Elizabeth and Kate exchanging looks of concern. At length, Kate broke the silence.

"Mom, who wants to hurt you?"

Shaking her head, Elizabeth didn't comment about who she thought was calling the shots or about her slashed tires, although her fear hung in the air, palpable and disarming.

A knock on the kitchen door caused them all to start. "Don't answer it," Elizabeth whispered.

Kate and Alex sleuthed to the door and took turns at the peephole.

"It's Obispa," Alex said, his face a pool of relief.

Opening the door and introducing herself to the shaman, Kate helped Obispa carry several mysterious rucksacks while Alex took her coat. Obispa instantly came to Elizabeth and surveyed her wounds. "*Madre de Díos*! But I can fix this."

Kate and Alex trailed Obispa into the kitchen, where the shaman pulled out two large kettles and dumped powders and liquids into them. She instructed Kate to place each kettle on the stove and turn on the gas. As the potions came to a boil, an acrid odor whirled through the house. Kate held her nose. Alex blinked.

"What're you making?" Elizabeth asked.

"Herbal tea and a poultice for your scraped hands. These medicines will also relieve your ankle pain." Obispa swiveled to face Elizabeth. "What you must do now is bleed. Push on your cuts."

Kate snickered. Elizabeth put her finger on her lips to hush her. From the purple sack on the floor near her feet, Obispa pulled out two vials, three jars, a mortar, a pestle, and several gourds painted with fire symbols. She arranged the items in a row. "I will prepare Spider Lily, the strongest remedy for cuts known to those who practice The Craft."

"The Craft?" Blowing a runaway strand from her forehead, Kate sauntered closer and watched intently. "Witchcraft, you mean."

Obispa's violet orbs narrowed. "I am not a witch."

Unabashed, Kate kept it up. "But you act like one."

"A *curandera* is not a *bruja* ." The shaman stirred her potions, but her attention remained on Kate. "And now you will help me make medicine, Kate Grant." Obispa thrust a gourd bowl at her.

"So, I get it. You're like a one-woman pharmacy."

Obispa ignored Kate's wisecrack. "Take a spoonful of vitamin C and myrrh from these vials. Mix them with powdered rosemary and pour everything into this green salve." The shaman stuck her fingers into one of the jars and jabbed a gummy glob into the gourd.

"Okay, then." Kate surveyed the ingredients, asked a couple questions about the amount of spices, then mixed the conglomeration with great energy. She seemed to enjoy the task.

Elizabeth began to relax until Alex fell into the chair beside her, elbows on the table, head in his hands. She lightly touched his arm. "Alex?"

"I wish Fernando had told me more," he said in Spanish.

"What did Fernando say to you?"

He shook his head and stared at her palms. "Make them bleed, *señora*," he said in Spanish. "It stops you from getting sick. Father Chiabras made us do it every time we were cut."

Obviously, Alex didn't want to tell her what he believed he'd heard from Fernando. Elizabeth decided to let it go. She didn't want to cast doubt on a conversation with his dead brother, and while Elizabeth considered what to say next, the shaman waved a clean dishrag and glided to the table with a vaporous concoction.

"Dip in the bowl with this rag, then clean your hands."

Wincing, Elizabeth squeezed her scraped palms until blood oozed out amid flecks of gravel. She took the rag and dipped it into the heated liquid while Obispa removed a garlic clove and some long green leaves from the pocket of her apron. She handed them to Alex.

"You need to calm your nerves, Alex. Crush the garlic and echinacea for me."

With a hangdog expression, he took the ingredients to the counter, dumped the garlic clove and the leaves into the mortar, and ground them with the pestle.

"I'm finished," Kate said, eying the goop she'd just mixed. "It smells kinda good."

Alex held up the mortar. "I almost," he said.

Obispa fluttered around him, examining his work as he ground the herbs. She poured Alex's ingredients into one of the kettles. Speaking to Kate, she said, "Put the salve on your mother's palms and bandage them with this gauze."

"Gotcha," Kate said, smearing a translucent lump of salve that resembled green, radioactive Vaseline onto Elizabeth's hands.

Alex delivered the mortar to Obispa, then he focused on Elizabeth. He bit his upper lip, his forehead creased into a frown.

Glancing at him, Kate said, "We're going to do everything we can to help you, Alex."

"I do not need help." Alex said in halting English. His face marbleized, his shoulders stiffened. "Good night." He left the room.

"What did I say?" Kate asked.

Obispa patted her arm. "We must be patient. Alex is a proud boy. He wants to succeed on his own." She handed Elizabeth a cup of liquid the color of chicken broth. "Chamomile tea with special healing medicines."

Settling across from Elizabeth, the shaman said to Kate, "I must talk to your mother alone."

"Sure," Kate said. "And it was nice to meet you. I'll go check on Alex."

Elizabeth blew her a kiss before she left the kitchen.

The salve and herbal tea calmed the painful protests of her scrapes and aching limbs. Maybe the medicines would completely cure her by seven a.m., when she planned to hop the company plane to Austin. As she sipped her tea, Elizabeth wondered what the shaman wanted to say, but she knew Obispa would reveal it in her own time. "You must be tired," she said.

Nodding, she sighed. "Alex was right. It was a very dark night."

"Man, was it."

"More than you know, Elizabeth. Earlier this evening, I could not dispel my concern for Mariella." She leaned forward. "I know Tulio Mola drugged her with *La Rocha*, so she will have sex with him, and God knows what other men."

"The date-rape drug."

"*Sí*." She scowled. "I went to *Carnivál*, hoping to find her. At the front door, there was a bouncer who would not let me in. When I left for my car, he called to me, 'We know where you live, Navidad Maria Cid.'"

"They're trying to stop us both."

"Yes, they are, but I will stand up to Mola for the sake of our people. We cannot allow his cantinas, his filth, and his drugs."

"We can't and we won't."

Obispa's circled eyes flickered. "When I returned from *Carnivál* to my House of Light, there was an effigy of me swinging from a branch near the porch."

"Mola's a persistent pervert, I'll give him that."

"Yes, he is. And now he has sent his gang for you."

"I know." Elizabeth groaned. "How did you know I was attacked?"

"After I called the police about that effigy, I lit a candle. In its flame, I saw a vision of you tumbling into Yawning Mouth."

"That's disgusting." Elizabeth intensely disliked the thought of falling into an open mouth. "What's a Yawning Mouth?"

"The jaws of death." The shaman leaned close to Elizabeth. "But tonight, it was not your time."

Elizabeth looked at her hands. She'd seen the jaws of death in the distraught face of Concepción's mother. "The people on your street must be panicked."

"They are." The shaman tapped the toe of her sandal on the travertine floor. "Johnny McCullough led the investigation about my effigy. But I did not trust him, so I called Javi Padilla, whom I have known since he was a child, and he must have notified Luke Santa Maria. They both came. Javi promised he would ask for a twenty-four-hour patrol in our *barrio*, but he said it would be hard to convince his chief." Sighing, Obispa pushed away from the table. "They do not help us because we are poor."

She strode to the kitchen and packed her vials, jars, and gourds into the rucksacks. "I must go home. When there is death and terror on our streets, many people will come to see me regardless of the hour."

Accompanying Obispa to the porch, Elizabeth was relieved to feel so agile. "Do you have a protection for me, like a talisman?" she asked. "I'm flying to Austin in the morning. I've arranged to catch a ride with some newspaper executives who are doing a day trip there."

"There is only one pilot?"

"Yes, but it's a short trip, perfectly safe. A commercial flight takes too much time, and after tonight, I need to get home as quickly as possible."

"I understand." The shaman withdrew a small woven sack from her neck and gave it to Elizabeth.

"Thank you, *mi amiga*, and thanks for coming all the way over here. You're a true friend." She started to express her deep affection to this strange and splendid woman, but embarrassment caused her to pause. Instead, Elizabeth hugged Obispa, walked her to the curb, and made sure she was secure in her car.

That night, Elizabeth dreamed she and Mariella were fleeing Tulio Mola, whose body warped into a yawning mouth. As they ran through a grassless yard, a small red radio blared, "*lloro, lloro, lloro.*"

I cry, I cry, I cry.

THIRTY-SIX

Dominic's legs cramped. He longed to wiggle his toes, but any sign of consciousness might agitate Marco. Patches of the floorboard smelled of piss, a telltale sign he wasn't the first victim crammed into this space. The lowrider's jerky motions, crawling, then lunging forward, made Dominic nauseous. He gulped the stale air but couldn't suppress the sick, green sensation taking hold of his gut.

"Shit, man, the dude's throwing up," Marco said to the driver.

"Not for long," came the voice from the front.

The car slowed. Dominic suspected they were in line at a Juárez crossing. His mind raced for a way out, but all he could do was prop his head to keep from aspirating a chunk of undigested nacho. *"Sucking in your own vomit, a bad way to die, son, a bad way to die,"* his father had once said when Dominic had been seriously hungover. Dominic had laughed, wondering why the hell his old man would ever say such a thing. *Funny the memories that come to mind when you're about to get snuffed.*

"These fucking lines," Marco said. "I hate these fucking lines."

"Take it easy, man. We'll be in heaven soon."

Within minutes, the soft thump-thumping sounds of a bridge surface suggested they were crossing the *Rio Grande* and approaching a Mexican checkpoint. This was Dominic's chance to throw off the serape and yell for help. But his plan dissolved when the car halted, and he overheard the driver talking to someone, definitely not Marco.

"We have our cargo," the driver said.

"Before you pass, I'll count my money," a man's voice replied in a dry tone.

"Count it fast, you sonofabitch."

Dominic pictured a greedy immigration officer relishing the bribe, eager to sell a life for a buck. When the motor hummed again and the lowrider lurched forward, he thought about the bridge they were passing over. He knew of three: Santa Fe, Stanton, and Cordova. If they'd crossed the Santa Fe, they'd now be on Avenue Juárez, nearing the History Museum, where he'd spent a few hours to decompress after Juana's funeral.

In his grim world on the floor of the car, he pondered his life, a bubble about to burst into insignificant specks and be splattered on streets of the ugliest city in Mexico. He had one chance—to blast Marco. A final desperate notion eked its way into his mind, a plan that hinged on an unlocked door. Searching his memory, Dominic found no recollection of Marco pressing the lock, and this old car wouldn't have automatic ones. Maybe he could escape before the driver had time to react. He visualized his gun resting above his right ankle, pressing into the lower part of the backseat.

With his hand creeping along his thigh past his knee to reach the Ruger, Dominic considered his other problem, one that had seemed inconsequential at first. The more he thought about it, the more he realized it was huge. The ankle holster where his gun rested was secured by Velcro, and all Velcro fasteners made a scratchy noise when opened.

Feigning another round of stomach upset, Dominic wretched and moaned as he ripped the Velcro strap. His sweaty fingers tore the Ruger from its holster, threw off the serape, and raised his pistol. Marco had laid the AK-47 on the seat, and before he could grab it or warn the driver, Dominic plugged Marco twice. The boy's shirt webbed in crimson rivulets. Twisting, Dominic tried to get a bead on the driver, who ducked and slammed on the brakes. No time to try again. He pushed down the handle. The door swung open.

He hurled himself from the car, rolled into the street, and scrambled to his feet. Dodging a smattering of cars, Dominic crouched behind a bulbous Toltec head at the front of the History Museum. He aimed at the lowrider, hoping to pump a bullet into the driver's head, but a garbage truck rumbled between him and the car. He tried to adjust quickly, but instead of hitting his mark, he popped the car's rear tire.

Dominic took off running. At the far side of the stately brick museum, he spotted the top-heavy garbage truck rambling into a narrow drive and disappearing behind the building. He could commandeer the damned thing and get to a telephone. But with no money and no ID, who the hell would let him use a phone in this besieged city? The museum was his best bet.

Sprinting to the rear, Dominic spied the truck cruise to a stop near a loading dock illuminated by shafts of ghostly light. Two men disembarked while a metal garage door at the rear of the dock opened. An armed guard emerged, rolling a white statue on a dolly. The fuckers weren't after trash, and the theft probably wouldn't be noticed for days in this condemned city.

With a *thump-scrape-thump*, the lowrider limped into sight, the sound of its wheel rim grinding against concrete. The thieves paused to stare at the car, so Dominic took the opportunity to duck behind a large plywood crate stuffed with white shredded packing material close to the dock. The lowrider lunged to a halt about twenty feet from where he hid, its headlights shining directly at him, making it tough to see.

"I'm after an escaped prisoner," yelled the driver as he jumped out, leaving the door ajar and standing behind it. He spoke perfect Spanish.

"You're a cop?" There was derision in the men's voices as they opened the jaws of the truck and loaded their contraband.

"US State Department."

"Nice car for the State Department."

The *rat-tat-tat* of an AK-47 filled the air. Hands flew above heads, causing the statue to topple into the truck, which triggered its mashing mechanism. To a rhythmic grind, the white stone was pulverized, devoured, and swallowed while the museum guard stood on the dock, mouth ajar, swaying back and forth.

From behind the crate, Dominic glimpsed the bulky upper torso and huge misshapen hands of the driver, Diego Velasquez. He hovered behind the open car door and pointed his weapon at the men. Glaring headlights made it difficult for Dominic to get a bead on Velasquez, and if he missed, his Ruger was no match for an assault rifle, a weapon Dominic knew held at least twenty-four more rounds. And Velasquez could easily have a banana clip or one magazine taped to the other.

"Change my fucking tire." Velasquez waved at the men.

Like frightened children, they scampered down the stairs. Velasquez opened the trunk and stood behind the car. Dominic couldn't see shit. All he could do was listen. One of the so-called garbage guys, the shorter of the two, stepped away from the car into Dominic's line of vision and edged his way toward the corner of the museum.

"On the ground, you sonofabitch." Velasquez's voice boomed from behind the open trunk.

Dominic could imagine the stubby little man's terror as he stretched out on the concrete between the lowrider and the dock, his head near the car, exactly as Velasquez had commanded. Within seconds, two shots rang out, and the small man's body flew into spasms before it wilted onto the pavement.

A bilious acid rose in Dominic's throat as if he'd been slammed in the gut again. The gun's report wasn't the deafening racket made by the AK. Velasquez had murdered the man with Dominic's SIG Sauer.

"Just to make sure you don't get any ideas," Velasquez said to the other man. Although Dominic couldn't see, he heard the clink of a tool. The surviving thief was most likely using it to remove the tire from the trunk. The museum guard watched, making no move to touch his holstered gun. Dominic didn't blame him. Velasquez was a raving psycho.

"Take a look." Velasquez flashed Dominic's badge at the guard. "You're going to help me find my man. He's tall, with a ponytail, wearing jeans."

"*Si, señor.*"

"He's armed, so shoot first. Ask questions later, as they say in the movies. If you kill him, my government will pay twenty-five thousand."

"*Si, señor.*"

"Search that side of the museum. I'll take the front."

When Velasquez took off in the opposite direction, Dominic suppressed an impulse to stand and shoot him in the back. Luke's words "*You're too smart for that shit*" reminded him that if he did so, he'd have to face the clueless guard, who now trotted past him and who'd just been offered a bundle to kill Dominic. His job was to get out of this with Velasquez in custody and find out who else was involved.

Dominic waited until Velasquez and the guard disappeared, then he crept to the dock. Once inside the loading area, he searched for a switch to close the garage door, but he found none. The thief glanced up from the tire project and yelled for Velasquez. Dominic dashed into the museum through a paneled door. In the flash before he locked and bolted it, he saw Velasquez hurtling toward him.

Gripping the Ruger, Dominic figured one shot into the alarm pad would set it off and might bring help. He aimed at the pad, but it wasn't his own gun he heard. Explosive fire followed by piercing alarms assailed his ears. Fleeing from the bullet-riddled door down a basement hall, he reached a wide stone stairway and sprinted upward three steps at a time. At the top, he scanned a large, square room dimly lit by outside lamps glimmering through pane-glass windows. White marble floors reflected the exterior light and made it easy to see arched doors between the columns bordering the other three sides of the room. No sign of an office or a phone. From his previous visit to the museum, Dominic recalled that the doors led to exhibition galleries.

Velasquez bounded into the room. Dominic braced himself behind a column. As Velasquez circled, coming closer and closer, Dominic darted for the nearest gallery, found its door locked, and spent two bullets blowing it open. The shot caused a delicate chandelier in the main room to fall and shatter onto the floor, a tinkling crash above the alarm's piercing din. As he ducked into the gallery, Dominic heard Velasquez fire. Another chandelier bit the dust.

A hissing sound followed. Spurts of cold water jetted from strategic spigots, and there was no escaping the deluge. Shirt, jeans, and hair drenched, Dominic adjusted his eyes to the gray gallery and walls filled with Francisco Goya prints depicting the horrors of war. Dominic had seen a similar exhibit at a Madrid summer program for Hispanic kids, and he'd never forgotten the haunted faces of Spanish soldiers being executed by the French.

Now here he was, caught in his own little war. Any second, Velasquez would be in the gallery. There was no other exit. Dominic fell to the floor behind a bench situated in the middle of the room. He had clear aim at the doorway and would nail the bastard the instant he showed himself. Screw the high-minded idea of taking Velasquez alive.

Through the downpour, Velasquez peered around the doorjamb. Dominic fired. His mark disappeared for a second, then Velasquez plunged into the gallery, blasting his AK-47 around the room. Dominic shot again, three times in rapid succession. Velasquez sank to the floor, flailing for a brief time before he went still. Dominic waited for several minutes, then he made a cautious approach, circled from behind, and kicked the Russian weapon away from Velasquez's body, but as Dominic bent to search for his badge, Velasquez raised his left hand and fired the SIG.

Searing heat ripped through Dominic's femur. He popped two more slugs into Velasquez, puncturing his temple. The gallery whirled in a blaze of red pain. Dominic heard yelling and the clap of footsteps. His eardrums throbbed from the reports, and soaked strands of hair fell from his ponytail onto his forehead. As he staggered through the door, a horde of police charged him, weapons drawn, shouting for him to put down his gun. More crashing sounds echoed from the main room, and electrical sparks sent intermittent light into the gallery.

"I'm with the US State Department," he choked, waving the Ruger above his head.

Dominic didn't see the shooter, but he felt a bite in his chest as if someone had packed his lungs with dry ice. He careened onto the floor outside the gallery. Blood in his throat and a squeezing implosion each time he tried to speak hindered his chance to convince these men of his innocence. Last thing he saw was the uniformed guard grinning from ear to ear, the barrel of his gun ten feet from Dominic's forehead.

"There's no reward, *hombre*," Dominic rasped. "There's no reward."

THIRTY-SEVEN

Sometime before dawn, Luke awakened, startled, fumbling for the gun on his bedside table, determined to stop a tragedy. His dream had been haunted with his mother's voice. He was a kid again, bolting from his bedroom at the sound of her screams, her pleas, the last utterances she'd made before death. His skin crawled. Sweating, he sat up and looked around.

Dull with first light, Luke's bedroom was a peaceful contrast to his chaotic slumber. Hoping he could catch another hour's sleep in spite of the nightmare, he groped for his blanket, caught beneath the warm body nestled beside him. "That does it," he said, giving the cover hog a jab in the ribs and wrenching the blanket from his hefty new housemate. Andre snorted and peered at him with sleepy eyes, closing his lids as if dismissing Luke's annoyance.

Luke had fallen into bed at some unknown hour after he'd left the scene at Obispa's. But before he dozed off, he'd given strict orders to the Dane and to Dominic's hound, Horace, to sleep on the floor. At least Horace had the sense to obey, but then again, with his girth, Luke doubted if the basset could hoist himself onto the mattress.

Anxious about an ambiguous concern floating out there just beyond his reach, Luke gave up on the forty winks. He showered, washing the dream away but never the memory. After dressing in gray slacks and a white button-down shirt, he shuffled into the kitchen, poured the coffee he'd set on a timer the night before, and spent a few minutes at the breakfast table sipping his favorite Italian brew. At 6:30 a.m., he checked with his office to see if they'd identified the fax numbers Dominic had sent last night.

The department's night clerk had indeed traced the numbers that confirmed Randall Cole's theory. Just as the lawyer had predicted, the fax numbers were county health departments located statewide in Texas's large cities: Houston, San Antonio, El Paso, Ft. Worth, Dallas, and Austin. Regardless of Elizabeth Grant's opinion of Cole, he was useful to Luke.

Punching Dominic's cell, Luke got a recording and left a lengthy message.

"Yo, Lone Ranger. The fax numbers are urban health departments like your best buddy, Cole, told us. Arrange with Captain Leál, the *Federalis* in Juárez, to hold Velasquez for questioning. And by the way, Dom, great work." Luke chuckled. "And now, a surprise for you, man. I completed Horace's adoption forms after you left and brought him home with me like I promised. He can't wait to see you." Luke hesitated, thinking how to deliver the next piece of information without setting Dominic off. "Scope out the eateries down there, bud. I have orders to join you. See you around five."

Luke clicked off, thinking his partner must have had a long night. Usually when Dominic was in hot pursuit, he was up before dawn, high on the thrill of the hunt. Luke considered calling Lourdes Ortiz with El Paso PD to see if forensics had found anything interesting from Banderas's office, but he remembered she had a boatload of kids at home. He'd wait until at least 8:30 a.m., a more civil hour, to contact her.

Stretching his long legs, Luke reviewed the list of health departments until his cell phone vibrated. Dominic had probably been in the shower when he'd rung him. Luke checked the caller ID. Elizabeth Grant. Well, well. This should be good.

"You're up early," Luke said. "Have a good run?"

"The run of my life."

Still annoyed by her prickly behavior, Luke was tempted to send a zinger over the airwaves, but Elizabeth's voice quavered. As she described her running saga, he stood and poured more coffee.

"Mola was sending you a message," he said when she'd finished. "You must be getting under his skin."

"Did you have Sergeant Buendía follow me?"

"Never heard of the guy."

"He's with HPD."

"That would be Javi Padilla's work."

"Buendía said he was ordered to tail me last night, but HPD

doesn't have the manpower to watch me during the day." Her concern apparent, Elizabeth continued. "I'm on my way to Austin, and I'm worried about Kate. Can she check in with you today until I get home?"

"Sure." Luke worried about Kate's hostility last night. "If she'll speak to me."

"Believe me, she's scared. I told her and Alex to go straight to my mom's when they got up. I let them sleep in because they were up so late with me. I hope that wasn't a mistake." Elizabeth sighed. "I put the alarm on and alerted the neighborhood patrol."

"Give Kate my contact info," Luke said, and, as an added precaution, he scribbled Elizabeth's mother's number.

"I wouldn't leave town, but I have a hunch about the ownership of those cantinas," she said. "So I'm off to the state comptroller's office for some research."

"My secretary did a thorough ownership review and came up with zilch."

"I'm pulling into the airport now. How 'bout I give you details when I deliver the goods?"

"Fine with me," he said. "I'll call the comptroller's gatekeeper, Fernell Hollis, and tell him to cut you some slack. He can be very difficult."

"Thanks. I don't have much fight left in me."

Luke didn't want to hear Elizabeth talk like that. He'd become attached to her fight mentality and radioactive energy. "Take care of yourself, lady. You've been through hell."

"Thanks." Her voice snapped to a more upbeat note. "Oh, and Luke, Zadie Gutierrez agreed to see me tomorrow afternoon."

"You changed your mind?"

"I was wrong. You were right. She knows the murderers."

"Yes, she does, and Zadie's terrified of Mola now. If you can play that card, sell her on witness protection, it'd be icing on the cake for me."

After Luke hung up, he left a voice message for Fernell Hollis at the comptroller's office, and then for Javi. He was curious about the anti-gang director's reason for a tail on Elizabeth and why he hadn't informed Luke when they'd seen each other at Obispa's last night. But then, it had been a grisly day.

In dire need of a rote activity, Luke dished out scoops of dry dog food for Andre, drooling as usual, and Horace, who was sniffing the bedroom floor. At the mere sound of their food hitting the dishes, the dogs hammered into the kitchen, Andre galloping and Horace skittering across the hardwood. He coaxed the dogs into the terraced backyard, set their water and food in the shade on the patio, and hurried for his truck. Luke had a premonition things were starting to pop on this case.

It was seven a.m. when he arrived at his office, the Mickey Leland Building, a twenty-story dark-brick affair named in honor of the late Texas congressman. On the elevator, he checked his cell. No calls. After he'd settled at his desk, he rang Dominic again. Nothing.

"Luke." Abby, his assistant, peeked around the corner.

"What're you doing here so early?"

"Today's my son's spelling bee, so I came in at the crack of dawn to keep up with you before I leave."

"Tell him I said good luck," he said. "Things are wild with these two murders, and other crimes going down in the *barrio*. Dom's in El Paso, and I can't get a hold of him."

"That's weird." Abby cocked her head and knitted her brow. "Oops, almost forgot. Javi Padilla's on line three."

After the effigy ordeal at Obispa's, Padilla must be as tired as Luke, but a prickly irritation in the anti-gang director's voice told him something else was eating him besides a sleepless night.

"Someone got to Zadie Gutierrez."

"Goddammit."

"Cyanide. Looks like she took it herself."

Luke glanced at Abby waving from the doorway and shot her a questioning look.

"There's a teenage boy in the waiting room," she said. "His name is Alex."

"Padilla, I'll call you back. Something's up." Squeezing past Abby, he strode down the hall. His eyes scanned the reception area and landed on Alex Sifuentes, gawping at the poster of bin Laden, still hanging on the wall, the red X still across his face.

"Hey, Alex."

Alex jumped at the sound of Luke's voice. The boy's dark-circled eyes spoke of no sleep, but his hair was combed, still damp with water. He wore fresh jeans and a nice olive T-shirt, no doubt the work of Kate Grant, who'd hovered over him like a mother hen during their difficult conversation last evening.

"Come on in," Luke said, speaking in Spanish. He led the way to his office, closed the door, and gestured to a nondescript government-issue chair. Instead of going behind his desk, he leaned against it and remained close to Alex, who appeared frazzled. "What's up?"

"I've been thinking. Maybe, if we contact Father Chiabras, he can help us find Santiago."

"Great idea."

Tapping his foot, Alex jiggled his leg. Luke felt certain he hadn't come there to tell him about Father Chiabras. "I heard about Elizabeth Grant," Luke said, hoping to get the kid to talk.

Alex elevated his chin and drew a deep breath through his nostrils. "I had a bad feeling last night, and I should have warned her. But Kate and I left. I didn't know *la señora* went to run."

"How long have you known *Señora* Grant, Alex?"

"Three days."

"Then you may know she doesn't change her mind once she's decided to do something."

Alex grinned.

"So even if you had told her about your bad feeling, I bet she would've gone running anyway."

"It's possible. But I stayed up all night guarding Kate's room to make sure nothing happened to her." Stretching, he leaned forward with his elbows on his knees. "And nothing did."

"Now I see why you look so pooped." Luke was curious how the hell this Guatemalan kid had made it to his office on his own, but he thought better of asking until the poor guy got some groceries in his stomach.

"Have you had breakfast?"

Alex wet his lips, his eyes wide. "No, *señor* ."

Luke took the boy's apparent astonishment at his offer of food as a sign of how few people had been kind to him.

"Let's go. There's a great restaurant in the underground."

"I don't understand the 'underground.'"

"Tunnels underneath these big buildings where people shop, eat, and never have to deal with traffic or weather. You'll like it. I promise."

"*Sí, señor.*" Alex's answer held no joy, and when he stood, his hands trembled as they dangled by his side, brushing against the fabric of his new jeans.

They took the escalator to the basement, then meandered through the Louisiana Street tunnel filled with colorful storefront displays: trendy clothing, makeup, leather briefcases, and the ubiquitous cell phones. Because of the hour, iron burglar bars still secured their windows and doors.

Luke directed Alex into a funky breakfast hangout for Houston's early risers, yuppies, and those who had yet to go to bed. Sepia photographs of Main Street, circa 1900, and the vanishing Fourth Ward African American community hung above brown leather booths bordered with brass nails. A mint-green concrete floor gleamed beneath rows of bronze-colored globes shedding light from above.

Short-order cook and owner Aloysius Turnbull waved at Luke from behind the counter. Since the restaurant wasn't crowded, Aloysius brought menus himself, and Alex's eyes widened at the sight of the beefy black man dressed in a Hawaiian shirt, black pants, white apron, and starched chef's hat perched above his porcine face. As Aloysius bellowed the specials, Luke translated for Alex.

When he finished, Alex glanced Aloysius. "I learn to speak English."

"That's right, my man." Aloysius slapped his huge paw across Alex's back. "Welcome to the US of A. This morning, you're gonna eat real soul food. It'll put meat on those bones of yours. I recommend the short stack, grits, and the one-eyed egg."

Alex shifted in the booth and smiled.

The cook pointed at a plastic bottle filled with rich brown syrup. "Homemade molasses. Best you'll ever eat." After Aloysius informed Luke of the latest underground gossip, he lumbered off to greet other customers.

"Soul food is best prepared by African Americans," Luke explained. "It's their heritage, like tortillas are Hispanic." Then he read the menu aloud and urged Alex to order anything he wanted.

A quick study, Alex absorbed the culinary information, then decided on the special Aloysius had recommended. "*Señor* Luke," he said in Spanish after the waitress took their orders. "You're the nicest man I've met beside Father Chiabras."

"Well, thank you, Alex. I've heard how much you admire Father Chiabras, so I consider that a compliment." Luke felt buoyant, as if he were ascending into this kid's pantheon of saints.

A young waitress with cornrows tipped in red beads and silver rings in her nose smacked tumblers of orange juice onto the table along with a cup of joe for Luke. Alex stared at the huge plastic glass for some time before plunging his straw into the orange pulpy liquid. With his lips still wrapped around the straw, he cast somber eyes at Luke.

After a drawn-out sip of juice, Alex said, "In Guatemala City,

I was once a good fighter for the gang, but after three years, I'm afraid I've forgotten things." His voice fell into a whisper, and when he pursed his lips, the corners of his mouth slipped downward. "It's a long time not to fight. Still, I am my brother's keeper, and for this reason, I'll join the Latin Angels."

"Brother's keeper, huh?" Luke paused. His gut soured at the thought of sending a super kid like Alex into the Angels. He had to find someone else. "Let's wait a couple days," he said. "My partner, Dominic, has discovered evidence that may help us get to those gang leaders."

"I remember *Señor* Dominic from the cantina. He has a ponytail and tried to make that mean Zadie to shut up."

"Yep. That's him." Luke grinned in spite of his apprehension about Dominic's mysterious silence.

Alex poured a string of molasses over his golden pancakes, grits, and even the fried egg. While the kid scarfed down the pile of food, Luke picked at a bowl of granola, knowing full well if Aloysius spotted him, he'd get a mound of harassment. He swallowed a couple of bites, then punched Dominic's cell again with the same frustrating result. Lourdes Ortiz was next. As he looked up her number on his phone index, an incoming call caught his attention. At last. The rogue had surfaced.

"Luke?" Abby's voice was shaky.

"What's up?"

"You need to come to the office."

"Why?"

"Please, just come back."

"What's going on?"

"I can't . . ." Her sentence melted into muffled sounds.

"Luke?" It was James Clark, senior agent in charge of the Houston district.

Luke suspected what was coming before James ever gave the sketchy events leading to Dominic's murder. Luke's pulse raced. Pain throbbed in his chest, a deep sorrow cut through him.

"A cop shot him," James said. "A cop . . ."

Silence and more silence as Luke grappled for words. Dominic's grinning face swam before his eyes, and he heard his partner's voice somewhere above the clatter of dishes and chattering conversations. Finally, he said to James, "I want to tell his mother. He was her youngest son." Not waiting for a reply, Luke hung up.

Alex stopped eating, fork suspended in midair. "Something bad happened."

"Dominic is dead. Murdered," said Luke, stumbling from the booth. He pulled some bills from his wallet and handed them to Alex. "When you're finished, pay at the register and come to my office. Can you find your way?"

"*Sí.*" Alex nodded. "I know how you feel, *Señor* Luke."

"Yes, you do," Luke said. "Dominic was like my brother."

"It's a terrible thing."

"Yeah," Luke groaned. "You and I'll have a good talk later. For now, Abby, the woman you met when you came to see me, will drive you to Kate's grandmother's house. Kate's staying there too." Even in his grief, Luke felt a deep compassion for the teary boy who sat motionless in the booth. "And Alex, one more thing. Forget the Latin Angels."

THIRTY-EIGHT

The air was delightfully cool on this crisp December morning, the Austin office buildings adazzle with holiday lights and greenery. Elizabeth had been so preoccupied she'd missed the season altogether, but in spite of her aching body, she now tingled with the prospect of Christmas. Kate and Alex could help decorate the house, and maybe she'd even bake cookies—Obispa would like that move. She wondered if Alex had ever picked out a tree. Doubtful. This year would be different for everyone.

When Elizabeth entered the state comptroller's office located on bureaucracy row in downtown Austin, she came face to face with the gatekeeper Luke had mentioned, Fernell Hollis, a swishy little man who commanded the research center. He wore a pressed plaid shirt with sleeves rolled to his elbows, black wool slacks, shiny boots that looked like they'd never seen the pavement, and silver earrings in both ears. His sepia-colored toupee didn't match the brown hair on the sides of his pinched little head, and his birdlike features included a beaked nose, thin lips, and gray, darting eyes.

Fernell took her business card, dropping it on a pile, not bothering to read it. He snickered at her bandaged palms and dismissed her presence with a flick of his wrist.

"Work over there," he said, directing Elizabeth to a sterile cubicle where he issued brief instructions on how to locate a company. Thanking him, she removed her coat and began. An hour later, she was mired in computer hell with no new information. Elizabeth, a woman of action, preferred field investigations and usually delegated daylong research projects to underlings, but in this case, the stakes were too high to miss any clue. After another futile fifteen minutes, she glanced around the corner of the dreary cubicle to see if Fernell Hollis was busy. As far as she could tell, he was busy rearranging stacks of paper.

Armed with the list of cantinas, she approached him. "I can't find these businesses in your database," she said. "Could you help me?"

Fernell peered at the list, pranced to the computer where she'd been working, and plopped into the chair. "Corporation name, please."

Elizabeth's face flushed with irritation.

"I don't know the corporation name. That's why I'm here."

"Well, you must have something. Employer Identification Number?"

"No, I don't."

"Then, pardon my French, you are screwed."

He flounced back to his desk, and Elizabeth tramped after him. She dug her heels in, determined not to move one inch until he helped her.

"Did the State Department call you about me?"

"Nooooo," he said, drawing out the word until he sounded like a prissy teenager. Glancing at her card, he continued, "Since when does the State Department deal with reporters?"

"Agent Santa Maria should've called you. Maybe you have a message?"

"Haven't had time to check."

"I'll call him for you." Whipping out her cell, Elizabeth was so frustrated she could have slapped the little jerk right out of his chair.

"No cell phones allowed. Go outside to make calls."

Her ire ratcheted to ten on a scale of one to ten. Elizabeth turned off her phone and glared. "Look, Mr. Hollis, these cantinas promote child prostitution. They aren't the good guys here. I'm the good guy."

"Whah-ell, that's a new one." Fernell shifted his shoulders and uncrossed his legs. "Give me the names again," he said.

Surprised at his change of heart, Elizabeth trailed Fernell back to her cubicle, where she watched over his shoulder as he tried to trace ownership of *Zona Azul*, *Noche Azul*, *Hurican Azul*, *Caliente Azul*, *Carnivál*, and *Vocan Azul*.

"What's with this *azul* fetish?" he asked.

"It's Spanish for 'blue,' but I haven't cracked it."

Fernell concentrated on the screen, his fingers clicking faster than Elizabeth could think. She probed her brain for anything that could help him.

"I've done Google searches, but these places aren't even in the phone book, much less on the Internet," she said. "I've learned about them either by visiting myself or from people in the *barrios* who want to see them shut down."

After thirty minutes, he'd come up with zero. Fernell shook his head, and Elizabeth thought he actually looked disappointed. A queue of disgruntled people were waiting at his desk to see him or to be directed to other destinations.

"Be back in a bit," he said.

"Here's a copy of my list in case you think of something," she said.

"I'll be working on it."

Fernell tucked the information in his pocket and returned to his command center. Stretching her arms, Elizabeth longed to put her head on the desk, go to sleep, forget life for a while. Earlier she'd been energized by the anticipation of discovery. Now she was discouraged and flat-out beat. She checked her watch. Eleven a.m. Her eyeballs felt as if they were shrinking to pin size inside their sockets, and her stomach called out, *"Feed me, you idiot—a roll, a bowl of cereal, a bag of chips, anything."*

"Is there a café around here?" she called to Fernell.

"Yummy food just across the street."

"I'm taking a break," she said, glancing at the list of cantinas again before she filed it in her briefcase. She was missing something and just couldn't figure it out.

From the lobby, Elizabeth spotted flowered curtains in the windows of the down-home coffee shop Fernell had recommended. She buttoned her coat against a brisk wind, crossed the street, and ducked into the cozy café. After ordering a bagel, orange juice, and black coffee, she studied the street scene. The state legislature was in special session, so things were hopping, cabs darting up and down the street, and people bustling to and from the capitol building. Elizabeth downed two aspirin and wiped her mouth as her gaze wandered around the café. A plump waitress cleaning the countertop, oak chairs with tiny checked cushions, and Fernell Hollis dashing toward her, his gray eyes bugging.

"Ms. Grant, I just thought of something," he said, breathless. "Maybe there's a corporate name on the cantinas' liquor licenses."

"Of course!" Elizabeth's exhaustion waned with a fresh rush of expectation.

Within minutes, Fernell had ushered her into the Texas Alcoholic Beverage Commission, where he cut red tape with the TABC's taciturn receptionist. Elizabeth settled beside him in another sepulchral booth and watched his deft fingers dig into a database. Through Fernell's expert maneuvering, the computer screen revealed the cantinas' individual licenses, and then a corporate name.

"*Le Bleu Chèvre*," Elizabeth mused. "The Blue Goat. French this time. Located in El Paso."

"More blue. How apropos," said Fernell. "Says here, Rufino Banderas filed the forms via the Internet, so we won't find a clerk who can describe him. That sucks."

"But this is fantastic. Ever think about investigative reporting?"

He squeezed out a smile.

"Can I get a printout of the licenses?"

"Sure." He pranced off in his elevated boots, fading into the maze of drones—captives in a government hive. In Elizabeth's estimation, Fernell had just been crowned queen bee.

She returned to the computer, double-checking each license. Suddenly stymied, Elizabeth discovered that *Noche Azul* wasn't a company belonging to *Le Bleu Chèvre*. A further search revealed *Aqua Rabino*, the "Aqua Rabbi," was the parent of *Noche Azul*. The owner or owners had cleverly established two corporations. Elizabeth couldn't wait to tell Fernell, who'd been gone for an exasperating fifteen minutes. When he finally bustled down the corridor, his toupee tipped to one side as he waved a handful of papers.

"Printer backed up," he said. "So while I was waiting, I entered all the synonyms for blue: navy, cerulean, turquoise, you name it, into the database, and bingo!" He handed her a fistful of documents. "I found two other Harris County parent companies. Indigo Forest owns several upper-crust restaurants. And Sapphire Desire holds *vaquero* cantinas, probably a group of sleazy strip joints."

"And look at this one in Galveston," Elizabeth said, pointing to *Aqua Mar* on the computer screen. "This 'blue' obsession is freaky."

"Who else but a freak would prostitute kids?"

She caught a hint of the hollow-eyed look she'd seen all too often lately. Fernell cast his eyes toward the floor, and Elizabeth gently touched his arm. "This is a major breakthrough. I can't thank you enough," she said. "Next time I'm in Austin, lunch is on me."

His lips eked out a meager grin as if he weren't sure life would allow him to show a full-tilt smile. "Can't wait," he said, gliding to the door like a supermodel on the catwalk. "I hope you have a juicy expense account."

"Get ready for a feast," she called as he disappeared into the cubicle maze of the TABC.

Stashing the evidence into her briefcase, Elizabeth turned on her cell phone and checked her messages. She noted with alarm that Kate had called seven times. Without bothering to listen to voice mail, she punched Kate's speed dial button.

"Kate?"

Her daughter's voice shrieked into Elizabeth's ear. "Alex is gone. He joined that gang."

She took a deep breath, making every effort to sound calm. "What happened?"

"He called me from a pay phone. Luke's partner was murdered in El Paso last night. Alex said this killing was like his brother's death, and he's going to help Luke catch those guys, even though Luke told him not to join the Angels."

"So he talked to Luke?"

"While I was asleep, he borrowed money from my purse and took a bus to Luke's office."

"Are you sure? I just don't see how—"

"Mom! He's a street kid." Kate sounded as if she were hyperventilating.

Elizabeth's throat constricted, but she employed all her skills not to stoke Kate's panic. "Okay, let's assume Alex is looking for that gang. He may go to that cantina near Obispa's. I'll call the anti-gang director and ask him to have Alex picked up. They do gang sweeps every day."

"They won't hurt him, will they?"

"Absolutely not," Elizabeth said. She was terrified for Alex, and her heart panged with sorrow for Luke, but Kate's safety was paramount at the moment. "Now, tell me where you are."

"Still at home. I was hoping he'd come back."

"I told you to go to Nana's."

"But what about Alex?"

"Listen, Kate. They followed me last night. That means they know where we live. I want you out of that house."

"Yeah, but they could be out there watching."

"I alerted the neighborhood patrol this morning. Call them on the house phone and ask them to take you to Nana's. You're not going to hang up your cell until you get there."

Elizabeth listened the entire time while Kate phoned the patrol, packed a few things before they came for her, and finally arrived at Nana's house with no sign of a stalker.

"Thank God," Elizabeth said when her own mother's voice came on the phone. "I feel like an animal trapped in Austin while the world goes awry in Houston."

"If you don't find another job after this, I'm going to have a heart attack."

Elizabeth smiled. "You always say that."

"This time I mean it," Nana said. "Anyway, my car's ready. We're going to the beach house, and we're not coming home until this nasty thing is over."

"Mom, you're a jewel."

"Don't jewel me. Here's, Kate. She wants to talk."

Kate sounded shaky but more in control than before. "Call me if Alex gets picked up."

"You bet." Elizabeth heard Kate getting into her grandmother's car. The motor purred. She envisioned them pulling out of the drive on their way to the family home on Galveston Bay.

"Mom, I was thinking," Kate continued. "You shouldn't come back to Houston just now with those gang guys after you."

"That's a good idea, Kate. I'll stay here in Austin and call you tonight." Elizabeth paused. "I really wish I was with you and Nana." Awash with remorse for years of selfishness, Elizabeth was beginning to understand how lonely Kate must be with an absentee mother. Before she hung up, her voice cracked. "I love you."

"Love you too."

Elizabeth thoughtfully cradled the phone before she reported the cantina findings to her editor and requested that the *Chronicle* hold the info until the State Department located Banderas. In order to convince her editor, she had to tell her about the exclusive story Luke had promised. Sighing relief when she finally agreed, Elizabeth then left a message for Javi Padilla about Alex.

"He's a great kid, Javi. Keep him safe. Don't put him in a cell with the goons."

The last and most challenging conversation was yet to come. She cringed as she dialed Luke Santa Maria, and with an unsteady voice, Elizabeth expressed her condolences. He sounded weary, his distress palpable as he explained that he'd just talked to Dominic's mother.

"I promised her I'd accompany his body to Houston, so I'm

flying to the border this afternoon." Luke paused. "And I want to see that crime scene."

"God, Luke. Be careful."

"Dominic wasn't supposed to cross the border again. He called me from El Paso."

"Can I do anything to help?" she asked, alive with the grief and fear circling their lives.

"Yeah, meet me tomorrow night after I get home. I'll be in serious need of a margarita."

"I will," said Elizabeth, distracted by thoughts of whether to tell him about Alex.

"I'll call you," he said.

Perceiving a slight uptick in Luke's voice, Elizabeth decided to wait on Alex. Padilla would find him, then she'd tell Luke. Before she signed off, she explained about Rufino Banderas, who'd filed paperwork on the four "blue" corporations that owned the cantinas.

"This matches evidence Dominic discovered before he died," Luke replied. "We're getting closer, sweet Elizabeth."

"Yes, we are." After she said good-bye, Elizabeth sat in the cubicle and tried to recall if in the span of her adult life, anyone had ever called her "sweet."

THIRTY-NINE

Randall Cole took the morning off, remaining at his ranch for Velasquez's report about Dominic Fontana. Light fuzzy with dust motes filtered into his breakfast room, birds chattered in the water oaks lining the porch, and a crisp breeze drifted through open windows. *All's right with the world*, Cole thought, grinning to himself at the idea of Dominic's premature departure from this earth. Since high school, he'd despised the sawed-off, arrogant runt who'd run with the beautiful people in spite of his humble origins.

Muñeca and Mariella cleared the breakfast table, went to the kitchen, and nibbled on *pan dulce*. Cole was glad they'd hit it off. Nothing worse than a harem of squabbling women. He savored a cup of his finest boutique coffee, lit a *Cohiba*, and flipped through a Sotheby's auction catalog on a quest for a John Singer Sargent painting from when the artist lived in Northern Africa. In this particular desert scene, two blue-veiled women were drawing water from a well.

As Cole's eyes lit upon his intended purchase, Tulio Mola sauntered in wearing designer jeans that clung to the contours of his glutes, a gray turtleneck beneath his black leather jacket, and alligator loafers. The smirk on his face said it all. Dominic was dead.

Cole banished Muñeca and Mariella to their well-appointed rooms, where they could play dress-up all day. The arousal medicine he kept feeding them had both girls horny and humping. When he'd built the ranch house, Cole had installed cameras in every room, and one of the enjoyments he cherished was making videos of his girls. He was eager to see what these two did with their time.

Mola's shaved head held obsidian eyes so dark Cole couldn't distinguish the pupils, his stare was unreadable as a cat's, and his mouth hooked to one side as he spoke. The message he delivered was so astounding, Cole rose from his chair. After hearing Mola's account of Dominic's and Velasquez's deaths and the damage inside the museum, Cole threw up his hands.

"That charming museum. Was it ruined?"

"What the fuck." A muscle twitched beneath Mola's nose, his voice was a snarl. "With Velasquez dead, the Juárez Angels are fighting about leadership, and you're worried about a fucking building?"

"Some of those artifacts are irreplaceable," said Cole, refusing to give Mola credit for his accurate assessment of the Juárez situation. In an uneasy silence, Cole considered the significant void caused by Velasquez's untimely departure. "Velasquez was Sandoval's brother, right?

Mola nodded.

"Tell Sandoval to go to the funeral and take over down there until we decide on a replacement."

The gang leader poured a cup of coffee, then resumed his account of the debacle. "Before Velasquez entered the fucking museum, he called the homeboys for backup. When the Angels got there, at least twenty cops were inside shooting up the goddamned place, so they wiped out a garbage man, hot-wired Velasquez's car, and left."

"No witnesses and they have the car. Good."

Mola nodded, dumped sugar in his coffee, and stirred. "In the car, my boys found Marco's body splattered all over the backseat. He was just a kid but one of our best shooters." Mola's words were ripe with hatred.

Cole shook his head, concealing his lack of concern for a fucking teenage shooter.

"They found Fontana's cell in Marco's pocket. We will get his contacts off the SIM card. This afternoon, one of the *cholos* is flying into Hobby with the phone."

Cole had to admit, the dickhead had a brain. "I want the man who delivers the phone to go home immediately. Last thing we need is a Juárez Angel caught in one of Padilla's goddamned sweeps."

"Already covered." Mola sipped his coffee and settled at the table. "And my guy understands not to answer the cell for any reason."

"Who's picking it up from the airport?"

"I am."

"Good." Cole checked his watch. He had a host of afternoon meetings in Houston. "I need to leave. Call me when you get the phone."

Mola rotated his neck, then studied his fingernails. "Mind if I look in on the new cunt I brought you? I can teach her some tricks."

"Ah, you want the lovely Mariella."

Mola gave a half nod.

Puffing the *Cohiba*, Cole blew smoke rings and envisioned a video. "My proposal is this. Fuck Mariella and Muñeca together. Teach both girls your nasty little tricks."

"How generous." Stretching his arms, Tulio Mola stood and removed his jacket.

"Their rooms are down there." Cole gestured to a hallway off the kitchen.

Once in his bedroom, Cole locked the door and checked his video equipment to ensure it was running properly. He stepped into a steaming shower, where he relished the prospect of his late-night, two-on-one entertainment for the week.

*

Midday traffic was light on the way into Houston, and Cole arrived in record time to find Luke Santa Maria in his waiting room. Luke's expression was unabashed misery, burdened with the bad news Cole already knew.

"Luke, good to see you."

Luke shook his hand. "We need to talk in private."

"Of course," Cole said, inserting his security card and ushering the agent through the doorway leading to his office. "What's the matter? Lost your best friend?"

When Luke didn't answer, Cole was even more pleased with his cruel little quip. He imagined Dominic writhing on the floor, bleeding to death, a dozen guns pointed at his head. The fucking Mexican police probably didn't bother to take him to a hospital, since they thought he'd killed a US agent. But it wouldn't do to say those things out loud.

He closed his door and offered Luke a seat. "This must be bad."

"You and Dominic didn't share any lost love, but still, I wanted to tell you in person. Last night he was killed in the line of duty." Luke slumped into the chair.

Cole rounded his desk and mirror-imaged Luke's collapse by falling into his own chair. "You're right. We didn't always see eye to eye, but we go way back."

"It's hard to remember a time when he wasn't in my life," Luke said, filling in the details of Dominic's death.

In feigned anguish, Cole thumped his desk with his fist. "Let me fly you to El Paso. We'll bring him back in my plane."

"Thanks, buddy. The department will handle it. But I need your help on another front. Dominic may have located the owner of the Blue Agave, a man named Rufino Banderas."

"So you talked to Dominic before he died?"

"I missed his message, so the details are sketchy. But I think Banderas is a key link in the chain. I'd appreciate you putting out the word in your network. See if you can get a nose on the guy."

Like taking candy from a baby, Cole thought as Luke outlined what he knew about Banderas's vacant office and the fax numbers.

"Since his office is empty, he could be fictitious."

"If he is, a very competent person is behind the mask," Luke said. "One of my sources discovered information about ownership of those cantinas. Banderas's name is on the documents."

"What else did your source find?"

"I don't have the details yet."

Cole fought the urge to question Luke about the source. His mind raced for a solution to this dilemma. "Can you give me anything else on Banderas?"

"The info is sketchy. Velasquez was the manager of Blue Agave Tile. He could've been Banderas, and he may have been a lawyer. He filed legal papers via the Internet from a Houston-based e-mail service."

Cole nodded. Already his mind was searching for a way to eliminate Luke Santa Maria without bringing the whole fucking State Department down on his head.

FORTY

Alex reasoned that the neighborhood around *Noche Azul* was the best place to begin his quest to join the Latin Angels. Gripping the crumpled paper with Obispa's address, he asked several people which bus went to the *barrio*. He was amazed how many of them spoke Spanish. Within fifteen minutes, a bus with his destination written in the front window rumbled up to the busy corner where he stood. Alex admired its sleek white exterior plastered with new multicolor ads, so different from buses in Guatemala City, dilapidated vehicles navigating crowded streets, spewing sour fumes into ugly air.

When the bus stopped, he raced up the clean rubber stairs. With help from the driver, a skinny black woman, he inserted the correct coins into a meter, then showed her Obispa's address.

"My stop will get you close, but you'll have to walk a few blocks," she said.

Nodding, Alex tried to memorize her words. He'd figure them out after he sat down. Her voice was friendly, not like the drivers in Guatemala City, who would as soon spit on you as give directions. Something told him to be brave and speak English.

"You tell me when get off?"

The driver's generous smile revealed sparkling teeth between glistening pink lips. "Sure thing. You sit right behind me."

"*Muchas gracias, señora.*"

The bus was half-full, mostly Hispanic people carrying small packages, reading newspapers, or eating snacks from brown paper bags. No one threw trash on the floor, no one smoked, and there were no annoying goats or caged parakeets. America, so clean across the *Rio*. A picture of his mother edged into Alex's consciousness. She was smiling on him from heaven.

His sense of direction, not to mention the surroundings, told him they weren't anywhere near Obispa's or *Noche Azul*. The bus made several stops in front of towering glass buildings whose monster shadows darkened the streets. Rows of dull gray warehouses steadily replaced the tall buildings, and a freeway loomed alongside the bus.

Suddenly it hit Alex. The mean times he'd had in the Guatemalan Angels whirred through his mind, and now he was looking to join their *compadres* in the States. To stem his fear, he reminded himself how he'd been a super street fighter, adept with knives and quick with brass knuckles. His job had been to keep a rival gang, *La Sangre Roja*, from invading Angel territory.

Many of the older Latin Angels had prepared, moved, and sold drugs for Honorio Simón, a former trucking magnate who'd become the largest cocaine trafficker in Central America. The Sangres and other rivals envied the Angels' deal with Simón and were always trying to seize a piece of the action. In the end, the beatings and deaths were too much for Alex, and he couldn't stand the thought of Fernando becoming what he'd become. Finally, he'd left the Angels.

As the bus chugged on, Alex continued to second-guess his decision. He begged Fernando to appear and advise him. Glancing around, he spotted young boys giggling in the back row, two whispering old women, and a teenage boy reading a comic. No sign of Fernando. Alex closed his eyes and fashioned an elaborate prayer to the Virgin, but silence flooded his ears and a blank blue haze hung behind his closed lids.

"We're here, sugar," said the bus driver. "It's three blocks down on your right."

Alex shot from the seat. "Three blocks?" he asked.

"Yes, sugar. That way," she said, pointing in the direction of the bus door.

Alex's heart pummeled the walls of his chest as he stepped from the bus into a breezy morning and waved to the driver. "Thank you," he called.

Hesitant to move from the curb where he'd landed, Alex fingered the money in his pocket. Luke had given him twenty, plus twenty from Kate, minus bus fare and breakfast, left him with thirty-two dollars and change. Alex's shoulders slumped when he thought of Kate. He hoped she understood why he had to leave and why he'd borrowed money. With hands stuffed in his jeans, he shuffled along a cracked sidewalk toward Obispa's shaded *barrio* filled with houses much different than Kate's.

At the next corner, he spotted the House of Light down the block and *Noche Azul* on the far end. To avoid any chance Obispa might see him and try to persuade him not to join the Angels, Alex slipped over to the next street. Colorful clapboard houses with covered porches lined the road. One of the houses had a painted sign of an eye floating in the palm of a red hand. Alex decided a fortune-teller lived there. In another yard, a man working amid stacks of scrap metal used a hand torch to repair wrecked cars.

Farther down the block, a gnarled old woman dressed in a worn floral housedress sat in her yard encircled by racks of blouses, pants, and skirts. Interested people tried on clothes, sifted through blankets, books, and silverware, and carried furniture to their cars. Alex was drawn to a table piled with folded black jackets, maybe leather. Remembering the bills in his pocket, Alex moved closer, then touched a shiny jacket adorned with silver studs shaped like pyramids. To look like a tough guy, he needed this. Moments later, Alex dished out twelve dollars to the haggard woman, who didn't even thank him as she stuffed the bills into a beaded pink purse. In spite of her grumpy disposition, he felt jubilant.

As Alex slid his arms into the sleeves he sensed a new courage, but when he zipped the jacket, a silver stud fell from the collar onto the ground. Disappointed at first, he decided the flaw would give his jacket character. Alex picked up the stud, studied its sharp protrusions, and pushed it deep into his pocket. Now he was ready to find the gang.

Walking around the block, he noticed a big change in the neighborhood. Splintered lumber was heaped on both sides of the street as if a giant boot had crushed the houses. Alex stepped off the sidewalk to avoid broken beer bottles, passed deserted homes with boarded windows, and ended up at a vacant lot overgrown with weeds and littered with rusted cans. The road had come to an end.

Two teenage boys sat on a curb in front of the lot, cigarettes dangling from their mouths. The taller kid had a spiked purple rooster comb, the other guy's hair cascaded down his back in the longest braid Alex had ever seen. Now he was sorry he'd let Kate talk him into a haircut.

His mind dug into the neat hair problem and how to solve it if the boys were Latin Angels. He could tell these *cholos* he'd been forced to live with an American family who made him cut his hair, so he ran away. The boys would understand. And thank God his tattoo, the mark of an Angel, would save him. Alex sucked a quick breath and introduced himself in Spanish.

The boys' names were Chi and Howler, new initiates into the Angels. Purple-ringed eyes, bruised cheekbones, and scabbed knuckles told of the beatings they'd endured to attain their status. They spoke very bad Spanish but enough to communicate, so Alex kept at it in Spanish.

"You're on our turf, *hombre*," Chi said. His neat braid and short wrestler's body contrasted with Howler's lanky limbs, wild hair, and lack of any visible muscle.

"I've come to join the Angels," Alex said, showing his tattoo. "I escaped from Guatemala after a death squad killed my brother."

"That's heavy shit, man," Howler said. "The cops here aren't that bad."

Alex could tell he was making a favorable impression. Plus, he had mounds of experience over these beginners. "How do I join?"

"We're waiting for Sandoval, *el jefe*, to take us to target practice," said Howler. "He'll tell you."

"Target practice?" Alex asked.

"Guns, man," Chi explained. "So we can take out our enemies."

"Yeah," Alex said, disguising his ignorance of firearms. "Who are your enemies?"

"Rival *cholos* who sell drugs, pussy, or protection in our territory," Chi said.

"Up till now," Howler said, removing a white tube from his inside jacket pocket, "I have used my cement glue to blind and roll those fuckers, but our leader, Tulio Mola, says we must become shooters."

"You heard of him?" Chi slatted his eyes and came closer to Alex.

"No, but I'm new in this country."

"Don't fuck with Mola." Howler thrust his fist in Alex's face, the cement glue wedged between his fingers, the tip aimed at Alex's eyes. "Or you'll be a dead faggot with feathers in your butt."

"Yeah, don't fuck with Mola, or his main man Sandoval." Chi's eye drifted over Alex's shoulder. "There he is now."

Alex assumed the belligerent stance he'd perfected years ago, but when he got a load of Sandoval, his bravado faltered. The bald, muscled man glared at him as he stepped from a four-door black Mercedes. He wore a dark T-shirt with a colorful icon centered on the chest. At first, Alex thought the image was Our Lady of Guadalupe, but on close examination, he saw Santa Muerte, the old skeleton woman, worshipped by certain Mexican *Indios*. Santa Muerte posed as the Holy Virgin surrounded by light rays and standing on the head of a child's skeleton instead of a cherub.

Fists clenched, Sandoval walked toward Alex. Certain he would be beaten, Alex stood his ground, trying to think about Fernando's death, when he'd endured the ultimate pain. Sandoval gut-punched Alex so hard he tasted something foul rising from his stomach. Grabbing the collar of his jacket, the gang leader shoved Alex toward the back of the Mercedes.

"Open my trunk," Sandoval yelled at Chi, who immediately obeyed.

"Get the fuck in there," Sandoval commanded.

Alex crawled inside. After the door slammed, he curled his knees into his chest. His ears rang, and he thought he'd vomit, but at least he was away from Sandoval. He could hear the gangster dress down the boys for talking to a stranger. Suddenly, Alex remembered Luke's business card and Obispa's address stashed in his jeans pocket. In spite of the spiking pain in his stomach, he kneaded his fingers into his pocket and retrieved the incriminating information. He had committed Luke's phone number to memory, and he knew Obispa's address, so he tore up and swallowed the papers piece by piece. With every bite, Alex shuddered at the thought—if he forgot one digit of Luke's number, he'd lose contact with the only man who could save him.

Sandoval's car hummed as it began to travel at a moderate speed. Remembering how he'd calculated distance and time while enduring the trip *norte*, Alex concentrated. He'd need to tell Luke the approximate location of where they took him. They rode for about five minutes, so Alex estimated they were just a few miles from Obispa's house. Shortly after he made this assumption, the car halted and Sandoval opened the trunk. Chi and Howler stood behind him, both boys scowling, their friendly attitudes vanished. Without a word, Sandoval's close-set eyes scrutinized every inch of Alex's body. Out of respect, Alex didn't look at the gangster, nor did he flinch a muscle or indicate the terror that enveloped him.

"Get out," Sandoval said.

Alex pulled himself from the trunk. Standing straight as if he were a soldier reporting for duty, he thrust his tattooed hand at Sandoval. "I want to rejoin the Angels," he said in Spanish, not trusting his rough English and wanting to speak with utmost confidence.

"Take him to the pit," said Sandoval. His voice grated as if he'd had no sleep.

The boys jerked Alex by the arms and led him toward a metallic warehouse, its shiny walls glinting in the sunlight.

Alex surmised the pit would be a test to see if he had the courage to be an Angel, and he knew he did. When he was ten years old, he'd joined the gang, and since Fernando was only seven at the time, Alex had begged the Angels to beat him for both of them. He suffered a merciless thrashing, broken ribs, cuts on his face that became infected, and blood in his urine for days. Father Chiabras saw him dragging around the streets, gave him salve to heal his face and pills for the injury to his kidneys. After that hellacious time, Alex had become a skilled combatant, but he'd never flogged a kid at initiation, nor had he ever used the power in his fists on a younger boy.

Inside the warehouse, a damp musk odor greeted his nostrils. Steel girders crisscrossed the ceiling, and an eerie glow radiated from bald bulbs dangling from wires. Stacks of rectangular boxes stretched the length of the rear wall. Alex surmised the boxes contained weapons or drugs. To his left, a shooting range consisted of six human silhouettes lining the wall below a row of intense fluorescent lights. The floors were white linoleum except for a spot to his right, a roped-off section the size of a boxing ring. That place was, no doubt, the pit.

The three boys ducked under the ropes, and Sandoval leered from the sideline, his arms folded across his chest. He pulled a clanging cell phone from his pocket, spoke in low tones, and never shifted his hooded gaze from Alex.

Chi nodded for Alex to take a corner, while he and Howler faced him from the opposite side and removed their jackets. Alex watched closely to see if Howler palmed the cement glue, but he didn't. Slinging his jacket on the post behind him, Alex caught sight of a thin metal strip on the floor near his foot. He knocked his jacket to the ground close to the strip and grabbed the sharp metal, then he snatched the stud from his pocket. As he hung up his jacket again, he caught Sandoval's amused expression. Alex was certain the gangster had seen him pinch the strip.

Chi and Howler ambled toward him, Howler in the lead but walking with less confidence than his shorter, more muscular *compadre*. Alex surveyed Chi's balled fists and bulging forearms tightened into knots. Not a second to waste. The way to win was to get the jump, hit hard, finish fast.

Lowering his head like a bull, Alex charged Howler, who pivoted and crashed into Chi, tipping both boys off balance. Before Chi could push him off, Alex used Howler as a shield, forcing both boys into the ropes.

"Get off me," Chi yelled at Howler, but Alex had Howler around the neck and kept shoving. Howler seemed broken by Alex's preemptive attack. Alex felt the slack in the boy's body and the stumble in his steps as he took the stud from his pocket and screwed its point into the back of Howler's neck, causing him to scream and flail. Chi tried to shove him into Alex, but Alex held firm.

"I hate this," Alex said, removing the stud and reaching to the front of Howler's neck, this time stabbing him beneath his chin near the place where he swallowed. Howler lurched, and blood smeared onto Chi, still leaning into the ropes. In that instant, Alex backhanded Howler, a goner grasping at his neck and slipping to the floor, then he kneed Chi in the groin. When Chi doubled over, Alex seized him in a head hold and thrust the sharp metal strip at his throat.

"What are the rules here, *Señor* Sandoval?" said Alex, breathless, knowing full well if Sandoval ordered him to kill Chi, he couldn't do it.

Lighting a cigarette and stepping into the ring, Sandoval began to laugh so hard tears came to his eyes, then he made the Sign of the Cross, causing Alex to think the man was loco.

The gangster crossed the ring and jutted his lips to Alex's ear. "Let him go," he whispered.

Relieved, Alex loosened his grip on Chi, who stumbled to the corner near Howler.

Puffing his cigarette and stroking the green rosary beads around his neck, Sandoval breathed into Alex's face. His teeth were like the white squares of chewing gum, as if they weren't real, and he smelled of tobacco and fresh limes.

"Last night, I lost my brother and another Angel who was a great shooter," he said. "So I prayed to *Santa Muerte* to send me more good men. Today, she has begun to answer my prayers."

FORTY-ONE

It was early evening when Luke arrived at the El Paso morgue. He stood alone in a room permeated with formaldehyde, saying his good-byes to Dominic Fontana and remembering better times. Running his fingers across Dominic's cheek, he tumbled into melancholy, cursing the corpse, a betrayal to his friend's vitality, his offbeat ways, his very soul. Regardless of Luke's preaching about Dominic's outrageous behavior, Luke knew that his own drive had frequently fed off his friend's intensity, love of danger, and disdain for authority. Between them, they'd experienced a unique partnership, and now Luke felt a vast emptiness coupled with a conviction that no one could replace him.

His eyes stung as he gripped Dominic's shoulder. "I told your mom this afternoon."

When an ashen-skinned orderly wheeled another body into the room, Luke nodded, concealing his grief, and occupied his mind with details of Dominic's murder. He'd been shot three times, once with his own gun and twice with the museum guard's .38 revolver. The bullet wound in Dominic's temple indicated he hadn't suffered a lengthy death, and Luke found consolation in that.

"Don't worry about Horace, Dom, he's with me," Luke whispered. "And the kid, Alex. You were right about his courage. In fact, you were right about a lot of things."

Luke reminisced as if he were conversing with Dominic in person. They used to talk about the girls at Canyon City High School and their good times in Palo Duro Canyon where they'd hung out at

Randall Cole's ranch and on and on. *Enough*, Luke said to himself.

Reluctantly, he left the morgue.

A mellow white moon illuminated the night as he drove his rent car to the Juárez crime scene, hoping to assuage his grief and dull his anger by solving the senseless killing. He parked at the museum outside a cordoned area peppered by a cadre of Mexican police officers and military men, who were now showing themselves as guardians of the historic building, ensuring no looters would steal the precious artifacts. But when it came to protecting humans, their performance was pathetic. God knows, some of them could be members of the Juárez or Sinaloa cartels dressed in confiscated uniforms.

Through the museum's glass-walled entrance, Luke observed cleaning crews bustle around the main hall, sweeping glass and mopping water puddles. He recalled the magnificent collection of antique chandeliers, most of which had fallen during the firestorm. He surmised that Dominic had deliberately shot them to set off alarms, or maybe the gunfire had rattled them loose from the ceiling. If Luke had gone with Dominic to El Paso, would this disaster have been avoided? Would they be eating dinner at a fine Mexican restaurant at this very moment? He worked his hands into his jeans pockets as he contemplated his friend's death, not fully realized.

After showing his credentials to the captain in charge, Luke pushed through a smattering of cameramen and reporters who were taking footage for the late-evening news. Leaving the crowd, he walked the opposite direction from the media, then kicked around the loading dock, trying to catch a glimpse of Dominic's last hours. He must have been royally pissed off at Velasquez, as only Dom could be, and then Velasquez had set him up with the Banderas deal.

Lourdes Ortiz had sent the sketch of Banderas to Luke before he'd left Houston, and near as he could tell, Velasquez's photo held a striking resemblance to the elusive El Paso lawyer. In addition to Banderas, Luke believed there were higher operatives in this criminal network, and he would hunt them one by one.

He stared at the marked areas where the locals had discovered two dead men. The Juárez police had asked El Paso forensics to take tire prints and gather evidence, and the initial ballistics showed the first man was killed by Dominic's SIG Sauer at close range, but Luke knew Dominic hadn't shot an innocent man. Both Velasquez's and Dominic's prints were on the gun. The other man was shot in the street, apparently trying to escape from someone. His killer used a 9mm, perhaps a Niña, the pistol of choice for Latin Angels, but that gun was missing, as was Velasquez's car. At least, Luke assumed Velasquez had a car.

"I'm so sorry, Luke." A woman's voice floated into his consciousness.

He whipped around to see Elizabeth Grant standing beside a row of wooden crates. How the hell did she get past the cops? All he could do was shake his head as she strode toward him, her fresh scent hitting him straight on. A white sweater clung to her breasts, her slim hips swiveled in a tight blue skirt. She wore lower heels than usual, but still her calf muscles knotted into sensuous lines, her limp and bandaged palms reminders of the attack she'd survived the night before.

Elizabeth held out her hand and he gently took it. "How's the leg?" he asked.

"Up and running," she said. "After I finished in Austin, I decided to come down and cover the situation."

"Yeah. A situation." Luke glanced over at the bloodstained areas where the garbage men had been slaughtered.

"Found anything yet?"

"I've read the police reports," said Luke, averting his eyes from Elizabeth's gaze. "They surmise two men kidnapped Dominic and brought him across the border. The second guy probably drove the missing car from the crime scene after Velasquez went into the museum, and that's what I can't figure. Why didn't the other man go after Dominic too?"

"It doesn't seem logical." Elizabeth released his hand. "I have something for you." She dug her graceful fingers into a gray purse and pulled out a plastic bag containing an object wrapped in tissue. "I found this behind those crates."

Luke studied it with a curious eye.

She continued. "About an hour ago, the police let US reporters take pictures of the dock, then they issued a statement. Their spokesman wasn't saying anything I didn't already know, so I stayed at the back of the crowd and nosed around."

Her upper arm brushed Luke's shoulder as she unfolded the tissue, revealing a mint tin, probably Dominic's last repast before dying. "I know it's evidence, but I thought you'd want to keep it for now."

"You're a champ," he said, tucking the wrapped tin into his jacket pocket.

Elizabeth sighed and bit her lip, then continued in a halting voice. "I hate to tell you this right now—"

"What?" Irritated by her switch from soft concern to terse reporter mode, Luke considered cutting her off, but a harangue with Elizabeth was the last thing he wanted at the moment.

"Alex ran away. He told Kate he was going to join the Angels."

"I told him to forget the Angels."

"If it's any consolation, Javi's guys are looking for him," she said quietly. "But since they haven't found him, I wanted to tell you."

Grateful she wasn't blaming him for Alex's decision, Luke gazed at Elizabeth. Beyond her shoulder, he could see a yellow glow on the massive Toltec head near the museum entrance, and he felt a similar fire. "I'm glad you're here," he said. Barely able to contain his desire to hold her, he bent to kiss her forehead.

She turned her face upward and caressed his neck as he brushed her mouth with his. He held her face in his hands, then kissed her deeply. A forward jut of Elizabeth's body against his chest fueled Luke's yearning. He cupped her firm breasts, her nipples taut, and her hand slipped around his waist. For an insane moment, Luke imagined them lying together on the dock.

"Let's go," he whispered, burying his face at her neck.

"Sounds like a plan, Santa Maria." She swept strands of golden hair from her eyes.

"What's with the 'Santa Maria' thing?"

"My way of flirting, I guess," she said. "But before we go, I need to call my photographer, Joe, and tell him I'm leaving. He met me here. Came in from Houston." Elizabeth flashed a playful smile. "You remember him from *Zona Azul*."

"Yeah, I remember Joe." Luke's mind sketched the raid when he'd first sparred with Elizabeth Grant and desperately wanted to slap her.

He grasped her hand and led her to his car. While Elizabeth called Joe on the way to the Camino Real, Luke considered what he was getting into with a woman he considered to be as strong as he was, and as stoic and distant. Then he dropped this line of thinking and worried that she would be put off by his no-frills, government-budget room. At least he'd insisted on a king-sized bed. But when they arrived, Elizabeth didn't seem to notice the room as she dropped her briefcase and light-blue coat on the bed.

Tossing his jacket on a chair, Luke strolled to the balcony and opened it to city sounds, mumbling below them amid shadows of downtown buildings. A dense cloud drifted in front of the moon, and raindrops pattered on the windows.

Elizabeth came up beside him. Tracing water ripples down the glass with her fingers, she said, "I remember an old song. The words are something like this: '*I hear raindrops on my window, love is like the rain.*'"

"I like those words," he said, kissing the ridge of her ear, tasting her skin, and inhaling the scent of honeysuckle laced in her hair. She threaded her arms around his neck and he held her, gently rocking as if they were dancing to music only they could hear. Entwined in each other's arms, they sank onto the bed, and Luke nudged her coat and briefcase onto the floor.

"I like this room with no light," Elizabeth said.

"I like it better with you in my bed."

She ran her hands across his chest, causing a tremor in his loins. "You work out a lot."

"Lift weights all the time," Luke said, "to chase away my demons."

"Demons. I know about demons." She paused. "I run every day to escape them."

He guided her head onto a pillow as their bodies sank into the supple mattress, where they held each other for a long, hypnotic time.

"I've been wishing for this," Elizabeth whispered.

"You could've fooled me."

"Now, Santa Maria."

He smiled. "No more wishing for you."

Leaning over to meet her lips, Luke ran his hands up her ribs and traced the curves of her breasts, wondering if this intimacy would be the beginning of something between them. Don't think, he cautioned himself. Her cool breath caused a tingling sensation on his chest, a warm ecstasy in the undulations of her hips, their tender oblivion dark and swimming.

Sometime after eleven p.m., Luke wrapped a towel around his waist and ordered dinner. A waiter arrived with a pitcher of margaritas and mounds of Mexican food. Aromas of *frijoles, guacamole*, and *salsa roja* wafted through the room. In contrast to the fluidity of his lovemaking, Luke found it difficult to create a conversation as he awkwardly arranged their dinner on the desk and pulled up chairs. Elizabeth must have felt it too. She didn't talk as she settled into an armchair across from him, leaving her coat open, revealing soft curves. Famished, Luke tightened the towel, lowered himself into a chair and dug in. Nesting in the chair, Elizabeth sipped her margarita and nibbled on a *tortilla*.

"You're quiet," Luke said, unnerved by her silence.

"Yes," she whispered, picking at a *nacho*.

He tipped his glass. "To you, sweet Elizabeth."

She clinked her glass against his, then stood, languidly easing the coat over one shoulder. Lowering herself onto his lap, Elizabeth undid the towel wrapped at his waist, raised her thigh and straddled him. Stunned by her lithe and eager movements, Luke pressed against her. Again he was tempted to ask what she saw in their future, but instead he moved with the ebb and flow of her body.

For a long time afterward, Elizabeth remained on Luke's lap, her head on his chest. He kissed her hair and her trembling lips, trying to capture her attention, but she stared off, her cat-eyes focused on a faraway place.

FORTY-TWO

After midnight, Mariella tiptoed through the great room beneath shadows cast by animal heads looming on the walls above her. With sympathy, she looked up at the poor dead creatures. Everything Cole touched, he either killed or mutilated, and the pain of Mola's repeated abuse had jolted her into another truth. Cole was drugging her and Muñeca. No matter what happened in the next few hours, Mariella promised herself she would never be used again.

Since lunchtime, when Mola had left them in total misery, she and Muñeca neither ate nor drank anything but bottled water and a slice of bread. Mariella's hazy thinking had lifted, and vague memories of the past few days came in spurts too disgusting to dwell on.

Now Mariella moved quietly to Cole's bedroom, where she listened at the slightly opened door. It had been Muñeca's idea to collect Cole's pills and use them on him. Mariella could hear her friend offering him another drink and coaxing him into the bathtub. Cole accepted the drink. Muñeca had him in her power and wasn't in danger of being found out. Alive with nervous energy, Mariella set out to conjure some trickery of her own.

Near the veranda, she peered out a window at the only thing she loved about Cole's ranch, the glorious stars. In Panama City, a few stars had winked at her, sending futile messages of hope through the polluted night haze, but Mariella was making her own hope now. She'd escaped her father, a man as cruel as Tulio Mola, and tonight she would escape again or die an honorable death.

She approached the guards, who were settled at a poker table on the spacious front porch overlooking a shallow valley surrounded by pastureland. Confident of her superior position with these men, Mariella remembered the first evening she'd been at the ranch, when one of them had dug his fingers into her buttocks in front of Randall Cole. Cole had beaten the man with the butt of his gun and sent him away. In that instant, Mariella understood the order of servitude in Cole's domain. Next to him and Mola, she and Muñeca were top dogs.

"Texas Hold 'em," said one of the guards as he shuffled the deck, his short, knobby arms on the table.

The other man snickered, studied his dirty fingernails, then cleaned them with a toothpick that had been hanging from his mouth. "Texas Hold 'em is my game. Sure you wanna play?"

"You bet, Bronco."

"Tequila?" Mariella called in an innocent tone from the bar.

"Bring on the drinks, *Mami*."

Mariella busied herself. From her skirt pocket, she removed a packet of white powder and dumped it into the tequila bottle. To her dismay, the powder clouded the clear liquor. She frantically shook the bottle and stirred the tequila with a long plastic swizzle stick.

"What's taking so long?" one of the guards called.

Smiling, Mariella waved a paring knife above her head and began cutting a plateful of limes. When the tequila finally cleared, she splashed it into shot glasses, setting the bottle in the middle of a carved wooden tray along with the glasses, cocktail napkins, and lime slices. She moved slowly to the table, her back and thighs still aching from the last afternoon she'd ever spend with Tulio Mola.

After serving their drinks and chatting with the guards, Mariella stole from the porch. As she dashed down the main hall, Muñeca stepped from Cole's bedroom, carefully closing the door behind her. When she saw Mariella, she gripped her hand, a reassuring gesture at first, but Muñeca's saucer eyes and rigid shoulders revealed her friend's fear.

"You did it?" Mariella whispered.

Muñeca nodded. "Cole had enough pills in his drink to put down an army."

"Let's go then."

In their pretty pink room, the girls slipped into jeans, T-shirts, and double pairs of socks in order to fit the athletic shoes Mariella had lifted from the guards' quarters earlier in the day. They crept to the kitchen and opened a drawer where Cole kept the keys to his numerous cars and trucks.

"We'll take all the keys, so no one can follow us," Mariella said.

Opening the refrigerator, Muñeca removed three pounds of ground beef they'd laced with powder from Cole's sleeping pills. "The dogs will dream tonight," she said with a crooked grin, but her hands trembled.

Mariella nodded as she mused over seven sets of keys and stuffed them all into a small pack she'd found on a table near the shooting range. "We'll try each one to see which set works for the Mercedes."

"We're going to steal his Mercedes?"

"We're leaving in style," Mariella said.

While Muñeca fed the dogs, Mariella tiptoed to the porch and checked on the guards. Both men were sprawled across the card table, snoring in loud bleats reminiscent of her father. "*Buenas noches,*" she whispered, chuckling to herself. Then she went to Cole's study, where she'd discovered a stack of maps in one of the carved mahogany bookshelves. Although she couldn't read many words, *Houston* and *Texas* were easy to spot. They would need both maps to get to the big city, where she'd find her mother. Mariella imagined the comfort of her mother's arms and the thrill of being loved and wanted at last, but she couldn't think about these things now. First they had to escape.

Nerves on edge, she and Muñeca lingered outside the garage, afraid to leave until they were certain the dogs were asleep. Every minute or so, Mariella threw a rock toward their run, listening with dismay at their growls and snarls, so they waited and waited and waited.

"If Cole wakes up, he'll kill us," Muñeca said, removing Cole's gold watch from her pocket, her eyes clouding with concern. "It's twelve thirty. We have to go."

The girls entered the garage from a side door. Earlier they'd agreed Muñeca would drive, since she'd driven a car before in Mexico. Mariella had never driven, although she'd watched carefully when Soledad brought her to Houston. Many times since then, Mariella had wished to be dead, and every time she thought about Soledad's betrayal, her heart hurt.

The girls dashed to the shiny silver car, tried several keys, and finally selected the correct one. Muñeca turned the key to the right. The motor hummed. She played around with the gears, testing which was forward and which was reverse. Suddenly the car lurched backward.

"The garage door!" Mariella screamed, but a loud crunch told her their mission was doomed. Her neck prickled and she felt like crying, but she knew she must not panic.

"*Aye*, I'm so stupid." Muñeca banged her fist on the steering wheel.

"Go forward a little bit. I'm going to open the garage door at the wall switch to see if it works. After I do this, back out if you think you can make it."

Near the entrance, Mariella touched a white button and watched the door shudder as it rose up, but Muñeca must not have been paying attention again because the Mercedes blundered toward the door before it had completely opened. In horror, Mariella watched the car scrape its top on the ascending door and shoot into the driveway before it came to a shaky halt. The gnashing noise still echoed in her ears as she jumped into the front seat.

Muñeca threw the control lever into D. "Drive, *Mamacita*, drive," she said to the car.

Swerving from side to side, they fled along the gravel road they'd watched other visitors use when leaving the ranch house. Within seconds, they reached a closed iron gate, hovering like a spider's web to stall their deliverance.

Muñeca winced at Mariella. "I knew we wouldn't make it," she said.

"Go closer," Mariella said. "We'll climb over and run."

Muñeca eased the car forward, then thrust her foot on the stopping pedal. To Mariella's amazement, the gate was opening.

"*Un milagro*." Signing herself, she took this as an excellent omen.

The road outside the gate was narrow but smooth. They pressed on until their path dead-ended into a large street. Which way to turn? The girls studied both directions: to the left, pitch-black; to the right, a glimmer on the horizon. Muñeca nodded in favor of the lights. Mariella agreed.

But her stomach became heavy with the number of twists and turns, ups and downs, slips and slides they had to take. Still, the sky continued to brighten, and they remained on course toward what they believed to be salvation. After fifteen minutes, a highway appeared near a shining yellow Shell sign above eight gasoline pumps, signaling the opportunity for help.

Muñeca steered the injured Mercedes into the gas station. The car scraped a red pole, barely missed the first pump and careened toward the station's food market. She threw the gear into P, and both girls jolted forward, Muñeca's chin hitting the wheel as Mariella threw her arms forward to avoid crashing into the dashboard.

"We must put these on when we leave." Mariella tugged at her seat belt.

"*Sí*," said Muñeca, gulping deep breaths.

A man blinked at their staggering approach. He sat behind a thick glass enclosure in the middle of the station.

"He's a *chino*," Muñeca said. "Look at his slanted eyes. I'll try to speak to him in English, but he may not understand."

Maps in hand, the girls approached the man in the glass cage. He wore a blue striped uniform. His black hair hung in careless bangs across his brow, and his smile revealed a row of crooked teeth with brown spots in between.

"Quite a landing you had there," he said. "You girls drunk or high?"

"No. We are not," Mariella answered.

"Not what?" The corners of his eyes slanted even more when he laughed.

"Please, sir, can you show on this map Houston?" Muñeca asked.

"Put the map in the slot," he said, pointing to a metal conduit. "I'll mark it for you."

With a sense of alarm, Mariella grabbed Muñeca and whispered. "If we give the map away, he could steal it."

"*Sí*, you're right. We won't let him have it."

"Look, girls, this isn't rocket science," he said. "You're at I-10. It's a straight shot to Houston." He gestured to the left.

"Shot. Houston." Muñeca repeated two of his words and looked toward the highway.

"No, no, no." Pointing to the left again, he said, "Houston's that way."

"Houston?" Mariella asked with great excitement.

"Yes, Houston. Are you a retard?"

Squinting her dark eyes, Muñeca leaned closer to the window. "What is this 'retard'?"

"For Christ's sake. Houston's that way. I'm not going to say it again." He pointed, then folded his arms across his wrinkled shirt and glared at them.

"No need map?" Muñeca asked.

"No need a map. Now get the hell out of here."

FORTY-THREE

Elizabeth told herself she should stay curled at Luke's side. Instead, she was plagued with an urgent need to escape and tossed and turned beneath suffocating sheets. Voices from an inner Tower of Babel chimed in to elaborate on her fear of being mistreated by another man, fear of what her relationship with Luke would be like after they solved this case and weren't feeding off adrenalin, fear of how Kate would react now that Elizabeth was trying to be there for her.

Other niggling thoughts made her heart race. Luke made love to assuage his grief. She responded out of compassion for Dominic's death. Was this a disaster fuck? The roar wouldn't stop. She had to get out of that room.

Luke's long slow breaths signaled deep slumber, so Elizabeth stole from the bed into the bathroom, where she dressed, huddled near a dim nightlight, and composed a note on the hotel pad.

Luke,
Forgive me for leaving. I'm so confused. Please be patient.
Yours,
Elizabeth

She considered the word "yours" and all it could mean. Over the years, Elizabeth had signed a thousand letters that way. This time that miniscule word was the cause of her panic. With a last peek at Luke peacefully asleep, she carefully closed the door, expecting relief. But in the hallway, she felt more agitated than she had been in bed. Impatiently jamming the elevator button, Elizabeth resisted the urge to return to Luke.

Downstairs, a mammoth silver spruce glittering with Christmas lights and covered with golden angels stood as a lofty centerpiece beneath the Camino Real's domed glass ceiling. It was after four a.m., but the bell captain mustered a taxi to carry her to the airport. To Elizabeth's dismay, the first flight to Houston wasn't until seven thirty. She purchased an e-ticket and, after a painless trek though security, grabbed a double espresso from the all-night coffee bar. Emotionally frazzled, she folded herself into a chair near the gate. Her intention was to refine her notes about the cantina's parent companies and the tragic scenario at the Juárez museum, but in spite of a caffeine infusion, she found herself nodding into fitful sleep.

Elizabeth awakened to a brilliant desert sun peeking over a gray band of bald mountains that cut the horizon into a saw-toothed silhouette. She rubbed her eyes and spotted Luke seated across the waiting area. Talking on his phone, he faced away from her, and she surmised he'd sat that way deliberately.

Her brain clogged with remnants of the margaritas, she was mulling over how she'd explain herself to Luke when her cell rang. "Elizabeth Grant," she said with a sense of weariness.

"Mariella and a friend came to my house this morning." Obispa's voice quavered. "They have been kept as sex slaves by a man named Randall Cole. And of course, Tulio Mola is involved."

Elizabeth's mind cleared instantly. She scooted to the edge of her chair.

"You must do something, Elizabeth," Obispa continued. "I left messages for the DSS agent, Dominic Fontana, but I cannot reach him. These girls are in great danger."

"You know Dominic?" Elizabeth spoke in an overly loud tone as the Obispa-Dominic connection clicked in her mind. The shaman was a CI, and she was also Elizabeth's anonymous caller who wanted media coverage for the raids. "You're my informer."

At the sound of her voice, Luke whipped around, his eyes boring a hole in her heart.

Elizabeth mouthed, "I'm sorry." He scowled and looked away.

"Do you know where Dominic is?" Obispa asked, ignoring Elizabeth's CI statement.

Elizabeth froze, unable to answer.

At length the shaman spoke as if talking to herself. "It is the Black Moth."

"I'm not sure what the Black Moth means, but . . ." Elizabeth's eyes smarted and her chest ached. She lowered her voice. "Two nights ago, Dominic was murdered in Juárez."

There was no sound from the other end of the line, and she imagined the shaman with a taper in her delicate hand igniting a myriad of candles, creating an altar for Dominic.

In the melancholy silence that followed, the gravity of Obispa's message about Mariella sank in. "Obispa, are you there?"

"*Sí.*"

"I'm in El Paso with Luke Santa Maria. He's bringing Dominic's body to Houston. I'll ask him what to do about the girls."

Obispa described the sickening ordeals Mariella and her friend had endured and their escape from Cole's ranch. "I am very worried. I have no garage, and the girls parked Cole's Mercedes in front of my house. We cannot move it away because the streets are blocked."

"What's going on?"

"A great parade for the Feast of Our Lady of Guadalupe," Obispa said. "I am certain Mola's gang will spot the car and come for the girls."

"Get out of the house. Now."

"We could go to the church. There will be many people."

"Stay at the church. I'll get help. Just go."

After Elizabeth hung up, she rushed to Luke, his hair rumpled, his shirt wrinkled as if he'd overslept and hurriedly assembled himself. He gave her an explosive look she'd never forget, a mixture of hurt and anger welling behind a controlled stare.

"Luke," she said, breathless.

"You're not calling me 'Santa Maria'?"

"Did you get my note?"

"Yeah. I woke up to an empty bed and a few cryptic words on a piece of paper."

Elizabeth exhaled to calm herself.

"I guess I expected more from you, Elizabeth. Like maybe having a conversation about your confusion rather than 'The Great Escape.'"

Her imperative to explain Obispa's emergency competed for Elizabeth's need to explain herself. She inadvertently glanced at her watch.

"Excuse me," he said. "Am I boring you?"

"You never bore me, it's just that I can't think straight at the moment."

"I agree with that assessment."

"Please, listen to me. Obispa just called." Elizabeth sat beside him and whispered, "Two teenage girls escaped from Randall Cole's ranch, where he and Mola used them for sex slaves. One of them is Mariella, the girl Obispa and I tried to help, the one who disappeared from *Carnivál*."

Luke leaned back in the chair. "When I got up this morning, I decided you were a cruel woman at worst, a scheming one at best. Now I think you and that shaman are over the edge."

"Just hear me out, Luke," she said. "Remember I told you Mola and Sandoval wouldn't let Mariella leave with us? They could have taken her to Cole's ranch."

"Okay, she was with those thugs, I'll give you that." Luke said. "But if Cole were involved with Mola, I would've picked up on something over the years."

"Maybe not, Luke. Cole's got the ideal cover. Mola runs the cantinas, the drugs, and the trafficking. All Cole has to do is exercise his legal savvy and direct operations from his ivory tower."

Luke shook his head.

"You know I saw Sandoval in Cole's office. I don't think it was a coincidence." Be cool, Elizabeth told herself. If she held on to common sense, she could convince him. When Luke didn't respond, she continued in a more even tone. "How could those girls know Cole's name? How did they get his Mercedes?"

"Call Obispa," he said. "I want to question them."

"I hope she has her cell phone." She quickly explained about the blocked streets. "The Mercedes made them sitting ducks, so Obispa took them to the church." Elizabeth's voice shook.

"Jeezus." He drummed his fingers. "Why didn't you bring me the phone when you had them on the line?"

Luke was right, of course. She hadn't done it because she was mired in last night's stupidity. Now she stabbed the shaman's number several times to no avail. "No answer," she said.

Luke shifted in his chair. "It bears looking into."

Elizabeth's pulse thumped to the brisk beat of breakthrough, while Luke called for a warrant to search Cole's ranch and arranged for agents to pay him a visit. It all made sense. Cole was behind these crimes, she knew it.

Luke closed his cell and looked at her. His bleak expression made her sick with herself. Suffering his palpable scorn, she said nothing, remaining beside him until the nasal twang of an airline agent beckoned preboard passengers. Luke quickly rose and took her arm.

"Get on the plane. You're sitting with me."

"But—"

"That's an order. Until I say differently, you're a resource for the State Department."

"Doing what?"

"Exactly what I tell you."

"I have rights."

"Don't we all?"

FORTY-FOUR

At first light, Alex awakened in the warehouse bunk room where he'd slept on a top bunk, with Chi and Howler in beds below. Exhausted, he twisted his body into the most comfortable position he could manage on the hard mattress and tried to doze off. But his mind, bursting with yesterday's events, wouldn't allow him to sleep again.

After the fight, Alex had watched with amazement as Sandoval had put a pressure bandage on Howler's neck. He told the boys the dispute was over—forever. "You are brothers now," Sandoval said, kissing the silver cross on his rosary. "From now on, you will save each other's lives." Then he nodded at Alex. "A fighter and a thinker. I like that."

Although Chi had complied with Sandoval's orders and loosely clapped Alex's hand, the boy had sneered at him every time Sandoval wasn't looking. Howler, on the other hand, seemed in awe of Alex's prowess and hugged him with his scrawny noodle arms.

"Now we'll practice." Sandoval had gestured toward the seven silhouettes.

In silence, the boys had followed him to the shooting area of the warehouse, where Sandoval had removed four handguns from his small black suitcase. When he offered one to Alex, Alex stared him straight in the eye.

"I have never shot a gun, *señor* . In Guatemala, we used knives and knuckles."

"I'll teach you." Sandoval had twirled the pistol around his finger.

"This Colt Python fires .357 magnum rounds, six bullets on reload, and has the power to stop a drug-crazed zombie. As you'll see, it's slow to fire, but this *mami* will kill in one hit. I'll show you how to use the speedloader as you learn. The Angels use these guns when we fight close-up. We have many other weapons, too. You'll see them later."

Chi had passed out what Alex took to be music earphones, but Sandoval explained that during practice they'd need to protect their hearing.

"On the streets, there are no safeguards. Your ears will ring like fucking hell."

To his surprise, Alex had found himself fascinated with the mechanics of the gun and the skill required to hit a target. For over an hour, he practiced aiming at the heart, head, and knees. He made his mark half the time. When Sandoval called the practice to a halt, Alex exceeded Howler's score by over a hundred points. Chi beat him, but not by much. Alex could sense his latest success didn't go well with Chi.

In the late afternoon, Sandoval had driven the boys to a cantina for dinner and cerveza, then he'd told them they must spend the night together because they had an assignment first thing in the morning. Alex sipped his beer, taking care to stay alert. After a couple of tequila shots, Sandoval revealed his plans. Tomorrow, the boys would travel with him to El Paso and help with some business in Juárez. Alex's chest tightened at the thought of leaving US soil, but he could see no way out. And Luke's partner, Dominic, was murdered in Juárez. Could these happenings be a sign? Alex longed to ask Fernando's advice, but his brother's ghost didn't appear in the noisy cantina.

When they'd returned from dinner, Sandoval had showed them into the bunk room. "Go to sleep. I'll come very early," he had said.

It was very early now. Dangling his feet over the side of the bunk, Alex surveyed the room where Howler sprawled deep in slumber and Chi snored. As he waited for Sandoval, Alex tried to figure out how to contact Luke. If he used the black phone on the wall near the bunk room, he might wake the boys. His head spinning with ideas, Alex spied the cement glue on a table beside Howler's jacket. He doubted if he could squirt the stuff into anyone's eyes, but he dropped from the bunk and pocketed the tube.

Alex didn't have to hang on long for Sandoval's arrival. The gangster barreled through the bunk room door with a fiendish glint in his eye. He spied Alex and nodded a greeting.

"Get up, you *cholos*," he said to Chi and Howler. "Today, you'll prove you're worthy to be an Angel."

The boys threw on their shirts and jeans and shuffled behind Sandoval into the other room, where they assembled around an acid-washed steel table near the pit. It was the kind of table Alex had seen one summer when Father Chiabras found work for him cleaning a morgue, a most grueling occupation, if ever there was one. Alex bet the Angels had stolen this table from a mortuary, but he forgot that notion when Sandoval opened a satchel and spread pictures of two beautiful teenage girls on the table's smooth surface.

Catching his breath, Alex restrained himself from showing recognition. How could she be alive? He leaned closer to the photographs. Sitting on a bed, the girls wore ridiculous pink outfits, a fact that made Alex doubt his first impression, so he studied the images. He didn't want to make a fool of himself like he had with Kate in the Galleria, but his eyes didn't deceive him this time. The taller girl was Mariella Guzman, stuffed into a child's dress.

"No time to waste," Sandoval said. "These girls are your targets."

Alex gripped the rim of the steel table and tried to understand how this could be happening. So many events had occurred since he'd last seen Mariella in the desert, left to die by the bastard Santiago. And now, he was being commanded to kill her.

Outside the warehouse, Sandoval invited Alex to sit in the front seat of his Mercedes while relegating Chi and Howler to the rear. Alex started to protest but thought better of it. He dropped onto the soft gray leather as Sandoval passed the envelope of pictures to him.

The gangster slammed into reverse and said, "You're in charge of this hit, Alex. Memorize their faces. By noon today, they must be smoked." Sandoval zigzagged though the *barrio* until they reached an intersection near Obispa's House of Light. Row after row of white barricades obstructed the streets while hundreds of Hispanic people marched in procession, singing *Las Mañanitas*, the famous Mexican hymn. Some were dressed in native costumes, white garments brightly stitched in yellow, blue and red, while others were decked out in their Sunday best.

"The fucking Catholics." Sandoval slapped his fist on the steering wheel and stared at the barricades. "Okay. I have to think." He cocked his head, eyes closed, nostrils flaring.

At length, he spoke to the boys. "See that house with the silver Mercedes out front? The girls are hiding there. Two of you will go to the back, one stays in the front. You'll make Molotov cocktails and throw them into the house. I have the supplies." He nodded toward the trunk. "When the house explodes, the girls may die, but if they run out, shoot them and anyone else who gets in your way."

"Their clothes are weird," Chi said from the backseat.

"Never mind that. Do exactly as I say."

"But what did they do to deserve death?" Alex asked.

"They've disrespected our leader, Tulio Mola. For this, they will die like dogs."

"I'd rather go to Juárez," Howler said, his voice a nervous squeak.

Sandoval whipped in Howler's direction and repeated their assignment. "I will not say this again. Alex will lead, and you two will do as he says. Blow up the house and kill those girls."

Alex watched Chi and Howler nod, but he was sure when Sandoval was gone, he'd have trouble keeping them in line. Still, Sandoval had designated him to call the shots, so he had a chance to make sure the girls escaped. How he'd accomplish this, he didn't know, but being the leader gave him the advantage.

"Hand me my bag," Sandoval said to Chi, who passed him a leather attaché from the floor in the back. "Here are your babies." Before parting with the Colt Pythons they'd used in yesterday's practice, Sandoval stroked each pistol with an oilcloth as if it were the love of his life, but Alex knew he was erasing any trace of his own fingerprints. Alex took the weapon with bravado and stuffed it into his jeans.

"Do we get the speedloaders?" Chi asked.

"Of course. Put them in your jackets."

Sandoval again demonstrated how to use the speedloaders, but Howler stopped paying attention. Eyes widened, he stared at the House of Light. "Look! Those girls are marching in the parade," he said.

Obispa, Mariella, and her friend appeared in the yard but quickly melted into the crowd and disappeared into a throng of worshippers.

"They're going to the church." The gangster spat the word "church" as if it held a dirty meaning.

While Alex waited for Sandoval's next move, he felt ripples of relief. At least they weren't going to bomb Obispa's House of Light.

"I'll wait here, *homitos*. Find them in the church, waste their asses, and if someone spots you, run like hell. If, by chance, you aren't spotted after the hit, walk away like you're part of the group. Be reverent. No swaggering."

The boys left the Mercedes and huddled around Sandoval, who

leaned out the car window.

"Don't leave until you kiss my cross." Removing the rosary from his neck, Sandoval dangled it in front of them. They pressed their lips to the crucifix as he said, "Santa Muerte protects our kind."

Alex, Chi, and Howler left the gang leader and hopped the barricades. Pushing through the horde of marchers in the direction Obispa and the girls had taken, Alex observed people of all ages, some with dogs on leashes, while others carried costumed babies or pushed toddlers in strollers suffused with blue and white streamers. One man had a parrot in a cage strapped to his shoulders like a backpack. Middle-aged men swung placards with images of the Virgin followed by a cadre of old women draped in veils.

Alex eyed the mounted policemen directing the crowd. Even if he could ditch Chi and Howler, he didn't think it was safe to approach the police. The cops would think he'd lost his mind or, worse, arrest him. Even if they did believe him, it would take precious time for the police to check with Luke, and that would leave Chi and Howler with an open opportunity for murder.

Glancing over his shoulder, Alex saw that the black Mercedes had vanished. So if by some miracle they all did make it back to the intersection, the gang leader wouldn't be there. Sandoval had sent them on a mission to kill and be killed. Alex wasn't surprised.

FORTY-FIVE

Thirty minutes into the flight and an icy silence filled the space between Luke and Elizabeth. Sitting next to her in the first row, he considered her actions and couldn't figure the woman. She was beautiful, competent, passionate, and royally screwed in the head. Or maybe he was the problem. He should have asked why she was so quiet last night instead of picking her up, laying her on the bed, and making love again. But she sure as hell didn't resist. And the note. Elizabeth was way too old to be confused, but she didn't try to explain herself again and responded to this hush between them by shifting her shoulders to face the window.

The morning had been ridiculous. Waking up to a missing lover, muddling his way to the airport, and worst of all, standing by while the baggage crew loaded Dominic's body on the plane. Elizabeth's presence at the gate had distracted him, but now he allowed the grief to settle, recalling Dominic's antics at the animal shelter, his choice of Horace, and his deep anger at injustices wrought on young *Latinos*. Luke closed his eyes, but his misery fueled an unstoppable resolve—he'd punish the men who'd orchestrated Dominic's death. And Randall Cole might be number one on the hit parade, a bitter pill to swallow after their supposed friendship that had spanned decades.

Luke's eyes ached. He closed them and dozed until his phone vibrated on the tray next to his laptop. As he answered, he noted the attention of two businessmen seated across the aisle. He waved the cell at them. "State Department."

Startled by Alex's voice, he listened carefully. "Delay them as long as you can," he said. "Has Mass started?"

"No. The parade still happening. I talk fast, *Señor* Luke. I send Chi and Howler the other way, then I pay some guy to use his cell phone."

"Very smart." Luke shifted into Spanish to be sure there was no communication glitch. "Tell those boys you'll wait till after Mass to make the hit, when people are leaving the church. Say it'll be easier. I can be there in ninety minutes; right around ten o'clock."

"A good idea, *Señor* Luke. These boys, I think they will obey me." Alex sounded more confident than Luke expected.

"Try to stay in the rear of the church. I'll see if the locals can get there before I do."

"How will I know these locals? Are they police?"

"Police sharpshooters and the anti-gang team. They won't be wearing uniforms," Luke explained. "I'll have them find you. What are you wearing?"

"Yesterday I bought a black leather jacket with the money you gave me. It has silver studs. You'll like it."

Luke grinned in spite of the situation. "I'm sure I will, Alex. Now stall those boys and be careful."

Elizabeth's cat-eyes were trained on Luke when he disconnected. He spoke before she had the chance to deliver a barrage of questions. "Sandoval spotted those girls with Obispa. They were headed toward Guadalupe Church, so he sent Alex and two other boys to whack them."

Elizabeth gasped. To Luke's surprise, she didn't freak out in fear or gush with advice.

"I'll do my best to have the anti-gang team there." He called Javi Padilla and couldn't reach him, so he apprised Padilla's assistant of the looming disaster at Our Lady of Guadalupe. When he hung up, Luke said, "They'll make it before we do."

"We?"

Nodding, Luke made a split decision to take Elizabeth. "You'll warn Obispa, while I deal with the shooters." Elizabeth stared at him as he dialed Abby and gave her instructions to have an ALERT chopper waiting for them when they landed at Hobby Airport.

"Excuse me," Elizabeth said when Luke hung up. "What does 'ALERT' mean?"

"Aerial Law Enforcement Response Team, an HPD chopper. They lend it to State if it's not in use."

"What about Dominic's body?"

"Now it's twenty-questions from the lady." Elizabeth's query about Dominic stung, but he quickly answered to cover his pain. "They'll bring him off last. The funeral home takes over from there. My job right now is to deal with the living."

She smoothed the gauze bandages on her hands, then, lifting her chin, she asked, "Can Joe meet us at the church?"

"Jeezus, Elizabeth." Luke tried to be patient, reminding himself this was her work. "If he doesn't get in the way or take one goddamn photo until I say so."

"You're a champ," she said, eyeing his phone vibrating again. "Any chance I could use it when you're finished?"

"Now you're pushing it." Luke pressed the receiver to his ear. "What'cha got?" he asked the Katy sheriff's deputy. He didn't want this conversation overheard by anyone, so he trotted to the head and locked the door.

"It's not pretty, sir," the man said. "Sheriff Holland asked me and Frank to check the goings-on at the Cole ranch."

"That's correct, Deputy. I didn't catch your name." Luke had been in this business long enough to know how to question a yokel.

"Name's Cletus Arley, been with Katy Sheriff's Department nigh twenty years, and I've never seen nothing like this. Carnage is what it is."

"Tell me."

"Well, me and Frank had no trouble gettin' onto the ranch 'cause someone left the gate open. Mr. Cole must've left outta here in a goddamned hurry, and I can see why."

"Why, Cletus? I need to know now."

"Near as I can tell, we have eleven murder victims. Right off, we saw two bodies on the front porch. I'm assumin', and I ain't no detective, but I'm assumin' those guys were guarding the place and playin' poker, then someone smoked 'em in the head, professional-like. In the bunkhouse, we found seven teenage boys, more'n likely ranch workers. Shot in their sleep."

Luke winced. "And the other two bodies?"

"There's a kitchen in the ranch house, where these two middle-aged Mexican ladies were lying dead on the floor. Juevos rancheros and sausage still in the fryin' pans. Whoever done this sure as shit didn't eat breakfast." He coughed and spit, not bothering to cover the receiver. "Funny thing though. The killer turned off the gas stove, 'cause nothin's still cookin'."

Initially dulled by shock, Luke suddenly absorbed what Cole had been up to all along, right in front of Luke's face, laughing at the trust Luke had placed in him. "No sign of Randall Cole?" he asked, but he knew the answer.

"Not a trace, and I'd always wanted to meet that rich guy who come out here and bought up half our county."

"Look, Cletus, Randall Cole's a sonofabitch. He's hurt a lot more than the people you found at the ranch. The State Department thinks he's into child prostitution and human slavery, so I'm asking you to guard that crime scene with your life. Don't let anyone disturb the bodies until forensics gets there. Do you read?"

Luke considered the odds of poor quality police work out there in the sticks, but it didn't matter anymore. Lady Justice would be meted out at the end of Luke's SIG. Cole and Mola would get nothing better than what they gave to Dominic.

"Don't you fret about this crime scene, Mr. State Department," Cletus said. "Roger and out."

Luke's phone registered another incoming call, this one from Padilla, and his news was predictable. Javi had received Luke's message and gone to Cole's office, buzzing with business as usual, but the head honcho had gone missing. The receptionist described a man who looked like a thug leaving with Cole over an hour ago. Luke gave Javi the info about the Katy murders and the most immediate danger, Alex's peril. "See you at church," Luke said. Padilla assured him he'd be there.

Shifting into high gear, Luke laid out a mental plan. First he needed to alert Houston airports about Cole and Mola. He shot out of the bathroom, cornered the flight attendant, and showed her his credentials again. She took his badge and disappeared into the cockpit, closing the door behind her. When she reopened the door and motioned for Luke to enter, several wide-eyed passengers stared at him. They were still vigilantly watching when Luke returned from speaking with the pilots, but Elizabeth's ravenous expression said she was merely hungry for information. Luke was privately pleased he possessed details she'd kill for.

"It's bad, right?" she asked when he settled beside her.

Luke nodded. Buckling his seat belt, he took a long breath and tried to switch gears. Until they arrived in Houston, there was nothing else he could do about Cole or Alex, and, of course, Alex and the girls were top priority. No more kids would die today if he had anything to do with it. Cole and Mola were another story.

Elizabeth zeroed in on Luke, expecting more goodies, no doubt, but he was determined not to tell her about the slaughter at Cole's ranch just yet. When he didn't offer more, she shot him a homicidal glare, then leaned back into the seat as if she really didn't want to know, her palm casually open and relaxed in her lap. Searching his shirt pocket, Luke removed a small silver object and pressed it into Elizabeth's hand.

"My earring," she whispered.

"You lost it in bed," he said, closing his eyes.

*

Luke and Elizabeth raced through Hobby Airport, heading to a helipad where the ALERT chopper waited. The pilot, Neal Frazier, was ready to roll. Neal, in his mid-thirties, had flown Hueys in Afghanistan and now wore a dark-blue HPD uniform with various patches on his sleeves, his eyes hidden behind aviator glasses. After brief introductions, Elizabeth climbed into the backseat. Luke handed her a headset and mouthpiece so they could communicate over the engine roar. They strapped in and Neal took off.

"We cleared a grocery parking lot five blocks from the church," Neal said. "Couldn't get closer because of the crowds."

Luke checked his watch, 9:30 a.m. "Alex told me Mass was at nine, but I'm betting they'll start late. I think we're right on the number."

Elizabeth's eyes widened. "If we're late, Alex can't hold off that gang."

Neal turned to Luke. "Charlie Finn, FAA, on channel nine."

Switching channels, Luke listened.

"Fifteen minutes ago, Cole and a passenger named Hector Garcia took off from Hobby," Charlie said.

"Get me the flight plan, fuel capacity, and tail number," Luke said.

"You bet. We'll trace him till he leaves US airspace, and then, you know what Mexico's got—nada." Charlie sighed into the receiver.

"Yeah, zilch. Keep me posted."

Unable to control his frustration, Luke delivered the details to Elizabeth and Neal, describing the slaughter at Cole's ranch and his escape from the airport, where they'd just landed. "The flight plan says Cole's headed for Cabo."

"He can't make Cabo," Neal said. "He'll probably refuel in

Monterrey."

"All I can hope is the Border Patrol or ICE intercepts him before he clears US airspace," Luke said. "Or if he stops in Monterrey, the police there may detain him."

"I need to call the paper, get someone out to Katy, and alert our partners in Monterrey and Cabo," Elizabeth said.

"Why am I not surprised?"

"Get over it," Elizabeth said.

In spite of the crushing noise, she yelled instructions into her cell, while Luke leaned his head back and reviewed everything he knew about Randall Cole and Tulio Mola. *Why did they kill all those people at the ranch?* Their victims must have had damning information. At any rate, Cole's swift departure meant he'd had an exit strategy long before the girls escaped last night.

Luke abruptly spoke out loud to no one in particular. "Tulio Mola has strong connections in Guatemala City. If they disappear into that sewer, we'll never find them."

FORTY-SIX

Alex, Chi, and Howler loitered in the church vestibule as waves of children in embroidered costumes, colorful prisms in filtered sunlight, entered through an arched doorway. Their chubby hands gripped basketfuls of flowers. They scattered rose petals on the floor in remembrance of the Virgin's appearance to the poor *Indio*, Juan Diego, and her gift to him, roses in winter. Inhaling blissful scents and closing his lids, Alex committed himself into Our Lady's loving hands. When he opened his eyes, a bronze framed clock on the sidewall read nine thirty, and Mass hadn't begun. Luke would be there soon. Alex knew it.

Scanning the crowd for anyone who might be an undercover officer, Alex watched *los abuelitos*, the grandparents, grasping their grandchildren's arms to keep them in tow, and teachers herding classes of kids through the maze. After the schoolchildren settled in pews at the front of the church, a priest and eight altar boys dressed in blue cassocks entered. The priest wore a woven vestment and swung a gold container spewing smoky incense into the vestibule.

"What is that shit?" Howler whispered, pinching his nose with his fingers.

Chi slapped Howler's hand away from his face. "Shut up, you dick."

Alex made the sign of the cross as a cluster of broad-shouldered men marched past bearing a pedestal with the Virgin's statue. They lumbered down the center aisle, lowering the statue to the floor midway between the altar and the entrance. A group of veiled women walking on their knees followed these men. They remained kneeling in the center aisle as the priest sprinkled holy water on the statue and then on the women. Alex and the boys loitered in the rear along with latecomers who couldn't get a seat.

Chi thrust his elbow into Alex's ribs. "Why not find the girls now?"

"Be patient," Alex whispered. "We'll make the hit when people leave church, so we can hide in the crowd as they walk out. If we hit them now, we'll be easily spotted."

Chi scoffed. "So we just hang here and do nothing?"

"Look, man. I'm trying to save our asses."

Shifting from one foot to the other while picking his nose, Howler offered no comment to the debate. Alex suspected cement glue wasn't the only drug this guy snorted.

"I don't like it," Chi said.

Alex gestured toward the two side aisles leading into the church. "Since the veiled ladies are blocking the main aisle, you stand guard on the left, Howler on the right. If the girls leave, you'll have a clear shot. Otherwise we go in with the Communion line and take them out."

"What about you?"

"I'll go upstairs, see if I can spot them."

Chi seemed to agree with the plan. He and Howler separated and stood watch at the side aisles. Alex figured Luke would be there in ten minutes, so if Alex could locate the girls, maybe he could prevent someone from getting hurt. He bounded up the choir stairs and eased his way to the corner of the loft, every inch crammed with devotees.

He scanned the church row by row. The first several pews were filled with schoolchildren. In the second aisle behind the kids, Alex spotted Obispa with two dark-haired girls—the taller one, Mariella Guzman. His mouth went dry and his pulse threaded as he calculated the difficulty of warning them before Chi figured it out. Then, Alex freaked.

In the center aisle, Chi and Howler were entering the church on their knees, scooting their way into the middle of the veiled ladies, who smiled, pleased to have the boys join them. Alex rubbed his fingers over the gun stuffed in his jeans and tried to think. He had to stop those *cholos*. Pushing along the choir rail to the middle of the loft, he kept an eye out for Luke or anyone else who looked like a cop. No one came.

As a guitar group strummed *Ave Maria*, the priest, altar boys, and a cluster of costumed children formed a "U" at the altar to receive the men carrying the precious Virgin. When the men lifted the statue, Chi reared up from his place among the kneeling women, scuttled toward Mariella and Obispa, and fired twice into the crowd. Guitar music muffled the shots, but children wailed when a teacher collapsed. Obispa, the girls, and everyone else ducked.

"I am police," Alex announced to a sea of faces in the loft. When he withdrew the Colt Python, people started pushing and cramming into the single aisle that led to the stairs. Others crouched behind pews, but no one attempted to take his gun, so Alex faced the altar. Aiming at Chi, he realized there was little chance he could hit him from that distance. But he also surmised that if he didn't try, Chi could get Mariella and Obispa.

"*You must fly, brother.*"

Alex gasped. Fernando's grinning ghost floated above a huge iron chandelier hanging close to the choir rail. "*Fly! To save your friends.*"

Six curved arms of the light fixture fanned out from a single chain and were attached to a circular base. Without considering the consequences, Alex stuffed the gun in his pants, hopped onto the loft's ledge, and hurled himself forward. His hands clasped two iron arms. He strained to lift himself onto the base, but his weight tipped the chandelier to one side. The heavy chain creaked above him as plaster and dust crumbled from the ceiling. People looked up and shrieked.

"Move!" he warned those below as he released his grip and dropped to the floor near the veiled ladies scuttling out of his way. Howler had vanished, but Chi fired at Alex, his bullet finding a home in one of the devoted women. Alex felt sick. An innocent person was shot, and he didn't have time to help her. He ducked into a pew where frightened people stampeded away from him toward a side aisle.

"Alex!" someone hollered.

Alex saw *Señor* Luke, and he felt a shiver of relief. The agent slid into the pew and folded his large frame down next to Alex.

"Where're the shooters?"

"One of them is near the altar. I can't find the other one."

Luke squinted at Chi. "Got him." Keeping low, the agent snaked down the center aisle passing the four men frozen in place, still balancing the Virgin on their shoulders.

Alex's attention shifted from Luke to a purple flicker in the pew across from him. Howler hunkered dangerously close to the revered statue, and before Alex could stop him, he blasted the Blessed Lady at close range. A deafening shot. The air stung with soaring shards from the exploding statue. Stunned by the report, the men dropped the base. They started for Howler, but Alex barreled from his hiding place, tackled him, and slammed an angry fist into his jaw.

Our Lady's guards surrounded the boys. Alex pounced on Howler's stomach and clutched his neck. Fueled by a blind rage, Alex withdrew the cement glue, determined to squeeze it in Howler's eyes, but the cap was stuck. He pressed his thumbs into Howler's throat, harder and harder, until he felt a solid hand on his back and a voice speaking in rapid-fire Spanish.

"Alex, I'm Javi Padilla with the police."

Alex twisted to see a scar-faced man dressed in a fancy suit. Reluctantly, he released his grip on Howler and stumbled up in time to watch Chi zigzagging toward the costumed children. Luke dodged a bullet from Chi's Colt. More distressing screams followed. Chi shot again. Padilla and Alex flattened themselves behind the rubble that was once Our Lady of Guadalupe.

"The kid who's shooting," Alex said, "he'll die trying to kill those girls."

"Where is he?"

"I don't know. After I jumped from the choir, I couldn't see them."

Javi Padilla gazed up at the loft. "You're a brave man, Alex." He patted him on the shoulder. "Now let me handle it from here." Hunched over, he made his way to the right aisle, where he joined two men crouched behind the pillars. They held assault rifles with scopes.

"No!" A voice echoed through the church.

Alex scooted into a pew and peeked at the altar. The priest made a useless attempt to swing the incense burner at Chi, who'd grabbed a wide-eyed little boy dressed in a straw hat, striped serape, and emerald-green pants. The boy's hat tumbled from his head, and he began to sob as Chi clutched his neck.

"Shut up, you little shit!" Chi screamed.

Alex couldn't think of how he could help the boy. Then he heard Luke calling to Chi.

"Throw your weapon and lie on the floor with your hands on your head. No one will hurt you."

"Leave me alone, or I'll kill this kid!" Chi sounded like he was panting.

Alex could see Padilla and his men skulking between the pillars until they reached the last column nearest the Communion rail, about twenty feet from Chi. Their problem—the priest and children blocked their line of fire. With a sweaty hand Alex removed the Colt from his jeans and set his finger on the trigger.

Chi must have caught a glimpse of Padilla. He pivoted and fired twice, bullets ricocheting off the pillars, clipping the edge of an angel's wing. In that split second, Alex sprang from the pew and crab-crawled down the aisle until he was close enough to blast Chi in the leg without hitting the kid. Staggering, Chi released the little boy. Alex had to be sure the kid was okay. He rose to his knees, and when he did, the black hole of Chi's barrel sparked with a powerful pop and brute force knocked Alex onto the floor. In a red blaze of agony, he slumped.

"Fernando," Alex whispered. "Show yourself."

Barely able to raise his head, Alex searched the altar. The priest and children hit the ground as Padilla and his men rushed Chi, swaying backward now, firing as he went. Alex couldn't make out everything that was happening. One of the men with Padilla careened backward, collapsing not more than thirty feet from Alex. Then, on the left side of the altar, he spied Luke stand up in the marble pulpit. The agent fired once. Chi's chest exploded.

The church fell silent except for moans from the wounded. Holding his bleeding shoulder, Alex lifted his gaze to the crucified Cristo, and there, perched on an arm of the cross, sat Fernando, saluting him with a wide grin.

"The girls are safe, brother. You saved them."

Alex didn't close his eyes until his beloved Fernando had dissolved into the dark cracked wood.

FORTY-SEVEN

Just get them away from the shooter, Elizabeth told herself. In the chaos, she'd found Obispa and the girls huddled on the floor between the pews, and now she hustled the trio into the sacristy, a small room behind the altar where priests prepared for Mass. They piled into a closet crammed with vestments, Sunday missals, and other religious accoutrements. Elizabeth breathed through her mouth to avoid gagging at pent-up odors from vestments not cleaned in years.

The minutes passed like molasses dripping slow, arms and chests pressed against each other beneath a mantle of horror. When the sporadic gunfire finally ceased, Elizabeth wondered how many were injured, how many were dead.

"I want out of here," Mariella whispered.

"Not yet," Elizabeth said. Groping in her purse through a jungle of requisite items, she found the smooth surface of her cell phone. When she flipped it on, a sallow glow allowed her to see well enough to punch Luke's number.

"Where are you?" he said.

"I might ask you the same question," she whispered.

"Know what, Elizabeth? I'm sick of your mouth."

Surprised at Luke's angry tone, she hurriedly answered. "I'm in a closet behind the altar with Obispa and the girls."

"Stay there," he said. "The area's not secure."

"And Alex?" she asked, but he'd hung up. Frustrated, Elizabeth stuffed the phone into her purse and shifted her weight from foot to foot until she heard a shuffling sound followed by the slow turn of the doorknob. Obispa's clammy palm pressed against her arm. Elizabeth envisioned the girls, breathing through their mouths, licking their lips, gutting up for an unknown assassin.

"Javi Padilla. HPD. Come out with your hands above your head."

"Javi, it's Elizabeth Grant here," she called.

Abruptly, the closet door swung wide. The anti-gang director aimed an assault rifle at them. Mariella and Muñeca shrieked, hugging each other, even after Javi lowered his gun.

"*Muchachas!*" Obispa's voice was firm, but she put her hand on Mariella's cheek to calm her. "I have known this man since he was a child."

"Let's get out in the open so we can breathe." Elizabeth edged into the sacristy.

Still sniffling, Mariella and Muñeca ventured from the closet, followed by the shaman.

Javi's hyper-alert eyes darted to every corner of the room. "We're pretty sure all shooters are down, but I'm not taking chances. Take a deep breath, then get back in the closet."

Before Elizabeth could ask about Alex, the anti-gang director cautiously opened the back door and vanished into the parking lot.

Ten more minutes. Elizabeth couldn't stand it. She had to find Alex. Cautioning Obispa and the girls to stay put, she crept from the sacristy into the church. Medics were attending wounded children near the altar. *God, what a travesty.*

"This kid goes first," a medic yelled to a woman pushing a stretcher.

"There're bad injuries out front too," the woman responded.

Elizabeth spotted Alex lying in the main aisle, his shoulder swathed in a crimson-splattered bandage and a makeshift IV dripping in his arm. Dashing to him, she bent to take his hand. His trimmed bangs stuck to his forehead, his frozen gaze suggested shock, but he managed a wan smile when he saw her.

"Chi got me," he whispered. His gaze drifted to the altar as if he were looking for someone. "And Fernando told me—"

"Alex, Alex."

Mariella, Obispa, and Muñeca sprinted down the aisle at breakneck speed, Mariella in the lead. She knelt, scooting close to Alex, and the reunited friends spoke in a rush of Spanish.

"I thought you were dead," Alex whispered.

Mariella kissed his hand. "I still have your cross." Her lower lip quavering, she removed a silver chain, gingerly lifted Alex's head, and strung it around his neck. "It saved my life, and now it will make you well."

Obispa knelt beside Alex too. Withdrawing a bag of herbs from her pocket, she placed crushed leaves on his tongue as she had with the birthing mother. "This will stop your bleeding, *hermanito*."

"*Gracias*," Alex rasped. Then, raising his eyes, he gazed beyond Elizabeth. "*Señor* Luke!"

"You saved the day, Alex." Luke stepped in between Elizabeth and Obispa. Squatting, he placed his hand on Alex's forehead. "We'll have you fixed up in no time."

"I'm scared," said Alex, gesturing at his upper arm.

"Your bleeding will stop. Do not be afraid," Obispa said. "We will pray for you, dear Alex." Signing herself, she glanced at Luke. "And for Dominic, who has joined the angels."

Luke stood, looking down on Obispa, his body a tower above her, his lips clamped into a tense line. "I don't have time for prayers."

*

Keeping Luke Santa Maria in her sights, Elizabeth followed him through the churchyard, where deputies calmed hysterical families and medics ministered to children who cried out in pain. She called her editor's voice mail and dictated the story—a real no-no in the newspaper biz, but if she pulled off her next strategy to cover Cole's arrest, all would be forgiven.

"Where're you going?" she called after Luke.

"Hobby Airport." He kept his pace, tucking his hands into the pockets of his leather jacket.

"My car's there. Can I hitch a ride?"

Luke nodded. "You'll owe me."

As they approached the helicopter, it seemed the entire *barrio* had gathered. Officers waved at curious kids to stay away. Elizabeth hustled to the chopper and scuttled in behind Luke. He sat next to Neal, so she climbed over him into the backseat.

Neal turned briefly and smiled at her before blades began to whirl, then he passed Luke a headset. "Channel nine."

Luke clapped on the earphones. Elizabeth tapped Neal on the shoulder, pointing to the headsets. He handed her one, and she spun the dial to nine, but all she heard was static. The frequency was blocked.

"Hold the flight to Cabo," Luke said. "I'll be there in ten minutes."

After takeoff, Elizabeth's curiosity ballooned about what Luke was hearing on channel nine. She could hardly restrain herself when he signed off and flicked the headset to a channel where they could have a conversation. *Patience*, she cautioned herself.

"The FAA reports no sign of Cole's plane," Luke said. "He disappeared near McAllen, and Reynosa is just twenty miles from there."

"Reynosa as in Mexico?" Elizabeth asked, frequently confused about the multitude of towns along the US Mexican border.

"Yep." After offering this tidbit of information, Luke directed his eyes to Houston's crystalline skyscrapers and rode in a brooding silence. She decided it was best to let him strategize, since she had some strategizing of her own to do if she were going to travel with him to McAllen, Cabo, or wherever the hell he'd go next.

As the chopper approached Hobby Airport, Neal spoke to Luke. "I'm getting a bulletin, sir. A Cessna 210 crashed across the border from McAllen."

Luke chewed the corner of his lip. "Mexican officials confirm?"

"Not yet."

"I don't buy it."

Elizabeth expected Luke to erupt in anger at losing the chance to bring Cole and Mola in alive. Instead, he stared out the window at the flat ochre fields cut in two by Interstate 45, a gray streak snaking toward Galveston. As they approached Hobby, the chopper angled and dropped, droning over clusters of private planes parked outside silver-roofed hangars winking in winter sun, the place where Elizabeth had departed for Austin only twenty-four hours before.

Luke tapped his fingers with obvious impatience while Neal descended to a helipad, released the door, and lowered the step. After Elizabeth bid good-bye to the pilot, she scrambled from the backseat. Luke was several strides ahead when the whirring blades halted.

"Yo, Luke," Neal yelled. "Plane to Cabo's delayed for some other reason than your order. Won't leave for forty-five minutes."

Luke waved at Neal and hurried on. Elizabeth buttoned her coat against a brisk December wind as she ran down the runway behind him. He halted near a row of private planes. Brow creased in thought, he looked at her, but his focus seemed elsewhere.

"Go to your mom's in Galveston," he said. "I need to rent a plane, pronto."

"Maybe I can get one," Elizabeth said, stepping close to him.

"No delay, no hassle."

Luke nodded. "Ah, the company plane."

"Just two aisles over."

"It would save lots of time."

"If we get the plane, where're we going?" she asked.

"We are going nowhere."

"Please, Luke. This story is so important, the capture of men who traffic kids and use them as human fodder."

"Yes, that's a good headline." Luke put his hands on her shoulders. "But you need to understand, I'm going to get Cole, whatever it takes. And I'll die trying—"

"I've been in dangerous situations."

"If I say no, you won't help me with the plane."

Elizabeth shook her head. This scoop wasn't worth resurrecting her bad behavior. She had to stop sometime, and she guessed it was now. "If they'll give me the plane, it's yours. Just let me have the exclusive when you get back."

"Well, that's a switch," he said.

Turning, she took off for the hangar. Luke caught up and gently touched Elizabeth's arm. Glinting light reflected from an open window and froze in his eyes. "I know how important this is, so if you're crazy enough to go with me, I'm crazy enough to take you, but I call the shots."

"I promise to cooperate," she said, containing her excitement.

"I hope you mean that, sweet Elizabeth."

"I mean it," she replied with a grin.

FORTY-EIGHT

Elizabeth settled into the copilot's seat next to Luke. She'd sold the prospect of a riveting story to her editor, and the fact that there was a DSS agent to pilot the plane greased the way for the quick decision to allow them use of the *Houston Chronicle* Cessna 182.

Luke snatched a headset. "Hobby Tower, this is Cessna 5341 Echo, requesting permission to taxi." Listening, Luke started the plane and took it forward. "Be advised, Tower, I'm a student pilot."

"What are you saying?"

"Fasten your belt." Luke chortled as if he were having the time of his life. "Here at Hobby, if you tell the tower you're a student, sometimes they clear traffic for you."

"If you're a student, we're in deep shit." Elizabeth gripped the armrests.

Luke whistled as he studied the instrument panel and listened intently to the tower. "Roger. We're clear on five."

Surely Luke was an experienced pilot. He was just playing. Jitters coursed through her veins. Elizabeth shut her eyes as the company plane maneuvered onto runway five, gained speed, and after a few jarring surges, lifted from Mother Earth. When she finally raised her lids, the Cessna was heading north over dense patches of ponderosa pines that lined Interstate 45. This wasn't right.

"Last I heard, McAllen is way south."

"Yep."

"We're going north."

"Cole's family ranch is on the rim of Palo Duro Canyon. North Texas."

"So you think he went there," Elizabeth said, more as a statement than a question. When Luke merely nodded, she was taken by his haunted expression.

"Even though I lived in Amarillo," she said at length, "I never went to the canyon."

"It's beautiful, but for me, the whole area is a bad memory— particularly now."

Elizabeth stuffed her knee-jerk reaction to ask Luke more about his family. He'd lost everything—his parents, his best friend, and now the man who must have been like a brother.

"The canyon's over a hundred miles long," Luke commented, then fell silent for several minutes. When he spoke again, his voice sounded as if he were delivering a lecture, a disguise for grief, or maybe a lament. "Indians used to live in Palo Duro, but government troops forced them into Oklahoma. The buffalo were luckier. An army officer, Charles Goodnight—"

"I've heard of him."

"He protected the buffalo on his ranch in the canyon. The state still manages a herd up there."

"Did you see the herd when you were a kid?"

"Yeah." Luke smiled wistfully. "Cole's father, Mason, bought a ranch near Goodnight's place. Randall, Dominic, and I would ride horses over there on the weekends to see the buffalo."

Elizabeth could only imagine Luke's rage at having trusted Cole, who'd betrayed him in this most heinous way.

"How are you so sure Cole's plane didn't crash?"

"The crash was real, all right, but Cole's plane wasn't involved. He has the money and connections to arrange an accident using an identical plane." Luke smirked. "The giveaway for me was when his Cessna disappeared over McAllen right before he left US airspace."

"You're one smart *hombre*," Elizabeth said.

Luke slanted his eyes at her. "Smart enough for you?"

She searched her repertoire of spiffy replies, but before she found a retort, the plane hit an air pocket. "Oh God!" Elizabeth's breath caught in her throat as they plummeted into a downswing.

*

Weary from conversation, Luke was relieved when Elizabeth

dozed off, her head bowing forward, occasionally rolling from side to side. He scanned the stark and seemingly boundless plains of North Texas, Dominic on his mind, a fierce ache in his chest, revenge festering in the cradle of his gut. If Randall Cole wasn't at the ranch, Luke would hunt him down.

"Are we close to Amarillo?" Elizabeth asked in a sleepy voice, craning her neck toward the windshield.

"Fifty miles north." Luke withdrew his cell from a pouch on his belt. "I need to call the sheriff, let him know we're coming."

Elizabeth checked her watch. "You waited till now to call him?"

"The sheriff knows the airstrip on Cole's ranch. He'll be there soon enough." Luke's plans for retribution weren't far from his lips, but he zipped it. Instead, he considered the situation. "I'm going to need your backup. Hope you're ready." Immediately he saw the pile of concerns kindling in her startled eyes. "Look, Elizabeth, we didn't come here to enjoy the sunset."

"I know," she said quietly.

Elizabeth carefully folded her arms across her chest and seemed to concentrate on the control panel. The horizon, a dappled palette of yellow, orange, and red, cast ample light for Luke to determine the parameters of a dusty airstrip. On the runway near a clump of scrub juniper, he spotted Cole's Cessna.

"There's our man and his flying machine."

"He'll see us coming," she said. "And Mola's probably with him."

"More'n likely."

"So they'll have the advantage."

"Way I see it, we have the advantage."

"Sure," she said with a high-pitched hint of disbelief.

"No more talking. I need to concentrate." Luke vowed not to tell her the Cessna 180 was a high-performance prop that he'd had no experience in landing.

Dust blowing from the strip indicated the winds were up. Luke cut back the throttle to seventy knots, then, glancing at the wingtips, he lowered the landing gear until three green lights shone on the instrument panel, indicating all wheels were down and locked. He circled the north end of the canyon to be sure he was on target, then lined up for a straight-in approach. The Cessna kissed the earth with a slam. The plane, a bullet on hardpan, headed for the precipice ahead. Luke hit the brake. The wheels ground into the runway as the plane plowed over sagebrush and bluestem grasses and swerved to miss a cluster of skunk brush. Holding steady, he brought the aircraft to a choppy halt a short distance from the edge. As he backed up, Elizabeth let out a squeak. He was thankful this was the extent of her comments.

Cole's plane was parked away from the rim with its nose in the opposite direction, prepared for departure. Luke turned his aircraft as Cole had done but stopped near the rim several yards away from Cole's plane.

"Here's the plan," he said, pulling a Ruger from his ankle holster and passing it to Elizabeth.

She took a deep breath, unfastened her seat belt and scooted forward. To his surprise, she handled the firearm with confidence. "It's not my Glock, but it'll do."

"You own a Glock?"

"Tulio Mola has it now," she said. Elizabeth examined the Ruger's barrel. "I took lessons for a license to carry, but I need to take more."

Luke showed her the gun's features. "If Cole or Mola come near this plane, tap them in the head, just in case they're wearing vests."

"Tap means shoot?"

"Yep." Luke opened the door, but Elizabeth wasn't through with him.

"I want to go."

"Someone has to guard the plane," he said, noticing Elizabeth's flushed face and tense jaw.

"Do you know where Cole's hiding?" she asked.

"Bet my life on it."

As Luke disembarked, she leaned through the door. "I found this at the church. A protection for you."

Luke's fingers brushed Elizabeth's palm as he took the medal of Our Lady of Guadalupe, kissed it, and tucked it in his jeans. "Thanks. I need all the help I can get."

"Luke," she said. "I'm really sorry. Please be patient with me."

Rousing warmth filled him at the thought of her apology. "We'll talk when this is over."

"Yes, I want to talk."

Drawing his gun, Luke watched Elizabeth's silhouette, waving, closing the plane's door, and vanishing from his sight. Hunched over, he crisscrossed through clumps of mesquite and juniper until he found the trail. Seconds later, a twig snapped in the thicket behind a limestone boulder. He dropped, flattened himself on the caprock, and crab-crawled from the trail to a spot beneath a juniper's scratchy branches. Trigger finger ready, Luke waited. Any moment, Cole and

Mola would be in his sights.

The crackling sounds drew closer. Luke scanned the path, ready to take the men, but all he found were two mule deer foraging for leaves. In the gloaming, he could see the animals' razor-sharp hooves. Their coats had turned winter-gray with patches of white on their throats and rumps, and their large ears moved independently of each other. When the deer spotted him, they bounded off, all hooves airborne at once.

Luke pulled his jacket collar around his neck against a chilly wind from the canyon and sprinted ahead until he reached a limestone cabin nestled on a promontory surrounded by a split wood fence. He remembered when Mason Cole had it built, and how Luke, Randall, and Dominic had spent many nights there warmed by firewood they'd collected and piled into the hearth. There was no smoke from the chimney now, but Randall Cole was inside—Luke felt his presence.

He squinted at the cabin through the dodgy gray of early evening. A shadow passed the window. Gun at the ready, Luke crept on his elbows and stomach up a silted hill. By now, Cole knew he'd landed, and Luke didn't want to give him any more time to devise an escape plan. When he reached a rutted ditch below a sandstone outcrop near the front of the cabin, Luke stopped, recalling that the cabin had only one door. He crawled beneath a window next to the door, now warped and rotting, and he inched into a standing position, stretching for the handle.

A strident crack followed by a bullet flew through the window past his shoulder. Luke dove to the ground and headed to the ditch, more ammo winging above him.

"The girls are going to testify, Cole," Luke yelled. "Give it up."

"Fuck the girls and think about this," Cole called back. "I can make you a rich man, Luke."

"Not before I make you a dead man, Randall."

Luke waited for a response in order to pinpoint Cole's position inside the cabin, but all he heard were shuffling sounds and the howls of distant dogs. Minutes passed.

"Still mad about Dominic?" Cole finally called out. His voice sounded muted and faraway now, but Luke detected the amusement.

"You sick fuck!" Luke stampeded the door and fired at its wooden planks. Splinters peppered the air. But when he stormed the one-room cabin, Randall Cole had vanished.

FORTY-NINE

Elizabeth pressed her hand against the plane's window, searching the terrain illuminated by fingers of a dying sun and the hopeful presence of a three-quarter moon. Gunfire had come from the direction Luke had taken when he left her. Alarmed, she determined that, even if she wasn't a great shot, two pistols were better than one. Tucking the Ruger in her waistband, she fastened her coat over the weapon and unlocked the door. Elizabeth dispensed with figuring how to lower the footstep and dropped onto the sandy soil, causing her twisted ankle to smart. She momentarily rubbed her leg, then set off in the direction Luke had taken.

Her eyes adjusted to the stippled shades of endless purple in this vast, uninhabited place. Or at least she thought it was uninhabited until a mouse with a head as large as its body scampered in front of her and flattened itself into a crevice between the boulders. Avoiding piles of deer scat, Elizabeth followed the trail that led to a stone cabin balanced on the canyon's edge, its front door ajar like a menacing grin.

Luke was nowhere in sight. As the twilight dwindled, she dallied, cursing herself for not bringing a flashlight from the plane, trying to decide whether to call out to Luke, her mind not snapping to a quick decision.

A muzzle flashed. There was a pop and a whistle close to her temple. Elizabeth spun onto the ground. Inhaling a nose-full of dust, she stifled a cough. The shot came from the direction of the cabin, and she tried to quell a voice in her head saying Cole might have murdered Luke.

The silence that followed unnerved her as she waited for something to happen. At length, she stood and ran back toward the plane. Another bout of shots stung the air, a throbbing noise, her hearing dulled by the reports.

In dizzying pain, Elizabeth fell on her knees and crawled to a limestone outcrop where she huddled. Her fingers trembled as she wrapped her neck scarf around her head to compress a flesh wound on her ear, and with rare faith, she searched the heavens as if someone up there would help her. But the sky had become an imminent menace, blackened with bats.

The creatures flew helter-skelter, the night enveloped in their shrill calls. Fearing the bats might land on her, Elizabeth pulled her coat over her head as she pictured a horde of wolf-faced animals clawing at her flesh. Then, in a sudden twist of the already surreal moment, a more sinister animal gripped her shoulder. Stiffening, she peered from beneath her coat. Randall Cole, face blackened with soot and clothes bathed in charcoal, ground the barrel of his gun into her neck.

Elizabeth struggled to her feet. Her ear smarted, her vision waved, but her optimism soared. Luke must be alive, otherwise, this creep wouldn't be bothering with her.

"Move it," Cole said, his knuckles sharp in between her shoulders.

She played on her injured ankle to slow Cole down, dragging her leg as he directed her to a trail that led from the cabin seemingly in the direction of the landing strip.

"I'm a little old for you, aren't I?" she asked.

"Shut the fuck up."

Elizabeth pulled up her jacket, veiling the crown of her head against a bat attack. "Where's your boyfriend, Tulio Mola?" she asked.

He chuckled. "You'll see Mola soon enough."

*

Luke spotted an open window on the backside of the cabin. Dashing outside, he searched the perimeter. Cole had disappeared. When he rounded the last corner, a gust from the canyon hit his face. His hands were turning stiff and cold. Pressed against the stone wall, moving sideways, he continued to listen for movement.

In frustration, he reentered the cabin and pulled out his penlight again, this time skittering its beam across the planked floor sullied with a charcoal trail that led from the hearth to the open window. "Cole was in the fuckin' chimney when I came in," Luke muttered to himself. "And he escaped when I went outside. But where the hell's Mola?"

Bracing against the cold, he examined scuff marks below the open window to see if there were more tracks in the dry ground. Nothing. Pesky bats swept by, their haunted chirping calls stretching across the land. And then, below an army of marching stars, coyotes commenced with their howls until they were quieted by the sound of gunshots. Sprinting toward the shots, Luke flew down the path that led back to the airstrip. Muffled voices somewhere ahead of him rippled over night air, fell quiet, and then died.

Maybe Cole wanted Luke to chase him in the skies, a venue the miscreant lawyer was familiar with. And maybe Elizabeth had left the 182. Or Mola had rushed the plane and she'd surrendered. Too many thoughts, too many bad scenarios. Luke darted through the brush until he reached the Cessna—the door open, Elizabeth gone.

Scanning the area around the plane, Luke listened intently, the atmosphere suddenly full, heavy with the smell of dust and a nasty haze shrouding the horizon, obscuring the yellow moon. Dust storm, he thought, and wished he was wrong.

Movement on the far edge of the runway caught his attention. He climbed inside the plane and grabbed the binoculars. A half football field away, Cole strode behind Elizabeth as they neared his plane.

No way could Luke get an accurate bead on Cole at that distance. Even a marksman couldn't make the shot without a rifle and a night scope. If Cole took off with his hostage, Luke's only option would be to chase them in the 182, and he knew neither plane would be going far. Both were low on fuel. Infuriated at the impotence of his situation, he watched Cole hustle Elizabeth into the cockpit. Seconds later, her scream cut the clotted air. Luke cranked the motor, sickened by a persistent image—Tulio Mola in the plane with Elizabeth.

A roar bellowed across the high plateau, and dirt stirred behind Cole's plane as it taxied down the runway. But something equally as deadly as Randall Cole was heading straight toward the airstrip. A swirling maelstrom churned the earth's loose crust, a scene cut from Luke's boyhood, thick muck gathering into dense dirt squalls. Serious trouble.

FIFTY

Elizabeth shuddered. She couldn't stop gagging. The cabin reeked of a metallic, sanguine odor. Cole had forced her into the backseat next to Tulio Mola's body, strapped in, his bald head shining white as an egg, a bullet wound in his temple. The Latin Angels' kingpin—blood oozing down his cheek, bulging eyes focusing on nothing—his chest shredded from multiple stab wounds.

Clucking to himself, Cole started the plane as Elizabeth twisted as far away from Mola as possible. She fought waves of nausea, her scarf bandaged too tight around her ear, her ankle throbbing, and her stomach bubbling acid. Kate's face materialized in her mind, and Elizabeth knew she'd deceived herself all these years, insisting that she'd taken the dangerous assignments to pad Kate's college fund. What a crock. It was all for her precious career. Elizabeth sank into bitter regret, more raw than any wound. She had to get back to her daughter.

"You and Luke were friends," she said, strained and desperate. "He can help you."

Cole growled under his breath. She glanced at the back of his head, but it was the horizon that held her attention. A billowing cloud as black as death surged toward the plane.

"What's that?"

"A chunk of Oklahoma coming our way."

Cole gripped a rod on the dash. The plane jutted forward, its motor deafening, its vibrations intense.

"You can't take off in this," Elizabeth yelled.

"Watch me."

Thinking of how to delay, Elizabeth croaked a question, a lame attempt to distract him. "Is that a throttle?" she asked.

"You bet your white ass." Cole flashed a grin, but then he hushed, his bravado deadened as Elizabeth thrust the Ruger into the back of his neck.

"Stop!" she screamed.

"Fuck you."

Cole rolled down the runway toward the swirl of grit. Elizabeth gasped. If she killed him, she'd have to control the plane herself.

Her voice swelled into a fine-tuned pitch. "I'll blow your head off!" She clicked the safety, fingered the trigger, and scored a hole in the windshield.

"You bitch!" Cole eased back on the stick, gradually bringing the plane to a halt.

"Unlock the door," she said.

"Okay, okay. Take it easy."

Elizabeth crawled to the copilot's seat and kept the Ruger pointed at Cole, his gun in an unsnapped shoulder holster. Watching him, she worked the door handle. It seemed forever before it clicked. She cracked the door and her courage faltered. She couldn't shoot the man, but she couldn't allow him to escape either. *Remember Dominic*, she told herself, *and Mariella*. Okay, she'd shoot him. In the leg. No, the knee.

Blam!

There followed a montage of sight and sound—the Ruger's report, Cole's moan, a slit in the door with dirt blowing all directions—Elizabeth stuffed the Ruger into her belt and hit the ground, her bandaged palms scraped the hardpan, pain spiked in her ankle and hands.

Even in her misery, Elizabeth realized she must have missed her mark. Cole was still maneuvering the plane, turning it, aiming it at her, the prop whipping more dust into the already dirt-laden air. Elizabeth suddenly recalled the airport attendant pumping gas into the Cessna before she and Luke had taken off. She scrambled to the side and fired four slugs into the plane's wing near the fuel port.

Running like hell, she reached the canyon's rim, where she crouched and watched the explosion. After the blast, a smokescreen fanned from the aircraft. Elizabeth blinked at an orange inferno licking the plateau, and she thought she saw Randall Cole hurling himself from the plane.

To avoid the fire, Elizabeth tripped down a rock-strewn slope. The ground shook, sending shockwaves into the canyon, and everywhere along the rim, small boulders joggled loose, cascading into a landslide. Her eyes stung. Her footing unsure, she crept blindly forward until she found a clump of junipers, where she hunkered, bracing her back on a tree trunk against the rockslide. Even in the midst of the small avalanche, Elizabeth couldn't stop thinking. If the wind shifted and the fire swelled over the rim, she was toast.

*

"Elizabeth!" Luke called her name until he was hoarse. He circled Cole's charred plane through torrents of inky smoke, the Cessna a pyre of burnt umber belching wicked gasses. Luke's voice weakened each time he yelled, and finally he had to cover his face with a rag he'd grabbed from the cockpit. After rounding the wreckage twice, edging as close to the plane as humanly possible, he came up with nothing—no shoe, no clothing, and, thank God, no body.

Visibility resembled an old-time movie, black dots in the film, the landscape bizarre and unreadable. The charred fuselage cracked, its nose tipping downward, and a propeller torpedoed into the ground. Shifting winds continued to sweep dust at the flames, and to Luke's relief, the airborne dirt seemed to thwart the fire. The plane had been low on fuel, so Luke assumed something had caused a spark to ignite the vapors in the tank. On the passenger side, he explored the steep bank where Elizabeth would have logically landed if she'd been able to jump before the blast. He then rounded the plane again, methodically searching smoky culverts and ridges. Suddenly, a hand gripped his ankle.

Luke stumbled forward, holding a branch to stop his fall, twisting to see Randall Cole, eyes crazed in the eerie firelight. He lay on the ground, his pink skin blistered across his forehead, his leg a bloody disaster, and his gun aimed at Luke's crotch.

"Kneel down," Cole said in a rasp.

Doing as Cole commanded, Luke gritted his teeth. The fucker had nine lives.

"Scoot close. Throw the gun," Cole said. "Or I'll blow your balls to East Jesus."

Luke inched his hand toward his shoulder holster and slowly removed the gun. As he tossed it into a clump of nearby snakeweed, he heard a faint cry.

"Luke!" Elizabeth's voice welled up from somewhere in the canyon.

Propped on his elbow, Cole kept his aim between Luke's thighs. "Red Rover, Red Rover, let Lizzie come over," he said, spitting blood.

"Where are you?" she called again.

"I mean it. Get that cunt over here."

As Cole spoke, he turned slightly in the direction of Elizabeth's voice. Luke dove onto his bloody leg and rammed his fist into the wound. Cole slashed wildly, then fired a random shot before the gun slipped to the ground, but in his other hand, he held a buck knife. Straddling Cole's hips, Luke felt a shallow prick in his gut just below his belt buckle.

Luke wrenched the knife from Cole's weakened grip and tossed it to the side. Unable to control his rage, Luke repeatedly belted Dominic's killer. He pulped Cole's face, breaking his perfectly capped front teeth, then grabbing Cole's ears, Luke hammered his head on the ground until his victim quieted, eyes half-open, tongue licking cracked lips, tainted yellow lids swollen, the burns across his brow weeping a pale blood-streaked fluid.

As Luke scooted toward the brush, groping for his SIG, Cole's bloody hand reached his weapon. He fired a shot that found purchase in Luke's left bicep. With a piercing throb, Luke fell forward, the cold earth rearing up, slamming him in the face. He rolled in agony toward the spot he'd thrown his gun. Cole rolled after him.

"You don't have the killer instinct, son," Cole called, his voice too strong for the beating he'd just received. He inched toward Luke.

"You got those genes," Luke replied. His hand thrashed in the snakeweed. He meant to kill the bastard if he could find his SIG before Cole reached him. In that instant, Luke knew chances were slim that either of them would survive this night. Suddenly, his peripheral vision caught a silhouette illuminated by the plane's flaming strobes. Elizabeth dragged toward him from the canyon's rim.

"I should've killed you the first time," she said in a weak but determined voice. Her singed hair flew at her face as she aimed the Ruger with both hands and blew a crimson pit into Cole's forehead.

Eyeballs white and glassy, Cole went limp.

Although Luke's mind clouded as he held the oozing knife wound near his waist, he was able to work his lips into a smile at Elizabeth, her face blanketed with fine soot, her stunned gaze fixed on the lifeless body of Randall Cole.

FIFTY-ONE

Christmas morning ushered a crisp breeze through the open window. Alex lay in bed, watching sunlight patterns dance on the magnolia leaves that scratched against the screen. As a child, he'd held an ideal of America's pristine beauty and loving people, but the shootings at the church had changed his mind forever.

On a chest of drawers filled with Alex's new clothes, a small silver clock read eleven a.m. He stretched his right arm, still unable to move his left shoulder protected by a cast. *Señor* Luke was also wounded in his left arm. Was this was a sign about their future together? He'd ask Obispa.

Alex sat up and smoothed the ridges of the rumpled backpack he'd managed to keep with him all the way from Guatemala City. Its worn zipper and threadbare pockets reminded him of Father Chiabras, and inside was the precious photo of his mother and Fernando. He slid the picture from the pack to wish his family *Felíz Navidad*, and traced his finger over their faces, certain that Fernando and his mother were happy for him. Alex smiled at Fernando's impish grin, the expression Alex had come to cherish.

"Alex, you awake?" Luke knocked on the door. "We're due at Obispa's in an hour. Hustle up."

"I'll take a shower," he replied, amused at the American custom of taking many showers.

After he bathed, Alex dressed in jeans and an orange University of Texas T-shirt, then made his way to the kitchen. The back door was open. Balancing a stack of presents in one arm, Luke was loading the car with more colorful bags and boxes than Alex had ever seen. He hurried over to help, but Luke shook his head. "You might guess your surprise," he grinned and finished the job himself, skillfully using his uninjured arm.

Alex dared to wonder what the present could be, but he didn't ask. Instead, he fed Andre and Horace, herded the hounds into the backyard and played ball with the dogs until he and Luke left for the shaman's.

"You're very quiet this morning," Luke said as they rounded the corner onto Obispa's street.

"I am thinking about *extremos*." Alex tried to explain in his best English. "It is hard to understand everything that has happened. Last week, shootings and death. This week, *fiestas* and lights."

"*Extremos*. I'd say you're right on that one." Luke scrunched his lips. "Just for today, I'm going for *fiesta*."

When they wheeled up outside Obispa's House of Light, Kate was waiting on the red cement steps. She spotted Luke's car and skipped over to Alex as he opened the door. She smelled like fresh flowers, her arms wrapping around his shoulder, pulling him through the yard and up the stairs onto Obispa's porch. Flushed with a draft of embarrassment, Alex glanced over his shoulder. Luke was close behind.

"Alex's here," Kate called through an open window into the living room.

Garbed in white, her violet eyes alive with expectation, Obispa hugged Alex as he stepped through the door. *Señora* Grant, dressed in a long green skirt and flowing blouse, stood behind the shaman. All the furniture in the living room had been moved to make room for the *fiesta*, and delicious scents of carnitas, chiles rellenos, and chorizos circulated in the tiny space. A sea of smiles greeted Alex: children he'd met the morning he fainted at the cantina, a smattering of Obispa's neighbors, and by the tree. It couldn't be! The spry little priest held out his arms. Alex thought his heart would explode as Elena jumped out from behind Father Chiabras.

"*Feliz Navidad!*" someone shrieked, and the spinning, singing afternoon of a lifetime began. Out of the corner of one eye, he spied *la señora* holding Luke's hand and laughing. Kate joined Alex, sticking close to him, as Father Chiabras told the latest stories from *Casa Maria*.

"I'd love to visit and write about your work," *Señora* Grant said.

Father's eyes brightened. "You will be most welcome."

Alex glanced at the new watch Luke had given him. "When are Mariella and Muñeca coming?" he asked.

"The US Marshal promised he'd bring them over after he had his family dinner," Luke said.

Alex frowned.

Luke continued. "People are sometimes late on Christmas. Don't worry."

In mid-afternoon, Obispa and *Señora* Grant invited everyone to gather for the delicious feast. Glancing around the room, Alex memorized the magical scene. *¡Gracias a Dios!* After dinner, *la señora* pulled Alex aside and handed him two gift bags with gold cascading ribbons.

"A dress for you to give Elena," she said. "And a camera for Father Chiabras. He can send you pictures."

Alex threw his arms around her neck. She smelled just like Kate. "You are so kind to me."

"And you, Alex, have given me a new life."

Confused by her words, Alex started to ask a question, but Obispa rang a tinkling bell, the signal to open presents. She passed a gift to everyone. Paper and ribbons flew around the room. Elena pranced around in her blue velvet dress, while Father pored over the camera. At first, Alex found it hard to participate. He'd been given so much already, then, amused at himself, he opened a big box. It was a shiny silver computer from Kate, Luke, and *la señora*. He was astonished.

Kate gasped when she opened the box Alex had rewrapped three times to make sure it was perfect. She withdrew his silver cross and dangled it for all to see. "I can't take this, Alex."

"You must," Father Chiabras said, while capturing her picture. "I know Alex would only give it to someone he loves."

Hot blood throbbed in Alex's neck. He couldn't believe Father had said these words. "I want you to have it, Kate," he said quietly.

Kissing his cheek, Kate asked him to clasp the chain around her neck, and they sat for a long time together, holding hands and watching the children play.

When evening approached, Obispa passed *profiteroles* on a red tray and bowls of warm bananas, while *la señora* poured hot chocolate. Alex spotted Luke returning from the front porch, where he'd gone to take a phone call. Brow creased, jaw tight, he motioned to *Señora* Grant, who went outside with him. Shortly, he returned and asked Alex to join them.

"I'm going to tell you straight up," Luke said, placing a strong hand on Alex's shoulder. Then he made a guttural sound and didn't tell him anything.

Alex searched his heart. Everyone he loved was there except . . . "Is it Mariella?"

Luke's lips thinned into a line. "A US Marshal found Mariella's mother."

"But she didn't want to see Mariella or have anything to do with her," *Señora* Grant said.

"I must talk to Mariella right away," Alex said.

Luke's grip on Alex tightened. "Mariella took her life last night."

As Luke described the note Mariella wrote before she died, Alex felt a spark drain from his soul. He slumped onto the porch bench, buried his head in his hands and sobbed, feeling the warmth of Luke and *la señora* as they sat on either side of him. Alex finally raised his head. The whole group had gathered. They were silent with no words for this tragedy, or so he thought.

Fernando was the one to speak. Perched on the porch railing, he leaned against a column and smiled at Alex. "*Mariella will be with me,*" he said. "*She will be at peace.*"

"Don't leave me again!" Alex jumped up, almost knocking Obispa and Elena backward.

"*Sometimes you can't see me, but I never leave you,*" Fernando said. His brother's body grew faint in the evening twilight.

"Don't go!" Alex clenched his fists.

"Alex, no one is leaving," *Señora* Grant said. "We're here for you."

As he had done so many weeks before, Alex rested his head on Father Chiabras's chest and drew strength from the priest's embrace. No one spoke again for a long time.

Finally, Obispa squeezed Alex's hand. "Father and Elena are staying with you at Luke's house."

"For a whole week," Elena added in her husky little voice.

Alex studied Elena's ruddy cheeks and black inquisitive eyes. Unlike Mariella, she had a chance, and he must not ruin this special time for her by discussing Mariella's death. He would grieve alone. Tousling Elena's hair, he said, "We'll have a great time. You'll love Luke's dogs."

"Can I come over tomorrow and show you how to use the computer?" Kate asked.

Sighing, Alex nodded. *Extremos,* he thought. *How will I get used to this place of extremes?*

On the drive to Luke's, Alex sat in the backseat, Elena asleep on his shoulder. He was comforted by her small breath against his arm and the presence of the two most courageous men he knew riding in the front seat. Yet the words Mariella had written before she died dug their way into his heart: "*No more pretty in the world. No more pretty in the world.*"

Alex vowed to make it not so.

CPSIA information can be obtained at www.ICGtesting.com
Printed in the USA
LVOW130234141112

307203LV00003B/3/P